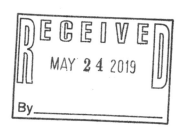

IT'S HOT IN THE HAMPTONS

IT'S HOT IN THE HAMPTONS

A Novel

HOLLY PETERSON

WILLIAM MORROW

An Imprint of HarperCollinsPublishers

IT'S HOT IN THE HAMPTONS. Copyright © 2019 by Holly Peterson. All rights reserved. Printed in the United States of America. No part of this book may be used or reproduced in any manner whatsoever without written permission except in the case of brief quotations embodied in critical articles and reviews. For information, address HarperCollins Publishers, 195 Broadway, New York, NY 10007.

HarperCollins books may be purchased for educational, business, or sales promotional use. For information, please email the Special Markets Department at SPsales@harpercollins.com.

FIRST EDITION

Designed by Diahann Sturge
Part opener art © Alex Rockheart / Shutterstock, Inc.

Library of Congress Cataloging-in-Publication Data

Names: Peterson, Holly, author.
Title: It's hot in the Hamptons : a novel / Holly Peterson.
Other titles: It is hot in the Hamptons
Description: First edition. | New York : William Morrow Paperbacks, [2019]
Identifiers: LCCN 2019009607 (print) | LCCN 2019012087 (ebook) | ISBN 9780062867384 (E-book) | ISBN 9780062867377 (trade paperback)
Subjects: LCSH: Domestic fiction. | BISAC: FICTION / Contemporary Women. | FICTION / Romance / Contemporary. | FICTION / Family Life. | GSAFD: Love stories.
Classification: LCC PS3616.E8428 (ebook) | LCC PS3616.E8428 I87 2019 (print) | DDC 813/.6—dc23
LC record available at https://lccn.loc.gov/2019009607

ISBN 978-0-06-286737-7 (paperback)
ISBN 978-0-06-291358-6 (hardcover library edition)

19 20 21 22 23 LSC 10 9 8 7 6 5 4 3 2 1

For women leaping into risk: You change the way the world revolves

IT'S HOT IN THE HAMPTONS

PART I

Summer Breeze

Chapter 1

A New Ghost in Town?

As Caroline faced a bright blue sky, the heat dispersed the city stress that clung like a relentless hangover to her body. Her father had taught her to appreciate this familiar Hamptons sun. Closing her eyes, feeling its warmth penetrate her skin, she knew it would turn bright orange in summer and dim to bluish-purple with the coolness of fall.

The scent of fried clams sizzling at the Dock House floated toward her in the breeze. On Sunday mornings after church, Caroline's father used to take her here to Sag Harbor's Long Wharf pier. They'd buy two plates of the seafood special and sit on this exact bench, agreeing not to tell Mom they'd eaten before lunch. It was now eleven in the morning, and her empty stomach sent a hunger pang up to her brain. The doors of the Dock House had just opened, revealing a bubbling, claw-foot bathtub filled with meandering lobsters. Caroline stood, unable to resist.

Ten minutes later, back on the bench, she dipped a steaming

fried clam into too much tartar sauce, which she had pumped into one of three little plastic pots, and crunched on it whole. She studied the boats starting to populate the marina. Even on the water, the traffic was beginning to get clogged.

Around her on Long Wharf, the echoes of seagulls trumpeted the season she ached for all year. For three solid summer months to come, she'd bite into sturdy and sweet tomatoes like apples, dig bountiful clams out of the bays, and allow the cooling salve of the Atlantic to splash over her body.

She'd arrived early to meet her friend Annabelle, wanting time to savor the last twenty-four hours of human civility before the unhinged New Yorkers were let out of their pens. The onslaught of *those* people en masse coming to the Hamptons for the holiday weekend would make moving around her hometown a stressful exercise. They'd sneak into her parking spots just as she was backing in, and honk at her when she didn't slam the accelerator the millisecond the red light turned to green.

Caroline had grown up in East Hampton, and reluctantly moved to Manhattan the day after she tied the knot with Eddie on the back lawn of his father's Elks Club lodge in Southampton. Eddie promised they'd move back home when they were ready to have kids. At the time, Caroline felt reassured her children would fill their growing lungs with the same salty Atlantic mist that had stuck to the windows of her family's small home on Bluff Road.

Only, it didn't work out that way.

On either side of the pier, several gargantuan yachts with fabric-covered navy bumpers were tied up to cleats. In anticipation of their .001-percenter owners who would board the next day, deckhands struggled as they loaded bulky cases of pink Moët & Chandon and Domaines Ott rosé onto the gangplanks. By late August the previous summer, the New York papers were lamenting the shortage of the most exclusive brands of rosé in liquor stores on the eastern end of Long Island. No fridge on these yachts would dare chill the Montauk-brewed beer that Caroline grew up drinking. Caroline huffed out as she pondered the whole urban lot of summer people, whining about their drought of pink drinks.

Looking out at the horizon, Caroline thought she recognized a profile on a small boat. A man was motoring a hundred yards out in a beat-up Boston Whaler near the mouth of the harbor. His Yankees baseball cap was tightly secured, and his sunglasses hid his eyes, but she was *sure* she recognized that nose and that square jaw, though the hair seemed longer. Heartbeats pulsated through her veins and thumped loudly in her ears. It couldn't be. It would be thirteen years this August since he'd drowned.

But that profile. Caroline recognized it just as any mother would her own kid's unique build out in right field. Only, before he'd perished in the roiling sea, Joey Whitten had been her lover, not her son. That profile she *knew*. Her fingers had lingered on his forehead, nose, and lips so many times. Since their first night together in high school, that was their way as she lay beside him. She'd massage his eyebrows with her index finger, then trace his sweet, soft nose, working her way down to his full lips, until he kissed her finger and grabbed it in his mouth, startling her every time.

"What the hell is with you? Hello?" Annabelle poked her shoulder.

"Nothing is with me." Caroline grabbed another fried clam, dousing it with lemon.

"I said hello two times, and twice you didn't turn around. Your face is stricken with something weird like you saw a ghost."

Caroline rubbed the back of her neck. A ghost? The man piloting the Boston Whaler was a perfect Joey Whitten replica. Even his shoulders slung the same.

"Sorry, I thought I saw something, or, I mean, someone. I just need a moment."

Caroline closed her eyes toward the sun, trying to will herself back to reality. She still didn't know what happened to Joey that day in the currents—no one did—and she couldn't shake the glorious thought of him returning to the living.

Annabelle rubbed Caroline's shoulders, and a series of pricey, tricolor gold Sidney Garber rolling bracelets jangled down her arm. The two friends had met on a hideous yellow couch outside Mrs. Blanchard's office at The Episcopal School, each with daughters who were having what the director euphemistically called a "challenging separation" from their mothers. Caroline and Annabelle bonded about raising painfully shy girls, and their mutual, prickly annoyance at the competitive moms in their class. Those women, yammering after drop-off over espresso at Via Quadronno, had spawned correctly adjusted children clad in smocked dresses and silly yodeling outfits as if they were von Trapps.

"What on earth is on your mind, honey?" Annabelle asked, sitting on the bench and turning to her friend. "Either tell me or let's take a walk into town to get it out of your head."

"Nothing at all, let's go. I need to polish off a project for a client before they arrive tomorrow, you know, shells, some poufs, knick-knacks," Caroline answered absently. "But you're right, and I do have to get my mind off something weird."

In the far distance, the Boston Whaler slipped out of view behind the jetty. Caroline assured herself that it was the heat of the summer sun that had resurrected visions of Joey Whitten. Or perhaps the fried clams had triggered a Proustian food memory that transported Joey from the past to the present.

"You're spacing out for sure," Annabelle said, interrupting her thoughts. "Let's get your client's final touches bought in town, then lunch, then go check on my horses. Over some good rosé you can tell me what's going on in your head."

"Nothing's going on . . . I just love this view," Caroline hedged.

Annabelle would think a Joey sighting was nuts. She continued, "I'd bring boyfriends here or friends, and we'd eat all the delicious food from that lobster shack." Caroline smoothed her hand along the wood. "Just sitting here with the clams gets me remembering sometimes. The menu and the taste haven't changed for, like, thirty years."

Annabelle wouldn't approve of fried anything for lunch in the same way she didn't approve of Caroline taking the 6 train down Lexington Avenue. *What about all the crazies down there in those filthy subways? Don't you know about them? They'll push you onto the tracks!*

Caroline didn't care which food choices her friend approved. Before she stood, determined to forget about the Boston Whaler, she dipped the last large clam into the third plastic pot of tartar sauce she'd demolished and chomped on it whole.

Chapter 2

An Immodest Proposal

"Before we go into town, let me focus your wandering mind on something a tad more captivating," Annabelle offered, brushing her corn silk hair off her face and turning toward the sun.

"I know that tone." Caroline stood up from the bench and threw the plastic food container into the garbage near the pier's edge. "You want me to do something I don't want to do."

"Please, I know you'll resist at first." Annabelle took her Tom Ford sunglasses off her eyes and folded them into a case in her bag. "Just breathe deeply, like in those yoga classes you hate so much."

Caroline let out a half-assed yoga exhalation and wiped her sticky fingers with a towelette. She stood before Annabelle, arms crossed, the corners of her lips lifting into a teeny smile. "Shoot."

"An affair," Annabelle declared.

"An *affair*," Caroline answered, incredulously. "I assume you aren't talking about a party, not a charity affair."

"You *know* I'm not. It's summer. 'Tis the season. And I'm very serious."

"You have something to get off your chest? You're not leaving that fabulous Arthur of yours?"

"I'll never leave him, you know that."

"Of course I do. Go on."

"And I have nothing to admit," Annabelle answered. "Not yet."

"Not yet . . ." Caroline nodded. She saw where this was going. She closed her eyes and turned to face that familiar sun again, not wanting to focus on her wearisome marriage today. Her father was up there somewhere; the man who never really approved of Eddie, even after he found so much success in Manhattan.

"We need it," Annabelle announced. "Both our husbands have splurged on extracurriculars, and it's time for us to stop stewing and act. See what it feels like to be with someone else. Look at it this way: at the very least, an affair will inform you."

"Inform me—interesting justification."

"An affair is a step to the breakup of your marriage, if there is one on the horizon. If not, well, at least you've done what Eddie has and won't care so much."

"Well, as of now, I'm still married. And, yes, Eddie did, but I wouldn't . . . it's not me."

"Oh really?" Annabelle prodded. "You almost did it once with an artist on some design job."

"I *thought about* it with that artist. I *almost* kissed him in a kitchen, Annabelle," Caroline corrected. "And I didn't. But he was great-looking, so I wasn't wrong to at least look at him twice." Caroline remembered he had cornered her against the fridge, his fingers brushing her hair back in the most sexual way.

"You're overdue, that guy was pre-kids, right?" Annabelle asked.

"Yeah, like ten years ago. It was right when I first suspected Eddie. I think I was about a month pregnant with Gigi. I locked myself in the bathroom after the artist in question almost kissed me, and I literally talked to myself in the mirror, 'Don't do this. Don't go there.' And I didn't. Eddie and I went to therapy, and I confronted him about straying, telling him to cool it. So, one: that doesn't count. And two: since it doesn't, your point is moot."

"My point is you came close at least once."

Annabelle, six inches taller than Caroline, stood up and put her hands on her friend's shoulders for that added domination she loved. "Somewhere between, what, two and however many (maybe six?) women later on your husband's scorecard, and you're not super pissed you haven't?"

Caroline opened the last package of chowder crackers and threw them at the seagulls one by one. She vowed to take the heat off herself and put some on her friend. "You always overlooked Arthur's affairs; you always said you were going to forget that one French colleague, that masseuse and, instead, focus on the fact that he's the most attentive gentleman out there . . . which, I do agree, he is. So what's changed?"

"Emotions evolve. I feel resentment building," Annabelle answered, pursing her lips, and sitting back down on the bench, elegantly crossing her grasshopper-long legs.

Caroline shielded her eyes with both hands from the harsh sun to look at her statuesque friend. "And how do you factor in breaking a vow, an emotional tornado, and the daunting logistics of the thing?" Eddie deserved it, but one image struck at her heart: his expression if he found out. His plentiful cheeks would sag and deflate; tears would flow. There had to be a better way to leave, without hurting him so much. Part of Caroline wanted to be friends with Eddie, good co-parents, but no longer his partner. An affair was not a productive way to get there. "You're giving me that condescending look."

"What look?"

"That look I hate: that same look you give me when you dare me to do things I have no desire, or, frankly, the ability to do."

"My what's-wrong-with-you look?"

"Not everyone was a ski *and* tennis team captain at Dartmouth, Annabelle. I skied down that black diamond mogul run and almost broke several limbs."

"You want this."

"Says who?" Caroline asked.

"And sorry to fuck with your splendid memories of that cold Vermont trip, but you never made it down that black diamond run on actual skis: you shuffled down the sides of the slope on your butt." She placed her arm on the back of the bench triumphantly.

From day one in nursery school, Caroline found Annabelle von Tattenbach (née Digby) to be an exception and an enigma: a snotty newspaper heiress, but cool; loaded, but defiantly real; an ice queen, but emotionally present. Annabelle not only kept Caroline guessing but also kept her honest with herself, which she found she needed more and more these days. Annabelle was the best friend she'd always yearned for, in a form she'd never imagined possible.

"Even trying to return one of your tennis serves isn't fun for me and, metaphorically, you could say, this is the same: making me handle something I can't handle. I don't gracefully swan dive into daring waters like you do. And, besides, Eddie couldn't take it."

"Would you stop always giving that bully his way before yours?"

"I don't always . . ."

"You do always. You know that. Take care of yourself for once," Annabelle answered. "It's simple. We both agree to sleep with someone else this summer. Someone safe, of course, but, nonetheless, someone *else*."

Caroline tossed her Diet Coke can into the recycling bin before adding, "Finding someone safe is modern fairy-tale bullshit."

"By the end of summer, you need to decide *if you are staying* and I, well, I need to decide *how I'm going to stay*," Annabelle added sternly.

"That's the only thing you've said today that makes sense." She walked a few paces toward the edge of the pier now, free from Annabelle's spell casting. Looking out for that long-gone Boston Whaler, Caroline flung her purse over her shoulder with a little extra force. Resisting this woman was almost impossible once she got going.

"If my marriage with Eddie is over at some point, I need to do what's right for the kids, what Theo and Gigi really need." Caroline turned back to her friend. "And, whether I leave him or not, I fundamentally believe my kids belong in the surf and sun and sand out here in their school years, instead of marching around in loafers and school uniforms on city concrete. Eddie promised me we could move back when I had kids. This very fall, Theo could start kindergarten out here; Gigi fourth grade." Caroline looked back at the glistening water. "I mean, c'mon, they don't even play on the bay beaches I grew up on."

"I promise, a summer affair might finally give you real answers to where all that anxiety is coming from: the city, Eddie Clarkson, or both." Annabelle raised her eyebrows at Caroline, forming that expression that often helped her crush life's opponents.

"Well, I'm different that way," Caroline stated, as she looked out at the harbor again, disturbed there was no Boston Whaler in sight. Though she would not admit it to Annabelle, an affair was, in the here and now of a summer's twilight, something she might consider. Eddie was a good, playful father and surely in love with her. But it was impossible for any partner to satiate his appetite for attention. And when she couldn't, he'd gorged elsewhere. And, yes, it made her furious and humiliated her.

"I *might* readdress your ridiculous plan at some point down the line," Caroline said, finally. "You're right about one thing: I'm sure I need *something* to change. Especially today. I'm feeling so strange suddenly."

She grabbed her cracker wrappers and napkin out of her pocket and crumpled them into a tight ball as if that would help her resolve.

Chapter 3

The Titan Treatment

Caroline's husband, Eddie Clarkson, laid his head back on the white leather Philippe Starck desk chair he'd bought at Art Basel Miami this past fall. He adjusted his headset and microphone, deciding he'd listen to exactly two more minutes of horseshit excuses.

He closed his eyes to temper his frustration while his partner in the Hawaiian poke bowl fast-food venture droned on, "I promise you, Eddie. We just need another infusion. I know I said three years to profitability, but it's gonna take four. We have franchises to develop, and, in time, they're going to make us strong gains. I'm telling you, the rare tuna, the cauliflower rice for all those low-carb freaks. What do you think all those women who take all those SoulCycle classes want for lunch? Poke bowls and poke bowls. Every single one of them."

"I don't know what idiot declared that the entire country should be fuckin' gorging on cauliflower all of a sudden," Eddie pointed out.

The window in his corner office on Fifty-Second Street looked down Park Avenue toward the building that stood above Grand Central Terminal. It used to say PAN AM in blue lights on the top when he was a young kid and visited Manhattan with his uncle Charlie. No one in his immediate family back in East Hampton ever went to the big city; they didn't see the need, nor were they interested. And Eddie saw where that provinciality landed his parents: his mom stuck driving an assisted-living transport bus and his dad an oil delivery truck, making dirt money their whole lives. Uncle Charlie understood the city was the key to real cash flow. He taught Eddie that it was just a matter of figuring out how to get close to the people who had a shit-ton of it.

"And if you look at column four, admittedly, the projections were a little off, but . . ."

Time's up. Eddie opened his eyes and placed his elbows on his glass desk. One phone, one small glass cube holding a dozen silver Cartier pens, and one small laptop lay before him. He wasn't into paper. Eddie didn't like records or reminders; it was always verbal with him, and everyone knew that by now.

A seating area with a white leather couch and two metal Knoll armchairs with white leather strips for seats stood on the other side of the desk. A spotless glass coffee table anchored them in a half circle. He demanded that his dark chocolate rug be vacuumed in the same direction every morning so he could see linear grooves when he walked in. That kind of thing made his day, boosted his mood, and got him ready to tell assholes like those on his phone right now to piss off.

"And on the next page, you see the P and L of . . ."

Eddie breathed in deep through his nose like a parent summoning patience with a three-year-old who wouldn't get dressed. He rubbed his evenly cropped haircut, which was as carefully groomed as his rug. As the team's justifications poured into his headset, he stood his stocky build up and walked over to the electric blue Yves Klein Venus statue in the corner.

That brunette lesbian art adviser told him to buy it and hold it for at least ten years. Too bad she didn't respond to his jokes about having a threesome with one of her girlfriends if he bought the art she pitched. She answered that every banker client in the city made the same proposal. And that he was "profoundly pedestrian" in his assumptions.

He wondered if her instincts about Yves Klein were golden and he'd cash in as she promised. He massaged the blue goddess's breasts with his fingertips, though he was told that his prints would mar the surface of the pigment and decrease the statue's value.

He did it anyway because the image of lesbians and their nipples rubbing up against each other got him stiff in his pants, even if only for a brief moment. Then, the thought of that lesbian art adviser kicking him in the nuts if he asked her how she got her own nipples hard caused his erection to wilt.

Out of nowhere, he barked into the phone. "Shut the fuck up with this speculative bullshit. I've had enough. I'm out."

Eddie punched the END CALL button hard with his index finger.

"Eleanor!" he screamed. "They are going to call back. Tell them when I say *fuck off*, I actually mean *fuck off for fuckin' real*." He shook his head.

Eddie had a feeling this deal would never work. He'd write the Hawaiian fast-food disaster off on some tax loss statement. If Caroline and her friends didn't order tuna tartar so much every time they went out, he'd never have put a penny into this poke bowl food scheme to begin with.

He needed some tax write-offs anyway, so even if the three poke bowl franchises in this cockamamy deal were booming, he'd have been out and figured a way to make it look like a loss. The partners didn't know that. They didn't need to. So many things people didn't need to know. That was a primary goal in his business life: remembering the link between limited knowledge and limited fallout. Uncle Charlie, Lord rest his soul, taught him that too.

"Eleanor!" he yelled again. "Get the car outside. Tell him I'll be down in five, and I hope the company sends that amazing driver."

His assistant knew when to push her boss and when to hold back. Every day, for thirty years now, Eleanor used the same thick tortoiseshell clip to firmly nestle a short bun just above her neck. Today, she'd chosen one of her bright suits, peach in hue, with a white silk blouse, and sensible heels that helped support the weight of her sizable calves and ankles.

"You have the people in the waiting area," Eleanor said. "We canceled on them three times. Remember they helped you last year: your lawyer's cousin's friend. I think this time you should . . ."

"Really? They gave me shitty advice last time. Put them in the conference room, and I'll talk to them from the car. I'll FaceTime you once I get downstairs. Show my face on the video conference projector. Just as good."

Eddie pushed open the glass door of his office, marched out, and pushed the elevator button. He stared at his reflection in the bronze-mirrored panel. At five feet eight, he may not precisely tower over people, but, he figured, his strong limbs, cropped brown hair, and large, full lips and eyes, made him a damn good-looking male specimen.

He was wearing a Thom Browne suit that hugged his crotch a little too tightly, especially when he got a hard-on from imagining frisky lesbian art dealers, but he'd lose the weight soon. Though that stylist at Barney's explained Thom Browne designed for lanky models, not men who cut such a muscular girth, nor with such thick thighs, he ignored him. Eddie figured the suit would fall better with the ten pounds off. That was two years ago.

He adjusted his testicles a little and then loosened his flashy purple Prada tie. Caroline never liked that tie and told him he looked silly in it, like a disco dancer, like John Travolta in the old days. She would have liked it a lot less if she knew Hélène bought it for him. He always wore it on the Thursday before Memorial Day weekend. Hard to believe, but it was the tenth anniversary of that very, very bad day.

Waiting for the elevator, he looked at the strange geometric lines and shapes in the drawing he'd bought at the recent contemporary evening sale at Sotheby's. He couldn't ever remember the artist's name. He looked again at the plate: Julie Mehretu. That's right, *Mehretu.*

The three other companies on this floor didn't seem to care about what art Eddie hung in the public spaces. They didn't have any taste anyway. All he knew was Goldman Sachs had a big Julie Mehretu painting in their lobby on West Street in the Financial District. His company wasn't exactly Goldman, but the feel of his entrance should match the lobbies of the Wall Street giants.

Marcus McCree was waiting downstairs for him, out front of the Lever House restaurant where Eddie and every other power *macher* in Midtown ate lunch. Marcus rarely chauffeured anymore, but when he did, he always drove one of the two navy-blue Maybachs in his fleet.

All through high school, Eddie had driven a navy-blue Ford F-150 pickup. Uncle Charlie had agreed to split payments with him, as long as he did well in school and worked hard at his summer jobs. Eddie's father had only driven that oil truck his whole life, no reason he had to be so tough on his son. Charlie thought it wasn't the kid's fault Jake drank himself into oblivion all the time.

Jake Clarkson egged his son on every time Eddie walked through the door of the home he'd bought for them. "Why don't you come home more often," he'd slur from the worn, rust-colored corduroy Barcalounger he'd installed front and center in the new living room, despite his son's disagreement. Or rather, because of it. "You too good for us, now?" There was nothing much Eddie or Caroline could do to appease him, not that he was ever sober enough at night to hear them. When Eddie would splurge on anything— from a navy Mercedes AMG S65 to a set of soft, navy Louis Vuitton loafers—he often did it to spite his dad. Just to prove he could live any way he pleased. Most material things in his life had that instant ability to make him feel like a badass motherfucker. Especially navy blue things, the color of winners.

"Hey man, good to see you; glad it's you today, Marcus." Eddie slapped the driver's shoulder and stepped into the quiet womb of the plush back seat. "Take the FDR Drive, would ya? I hate the lights, even if that traffic app tells you to take First Avenue, just ignore it. Jesus Christ, it's hot today."

"You got it," Marcus said. "We'll take the drive." After sealing Eddie into the back, he moved like Fred Astaire as he walked to the driver's side. Marcus McCree ran the Executive Coach enterprise with sixty cars and a hundred drivers with different shifts.

Marcus served in the police force for a dozen years, which allowed him to watch things, speculate intelligently on things that weren't right. He was shrewd in many areas, not only in starting a business from scratch. A forty-year-old African-American man with a shiny, clean-shaven head and an elegant, slim frame, he looked even taller than his six-foot-three height. Marcus didn't drive anymore because he ran the enterprise. He only started driving Eddie because he'd gotten that phone call to check on him. He knew that he was in a position, like the man who'd called him, to tidy things up, and to protect people.

THE MAYBACH CROSSED the hustle of morning in Midtown and entered the FDR Drive downtown at Sixty-Third Street and the East River. The car hovered over the jagged cracks in the pavement and the deep potholes as if on a sea of clouds. Eddie FaceTimed Eleanor from his iPhone. His image appeared on the office video screen; Eddie could see the three losers in suits sitting around his conference table. He yelled into his phone, "Go ahead with the pitch. You got ten minutes."

His personal cell phone rang twice, and he rejected the call before Brittany could get through. She was a little needy sometimes, and it made him nervous he'd be found out. He hoped the man—or woman—upstairs in the sky wasn't watching through the sunroof. Eddie often got superstitious, and he looked for signs.

Birds were always telling him things, swooping down and sending him messages. Rain always meant good luck. After big pitch meetings, he'd make sure every little thing the rest of the day was done with good intent, energy, and generosity. If he saw a wrapper on the sidewalk, he'd pick it up and throw it out. Sure, sometimes he'd walk past it, and then huff and go back and get it. He'd give up a taxi he'd hailed to a woman waiting, or to a man, and even hold the door for the woman or the guy—even though it made him look super gay. Eddie didn't believe God controlled the cash flow, but he felt someone was watching. Someone was judging him, he knew that much. Like Uncle Charlie said, *You earn your luck.*

The Maybach rounded another curve near that tacky restaurant on the water. Those lousy shrimp puffs from that sweet sixteen entered his mind—he had to go, the father was an investor. Eddie opened the window and stretched his head out. It felt as if he'd stuck his face near an open oven door, but the wind dried the sweat on his forehead. Another masterpiece banger of a song came on.

Alejandro, Alejandro . . .

Marcus glided off the FDR Drive at the Avenue C exit. A few twentysomething men played handball in gated, worn-down courts. Girls in booty shorts and colorful halter blouses sat nearby on overturned white painter's buckets. Travis Scott blared from a speaker by their side. As Eddie and Marcus drove into the depths of Alphabet City, near Tompkins Square Park, they passed twenty-four-hour bodegas selling cigars, vaping paraphernalia, soda, and chips, alongside trendy restaurants with French names he couldn't pronounce.

The high and low pulsing in this great city was awesome. Caroline, for some reason he could never understand, wanted to move back to the wood-and-sand hinterland of Long Island. Another million in his bank account might help sway her; although he knew she didn't care about all the cash like he did.

Marcus stopped a block up on the corner of Avenue B and Sixth Street by the Le Chien Noir bistro. Eddie opened his own door. This is how he always wanted it downtown. This area was half hipster, half somewhat poor, and he didn't want to look like a bougie banker guy. He'd instructed Marcus the first time they came to this block to never forget how he wanted it done: wait behind the wheel and stare ahead. *Don't even look sideways.*

Eddie walked into the small French bistro, one with a down-and-out, seedy decor that surely took more time to curate than a spanking new one. Above the counter, the menu was written on a blackboard with white chalk in letters that looked a tad too French and swirly for his taste. He didn't really get the French, or even twentysomethings these days. The place was hip, but red linoleum chairs looked pretty down-market to him. At least, he didn't need to order and try to figure out what the menu said.

He sat down in the far corner. Véronique brought over his French grilled cheese, ham in the middle, white sauce inside, as usual. It was called a croque something, but he didn't like to try to say it. He cared far more about the fact that Véronique's leggings looked as though they had been plastered onto her bulbous beach ball of an ass. He loved that her blouse was strategically buttoned at the very bottom of her lace bra, right where her messy blond curls ended. She leaned her bountiful tits into his ear. "Your Tabasco is by the napkins. You want a regular Coke again or you want to be a little wild and have a 7UP," she asked. Her butt rubbed his shoulder firmly as she turned away.

Uncle Charlie had told him only safe women could be indulged in. "Safe" meant a woman who would lose as much as you if word got out. But sometimes Eddie slipped a little: just that one blow job from Véronique, that one time. Life was too short not to experience those comic-book-level lips around his cock once. Just like Veronica in the Archie series, he kept telling her.

No matter how hard Véronique tried to seduce him again, Eddie promised himself he'd resist. Uncle Charlie was right: you only screwed women who were safe. Véronique was not only single, but looked at him with longing. Also, she didn't have any money, and now, he had way too much: the very definition of unsafe. Uncle Charlie up in heaven was wagging his finger: *Stay away from that French woman, they're all seductresses.*

Still, he wasn't to blame for treading into dangerous territory a few times since he got married. What the hell was he supposed to do when he wanted a little activity and minimal risk? Do a rich housewife with equal standing? Women in velvet Gucci loafers didn't turn him on, even the purebred hot moms in his neighborhood. He didn't see why Constantine, the doorman, called them yummy mummies. He and Constantine would argue over whether the moms were horny. Eddie always maintained it had been a decade since most of them had come for real. The cruder he got, the more Constantine laughed.

Véronique returned with the sweet potato chips he loved, even though he hadn't ordered them. He pushed them aside and adjusted the waist on his tight slacks. "Thanks, but not today, baby." He patted Véronique's ass and, studying it for a moment, figured it was the size of a basketball, not a beach ball. The kind of thing you could cup in one hand.

"Where is my man?" he asked her. "I've been here five minutes already."

"You know the drill, honey. You made the rules, now you forget them? You eat your croque monsieur. You drop the napkin on the plate. I get it. He comes in when you're done. You told us you don't like to eat and do business. You like to eat, *then* do business, or do business and *then* eat. So, if you tap the table like you did when you came in, I bring the food, and Thierry is going to chill outside near the lamppost." She nodded toward the opposite side of the street.

Thierry Moinot saluted. He was wearing straight-leg jeans, a fresh pair of black Nike Air Force 1 sneakers, and a gray bomber jacket. His ponytail stuck out of the back of his plain black cap. At thirty-seven, and a very slight man, he didn't want the balding part to show. Thierry kept the hat on all day every day when the sun and lights tended to highlight the thinning hair on top. He wasn't too successful with the ladies. Anything to help.

Once Eddie had demolished his croque monsieur and inhaled the chips he maintained he didn't want, Véronique cleared the table. Thierry got the signal and crossed the street slowly, like a fighter readying to duel. He was the son of one of the greatest polo players ever to play in Europe. Certainly, the greatest to die in debt.

When Thierry sat down, Eddie asked, "What's with the attitude? I'm paying you."

"Given everything, you have no right to discuss my mood," Thierry stared flatly. "I've done everything you and Philippe asked me to do. I play ball, and I deliver."

Eddie nodded. "Well, you got everything?"

"It's Philippe who got everything for you. I believe it is as you wish. Fifty-three prized animals in your new stables in Bridgehampton."

"And all the equipment? The bridles? Every fuckin' fake Hermès saddle I ordered from his bullshit replica people who charge me close to full fare?"

"No one will know the difference; he promised you that. All the equipment is out there. I've been working all week. It looks like the fanciest vineyard in the world, not a stable for horses. Just like you planned. And ready for the Memorial Day weekend." Thierry was thinking it was a pretty shitty thing to sell clients fake Hermès who could afford the real deal anyway. Nothing made sense to Thierry about Philippe and Eddie's arrangements on the whole horse complex. He was only doing his best for little Rosie.

Back in his Maybach, Marcus McCree snuck a sideways glance. Something was up today with Clarkson. He wished he could read lips as well as his deaf little sister. Next time they drove down here, he'd tell Justine to rush and sit discreetly again in the bistro. While Eddie Clarkson ate his two-thousand-calorie French sandwich, Justine had translated all his crazy shit twice now. By the look on Thierry Moinot's face, he could tell there was much more he needed to understand to protect that Caroline Clarkson. She was always too nice to everyone, including her husband. Marcus vowed to stick behind this wheel, for this client only, until he had it all under control.

Chapter 4

Strange Stroll

Let's go get your work stuff done," Annabelle said as she and Caroline left the pier. "One more thing, though: Why did you keep saying you felt strange on that bench? Don't think I didn't notice you evaded my question."

"You're going to think I've lost my mind," Caroline answered cautiously. "But I'm a little off today because I honestly thought I saw Joey Whitten." Her heart plunged into the depths as she admitted this out loud; she kept picturing Joey's stubbly beard and his firm, square jaw. And then, imagining the waves overtaking him, that beautiful face sinking.

To this day, she'd sense Joey's presence in the room sometimes, and would hold her arms tight to her body, feeling him. She whispered to him when she walked on their beach off Atlantic Avenue. Many times during a random hour on any day, she still felt an urge to tell Joey about something funny or stupid someone had said. But, as her grandmother on the Henderson side told her at his funeral: *We don't end up with the one we love the most.*

That was the saddest thing she ever heard.

After an emotional year of walking around in a virtual zombie state after Joey's death, Caroline finally fell into Eddie Clarkson's arms. Eddie had pursued her relentlessly since they were in the ninth grade. When their algebra teacher kicked him out of class for a rude, rebellious comment, as she did pretty much every few days, he'd smile at Caroline on the way out. No one her age had ever shown off for her, winked at her and meant it. Eddie's insurrections had made her ache to know him better. Finally, one afternoon in his attic, they made out so hard her lips stung for days.

Since that one kiss, that one Algebra class, Eddie had never once fallen for anyone else, even during the six years she was with Joey. Eddie had told her that about five thousand times ever since. When he teased that he was her rebound man, the joke always made Caroline uncomfortable. A year after the tragic drowning, it felt good to be held so tightly, to succumb to a strong man she'd known for a decade, who loved her fiercely. And no man would top his marriage proposal, on his knee in that insane medieval costume.

"He's gone, honey," Annabelle reminded her as she tapped on a restaurant window beside her on the sidewalk. "Once we get your work done, let's have lunch here, then to Eddie's stables to check on the ponies." She hoped Caroline wouldn't detect that she really wanted to check up on that new polo playing trainer, Philippe de Montaigne. What a delicious name. The body was *beyond*. She went on, "And, sorry, what's possibly going through your mind that would make you believe you saw Joey Whitten?"

Caroline's face turned more serious, as if honoring something precious. "I saw a little boat like his, a Boston Whaler in the harbor. The guy had his exact profile. And I'm remembering everything . . . even the feel of his face."

"The feel of his face? What are you talking about?" Annabelle asked, never a big romantic. "I mean, I get it, he was dreamy, but why would you think you saw him? Kind of ghoulish, no?" She knew Caroline was always more emotionally affected by things big and small. One memory could launch her friend into a completely different mood.

Caroline thought about the old bed in his grandfather's beach shack, how the lights never worked, and how the ocean breeze wafted through the windows and always blew out the candles. How that annoyed Joey because he couldn't see her nude any longer, beneath him, beside him, over him. Afterward, they'd laugh about how the wind was always strongest right when they were in the height of it, not the time to stop and relight candles.

Caroline huffed. All of it, too sad. And so fresh in her mind, even the smell of the blown-out candlewicks.

"Are you going to answer me, or are you going to walk into this piece of metal?" Annabelle asked, as she yanked Caroline closer to her, saving her from the sharp edge of a street sign that nearly cut her head. "Just because you saw a Boston Whaler, literally the most common boat in any marina on the Eastern Seaboard, and some guy with a handsome profile driving it, doesn't mean Joey's come back from the depths of the sea to screw you."

"Stop." Caroline laughed. "It's been thirteen years, and I still remember everything about him: his voice, what made him laugh, every second of being naked with him." Even the scent of sex seemed to be heavy in the humid air around Caroline today. "He used to make me smile just by walking in the room, and that guy on the boat, just like Joey, had these kind of sculpted arms, curved in, slumped shoulders, that . . . I don't know; there are men that just linger in us, forever."

"C'mon, you're never going to get over that one," Annabelle replied. "He's gonna linger, Caroline."

The deckhands holding brushes and rags stopped working as the two beautiful women walked down the pier. Caroline, at a young-looking thirty-eight, was round all over her short, tight body, with balloon breasts and a full behind. She could sense men and women alike watching her piercing blue eyes and her curvy build when she walked down the sidewalk or into any restaurant. Even when Caroline was little, her mother used to say she stopped traffic on Main Street with her fair skin against her Snow White, jet-black bob.

Meanwhile, Annabelle, at forty, walked like a ballerina, even though she never took one dance class in her life. At a lean five foot ten, her straight, Nordic blond hair fell down her back and ended in a manicured line that swayed side to side as she moved, like a freshly cut hedgerow. The muscles in her thighs were outlined through her tight, white jeans, especially when she knelt in that way she knew highlighted her body.

"You're thinking about Joey because summer is starting, and you both loved the beach, and then when I pressed you about our affair plan, it got worse," Annabelle reminded her, wrapping her rose cashmere sweater around her shoulders like a true American aristocrat.

"*Your* affair plan."

"Okay, mine, but possibly yours too. That got you thinking about the crazy sex you said you always had with Joey. And besides, if you're going to sit on a bench for a long time and get all insane and depressed, then you can easily imagine some shadow out on the water is something it isn't."

"I'm sure you're right," Caroline said.

AND NOW, WAY out of the women's sight on the other side of the Sag Harbor town bridge, that Boston Whaler idled offshore, Joey Whitten at the wheel. With his Yankees baseball cap tightly pulled down over his face, he drove that boat in a similar daze. He had seen Caroline too, and he knew she was no ghost, but his raven-haired love. Those twenty worn photos he'd touched and caressed every day, now curled at the edges, white scratches crinkling the surface, didn't show the real story. In the last thirteen unlucky years, Caroline had become even more beautiful than he ever remembered.

Chapter 5

It's Très Chaud *in the Hamptons*

As a delivery truck exited Eddie Clarkson's equine complex, Philippe de Montaigne drove his clementine-orange convertible Porsche toward its rear gate. The fresh air blew back his floppy French hair, and he wondered if the rushing wind might flatten his natural waves a tad too much. The former polo champion pushed his new Persol sunglasses down his nose a bit and stared at his penetrating bedroom eyes in the rearview mirror. Was it possible these glasses made him even more handsome than the vintage Ray-Bans he'd worn for decades?

As this megalomaniac stared at himself instead of the road, his car veered across the center line, while a delivery truck roared down Spring Farm Lane toward him. The truck driver honked loudly, just in time to avoid a head-on collision. *"Merde alors!"* Philippe screamed out the window, blaming yet another American who couldn't drive. He would not recognize the delivery driver, nor know that the man had no business being anywhere near Sea Crest Stables.

Philippe punched in the code to the back entrance. This gate was constructed of plain steel rails, far inferior to the white basket-weave woodwork entrance that welcomed clients out front. Philippe was the head trainer of Sea Crest Stables after all, not a junior employee. He imagined his grandmother watching him now, trying to fathom a world where her grandson, Philippe de Montaigne, had been formally relegated to the service entrance.

Eddie Clarkson insisted anyone making an actual salary at his new equine complex not sully the front area with cars and their resultant dust. When Philippe complained about parking his vintage sports car in the back near the hay bales and porta potties, Eddie answered, "Yep. The back. It'll set an example for the rest of the staff. You know, that you're *on their team.*"

Since his infamous polo accident had put an end to his modeling and sponsorships days, Philippe was exceedingly low on funds. He needed this job, but he didn't remember Eddie explaining that he would be treated like the guys who raked up the horse shit. He had, after all, introduced those polo playing investors to Eddie in the first place. Upon hearing the entrance rules, Philippe had raised his right eyebrow in that way that made women weak with desire. He asked, "The back, I see. If you park in the front, does that then mean you are *not* on their team?"

"I own shit, I run shit, and I drive where I want," Eddie replied.

Philippe had considered telling Eddie to suck his huge French dick right then and there. Americans were like that, always categorizing people by how much money they had. Philippe's ancestors were barons and counts, and inside the circles of refined people on the other side of the Atlantic, breeding, not one's financial assets, mattered most.

Philippe parked beside a stinking manure pile and slammed the door of his Porsche shut, rattling the car with a tinny bang. The door handle was a bit loose, but he didn't have the money to spend on an overpriced mechanic. It had been three years of hell with his endorsements gone and income dribbling in. No company wanted a forty-five-year-old with a leg limp as the face and body of their products. He walked through the dirt, the pain from the iron rod in his left leg constant. His right arm was so mangled from the collision of seven horses that it still hung awkwardly from his shoulder. Thank the good Lord his fingers still worked on the crucial lady parts. That light, butterfly fluttering touch of his caused women's eyes to roll into their heads, and to moan like wounded donkeys.

Philippe's polo accident, replayed on YouTube 493,238 times so far, was known in elite horse circles as "the big one." In the smash-up two years before, all the riders were jettisoned from their saddles, and several horses tumbled onto their sides. Philippe was thrown as if he'd been flung from a giant medieval slingshot. He lay in the dirt for minutes, his limbs splayed like a starfish's, before anyone, including the EMTs, dared to move him.

His polo days over, this trainer job made sense on numerous counts. The French partners that basically owned Eddie Clarkson had told Philippe to leave everything to the Americans, that the deal would flush him with cash. It was Maryanne who would keep everything running smooth and on the down-low. Eddie Clarkson was a diverting sideshow. Everyone knew that.

As for Eddie's side, when the French investors pushed their man Philippe as a watchdog employee, he agreed right away. Eddie knew his clientele well, the main key to his success in real estate. Philippe's bad boy brown hair and doe-like eyes would not only provide the right cover, but lure clients in—especially the fortysomething moms heading full throttle toward adultery and divorce. He'd told Maryanne early on, "That's the kind of polo-playing playboy I want as the head trainer: catnip to all those unhappily married felines."

As PHILIPPE ENTERED the center hallway of the main stables, his proximity to Earth's noblest creatures started to repair his sour mood. He reminded himself that an entry gate did not count in life, only manners and penile girth did, and to put his ego aside.

Watching the moms' asses bouncing in their tight horse breeches would make Eddie's idiotic rules easier to bear as well. He liked to complain, but the reality was this: as he strolled by the prized animals he trained, he could hardly wait for summer to begin.

THE STABLES BUILDING, made in the shape of an X, housed forty stalls in each of four long halls that met in a middle, circular room. A fountain punctuated the center with navy and white mosaic tiled walls that rose to a cathedral ceiling with flying buttresses. Eddie had picked a deep blue to match first-place ribbons, his lucky, winning color.

Philippe stopped at the third stall on the right, *Seaside* engraved on a brass nameplate on the door. A prima donna worthy of his fame, Seaside's balletic stride earned national championships in the prestigious amateur-owner hunter divisions. The animal, belonging to that American delight, Annabelle von Tattenbach, stood imperiously in his housing, playing hard to get.

Philippe grabbed a huge, deformed carrot out of a bucket and snapped it in two. The gelding turned quickly for the treat, suddenly finding his trainer worthy of attention. Philippe fed a piece on his outstretched palm and patted the distinctive seahorse-shaped spot on Seaside's face. He then grabbed both sides of the bridle and planted a kiss squarely on his nose. "You snob," he said. "You only talk to me if I feed you. I love you anyway."

Philippe heard the wooden barn doors at the far stable hallway slide open. That very Annabelle von Tattenbach strolled toward him, her slender legs slicing through beams of sun and clouds of dust. Eddie's beautiful wife walked beside her. Grading Caroline's physique, he decided she was too fleshy in the hindquarters, too roundly American for him—a good thing since she was married to his boss. A bit disgusted by her full thighs, he thought, yes, resisting Caroline Clarkson would be easy. He fancied women with coltish legs, long necks, and a more aristocratic way about them. Women should be tightly formed, but with muscles that weren't too defined.

"Philippe!" Annabelle said, as she removed her sunglasses and approached him. She pulled her blond, shiny hair from a clip. It was thick and straight like a horse's tail, as it fell suggestively around her face.

Philippe delicately touched her hair and guided her toward him with his left hand on her upper arm. Annabelle pulled back, feigning surprise at his boldness. He held on tight and forced a soft hello kiss near her ear anyway, burying his nose in her hair. "You smell so lovely, like spring," he whispered, raising his left eyebrow. "When is our lesson?"

"Seaside looks so happy in his new stall, don't you think?" Annabelle motor-mouthed. "How could he not? He's such a beauty. And One Hot Pepper, Mouse, Cappa, and Parker are ready for my daughters, I see! Will the rings be available for my girls on Sunday after the party? Or, because it's a holiday weekend, will they be in group lessons with everyone else?"

"We can work out anything you like," Philippe said. "The plan is yours to decide." He smiled. "Before the party, after the party, the next day. I'll cancel everyone but you and your girls."

Caroline, speechless again at this man's constant audacity, put her hands on her hips. This was no good. She tried to act stern, but she had to bite her lip not to laugh at him.

"I'm happy we're done with the old, crowded rings and that nasty trainer from the barn where we used to ride. I won't even mention his name," Annabelle answered, referring to her four equestrian-obsessed daughters—Lily, Liza, Louisa, and Laetitia (aged eight to fourteen, two years apart)—and the other stables they'd used for years. "And, yes, I'd love to set on a training regimen for the girls. The danger of all the horses jumping in two small rings was terrifying, and the reason why we moved the ponies and horses to the more spacious Sea Crest to begin with. I thought the girls were going to have terrible accidents." She looked down. "I mean, not a major collision like yours, Philippe, but still. It looked dangerous to a mother."

Caroline knew competitive horse showing was often a shady and shifty sport, and Philippe was just another sleazy player in the game. She'd warned Eddie about him and had pushed him to hire a woman she knew and liked instead. She was conflicted enough about allowing her nine-year-old daughter, Gigi, to ride in this elite sport at all, and Philippe as a trainer made it worse.

"Your husband has created a masterpiece. You know that," he said to Caroline, bowing slightly. "Please excuse me, ladies. I've got too much work to do to get ready for the party, all the crowds coming this weekend for their first inspection." He brushed the side of Annabelle's cheek with the back of his hand as if he were already her boyfriend, and then said softly to her, "I can't wait to hear your plan."

When the women reached the end of the hallway, Caroline turned to her friend. "I came here to let you check on your cavalcade of ungodly expensive show ponies and horses, *not* to watch you salivate over that hopeless lothario."

"I'm just checking out the merchandise, not purchasing."

"You better not," Caroline warned, knowing a dare only got her friend more motivated.

The women watched Philippe at the far end of the corridor in his white breeches, caramel riding boots, and tight, navy polo shirt. Despite his accident, he had managed to keep his muscular build very powerful and solid. The way he swung his left leg around to walk gave him a slight air of vulnerability that he played all too well with the ladies.

"Jesus, look at him," whispered Annabelle, in a bit of a trance watching Philippe depart. Slowly, she added, "What a very, deeply, astoundingly serious piece of ass."

"That is the type of person who would really fuck up your little affair idea this summer. Discretion is key."

Annabelle chose her right to remain silent: innocent until proven otherwise.

Caroline continued, "Discretion means *not* a well-known pussy hound. You need a lovely man who needs a little action: someone wealthy and single who doesn't want your money. That is the *only* way your whole idea can work."

"I have stiff-upper-lip breeding, and I'm not falling for anyone, so it's a little easier for me just to get laid with whomever as . . ."

"No, you're warped. Not *whomever*." Caroline looked at her friend and smacked her shoulder playfully. "You stay away from Philippe."

"When I have a feeling, you know how I get," Annabelle said. "I predict we both meet our affair-mates this weekend, even though you're not ready to admit you're already game."

"I never agreed to anything," Caroline reminded her, not honestly sure if Annabelle's affair pact intrigued or terrified her.

"And besides, he's a trainer who's well-trained himself," Annabelle added. "I can tell by the way his hand grazed the back of my neck. I'm sorry, but that was hot."

Chapter 6

Party Prep

A day after that slightly charged meeting with Thierry Moinot in Alphabet City, Marcus drove Eddie to his new real estate project in Bridgehampton. At 32 Spring Farm Lane, the gate opened on a property with undulating hills, four pristine horse rings, and four long stables. Thierry was right: Sea Crest Stables resembled an opulent Napa Valley vineyard more than a home for animals.

Naysayers told Eddie that developing the thirty acres was risky, and finding infusions of cash had been a grueling battle. Lending banks balked, concluding that his vision for the barn was too grandiose. Investors were skittish because he wanted to build the complex on the north side of the Route 27, the "wrong side of the tracks" in the Hamptons. They pointed out that all of the important homes, south of Route 27, were owned by families who "mattered." This estate section of town, near the ocean, allowed them entry into country clubs and parties with like-minded folk. Their stables should be close by.

"Guys, trust me," Eddie had disagreed. "I need thirty acres to build this dream. I found a lot on the north side: the seller is desperado, I'm telling you; we can rape him on the price.

"And don't forget I grew up out here and I live on Fifth Avenue now. My uncle Charlie drove me by every home out here since I was ten. He used to explain to me what land rich people buy to make them look rich, where they social climb and party, and the townhouse condos where they fuck their girlfriends. I got this, guys. You in or not?"

As the Maybach's wheels crunched along the cinnamon-colored pebble driveway, Eddie inhaled slowly, feeling grand self-adoration at the boldest real estate play of his career. Marcus opened his door. "I'm going to take a look around if I might?"

"Of course, Marcus! Be my guest, rifle through anything you want!"

Rifle through everything? *This clown's got no idea what's coming his way.* Eddie believed Marcus had chosen to drive him on occasion just to be a party to his inimitable, irresistible conversational skills. Eddie, oblivious, walked up to the main office of what he knew would become the Hamptons' premiere equine facility, knocking every other barn off its pedestal in one short summer.

A few celebrities, several of the wealthiest equestrian families, and one world-renowned trainer had signed up a year before Sea Crest was even finished. The stables would not only offer stalls for horses, and training lessons, but parties and championship horse shows. Rolex and J.P. Morgan had already put up purses for Saturday competitions for the best child and adult riders on the East Coast.

A Whispering Angel rosé bar would cater to the overwhelmed Hamptons housewives, all naturally exhausted from micromanaging both the decor and snacks on their helicopters. With *everything else,* it was downright *taxing* to find brown Pratesi cashmere throws that matched the muted Ultrasuede seats, and to tell the nanny to pick up those divine homemade potato chips from William Poll on Lexington Ave! And these women would flock to the rosé bar, because, well, who didn't need a drink after reminding their housekeepers, *for the tenth time*, to save the Frette powder room linen with the shell stitching *only* for guests, *never* for family.

Eddie dictated everything from the brand of mozzarella for the caprese salads at the café (buy it at Red Horse or don't serve it at all), to the bright purple bougainvillea whose abundant vines already climbed up the sides of the stalls. The landscaper, an old friend from fourth grade, explained that the plants Eddie coveted only flourished in warmer, dryer climates. "You can't have bougainvillea here, Eddie," he had said. "It'll never work. Give it up."

But the image of violet blooms on dark wood had stuck in Eddie's mind. It conjured up images of estates in the Caribbean, which, in turn, were reminiscent of the colonial tone he was after. In an *Architectural Digest* he'd saved from a dozen years ago, C. Z. Guest's home in Palm Beach burst with bougainvillea everywhere, and Eddie had thrown the article at his landscaper buddy, exclaiming, "I don't care how much this costs, or if it dies by September every year. This woman was the queen of society, and the closest to American royalty we'll ever get. Get me those gorgeous vines, growing up every column everywhere! Fly it in from Barbados if you have to."

Eddie walked straight to the smaller office in the back of the main entrance. "Maryanne, listen to me: the setup for the barn party tomorrow still feels half-baked. I want it all looking like a wedding. I told you that on Monday."

Without looking up from the wire reading glasses perched on her pointy nose (that matched her angular limbs) the middle-aged woman behind the desk answered, "Edward Clarkson: please don't use that tone with me." Maryanne had been the administrator of

Eddie's middle school twenty years before and had been just as harsh back then. When Eddie Clarkson was young, teachers wrote off his need to pummel his rivals as *grit*. Manners were never Eddie's strong point, in the same way doing the dishes or playing fair wasn't his thing, either.

"Don't talk to me like I'm late to class again, Maryanne."

"I'll call you by your full name when I want. I've still got many years on you." Maryanne refused to look at him. "Doesn't matter if I work for you now, we agreed that you would improve the way you talk to me." Maryanne's pageboy gray hair was styled neatly around her protruding cheekbones, and she took a few moments to neaten up the back, stalling to regain her patience. "We've got one day before the guests arrive on Saturday for your big opening," she explained, finally looking up at him. "The caterers are all here already; the tables are arriving soon. You wanted low-key class, and despite the injustice of this, may I inform you that you're not actually the sultan of Brunei."

"I'm not trying for showy! You don't get it!" Eddie responded.

"Oooh, I get it loud and clear." Maryanne wouldn't indulge him.

Though rather short, Eddie splayed his arms out on her desk like a giant. "I want this looking like a Rothschild vineyard from Bordeaux. All these rich families with little girls wanting to ride. All the Hamptons housewives who love horses and need a respite from never working a fuckin' day in their lives."

No one at Sea Crest had ridden in serious competition yet, but dozens of horses and ponies had arrived earlier in the spring. They were housed in polished mahogany stalls, each with a brass nameplate engraved with the horse's name. Eddie had built four rings outside. The inside show ring had climate-controlled viewing rooms with cushioned stadium chairs for spouses, partners, friends, and parents in the rooting section.

Eddie had even constructed an upstairs media room set up like a sports bar with several ESPN channels streaming on large screens. He called it the "Branch Water Lounge" (the name serious drinkers from Kentucky call their whiskey). Again, he knew his clientele: bored fathers, pretending to watch their eight-year-olds jump a pony over a six-inch rail, could slip away to catch baseball, golf, or football. Many of them might need a stiff one after writing checks in the hundreds of thousands of dollars to buy an animal their spoiled kid would get bored of in a year.

A designer who'd previously staged Ralph Lauren stores went to flea markets and found worn, leather viewing chairs, primary-colored horse blankets, winning chalices. Championship ribbons from horse shows Eddie had never heard of (nor had the designer) adorned the walls. At the bar, he had dozens of crystal low-balls lining shelves and he served only one whiskey, and only the best: Pinhook.

"It'll be fine, Eddie," Maryanne answered calmly, looking down at her ledgers. Payroll for all the grooms and trainers was due this very afternoon, and she was busy. She took out the calculator from her desk drawer and slammed it closed. "You've done all you can, little rich kids and adults leasing and owning animals, and your own ponies and horses for the local kids, charging thirty-five dollars an hour for their lessons. *So everyone gets to ride.*"

He slapped the end of Maryanne's desk to get her attention. "How is the vegan juice bar, all the boosters and shots ready?" He started counting on his fingers, "I told them I want MCT oil, all of that, spirulina, chia, flax, macha, mucho probiotic, whatever-the-fuck Gwyneth Paltrow bullshit in there."

Maryanne looked up at him over her reading glasses. She could only shake her head.

"Those famous women who ride, that Olsen twin—who can tell which one it is, but one of them rides—Matt Lauer's hot ex-wife, will make horseback riding more appealing than sweating your tits off on a bike in a dark, smelly room with bad disco, don't you think? Those candles in those friggin' spin classes make no sense! You're not chilling, you're sweating your balls off! Speaking of sweating your balls off, I mean, c'mon! Think of the *E. coli* on the seats alone!"

Maryanne stood up and walked over to her files, Eddie trailing her like a puppy. A folder in her hand, she turned to go back to her desk, Eddie now blocking her way. "Could you just give me some personal space and move?" She sidestepped around him.

He paced around in small circles and jabbed at the floor with his foot. It screeched from the rubber on his new navy JP Tod boat shoes. "I want it to look rich, but like I didn't even try."

"But you did try, Eddie. It's almost all you've done for two years now."

Eddie turned his head in circles to crack his spine. He closed his eyes for several seconds. His nostrils flared as they took in more air.

Maryanne hadn't even started logging up costs for the feed, hay, and deliveries that would arrive any minute now. And though she vowed to work on his manners, she also knew that people don't ever really change. As far back as his tenth-grade year, she had heard that Eddie would surf the bigger Montauk breaks when he was too young to be welcome. He'd think nothing of dropping in on the best rides from guys who considered that section of the Atlantic their sacred territory.

In the years since, Eddie's classmates, many of them rival surfers still pissed off at his selfish ways in the water, had become landscapers, architects, teachers, and restaurateurs. They had their own families now, from Southampton to Bridgehampton, East Hampton to Amagansett, all the way to Montauk. And the locals stayed close in the long months of winter, nursing beers in small bars, laughing about old times, and complaining about all the cheap dickheads from the city who questioned every line item on their bills.

It made Eddie feel good—magnanimous even—to hire a few of these old friends at Sea Crest Stables. He wanted to throw them a bone, even though Caroline cautioned him against working with any of their former schoolmates.

"The economic divide is too big now, Eddie," she told him. "They're going to resent you more than they will feel grateful. Don't do it; I promise it'll turn sour."

But Eddie didn't listen to his wife. He hired an elementary-school buddy to be the landscaper in the stables' driveway, and a painter he knew from tenth grade to do his office in gray, with French plaster, so the walls shone with a little expensive texture that only he noticed.

And when these men earning solid middle-class incomes heard that Eddie flew violet bougainvillea in from Barbados that would die in twelve weeks, they talked. And they watched, and they waited. Something would happen to Eddie one day.

"On the counters, let's get CBD! Sea Crest branded CBD Chapstick, creams, ointments! CBD everywhere!" Eddie knew he was pushing Maryanne. But what did he care? He was paying her, and she stood to profit big-time if everything went according to plan.

Maryanne slammed her hand on the desk. "You're like a bride, Eddie Clarkson. Just breathe. You've developed plenty of properties since you left town. This is no different from your little Rice Krispies enterprise in school. Take slow steps, and it'll all go according to your business plan."

In sixth grade, he'd bring Maryanne snacks he'd concocted when he was late to bribe her to take his tardiness off his record. Eddie the Entrepreneur (as he was known even in middle school) started an after-school Rice Krispies cart with flavors ranging from blueberry to caramel and chocolate chip. By eleventh grade, he'd hired three restaurant workers to make the treats, wrap them in plastic and ribbon, and sell them at schools along the Long Island coast and in gourmet shops in the ritzy towns. Maryanne used to tell him he'd be the next Paul Newman—except that she knew he would never give all his proceeds to charity.

"Eddie," she used to tell him, "if this Rice Krispies business doesn't work, you're going to make a lot of money with something else. One of these things is going to go big, and when it does, you'll have to admit I told you so."

"You'll be my first hire," Eddie always answered. "You'll watch me make my first million."

And back then, Maryanne, who was forty when Eddie entered the eleventh grade, had a feeling he was right, that he would actually hire her one day. He would help her get out of the school system just when she was ready to collect her pension and do something new. She was sure she would watch him make his first million. And his second.

However, Maryanne hadn't counted on making her own million. He threw that at her to keep everything very, very quiet. For as long as she lived.

Chapter 7

A Truck Driver Who Is Anything But

While Maryanne and Eddie bickered in the front office, a large, white delivery truck entered the service area of Sea Crest Stables. The driver wore a Yankees cap, the brim pushed down on his face. He wished he'd grown a beard so as not to be recognized. He worried his T-shirt didn't cover him enough, but it was hot, and he would look strange if he wore a hoodie.

The driver and three other men stepped out of the truck near the hay lofts by the back of the complex, preparing to unload feed before the holiday weekend.

"I have to check on something near the stalls. I'll be back," the driver told them, grabbing a clipboard from the truck. In a movie, he had seen an undercover investigator say you had to carry a pen and clipboard to look like you belong, and to arouse less suspicion.

He had answered the ad for a driver of a horse supply company four weeks before, as a way to gain access to Sea Crest. He'd explained to the owner that he had been living in Colombia for a while, helping to stock the restaurant of an eco-lodge, and that he had picked up Spanish down there. Many of the grooms were Hispanic, and many of them didn't speak English. After convincing the owner that he would be good with logistics and that he could speak to many of the laborers on the horse circuit, he got the job for the busy summer only, all cash.

When the driver entered the stable, he paid careful attention to the navy wooden trunks in front of each stall. A brass oval name-plate of the rider was nailed to the center. The barn shipped these trunks with the horses when the riders competed in shows in Pennsylvania, Lake Placid, and Florida. Peeking inside one trunk, he found helmets, bridles, sunscreen, gloves, and spurs. A drawer that slid across the top was piled with peppermint candies for ponies, bags of carrots, show ribbons, hair elastics, bottles of Gatorade, and protein bars that had melted from the heat.

A groom walked into the hall, and as he approached, the driver flipped through the pages on his clipboard and scribbled some fake notes, as he pushed his Yankees hat down further on his head. He was relieved when the groom made a left. Not able to find anything incriminating in the trunks, he now searched the tack room where bits and bridles hung on hooks. Very-expensive-looking saddles rested on polished wood bars. Nothing there, either.

Half an hour later, the driver steered his truck out of the massive equine complex, slouching so as not to be seen on the way out. He was annoyed he hadn't found anything. Maybe his source was wrong about the trunks. Still, he would have to find the goods somewhere else. Maybe Marcus McCree would have to come help him in person.

Anything to bury Eddie Clarkson in his own horseshit after all these years.

Chapter 8

He Built It, They Showed

SATURDAY, MEMORIAL DAY WEEKEND, BRIDGEHAMPTON

The day party for the launch of the Sea Crest Stables complex was packed; more than a hundred people showing up in the first hour alone. Faint notes of honeysuckle trailed through the persistent scent of hay. At the entrance circle, valets ran around opening car doors as if their lives depended on it. Cars from Priuses to Ferraris inched up in a line, announcing the income of those inside. No matter which chariot brought them, each guest stood awestruck at the exquisite barn and stables that Eddie Clarkson had created.

Parents huddled in groups or chased their children around the hydrangea bushes near the horse rings. A half dozen food and drink tents circled the main lawn, now filling up with guests nibbling on designer chips and mini lobster rolls, sipping rosé and mint lemonade, or queuing up to order a vigorous ginger shot.

The anticipation of summer simmered in the excited mood of the crowd. Pieces of conversations flew around the grassy fields and horse rings: *What kind of influx of cash did this take? How did that*

Eddie Clarkson develop this so fast? What percentage does that Eddie actually own?

Alongside several gated horse rings, pristine white cocktail tables stood on the green under large market umbrellas. Tented food and drink stations were scattered around the edges of the entertaining area offering sushi, mini sliders, sandwiches, and gelato in a dozen flavors. A truck pumped out thin-crust gourmet pizzas with truffled Italian cheeses and artisanal organic toppings. A rosé-tasting tent from the local Wölffer vineyard stood in one corner of the massive front lawn, a regular bar in the middle, and on the opposite edge, the fresh-pressed juice tent for the health-obsessed Hamptonites, already the most crowded.

Caroline still felt like an impostor with all this new wealth, and today, to mitigate any showiness (especially in front of old schoolmates who might come), she wore white jeans and a blue button-down she'd had for years. Eddie, meanwhile, marched around his manor in spanking new lavender JP Tod's moccasins and a matching lavender linen shirt. He shed his local East Hampton skin like a snake, allowing any sign of his past to wither up and turn to dust.

As Caroline leaned against a tree, checking her phone, figuring out which group to approach, Eddie had grabbed her hips from behind.

"Stop," she said, unpleasantly spooked.

He cuddled her and kissed her neck. "I want you by my side."

"You know I hate it when you come up to me like that," she told him. "I'm so proud of you, but don't scare me like that."

"C'mon, beautiful, off your phone. I know how you get all apprehensive. Lemme walk around with you."

"Well, maybe," she answered, knowing he got her ticks better than anyone, social anxiety and all. "You don't think I'm going to take away from your bro moments, working the banker guys out there?"

"I could introduce you to their wives, maybe some you haven't met?"

"You know the deal," she said, nodding. "Those horse moms think I'm some local yokel in the wrong clothes."

"It's high time they didn't."

"Let's get a smoothie over at the Juice Press bar, and just allow me to settle in at my own pace. I'm good."

Just then, Pierre Huntsman, a dashing Belgian billionaire now living in London with a boatload of children from several wives (and a gorgeous new husband he'd just married at his estate in Moustique), walked by. Eddie couldn't help himself. "Pierre, wait up!" he called. "I gotta talk to you! Your kids would fit right in!" And then, turning to Caroline, he said sweetly. "I'm sorry, you're right. This guy loves horses. He is *the central fuckin' fixture* of European social life. Lemme go work on him." He pinched her arm. "And if you're going to Juice Press, would you get me the Pink Dragon smoothie? And, honey . . . don't forget the turmeric booster. Makes me feel extra alive." Before going into battle to charm the Londoner, he pounded his chest like a gorilla and winked at her.

Next, Caroline walked to the lemonade stand where her nine-year-old, Gigi, and her favorite summer friend, Rosie, waited in line. "Girls, let me take you to go help with the pony rides, like we planned," she told them, as two men furiously cut up lemons, limes, and oranges before them. "A lot of the younger children will be scared to be in a saddle, and it's good to have other kids reassure them. Scooby-Doo and Sauerkraut are sweet ponies, and you know them better than anyone."

"We are, Mom!" Gigi said defensively.

"I'm just reminding you that you're the best helpers here, and the grooms could use you." Gigi was so sensitive these days, more so as she entered her tweens.

Caroline had allowed her daughter to ride ponies for three years now. The girls met at Gigi's old barn last summer, Rose Patch, where Rosie's uncle Thierry had served as a barn manager for the two dozen ponies stabled there, working for that well-known blond beauty Jenna Westlake, who served as head trainer. Rosie's mother had passed away when Rosie was a baby, her father had abandoned them, and she had lived out here with Uncle Thierry all of her life. Once the barn was complete, Eddie had poached Thierry to run the logistics and coordinate the horses at his own Sea Crest Stables year-round.

"I know you get it, honey: you ride, but you also love the responsibility of taking care of an animal. You're just like the working students here, who work for their lessons," Caroline said, kneeling down to face her child, brushing her long brown hair behind her shoulders. This time Gigi cuddled up against her for a tight, warm mom hug. She was glad Eddie had bought enough animals for the thirty-five-dollar lessons for all the local kids, so it wasn't only city kids here with cash and their own horses.

As she embraced her child, Caroline heard men arguing in the stable halls. She thought she heard the voice of that lovely Marcus McCree, who ran Executive Coach, inside. His voice was raised, which seemed odd. If someone were being terribly rude or rough, Marcus had that natural elegance that would diffuse the tension. She told the kids, "Girls, get your drinks when they're ready and wait for me a sec, then I'll take you over to the pony ring."

Caroline walked thirty yards closer to the barns near the tack room. She saw Eddie's two main employees, Philippe and Thierry, arguing with Marcus. None of them saw her, but she was close enough to hear garbled phrases.

"Why were you . . ."

"I was returning horse treats she'd . . ."

"Why the hell do you need to be in here at all?"

She crept up to the wall beside them and pretended to be on a call with her phone to her ear. Looking toward Gigi and Rosie, she waved and pointed at her phone, and held up her hand, indicating five more minutes to the girls. From this vantage point, with a window open to the tack room, Caroline could hear the conversation, or most of it. Philippe was somehow accusing Marcus of something. Nosiness? Theft? Impossible. What on earth could he have stolen? A bag of carrots?

"You never come in the tack room. No reason for you to be here!" Philippe screamed. "What do you need with the children's things? Do you ride horses? You want a saddle too?"

"I was just doing an errand in here, buddy," Marcus explained calmly. "Mrs. Clarkson asked me to check on her daughter's trunk. She's missing a jacket that I thought was in my car. And I got horse treats here."

"What kind of jacket?" Thierry asked, far more gently than Philippe had. He did, however, sound equally agitated. "He's right. You don't need to be here. Why didn't you just call?"

Caroline peeked around a pillar and saw Philippe jab his palm into Marcus's upper arm to make his point. Even though Philippe was five foot eleven, Marcus towered over him.

Marcus stood his ground and spoke softly, and in his calm, practiced manner said, "You all can please just keep your cool. It's your boss's big party day. He doesn't need any problems."

"But why did you come on a Saturday?" Thierry asked, still wary.

"I told you, man. I just had some horse treats from the city that his daughter wanted, and they were in the pile to come out here, and I figured they should be in her trunk, the girl would want them here. And, also, the wife said she needed the dry-cleaned jacket out here. I'm sure it was expensive and she doesn't want to have to replace it. You guys get that."

Thing was, Gigi's jacket was already dry-cleaned and folded in her trunk. And she never asked Marcus to bring horse treats from the city because they were never in the city in the first place. Plus, she would have called his executive car company in general to make a reservation for a car and driver, not the owner specifically. He didn't get involved in her mothering errands, she wouldn't even think to bother him with them.

Philippe pushed further. "Look, here's the deal: we don't want anyone who doesn't work here ever touching anything in this barn."

"These trunks belong to the girls, all thirty of them. Each girl has her boots, sunscreen, helmets, and extra crops in here," Thierry added, in a more conciliatory tone. "They don't need anyone moving things around. Same for the tack room. If they end up missing something, it'll be a safety issue."

"What kind of safety issue is a horse cookie or a jacket exactly?" Marcus wisely asked. "And I didn't touch any bridle."

Caroline decided it was time to intervene. She walked around the pillar and said loudly, "Why thank you, Marcus, for coming all the way out here on a holiday weekend. It's the big opening party, and we really needed those piles of treats and the jacket we had in the city front hall." At that, she shot Marcus a look.

He looked down.

"And one more thing, all of you . . . I really don't understand," she had to pry, "Marcus owns a large business he tends to, he drives our family sometimes only because Eddie pushes until he just relents, I'm sure. So what are you both accusing him of, exactly?"

"We weren't," Philippe said. "We just have to keep track of the horses' supplement intake. We keep some of their medicine in the girls' trunks. And bridles are particular to each animal, and I know them all so well."

"He wasn't touching bridles or medicine, he was just . . ." Caroline didn't finish, she knew all three men were being dishonest: Philippe and Thierry on one side of a lie, and Marcus on the other.

"You are so very, very right," Philippe answered obsequiously;

the snow job he did on most women possibly not as effective on Caroline Clarkson.

Thierry added, "I'm sorry. I agree." He reached out to shake Marcus's hand. "Sorry, sir, she's right. I worked hard to get the barn ready and I don't want to have any disorganization here. It's the first weekend of the season, just stress." He looked away and edged his jaw to one side. Caroline studied his expression, knowing people often make strange facial gestures when they aren't telling the truth. To mitigate the awkwardness among everyone, he said to her, "Thank you for taking Rosie today. She is going to ask for a sleepover, which obviously you don't have to agree to." He yanked at his ponytail, separating it in two to tighten it against the band.

"It's fine. They haven't asked, but that's good to know. I'm expecting some good behavior from them and, if they do well, that'll be the prize."

Caroline walked away, concerned. Something more than stupid male territorial pride was going on. She liked Thierry Moinot, they'd organized playdates for the girls for three summers now after the girls rode in the other barn he'd managed. She admired him for taking his niece Rosie on, with both her parents gone, but he was acting shifty in a way she'd never seen.

Adding someone with Philippe's temperament to the stable staff was a horrendous idea. He had manipulated Thierry into a cohort of some type—just like a seventh-grader who could transform a nice, docile friend into a bully.

She walked back to the girls who were waiting by the tent. "Thank you, girls, for being so patient."

"That was, like, ten minutes, Mom."

"I had to do something, honey," Caroline answered, feeling a bit sick to her stomach. "You guys can go get extra treats from your horse trunks and give some to the lesson ponies."

"Let's give them only peppermint candies. Ponies don't like the cookie ones," Rosie instructed, in that bossy manner she always took with the more pliant Gigi.

As she and Rosie walked off, Gigi turned back, her light eyes sparkling against the fair skin that Caroline recognized as her own. Gigi was becoming the mini-me everyone said she was. "Also, if we do a good job, can Rosie sleep over?"

"Of course."

Caroline watched Rosie walk with her tough girl stride, her thick limbs and middle section giving her a certain sturdiness and strength, and that hint of bullishness perhaps born from a life coping without a mother. Gigi walked beside her, more slight in body and manner, often deferring to Rosie's lead. Though her uncle Thierry had a network of aunts and grandmothers helping, he was unmarried and the sole guardian and parent.

Caroline took extra care to smother Rosie with maternal attention when the girls played at her home, dedicating extra time to do art projects or bake with them. When Rosie would talk about science activities at the beach, or hanging out at the barn after school, Caroline felt a pang of jealousy for her own child, who was boxed up in that horrible, cinder-block city jungle all week.

Chapter 9

Free Fall

At the juice bar, the way he raked his gray-flecked hair over his ear felt familiar to Caroline. When he wasn't looking her way, she managed to study his features through the crowd. His face was kind and weatherworn, tan already in May. She racked her brain searching for his name, but ultimately found nothing—a feeling not unlike a sneeze that faded and grew and then faded away entirely, leaving a sense of annoyance and dissatisfaction.

They might have walked by each other in a high school hallway when the bell signaled a harried change of classes. Or maybe they sat on the same bleachers at a basketball game. When he turned toward her, her eyes darted quickly away and she pretended instead to be judging the wait in line for the smoothies.

He walked around the far end of the counter, beyond the mason jars and baskets of vegan chia chips, and politely ordered. "I'll take a Clean Green Protein smoothie, please. Do you mind going easy on the ice? Sorry to be a pain," he said. His gracious manner made her wonder what it would be like to be with a docile man instead of the impetuous bulldog she'd chosen. Maybe she'd like it. Or, maybe she'd be bored.

He pulled a water bottle out of an ice tub before him and opened it. Something about Caroline, or, perhaps, just sensing a past connection, made him startle a little as he sipped. He attempted a little nod, something that said *I-know-you-too-but-I-don't-know-from-where* expression at her. This small motion back at her while he drank sent some water dripping down his shirt.

Caroline mimed *hello* and *sorry* at the same time, because she had a feeling her not-quite-normal level of staring at him caused his spill.

The servers hurriedly mashed kale, green apples, and carrots into loud, whirring machines, trying not to lose a finger in the process. The New Yorkers waved their hands high in the air, straining to get noticed.

Regardless of their placement in the line, they were all thinking the same thing: *I should be able to cut.*

He stood a few inches above most of the men there. One woman beside him at the counter thrust her drink in the air and demanded, "Could you redo this? I think you forgot the activated charcoal." Deep wrinkles fanned out from the edges of his greenish eyes, and he seemed to be considering whether or not to push his way around these people, who had turned his hometown into their opulent summer playground.

He rolled up the sleeves of his white button-down, and a vein crossing his left forearm showed across the counter. From ten feet away, Caroline noted the band on his left finger.

At the counter, the employee finally fit the lid on his smoothie. She mistakenly handed it to another woman who hadn't ordered it. She sipped it, knowing it wasn't hers, but claiming it triumphantly. He rolled his eyes while looking directly at Caroline, remarking on the wave of entitlement rolling into the tent like thick fog. The look alone told her that he assumed she had grown up out in the Hamptons as he had. She opened her eyes wide and round back at him, her expression saying, *City people can be such assholes when they want something right now.*

He then grabbed another cold bottle of water out of the tub of ice on the counter, and raised it in the air.

"Yeah, thanks," Caroline mouthed across the bar, even though she wasn't thirsty. It's only water, she told herself, and she wanted to find out where she knew this guy from, anyway.

Weeks later, Annabelle would remind her over lunch, "You could have whispered 'no thanks,' and gotten your own bottle of water." She then poured a little more rosé for Caroline and prodded her to take a sip, as if coaxing acknowledgment from her would take a little alcohol. "Yes, your husband's behavior warrants you having a dozen boyfriends, *simultaneously*. But I'm just saying, it didn't just happen. When you saw Ryan Miller in the tent, the descent was fast and slippery; you didn't fall into the rabbit hole, you jumped into it."

So, when Caroline agreed to move on from that bottle of water to a frosty Corona and lime with Ryan at yet another drinks tent, she hadn't tripped into a hole. It was a deliberate cannonball, an explosive splash echoing its intent.

Chapter 10

That Briefest Little Touch of a Finger . . .

"They've got a dozen food and drink tents here, and we picked the most crowded one." These were the first words Ryan said to Caroline at the barn party.

As he handed her the cold water bottle, his finger touched her hand and she pulled it away too quickly. "I didn't mean to stare. I do that when I can't place someone. My kids say I do it too much . . . my name's Caroline." She didn't include her last name on purpose.

"Ryan Miller. I think we were in school together, must have been. I know it's been a very long time. Maybe you were in my younger sister Katherine's grade?"

Caroline pulled her hair into a ponytail and let it fall down again just to have something to do. It was a tick of hers when she got nervous. An image from the past flew around in her mind: an art class from way back. "I was a Henderson back then. And, you know," she said, smiling a little. "I just remembered: I was in East Hampton middle school. You were in high school, and your class had our art class in to view senior-year projects. We were studying something Latin- or Greek-oriented, and I'd made a Parthenon type of structure that was listing sideways. You had this group of buildings you presented us with, they were so well done, and so high school-y."

"My senior-year architecture project: a beach stand, a complex or sorts," he said, laughing. "That was my career pinnacle, I imagined it built on a cliff. Or on a dune, actually."

"I'm just recalling your sister as well now. She was always so intimidating. She scared all the girls in my grade," Caroline said.

Ryan now recognized more about Caroline's face, her very dark hair against her porcelain skin. On weekend nights during high school he would often wait for his sister by the curb outside some house where a party was emitting deafening sounds of revelry. Caroline might have stumbled by his car after too many beers, or clung onto some crush's arm to steal away alone. "Katherine was cool from birth. I wasn't cool. I was a nerdy artist," he offered.

"Can't believe that."

"Yeah, I had three friends all through school. They were all science geeks. When we weren't blowing up soda bottles with Mentos in one of our basements, we'd build model houses out of balsa wood." He smiled. "Your face is familiar too. But I can't say I remember talking to you about my project, or the Henderson name just yet."

"Well, you kind of lectured us one day. But we all looked up to Katherine Miller, and then, I guess you were the older brother, so cool, by extension possibly?"

"Never. You just got a false impression." He smiled.

Silence followed. Both of them fiddled with the caps on their bottles. A gentle smile parted Ryan's lips, maybe one he didn't even intend, and Caroline decided he was one of those people whose face came to rest naturally in a slight grin. She didn't know what to say to restart the conversation. Annabelle could talk to anyone, but she froze up in situations like this.

Ryan pulled back hard on his blond-gray curls and started rubbing the back of his neck. He wanted to relax a little, and he wondered if there was a place to get a beer instead of waiting in line for kale juice. More people had gathered at the bar, which meant more hands thrusting in the air around him trying to get the servers' attention. He finally said, "These city people in line are stressing me out. I don't usually drink alcohol at noon, but Jesus, I could use a beer. Look at them, so competitive about getting their juice. Their nerves are contagious."

Again, Ryan and Caroline took a few silent sips of water. The two stood side by side, a bit awkwardly in that way people do who've come together by chance in a crowd. She scanned the crowd around them, and though she didn't recognize a soul, she almost moved on, albeit she didn't want to. It felt funny to stand there and not talk.

They spoke on top of each other next. Caroline offered, "Okay, then, nice to meet you."

At the same time, Ryan asked, "Do you know where the real bar is?"

"Over there," Caroline told him. "Go ahead, sorry to keep you." Now she was embarrassed; it seemed like he was looking for an exit strategy. Now she wished she'd taken her husband up on his offer to introduce her around. If she'd done that, she wouldn't be wandering around on her own in a hot tent with men trying to find a polite way to stop talking to her.

But for now, she decided, it wasn't her job to wait in this hot tent to get Eddie a smoothie, *with a turmeric boost*. She should be greeting the guests and new clients alongside him, instead of serving him.

Eddie could be the most doting husband, or the most self-centered. Often, he'd initiate some gallantry, but then get distracted. Today, the lure of the European horseman and her floating the concept of a pink shake sidetracked him. Her marriage was the reason to keep at her therapy twice a week; she'd be full of rage at his selfish, thoughtless antics, then she'd remember how much he loved her, and how much, deep down, he cared. How, with those parents having raised him, he really couldn't help but want too much attention in adulthood, to get his way for once. The push and pull got very confusing.

As for Ryan, he and this woman before him were only old school acquaintances, one he still couldn't quite pinpoint, but a dash of melancholy entered his mood at the thought that he might not see her for another twenty years.

"I don't mean to appear too forward, but . . ." Ryan smiled, trying not to sound all lecherous. "My wife is . . . over there in the sushi tent with friends, and my son is hating that I'm even here. My mere existence on the planet embarrasses him. So I'm just . . ." Ryan paused before he added, "You want a beer? Or, you want to just stay here while I get us two?" He'd mentioned his wife, so he figured that gave Caroline some clue he wasn't trying to get into her pants.

Once Caroline realized he was not trying to escape, she pushed her sunglasses back on her head so he could see her face better. He now saw how pretty she was, wisps of hair flying back in the breeze, revealing crystalline eyes. She was short, but cute and round short. He liked her white jeans and loose blue blouse that matched her eyes, the bottom side seam moving a bit in the wind and showing an inch of hip flesh. Good hip flesh, not all boney like the skeleton women around him from Manhattan.

Caroline couldn't entirely ignore the tug to stay near him either, his posture so solid, and a man much taller than Eddie. She considered what it would be like to sleep with Ryan for the briefest moment, but rather than let a harmless fantasy float around her mind, the thought entered her brain with a thud and got stuck there. It made her anxious. She breathed in deeply and patted the back of her head twice as if to dislodge the thought.

Annabelle was too flippant about the ramifications of straying this summer. Infidelity had to be like a pebble thrown into a pond, creating ripples that went on and on. Besides, Ryan grew up in East Hampton. There were too many connections, too many possibilities to get caught. Ryan probably had hung out with Eddie at some point in their youth. Annabelle was indeed nuts.

"You know what?" she answered, deciding that just talking to Ryan was innocent enough. "I would like a beer. I'm not one for huge crowds and big social events. My husband is busy too," she added, wanting, even though she wore a ring, to relay that she too was married. "And yeah, I kind of hate horses, and the horse moms from the city even more. But my daughter loves it all, so she, well, she rides here, or will this summer."

"Wait, what's your last name now?"

"Clarkson." Caroline rolled her lips tightly together. Busted. Now he'd know she was the owner's wife. This would change everything.

"Wow." Ryan nodded. And then, very slowly, he added, "Eddie Clarkson is your husband . . . yep . . . all coming together."

"Yes. Well, yes, that Eddie Clarkson is my husband." They walked in silence to the other tent. Once again, Caroline wished she could just gracefully leap from topic to topic with new people she'd met. Not liking that she felt funny, not liking that the Eddie acknowledgment came out as if she were embarrassed about his newfound wealth or even his boorish personality, she added, "I mean, Eddie's done a great job here, seen it through, no doubt."

"No one could say otherwise," Ryan confirmed. "I knew him from way back. We used to surf the same local break. Out at Turtles. I'm an architect now, more a restorer . . . I . . . was curious about his barn complex here from a design angle. Let me get us a beer. How about you try for a table?"

Ryan's stilted way of talking about her husband dismayed her, but she wasn't surprised. Everyone who grew up out here knew Eddie Clarkson.

Chapter 11

When You Marry for Money, You Work for It Every Day

Under the bar and wine-tasting tent, Ryan returned with two cold Coronas with limes stuck in the neck of the bottles. Caroline had planted herself in a cluster of small cocktail tables in a far corner. After Ryan sat, she noticed he then pulled his chair back a few feet away from the table, a safer distance somehow. He crossed his ankle on his knee and clasped his arms behind his head, studying her.

As she took a sip of beer, Caroline discreetly noticed his plentiful midsection, and thick arms. He was wearing flip-flops, jeans, a tan belt, and a white button-down with the sleeves rolled up. He didn't look like a guy who worked out in a gym, more like a healthy man who swam a lot, or surfed every day like so many of the people she'd grown up with who lived and worked outside. He could lose ten pounds, but so what? He wasn't eighteen anymore, and he was in good enough shape. The structure of his face not chiseled like a model, yet handsome, he carried himself as if he'd never much considered his own looks. And that permanent slight smile made her comfortable now, as did his soft greenish eyes, deep crinkles lining out from their edges. Ryan's blond-gray hair was a little messy, curling out where a barber should clip, a little long in the back, but she liked that, thinking that unkempt hair in men signified rebellion somehow.

She now reminded herself no one could contend she was flirting, only analyzing the impression this man projected, or how it differed from city folk. Besides, she could sit here a bit, it wasn't as if anyone else at the party was dying to talk to her. Far from it, the horse moms would be either dismissive or unable to hide their envy of the barn with an aside.

"Oh, so Eddie must have *really* needed to raise capital to get this done. Right?" they'd ask with a bullshit smile, and then contort their lips as if they'd bitten into a lemon. Rich New Yorkers were constantly taking the daily temperature of each other's net worth. Always pretending to be discreet, but painfully obvious in their need to know how much something cost, or to reveal how much they themselves spent. Quiet Caroline was an expert in these techniques to show off, and she'd often listen, appalled, and collect the best zingers. Joey would have died laughing at their pretensions. Her all-time favorite? "Oh, it's wheels up at three p.m.," something women at drop-off said, in pilot's lingo, to denote they were flying private, just to make sure everyone knew the whole deal. Ryan was simply better company than the spoiled brats from Manhattan swarming around her like killer bees.

Next to them, a portly middle-aged man in a blinding purple Ralph Lauren polo shirt, khakis, and Loro Piana $935 "running" shoes barked at his wife. He looked like someone who considered sports to be a punishing round of golf with his clients. His jowls shook a little just from snorting his impatience at pretty much everything around him. His wife gingerly placed a bottle of beer before him, and stepped back an inch like a pet that had just peed on the kitchen floor. He scratched the top of his thinning hair hard, marveling at the annoying injustices perpetrated on him 24-7.

It was a hot day for May, and the man's cotton shirt had dark lines of sweat where it had gotten stuck into his rolls of belly. Caroline figured he had to be someone who had inherited daddy's business and nearly run it into the ground. Ryan shot her a glance that said, *He's probably going to abuse her verbally about now.*

On cue, the man said, "Honey, sorry, but what the hell?" feigning kindness and patience. "You know I find Corona so watery. I asked for one of those Pilsners they serve at the club. Am I mistaken? If I am, please inform me."

The wife squinted, as if that might help her come up with a logical reason she'd married him. The corners of her mouth tensed up. To anyone but her husband, she looked like she might impale him on a tent pole.

Ryan dragged his chair closer to the table so he could whisper to Caroline. He explained, "Let me tell you something that I always think about when summer rolls around and these people invade our territory: *When you marry for money, you work for it every day.*"

Caroline laughed out loud and pinged her bottle against Ryan's. "Yep. I've never had it articulated to me like that exactly, but that is so true."

"Isn't it?" He smiled, more excited that he'd made her laugh than he expected.

"The diamond studs the size of headlights on those women don't come cheap," she whispered, grabbing her ear and motioning for Ryan to check out the rocks weighing down the wife's earlobes. "There has to be a ton of soulless work involved in getting those 'for free,'" she added, making air quotes around the last two words. Her remark wasn't as clever as his and she hoped she'd come up with a snappier riposte next time he made a joke.

"It looks like a friggin' miserable existence to me." He shook his head. "So, you're in the city, but I'm gonna guess you spend every free moment out here?" Ryan asked, wiping some beer off his mouth with the back of his hand.

"In the beginning we were going to stay for just a few years," Caroline replied, nodding. "We got married and moved to Manhattan, Chinatown actually, the next day. But Eddie's work has changed everything, made it impossible to leave. Like you maybe, I spent my whole childhood in a normal smallish house, a few streets from the beach on Bluff Road, where I could hear the waves when I went to sleep every night. I miss it. All the time. It still feels like real home out here."

"I get it: I can only take the city in small doses. I wouldn't know how to live without the beach," Ryan said. He would go into Manhattan for meetings or for a show, but he'd always be relieved when he was driving down the Long Island Expressway on his way home. He edged the sliver of lime out of the neck of the bottle and bit into it, wincing and blinking hard. "Where did you live in Chinatown? In architecture school, we studied those Lower East Side buildings. I worked on a small apartment once on Forsyth and Grand."

"That's very near where we were as newlyweds," Caroline said. "We lived above a noodle shop in Chinatown our first few years. I remember trudging up those dusty steps in our building and smelling the boiled pork from the restaurant on the ground floor." The restaurant exhaust would invade her nostrils, often waking her when they started cooking at four in the morning. Eddie could always snore through the city's sensory overload, but noxious fumes and the fiery tirades of taxi drivers outside rattled her night after night.

"I bet Eddie loved it. I mean, look at where he is now." Ryan shook his head.

She wanted to change the focus away from Eddie's wealth.

"And back then, living in that crappy building, I would lie awake wondering if my job greeting clients at a furniture gallery would ever get me ahead."

"You still work in the art world?"

"Nope, it was half gallery, half design firm, but I wasn't moving up at all. New York is so brutal that way. So I moved into full interior design, got a degree in a year, and landed some clients pretty fast after that. They've been smaller projects ever since—doing a few rooms at a time for people, mostly, which is fine with me. It lets me still spend time with my kids."

"Show me," he said. "Show me some things you did."

"Really?"

"Yeah." He smiled.

She took out her phone and showed Ryan her inspiration boards for the seven client jobs she had going. One by one, he asked questions about color, fabrics, and materials. They agreed that rafters and beams repurposed from old churches and installed in new ceilings was their favorite way to finish off a beach house. Caroline had recently found a very inexpensive source in Pittsford, Vermont, where an old Methodist church was being demolished. They had birch wood they'd salvaged in excellent condition.

Ryan asked that she send him the link.

She asked for his number without looking at him.

He gave it to her.

She sent the link.

"Again," Caroline continued nonchalantly, careful not to acknowledge that they now had each other's phone number. "I don't do much architecture work, but sometimes a ceiling needs help. So the guys in Vermont, about fifteen miles from Killington, send it in any amount you need, no minimums. My commissions are the normal trade rate, and I charge an hourly fee, so I'm not raking it in, but it's gratifying when the rooms are done."

"The work I do in architectural restoration earns a small percentage of the money I could make elsewhere," he said. "Can you imagine if I designed those monstrous ten-thousand-square-foot McMansions out here that pop up on potato fields like mushrooms? Fifteen percent on the construction costs, over and over again, like so many of my colleagues?"

"You could do that, you know," she offered.

"Yeah, then I'd be driving a Range Rover instead of my old pickup," he joked. "But I'm not. My paycheck hasn't much changed in a dozen years. I'm doing what I want, too." He smiled at her. "So, yeah, I get it."

Chapter 12

Stuck Together and Rather Happy About It

"You should go. I don't want to monopolize you more than I have," Ryan said. "I mean, you *are* the First Lady of Sea Crest Stables."

She threw her napkin at him playfully and said, "Don't ever call me that." Caroline looked over to see that Gigi, Rosie, and Theo were now at the arts and crafts area with the sitter, Francis, getting their faces painted. Thankfully, she could stay.

Ryan placed the beer bottle on the table and leaned back, clasping his hands behind his head again. He studied Caroline's features: the delicate mouth, the large blue eyes, the black hair against her fair skin. The curves on her upper thighs were more prominent the way she was sitting now. She was really pretty, but not seductive. Just really pretty. Period. Again, he said, "Honestly, don't you think you should . . ."

"No," she said, shaking her head. "It's fine. I'm good."

"Okay, then let's just chill here," Ryan said. He was relieved. He didn't want her to leave, and he didn't want to toddle after her into the crowd either. He wondered about going out to The Palm for dinner with Eddie and Caroline, and bringing his wife, Suzy.

It wouldn't work. Eddie Clarkson wouldn't be able to hide his disdain for people like Ryan, who reminded him of where he came from. Besides, Suzy would wonder why they were socializing with Eddie and Caroline all of a sudden. And be alone with Caroline? It wouldn't be easy to come up with an excuse to see her, or make it seem normal. He didn't do that kind of thing, flirt with women, or lead them on. Now that he heard Caroline's last name, he knew the whole story. He considered mentioning it right away, but instead he started slowly. "It's nice to hang with someone from school," he said. "I'm sure we have a ton of people in common."

"Like who?" she asked.

"And, just, uh, there's something I figured out when I heard your last name. I didn't want to mention it at first, but . . ." Ryan looked down at his feet and shuffled his foot back and forth across the grass.

"Go ahead," Caroline said. She wondered, *Has Eddie done something horrible to this guy in a real estate deal? Have they crossed paths?*

"It's kind of depressing in the midst of this beautiful, almost summer day, but Joey Whitten was on our Ocean Rescue squad," Ryan said. "I used to be the older kid sending him out on drills."

"Wow, yeah, then you certainly did know him," Caroline said. She tried not to show any reaction. She wasn't sure how to talk about Joey, but she was also glad Eddie hadn't been too much of a brute with Ryan at some point.

"I didn't really hang out with Joey because he was years younger, like you, but I knew him," Ryan said. "I knew he was a great waterman, even back then. By the time he was in college and really in charge of things on the beach in summers, I was in grad school."

"Wow," Caroline said again. Wow was not a word she usually used, and now she wondered why she had said it twice, as if hearing that Joey commanding a beach was extraordinary. He practically lived there.

Ryan balled up his sweater and leaned his elbow on it. "I really liked that guy, and I just want to say that to you," he said. "I mean, we might have become friends if we had hung out when we were both in our twenties. Not that I acted like an adult in my twenties." He paused and added, "You know, we might have been good friends if all that terrible shit hadn't happened."

"Yeah, well, that was a really screwed-up summer for me," Caroline said. Just then, the image of the Boston Whaler from days before flashed across her mind. She welcomed a connection with someone who had lived through the vestiges of the same tragedy she had. She pulled her hair back into a ponytail again and let it drop, brushing the top of her shoulders like a comforter.

"Let's just hope that was the single most screwed up summer of your life," Ryan said. "But, listen, you don't have to talk about it." He was surprised he hadn't made the link earlier, just seeing her across the juice bar: *Joey Whitten's girlfriend, of course. Then, for whatever fucked up lining up of the stars, Eddie Clarkson's wife.*

Ryan told her she didn't have to talk about it, and she didn't talk about it. She looked off toward the kids again and it gave him an opportunity to study her face a bit more. It hadn't changed so much in, what, the twenty years since they'd been in school. Caroline's features were nineteenth-century beauty material, he decided. But it was almost as if she were hiding it. He could detect no makeup, and that thick hair covered her gorgeous cheekbones.

Caroline waved to Gigi, and yelled out, "I'll be over when you're done, honey!" To Ryan, she said in a quieter voice, "And no, I don't mind talking about Joey, it's fine. I actually like it sometimes.

"My kids are happy. Eddie is in heaven welcoming the crowd. I secretly hate horses," she said, laughing a little. "I'm convinced they're going to chomp my shoulder if I get near them, and I always walk, like, ten feet behind them so they don't buck me. But my daughter loves them, so she walks them right over to me, at the fences, guiding their heads too close to me on purpose. She wants me to kiss them, which she knows terrifies me." Caroline felt that was a boring thing to say, made her look kind of flaky somehow, which she wasn't. She looked over at the kids again, and sipped her Corona. She crossed her arms and placed her foot up against the bottom of the tent pole, searching, in vain, for a position that made her look relaxed. "Plus, I hate the bullshit small talk that crowds always share. I freeze up, and my husband wonders why I'm acting shy. It's like, say what you mean or be quiet—that's just how I am. I don't like wading into a sea of moms talking about their Gucci sneakers and Balenciaga totes, don't feel I have something to add that they care about."

"No one's more out of it than I am," Ryan said. He looked over his shoulder for his wife. He saw her talking to girlfriends at a cocktail table. She saw him and he nodded to her. He turned back to Caroline and crossed his own arms, venturing no closer. He started wondering if he should leave, if this was a conversation he should not be having with someone he should not be having it with. He asked, "You sure it doesn't make you uncomfortable if I ask you more about Joey?"

"It doesn't. Not at all."

"I think about him sometimes, still. Especially when I'm on Atlantic beach. In fact, I always think about him there," Ryan said, unfolding his arms. "His drowning never made sense to any of us. I mean, that kid could have swum to Europe if he had to. I remember the whole thing. Most of us who grew up out here remember it too. And your part in the story is coming back to me. I can't believe I didn't place you at first."

One thing he didn't tell her: he didn't say that everyone had found it weird that such a pretty girl went from such a nice guy to such a dick. Maybe that's just the way things go. The coolest girls go for the worst guys. Suddenly, he felt a little fed up with life.

He said to Caroline, "Do you remember that fight Eddie and Joey had?"

"At the Ultimate Frisbee game," she said, nodding in an exaggerated fashion, to relay, *who didn't remember that game.*

"In the corner of the high school field. It took like five of us to get Eddie off of Joey. I thought he was going to strangle him. You know, he had his hands around the guy's neck, right?" When Caroline didn't say anything, Ryan felt like he'd been too harsh, and added, "I mean, in some way, I'm sure there was a reason for that aggression. We just didn't understand, is all. It obviously wasn't just a Frisbee game. It must have been some girl they were fighting over."

"It was. Of course it was. Joey had taunted Eddie, telling him he'd never get me," Caroline said. "I was all his at the time, and I guess, you know, Eddie had really strong feelings for me too back then, when I was with Joey. Eddie is kind of, you know, insanely competitive, not just in Frisbee. Yeah, that huge fight really sucked."

"Sucks to be in demand?"

"Stop," she said, and smiled. Boys had always liked her, but someone to fight over? No, she didn't remember it at all that way.

"Now that I realize you were that girl who was with Joey, I don't think I ever really talked to you back then, did I? Except for that architecture-class project, but guys would mention your name a bunch."

"Oh?"

"You know, a girl guys wanted to be with."

Ryan stood. It gave her an opportunity to leave, but she didn't take it. "I'm getting more chips," he said. "You want some?"

"Sure," Caroline said. She watched him wander over to the bar. He was exaggerating. Some guys had crushes on her, but she wasn't the kind of girl who was noticed by kids in other grades. It was only after Joey died that they paid attention. Her hair was so much longer then, bohemian tresses extending to her waist. It was different now, chopped at the shoulders, framing her face, but maybe the old way was more alluring somehow. She liked her thirty-eight-year-old mom hair fine.

A woman she barely knew came over to say hi. Caroline stood and talked to her, hoping she'd linger a little. She didn't want Ryan thinking she literally couldn't talk to anyone. But then the woman excused herself and headed for the bar. Caroline was alone again.

She saw Eddie in the distance. She waved to him, but he didn't notice, too busy guffawing over some joke he'd told to a bunch of Wall Street veterans. They gathered in a tight, protective circle, like football players in a huddle around their quarterback. With the kids settled, and her husband working the crowd, Caroline figured she could safely catch up with an old high school guy she sort of knew.

When Ryan came back, he brought a huge basket of chips and a pail of guacamole. "My family is still over there," he said as he sat down. "They may wander over." The reminder of his marital status was more for him than for her. "I'll introduce you when they're done gabbing."

"No rush, and thanks for the chips," Caroline said. She upended her bottle of beer and drained the last drop. She didn't usually drink during the day, but the tart bubbles sliding down her throat like soft little clouds made her wonder why she didn't.

"You know, I rarely get to talk about Joey and that summer. I kind of *like* remembering," she said, the beer making her feel a little looser. "It's funny, though, between a girlfriend last Thursday and you today, I've talked more about Joey Whitten than I have in months."

Ryan placed his elbows on the table and leaned in to reach the chips. Between chomps, he said, "Remember that dog he had? Lucky?" A bit of guacamole fell from his lips to his sleeve. "Jesus Christ, you must think I'm a slob." His shirt was still damp from spilling water at the juice bar and now this. He wiped up the guacamole with a napkin, spreading a green stain even wider.

"That dog was unbelievable. Lucky never left his side, even that day."

Ryan crossed his arms over his chest and leaned back—and that gesture somehow hurtled Caroline back in time. Now that his flexed arm was just a foot from her face, she could see he was really strong. An image flashed before her of him walking around town during high school. She remembered: he *was* a cool one back then.

"You know how they say dogs know more than we know?" he asked.

"Know what?"

"You're spacing out," Ryan said, chuckling.

"Sorry. Busted. I was just . . . ."

"Don't worry," Ryan said. "I do that all the time in conversations. I start thinking about something someone said and I get deep into it in my head and never hear the next thing the person says. I was asking about Joey's dog, how he knew something was wrong."

"Yeah, that was heartbreaking too."

Ryan touched her upper arm. "I know he was howling by the shore until God knows what hour, waiting for Joey to come home. That sound stayed with so many of us for so long. That dog crying out, it was so futile. It really scared me, and haunted me for years, still does I think. It was like the dog knew."

Caroline sniffed in, and rubbed her eyes. She wasn't crying, it was just a reflex.

Ryan backed off. "Oh, who knows what dogs know, right?"

"Maybe he didn't know what happened to Joey. Maybe he just missed him," Caroline said. "Or, sometimes . . ." her voice trailed off.

Ryan smiled and took a gulp of beer. A drop seeped out of the corner of his mouth. He wiped it as quickly as he could but it made him remember again the mess on his shirt. He bent his left arm across the stain on his chest.

His self-consciousness—about his clumsiness, about bringing up Joey, about talking to her in the first place—made Caroline think that even if she ever did agree to an affair, it would not be with this man. He was too safe, too kind, too married, too close to home. Maybe someone like him, though. She thought about all the possibilities. Who and when?

No. Not at all was better.

"And, and . . ." Ryan said, making circle motions with his hand, encouraging her to actually finish her sentence.

"Sorry! Anyway, just, who knows what Lucky knew or didn't," Caroline said. She looked out in the distance for her husband again. She'd barely spoken to him all morning, and she never did fetch him that pink smoothie. "Anyway, you work as an architect ever on the big houses?"

"Yes and no. I mean, I'm in a firm and I focus only on the small cottages and restoration work. But we have architects who are building houses that are so huge you could fit a basketball court in the foyer, you know, for everyone out here who is just interested in the shiny and new."

"Exactly," she said. "That must drive you crazy. Like, this one client just asked for curtains with a little sparkle in them and I tried so hard to explain that sparkly fabric is for a high-rise condo in Manhattan, to match the twinkling lights of the city at night, not for a bungalow out here, with the blue of the ocean and the ochre of the sand. You know?"

Caroline felt she was talking too fast. As Ryan explained his favorite preservation techniques in old homes, she glanced at his thighs, and noticed that they splayed out on the chair. She liked meaty men, and had never been with a skinny man. Joey was lean, but he wasn't slight. As every second ticked by, Caroline's mind and body were warming up to the idea of Annabelle's maybe-not-so-insane plan.

As Ryan gazed across the field, she took note of his nose, strong and sturdy like a Greek statue's. When his wife waved to him, he jumped up so fast he shook the table.

"Nice talking to you," he said, a little more coldly than she would have liked. Maybe his wife beckoned him because she felt he had stayed too long at the table, alone with a woman she didn't know. Maybe Ryan hurried off because he felt he had stayed too long too. Either way, Ryan knew what he was doing: his abrupt departure threw some water on whatever fire had been kindled between him and Caroline.

Chapter 13

The Citiots Are Here

With Ryan gone, Caroline really wasn't in the mood to play the one-upmanship games that dominated conversations with people from the city. Even when these women dressed down in T-shirts and jeans, they had to wear pre-distressed five-hundred-dollar Golden Goose sneakers in case anyone forgot they were loaded. Any fake conversation she would have now would just annoy her.

Right on cue, Linda Cockburn approached her table. She wore the requisite Memorial Day white slacks with a green, horsey H Hermès belt, even though she'd never been fifty feet from a saddle in her life. On her feet, a silly choice: hot red suede Gucci slides with fur outlining the soles, already destroyed by the dust and mud of a stable. Locals called idiots from Manhattan *Citiots*, and though Ryan had left, she bet he would have made that call once he witnessed the filthy Gucci fur lining.

Linda saw a need to rearrange the wildflower bouquet on the cocktail table next to Caroline's. Her substantial and perky breasts (unusually so, for a woman with four children) exploded from her blouse, their points resting just under Caroline's nose. "I don't know why messy is so in. I'm a genius at flower bouquets," Linda said. "You should have called me to help. You should have hired me! Party design can be *very* tough." It was always the same: Linda bombarding Caroline with a fusillade of advice on how she could live better, more like a real city person.

"Hire you? That's an idea," Caroline said. The trademark silver trim on the collar of Linda's pale pink Brunello Cucinelli blouse announced its exorbitant cost. Annabelle had taught her to spot one, informing her that the shirts cost over a thousand dollars. "And, by the way, I just love the *new toy*."

Linda had arrived the previous night on a black Sikorsky S-92 copter. She'd posted an endless Instagram story of her kajillionaire family being ferried from the city in her "new toy," as she called it, eating pretzels as if they were at a Met's game at Citi Field. As she descended from the helicopter, and as pilots rushed toward her with outstretched arms to assist her down the stairs, she continued to document the journey on her shaky, shitty, self-aggrandizing video story.

The week before, Eddie had insisted they go to Linda and her husband Henry's for dinner at 71 East Seventy-First Street, a ploy Linda used to give the side entrance of her building, as if to pretend she didn't want anyone to know they'd bought a sixteen-room apartment at the infamous 740 Park Avenue. This historic building was inhabited in the early 1900s by robber barons and Rockefellers and now by present-day hedge fund magnates. Saying please come for dinner at 71 East Seventy-First Street was the Upper East Side equivalent of saying you went to law school in New Haven or Cambridge. Inane pretentions aside, there was no denying the lily-white Park Avenue neighborhood they'd lived in for three years was now packed with people who made "very serious money," as Eddie put it. It seemed everyone on her block had chosen lifestyle over love.

Just like Ryan had said.

At that dinner, Caroline had been seated next to Linda's husband, Henry, who boasted about all the employees he'd magnanimously fired. As he did, Caroline contemplated the meaning of Henry's last name: Cockburn.

A fork clinked against a crystal glass. Linda, having interrupted six conversations around her table, took it upon herself to instruct the entire group that it was now time for "general conversation, people. New topic, people! *How to vacation.*"

Caroline remembered digging her fingers into her thighs. It was all she could do to remain silent.

"It's all about Nicaragua now," Linda said, closing her eyes as if contemplating the momentousness of her observation. "There's the greatest new resort called Mukul, but to get there you have to fly private at the very least from the Managua airport to the resort, otherwise the two-hour drive is just torture!" And now, she was almost screaming her guidelines, "*That's how you have to do it. If you don't have a plane, I'm telling you, saving you!, NetJet it.*"

Caroline had considered announcing to her hostess that NetJet was a private plane *rental company*, not a *verb*.

And now, at the Sea Crest Stables party, Linda explained, "You know, yes, hire me next time. You can work in design with no degree or special experience!" she added, overlooking the fact that Caroline had spent a year in design school and had worked in the field for more than a decade.

The air in the tent was now sweltering, as more people crowded inside. Like those late-August peaches at the Hamptons farm stands, Caroline was feeling a little overripe, and overdue for change.

Chapter 14

High-End Home Life

Caroline's family slept soundly. With school getting out at the end of the week, she would be moving the brood out east for the summer. Five large duffel bags stuffed with bathing suits, flip-flops, shorts, sweatshirts, sun hats, and sunscreen lay side by side next to the front door. Plastic bins were packed and ready, filled with kitchen items she liked to move back and forth (the juicer, the good blender, the bright pitchers she used to serve iced tea and sangria). She also packed up half-full bottles of the more expensive condiments. Eddie always teased her about her compulsion to never waste food: "Were you raised during the Depression?" Caroline preferred to stock the cabinets in the Hamptons house with staples she already had instead of buying new ones.

She'd packed until two in the morning. Now in the silence before dawn, she was awake again, sitting on one of the duffels and resting her face in her hands. She scolded herself for acting like this was the exodus out of Egypt instead of a temporary move from one apartment to a beautiful beach house. Annabelle would tease her about how she had changed more than she recognized, and about how silly it was to stress over packing half-empty jars of mango chutney and those cornichon pickles that Theo inhaled. Caroline shook her head and stood, resolved to get a grip and be done with obsessive organizing.

Her husband was still in bed snoring, an affliction that he had acquired after gaining ten pounds over the past few years. Caroline went to go check on four-year-old Theo, who was asleep in his usual position—crunched up in a ball. She sat on the edge of his bed and neatened his Sponge Bob sheets. His thumb was bobbing in his mouth with rhythmic sucking; she smoothed his curly blond hair, always wild. His hairstyle was a defiant screw you to the uptight matrons at his city school who didn't understand or appreciate him. Theo didn't care who "got" him and who didn't. At school, he bounced between blocks and paintbrushes, oblivious to the teachers' demands to "focus on one activity" and to stop being so "bouncy."

Their forty-thousand-dollar-a-year nursery school had fed the little ruffian into the Buckley school for boys, where they were about to pay fifty thousand dollars for his upcoming, *very high-end* (as Eddie said) kindergarten. Caroline remembered that her science classes at East Hampton elementary were held outside, often on the beach, nature their lab. She imagined the scene of her schoolmates in blazers and yellow ties tussling in the sand, learning about turtles and piping plover nests. If they moved back home soon, there was still time for her kids to socialize with normal kids who skateboarded home.

In the next room, nine-year-old Gigi lay on her back in her pink bed, her head resting against the pillow like an angel, her brunette hair cascading down her shoulders. Caroline sat by her daughter's side in the darkness, hoping she'd shed her natural shy skin as she grew older. Maybe, with a move to a more low-key school in East

Hampton, she'd be more confident, speak her mind more, not let playdates push her around so much and dictate the activity.

After checking on the kids, Caroline made tea. She placed the pot and honey on a tray, and plunked herself on the navy-and-aubergine-purple-paisley couch in the library. A striped red and ivory throw lay beside her. As she sipped, she marveled at the blue, built-in shelves lining the walls. She herself had painted twenty square patches of different blues on the wall, attempting to match her favorite worn-out pair of jeans from high school. The room was her first real design success, modeled after Matisse's palette in Nice with gemstone paisleys layered against thick stripes and an Oriental rug.

She had to admit one thing to herself (but never to Eddie): her design game was better in Manhattan. The city and all its aggressive competitiveness forced her to be better—more honed, tighter, clearer. New York City brought her more diverse clients and all the resources to please them, which, in turn, developed her own tastes. The apartment she'd designed was warm, stunning, and bold. And yet, even though the rooms she'd dreamed of in her first year of design school were now complete, paid for, and *hers,* she'd wander around the vast apartment on mornings like this, feeling something was *off.* What was it? Maybe that she'd never agreed to live in New York City in the first place.

Just last weekend, her mother had again tried to entice her and her family to return to East Hampton full time—as she and Eddie had initially planned. Her mother pushed the issue, even though she understood that Eddie had gotten sucked into the mad, money-making vortex of Manhattan. "Eddie," she said, "New York City isn't one big life-size Monopoly game: you don't need to acquire anything and everything as fast as you can, and build on it. Let someone else have Marvin Gardens. When is enough enough, son?"

"Not yet," Eddie said. He didn't even look up as he jabbed at that hanger steak she always made with extra force. Though he told her he preferred a good New York strip, she never gave in, relishing serving him the cheaper, thinner hanger every time. "I have clients and partners. I can't just walk out on them. It wouldn't be right."

This morning, as Caroline surfed between the maniacs on MSNBC and the lunatics on FOX News, she thought about the upcoming summer. Could she and Eddie be married and live separately if she stayed in East Hampton through the school year? She felt a rush of anxiety pulse through her as she sought out the hard-core truth: Would they even be married when Gigi hit middle school in two years?

They'd had a bad fight the night before. As always, something little would turn their anger nuclear. Eddie had read to the kids, as he insisted on doing as many nights as he could. Putting them to bed, he felt, made up for his absence during the day. He wanted to be the last thing on their minds as they drifted off. Caroline was in the kitchen making herbal tea, hoping for a quiet night. Like most moms across America, she was exhausted by the events and activities of the last week of school.

Eddie marched into the kitchen. Caroline could tell he was already at fever pitch. She hoped it was for a good reason, and not because of item number eleven on her improvement list for him: don't panic over nonsense and infect the household with your demands. He roared, "My leather pencil holder for my desk. I had T. Anthony engrave a new one. See?" He put it two inches from her nose. "See? E. J. C.?"

"Eddie, I know your initials," she said, pushing his hand away. "Don't get all whacked out of shape over the . . . we talked about prioritizing major versus minor—"

"What the fuck? You don't care that these guys do shoddy work and rip me off? I mean, my whole desk sucks. You say it's a little thing, but it isn't. *You know I can't work if my desk isn't right.* I put the kids to bed, want a nice night with my wife, and you gotta be all aggressive?"

She was afraid he'd wake the kids. "I'm aggressive?" she asked. And then, very slowly, added, "Interesting." Her calm tone reminded him of that first-grade teacher who had traumatized him. It only incited him more. Caroline knew what she was doing.

This was one of those moments they'd discussed in therapy: they drive toward a cliff, with ample time to step on the brakes, but instead accelerate, pushing the pedal to the floorboard.

"Look, my initials in gold?" Eddie held the pencil holder up against her nose again. "See on the *E*, the little leg on the bottom, it isn't the same font as the little flipped up thing on the edge of the *C*? You know the little dangly thing on the edge of a letter, they call it 'sans serif' or something?"

"*Sans* means 'without' in French. Sans serif would mean a letter *without* a dangly thing. It's just serif if it has a dangly thing." Nothing made him angrier than when she took that teacher tone with him.

And from there, the dispute turned into a full-on flight into the Grand Canyon as they drove off the cliff at a hundred miles an hour. All because of a pencil holder.

And this morning, with the day's sunlight beginning to stream through her steel, prewar windowpanes (that Ryan Miller would adore for their 1920s authenticity, she now realized), Caroline tried to keep her mind off the argument. She and Eddie had made up, sort of, before they went to bed. It helped that she apologized for comparing him to that "hedge fund asshole" who lived a floor above them.

Caroline nestled her elbow into the curve on the back of the library sofa, and faced the window. She poured herself more tea and cupped her hands around the mug as she blew across its surface, making it ripple. She'd have to make some decisions: Ryan Miller with the meaty thighs and kind eyes or no Ryan Miller; an affair with someone else or no affair with anyone.

Thank God she was half good at her job. Or more than half good. She'd still have a life if she left Eddie, a career, and a means to support herself if he lost his fortune or if he got crazy in a divorce. She watched as lights came on in the apartments across the interior courtyard.

Ryan had texted her the day after Memorial Day and she looked at the conversation on her phone now.

> *Great meeting you, or re-meeting you . . . after 20 years.*
> *I had a nice time talking.*
> *Really nice.*

Caroline replied:

> *It was nice re-meeting you.*

Then, three little dots had appeared, indicating he was typing. After a full minute or two, these words appeared:

> *I can show you when the wood beams are in place.*

She had responded quickly—she didn't want him to think she was worried about how her comments sounded—

> *I'd love to see the little cottage anytime.*

Ryan answered:

> *Sure thing . . . that would be nice, really nice.*

Chapter 15

To Cheat or Not to Cheat:
That Is the Question

Caroline whispered Ryan's text to herself: *That would be nice, really nice.* Maybe it meant something else.

It had been ten days and he hadn't contacted her once since asking for the beams. Maybe he wouldn't, but she'd been checking her phone often, wondering. Perhaps he was waiting until he installed the wood? This was all Annabelle's damn fault. She was the reason Caroline found herself on her couch in the early morning, wondering about another man; Annabelle, her friend who could better handle an affair, was tougher than she was.

Caroline swirled a full teaspoon of honey into her tea. She should be focusing on Eddie and her marriage, not some guy who hadn't texted in ten days. When she was in her twenties, it was much easier to hold on to the Eddie Clarkson roller coaster, but after so many years, her hands had become calloused from gripping so hard on the rail, desperate not to fall off.

Shit, Caroline thought, *marriage is hard.*

She closed her eyes and tried to summon real love for Eddie, to feel the way it once had. After Joey died, all she wanted was to feel strong arms around her and have a chance at a happy future.

Her memories drifted to the morning that had landed her on this couch. She was twenty-eight. It was late May. She and Eddie were at a small hotel in Greenport, on the North Fork of Long Island, celebrating the one-year anniversary of their first real date. They were staying in a beachfront room with an outdoor staircase that led from their porch to the sand. A view of the Long Island Sound flooded their windows.

At about eight in the morning, Eddie drew the curtains to send the room into total darkness again and grabbed the car keys. Caroline thought he was acting a little strange, so she pretended to have gone back to sleep as he gingerly left the room. The sound of someone scooping ice from the hallway icemaker at that hour gave her the first clue he was up to something. About a half-hour later, the sound of metal clanking against metal on the outdoor staircase that led to their balcony woke her.

She peeked through a crack in the curtains.

What the hell?

Someone was on her stairs in full medieval knight's armor as if just arrived from a film set (or battle in Constantinople). Her crazy boyfriend inside struggled to hoist the heavy armor up each step.

A bucket of champagne under one arm, the knight grabbed the rail with the other. Each labored step came with a thunderous clang.

As the gallant knight finally reached the top, his cumbersome armor finally won the battle. He tripped, sending the ice and champagne bottle skyward. The bottle landed on the porch floor, unscathed, and rolled against the wall.

"Shit!" the knight said, the sound echoing inside his helmet. He was outside on his stomach now, his face still hidden under the armored helmet. Caroline watched him crawl across the balcony; he seemed to be searching for something. She jumped back into bed and closed her eyes, her heart beating madly and trying not to laugh.

She'd figured it all out way before the full ten minutes it took him to gather up the ice, now in a dirty pile on the floor, put what he could back in the bucket, place the champagne bottle in, and hide the diamond ring inside.

What woman could possibly say no to that?

And so, Caroline said yes through her laughing tears.

And today, Eddie was still barreling Caroline through life on that same surprising ride. Only now it was so much more work.

Fuck.

She placed her thumb and forefinger on the silk curtain trim and slid them up and down. Settling for an okay marriage to an exciting man didn't feel right today. Maybe it never really did.

Caroline looked into the apartment across the interior courtyard. The beautiful woman in the apartment below hers had that lifeless stare when she said hello in the elevator. It couldn't be easy living with her gnome of a husband, who barked orders at her in front of other residents.

Unlike Caroline, that woman was stuck in her marriage with no eject button. Unlike Caroline, she'd married that gnome when he was already rich. Caroline and Eddie had been broke in Chinatown, moving to East Hampton in a few years to live, what she had imagined, a nice, middle-class life, or maybe upper-middle-class at best. She reminded people of that often, just in case they viewed her as one of those women who worked every day, in soulless ways, for cash her husband earned.

But her neighbor had it so much worse: she didn't have gainful employment outside the family like Caroline did, nor even a plausible roadmap to making a living on her own. They made small talk recently, and Caroline asked her what her hobbies were. The woman answered, the upkeep of two homes and a huge yacht took all day and all her energy. Park Avenue could be so dreary for those entrenched in it; Ryan was right about people who'd married into big-time cash. It was now a life Caroline was trying to get out of, not land into.

She got up and walked down the hall toward the sound of snoring. Eddie's alarm would ring in forty minutes.

She had plenty of time.

Eddie seemed more distracted lately. He was canceling plans with her at the last minute. He didn't have many colleagues, but he was often "hung up" at the office for meetings.

There had been two periods like this before. There may have been more but she knew chasing after young children only boosted her ability for denial. No reason to shield her eyes anymore. It was almost the summer solstice, an excellent time to shed light on her future.

Caroline went into the study and took Eddie's iPad out of his briefcase and entered the passcode: *3-6-1-6-3 7* . . .

She had nervously written the code on an index card after looking over Eddie's shoulder the night before, right about the time he started complaining about his pencil holder. He changed his code every week. She'd never believed in reading a spouse's texts, so she'd never tried very hard to follow his fingers on the screen.

As Caroline glanced at the bedroom from the corner of the study, her heart pumped so hard the blood pulsing in her brain gave her a headache. At first, she slammed the iPad cover shut, not sure she wanted to know after all. She tiptoed to the hallway. Eddie continued snoring like a grizzly bear. He'd never once woken before his 7:10 a.m. alarm. It helped that he'd had a vodka the night before. He always slammed the bathroom door when he went for his morning pee.

She needn't worry so much; she'd have to be braver and bolder. His routines would never change.

Caroline grabbed the iPad again and entered the *3-6-1-6-3-7* code once more. She opened Excel. Looking for financial folders, it took her ten minutes to home in on the document she wanted. Her fine arts degree from SUNY did not include math. She examined all the columns. Twice.

There was so much more money than she knew.

Holy Jesus.

Next, she opened the iMessage texting app on his iPad. Eddie was too much of a hothead for technology. It frustrated him, and he often threw devices toward her, asking her to fix something. He wouldn't know that the text messages on his phone would sync to his iPad if someone had his Apple ID.

Men, supposedly so much "better" at math and science than women, were such technological idiots sometimes. Eddie Clarkson's phone was now mirrored on his iPad. Many women she knew checked their husbands' iPads whenever the men seemed to grab their phones too quickly to read an incoming text.

After Eddie admitted in therapy the first time he'd strayed, he was apoplectic. She hadn't snooped that time, she just knew. "But, honey. I just told her to piss off," Eddie said, when they got back home from the appointment. "I'm not into it, I swear. I love you!" Eddie had grabbed her shoulders, while Caroline shook her head.

"How dare you act like this is routine!" she said.

"It was just fucking, that's it. Zero attachment, I don't even like her!"

Caroline believed him, though she didn't admit it. Eddie wasn't attached to the woman. He loved only Caroline. She wondered if it was the same for his current object of affection. She scrolled through several pages of texts before finding a female name that wasn't an employee's. But then, the names—the *single* names—started piling up.

There was a Brittany (that sounded like a Hooters waitress for God's sakes) to whom he'd texted:

Great seeing you baby.

And to a Linda:

Can I try that again?

And to Jennifer he wrote:

See you later?

The conversations were sultry, but not conclusive. He'd deleted most of the conversations, so Caroline could only see a cryptic few lines. It wasn't necessarily actual sex they were referring to, with a time and a place. Knowing Eddie's voracious appetite for attention, there was a minute chance these were flirtations, not actions. But still, the texts were very suggestive, and certainly not something a person wrote to a colleague, or even to a friend.

So many more women than she suspected.

First, Caroline briefly considered throwing the iPad onto rushing Fifth Avenue traffic. But she feared she might hurt someone. What she really felt like doing was throwing up.

Then, knowing that Eddie Clarkson loved a good competitive game, she decided it would be much more fun to get even.

Chapter 16

Meanwhile Down the Avenue . . .

On Fifth Avenue, a few blocks south on Seventy-Eighth Street, Annabelle von Tattenbach heard her phone ping at 6:18 a.m. This surprised her; a text unusual at this hour. Down the hall, her four blond daughters were enveloped in their nineteenth-century canopy beds, inherited from Arthur's family estate in Düsseldorf. Each majestic bed frame was draped in Cowtan & Tout pastel toiles and velvet ties and borders. When Annabelle checked on the girls at night, they were hard to locate among the mounds of plush down comforters and pillows. The little princesses were still asleep, blissfully unaware a new day had begun.

Annabelle's friends never texted before eight in the morning. They all knew about Arthur's spritely sexual appetite that had to be serviced before he left for work. He claimed the release helped him focus better on market volatility.

The prognostications on Fox Business News from his study one room down seeped into their master suite. Arthur, who had left the bedroom an hour earlier, was surely scrutinizing the four computer screens on his desk. The European exchanges had been open for hours already, so he was executing trades to enhance his colossal family fortune.

Annabelle reached across her moss-green, snakeskin table for her phone. She was correct: this was not a girlfriend checking in. The text came from Philippe de Montaigne at the barn. Her complexion now matched the blush Pratesi linens surrounding her. She pulled the soft covers over her head and breathed in deeply through her nose—the way her meditation coach, Bob Roth (whose client list included Stella McCartney and Michael J. Fox), had taught her.

Blindly, from under the goose down comforter, she reached for the teeny clicker on the table next to her in the little leopard skin bowl. She aimed it at the fireplace in front of her bed. After the regular three-second delay, a burst of gas and flames erupted behind the glass partition. The fire warmed the room, and the gentle, flickering light illuminated the Sister Parish sagebrush wallpaper just as her designer had promised. Even in June, the warmth helped put her in the mood. The request from Arthur's mahogany dressing suite would come soon.

When Philippe told her that he'd like to stay in touch via text from his personal phone, she shouldn't have whispered back, "Sounds perfect." She wished she'd been more standoffish, kept it on the professional more formal lines of communication through the barn secretary.

Philippe felt he was well-practiced in conversing with nuanced meaning, though his text this morning came off plenty direct:

> I'm glad our plan to stay in touch on text makes you happy.
> . . . there are so many ways to make a woman happy.

Annabelle got out of bed at that, needing to cool off or just move, and sat in the curved-back lounge chair in the corner of her peach marble bathroom suite. She lay her head back. The cushions were soft here too, and she grabbed the white cashmere blanket folded at the edge and curled up a bit, her hands warm and clasped between her legs.

Her mother, Bunny Digby's, warning rang in her head:
One's forties are a very dangerous decade, dear.

The text from Philippe had made her jumpy, and she felt an ache between her thighs. She considered whether to relieve it on her own or to allow Arthur the pleasure of pleasuring her. She considered Philippe's muscled and robust body. This was not good. Straying was too damn easy. This is why husbands do it all the time, she figured.

She could drive the Maserati out to the Hamptons this morning, screw the daylights out of that polo-playing, smoking hot piece of ass, and be back for cocktails with Arthur. Caroline argued Philippe was an unsafe accomplice, but Annabelle felt the opposite. In her view, since she wasn't seeking attachments, it was better to sleep with a playboy who was highly accomplished at discarding women. A gentleman might develop sloppy feelings for her.

Annabelle knew *all* about gentlemen. Though she wasn't trying to seduce them (besides showing off her pert breasts in those divine Saint Laurent evening blouses), men always fell for her when she sauntered into parties in velvet pants that appeared painted onto her body. Why remain flat-chested if you can't go braless at dinner parties? It wasn't her fault men were fired up by aloof women, by a teeny peek of a nipple through silk. Seated next to her at dinners, most men looked into her eyes in a way that made her want to slap some sense into them.

She'd be done with Philippe by August. That was consistent with Philippe's usual schedule as well, because he'd go on the polo circuit as a coach in the fall. He'd fuck her and be done with her—and she, for her part, was only looking for a slam-bam-thank-you-sir from him.

And *Arthur would never know.*

In fact Arthur had done just that a few years back with that French investment banker with the naughty librarian look from Société Générale. That skinny French bitch in the impossibly chic Dior suit looked so guilty when she delivered papers to Arthur's office that day and ran into Annabelle. Not to even mention the Croatian masseuse.

After ten minutes, Annabelle returned to bed, her desires still smoldering. The fire blazed before her, even though it was already sixty-eight degrees outside. The gold Tiffany clock on her bedside table read 6:55 a.m. The housekeeper knocked quietly on the door. Upon entering, Ghislaine placed a flowered Porthault breakfast tray atop metal stilts on Annabelle's lap and quietly exited.

Annabelle's mother had used this very tray as a child in New Canaan, Connecticut. When her eldest, Laeticia, was four months old, Annabelle's mother had presented it to Annabelle, along with matching napkins, on her first Mother's Day. Ghislaine had thoughtfully placed the *New York Post* and the Arts section of the *Times* in the slats on the left of the tray.

She poured her Harrods Irish breakfast tea out of a small Herend pot and into a delicate cup that had a lime-green butterfly wing for a handle. She swirled a dollop of blackberry preserves into the plain yogurt that Hans made every Sunday night for her. With the sterling silver mini ladle she'd inherited from her aunt Fiona, Annabelle sprinkled flaxseeds and granola into her bowl.

Meanwhile, riled from the overseas markets, Arthur stomped down the hallway in his velvet slippers and silk paisley Charvet robe to his dressing suite on his side of the master bedroom. He entered from the center vestibule, avoiding his wife. His mood was low, and there was no point in dragging her down with the world's currencies. The nonsensical trade wars made the international markets behave erratically, and they were too risky for his liking. He was holding today, stepping away from the chessboard for twenty-four hours until Singapore moved at least a pawn.

He thought a steam shower would cool him down. After ten minutes, the stress of losing several million dollars in the last hour had sweated out of him. He stepped out invigorated; he'd make it all back, and then some once Tokyo moved its rook.

He placed his heavy, strong body into the salted bath, which he always started to fill before he hopped into the steam shower. His shoulders were extremely wide, and he'd gotten a vast marble bath made custom. That genius architect had found a device that automatically filled the tub and switched off when the tub was full. He'd even taught that masseuse, Marjina, to draw his bath and pour in her salt concoction ten minutes before she finished working on him. Or rather, before she finished wanking him with her silken hands. Just sniffing that sandalwood oil she left for him got his fantasies flying in all directions.

Arthur laid back on a cushion at the edge of the black tub, dunked a waffle-weave washcloth in the water, and placed it on his strawberry-gray thinning hair. With the water dripping down the sides of his face, warming his short beard, he admired the masterpiece of marble before him. The slabs had been expertly sliced in Carrara. The architect had set them so that the veins kissed like a Rorschach test.

He lathered up his face with that special beard soap from Penhaligon's in London. Fox Business News blared out of the small screen embedded in the marble wall. Arthur had seen a screen like this at the Peninsula Hotel in Hong Kong and ordered his design team to copy it. He watched the bad news on the futures market and calculated even more losses. At least that Fox babe Maria Bartiromo delivered the bad news. He had always found the Money Honey to be an enticing and intelligent woman. Studying the curves in her pink suit, he felt another stirring in his loins that he encouraged with his left hand and some soapy water.

"Annabelle, my darling, come in here!" he beckoned.

"I can't, I'm reading," Annabelle answered. She sipped her tea resolutely and sprinkled more crunchy mix on her yogurt. "You know I need to have five minutes with the papers first." Annabelle mined Page Six of the *Post* for mentions of her friends.

"I'm feeling my morning urge here, darling," Arthur said.

Annabelle tied and untied the little string at the edge of her monogrammed neck roll. "You want me to get in the bath? Really? In there?"

She thought of her four girls. She wished they came into her room more often in the mornings before arriving at the breakfast table. Their presence could help her stave off her husband's need for sex. Unfortunately, Ghislaine and the nanny, Claudia, were too efficient at getting the girls ready in the mornings. They showed up at breakfast each morning in their Spence school uniforms, their knee socks properly pulled up, and their hair bows tightly secured. The older Spence girls, with little way to express their budding fashion sense in a uniform from an all-girls' school, shortened their skirts to pornographic levels and wore thigh highs. Arthur explained to Laeticia and Louisa that he'd disown them if they even got near a tailor.

"Darling?" Arthur said. "Did you hear me?"

Annabelle answered Philippe's text instead.

Making me happy isn't as easy as you might imagine.

She regretted sending the message instantly. It was not any of Philippe de Montaigne's business what made her happy.

Philippe took the bait, and was glad she'd bitten herself.

I'm told I'm very good at figuring things out on my own, but I always am open to instruction.
I have been told I follow directions well.

Annabelle blushed to deep red this time. *Oh God,* she thought to herself. Life was so much nicer when you could just tell the man what to do, and he did it. She wondered if Caroline had been right: maybe he was indiscreet, and perhaps these texts alone were no good.

Annabelle heard a robust sloshing and swaying coming from the tub.

"Darling?" Arthur asked. "I said I'm ready. More than ready."

She looked at her texts from Philippe again. She took a few screenshots, and texted the photo to Caroline and wrote:

> *I'm guilty of one thing: egging Philippe on. I feel bad, but not horrible. Haven't done anything yet and might not, but still . . . look how suggestive he is, I told you this would be easy. And don't worry—the way you do about everything—I deleted the text conversation with him already.*

Then she deleted the conversation with Caroline as well.

All good on technology.

The screenshots of the conversation with Philippe, though, still remained in her photo folder. Like most people either considering or executing an affair, she forgot just that one small detail.

Annabelle, feeling a tad guilty now, but strangely exhilarated, lifted her tray and placed it on the comforter beside her. She slipped down from her antique high mattress like an heiress from *Downton Abbey* and tied the sash on her Porthault flowered robe that matched her tray.

(When Bunny presented it to her, Annabelle had laughed, thinking it was a clever riff on WASP-dom. Her mother, relentlessly earnest with little penchant for humor, only asked, "What's so funny, dear?") She then walked into her husband's bathroom. He was leaning with his back against the sink, his midsection at a twenty-year-old's full mast.

"I love you, Arthur, but I can't spend a lot of time on you," she said. "Literally, honey, seven minutes."

"I'll come back to the living in six. I placed a towel on the floor, so you don't hurt your knees," he whispered, closing his eyes. Then, opening them, he asked, "Or, if you'd like the full extravaganza, I'm happy to take you to bed and pleasure you to your heart's content. *The choice is yours, of course.*"

Chapter 17

Not So Cheery at the Clarksons'

When Theo appeared in the doorway of Eddie's study at 6:37 a.m., Caroline was so spooked that she let out a strange little scream and banged her elbow against a chair. She slammed the cover of her husband's iPad shut and placed it where she had found it: precisely two inches from the edge of the desk. She had wanted to re-read the texts and figure out if they meant he was fucking these women or suggesting he'd fuck these women. And who was Brittany? Surely, he'd shy away from a Hooter's employee.

It was her husband's nature to flirt. Whenever she chastised him for it, he'd say that it was part of his knight-in-shining-armor charm, and she couldn't deny that. Eddie would tell older women in particular how beautiful they looked—he felt they rarely received this type of attention. Or he'd wink and say, "Now, how come a stunning woman like you can't . . ." Maybe his texts were mere flirtations. Maybe it's just what today's knights do.

Yet, who calls someone "baby" if he's not shagging them or trying to?

Baby, I'm telling you, I'd love to talk later when I can see you in person, he'd written.

Theo watched her.

"Go back to bed," she said sternly to him, scaring him and making it all worse.

Theo began to whimper. He jammed his thumb into his mouth and shook his head as tears streamed down his cheeks, his little curls shaking a bit as he did. "Why are you being so mean?" he said. "I didn't do anything!"

Her heart broke, she loved this child so much and hugged him hard, willing those tears away. The Excel program was still open on that iPad, Caroline hadn't had time to close the spreadsheets or delete the texting app. She wondered if Eddie did wake up, how long it would take the tablet to fall asleep. She comforted Theo more and laid him on the sofa, placing a blanket over him.

"Why are you covering my head?" he asked.

"Because, honey, the light, it's going to keep you awake," she whispered. "Just lie under there and rest. Promise me you'll rest."

Caroline walked back to the desk to undo what she'd done to Eddie's iPad so it would look the way it always looked when he saw it next. She opened the iPad and, indeed, the programs were still up and running. She told herself not to panic, that she had time.

"I can't breathe," Theo said. He pretended to slowly asphyxiate under the blanket on the couch, struggling for air, choking on nothing.

Caroline kneeled beside him and begged her four-year-old, "Honey, you can have whatever you want. Bad cereal, the kind we only eat on vacation in those little boxes. A chocolate chip cookie. A *huge* one. You name it. It's a special day, and you can have whatever you want for breakfast if you lie here quietly for five minutes. Under the blanket. Five minutes more. Okay?"

Theo yanked the blanket off his head. He squinted at her and whispered, "Lucky Charms. We don't have any of those cereals in the house. How are you going to get some before my breakfast?"

"Lucky Charms." She nodded. She would have poured a dump truck full of them into his room if he had agreed to lay under the blanket. "I'm, uh, honey, I'm going to actually run to the Food Emporium in about six minutes," she said. "You are going to wait here under the blanket. You don't even have to keep your head under it, once I go."

"I don't?" He kicked the blanket off.

"No," Caroline said. "You do actually, for now."

"You said I didn't."

She needed to get back to Eddie's desk before he woke up. Her mouth was so dry, her tongue felt like it was sticking to her teeth. If Eddie knew what she'd seen, she would lose all her power. She wanted time to respond on her own terms.

"You do, honey," she said. "You actually do need to lie here under the blanket and cover your head for five minutes. I have to do one quick thing, but don't worry—I'll be in this room. And then I'll pull down the blanket. In a little bit, I'll run to the store for Lucky Charms, and if you need anything before I get back, you can wake Daddy, okay?"

"Daddy doesn't like it when I wake him," Theo said. "And don't touch his things, that makes him really mad."

Caroline nearly hyperventilated. She wasn't sure what Theo had seen, but now she knew. "Touch his things? Oh no, honey. I just left something here. Besides, you know that Daddy's things are my things too, and my things are Daddy's."

"That's not what Daddy says."

She placed the blanket over Theo's head and dashed to Eddie's desk.

She opened the iPad again and sat in her husband's chair. She closed the spreadsheet. She erased all the recent history too. She closed iMessage. Caroline figured she had covered her tracks.

Now, off to fetch some Lucky Charms.

Chapter 18

Kitchen Confrontation . . . or Not

Caroline watched the illuminated numerals of the floors morph, one into another, as her building's paneled elevator rose. It felt like a tomb this morning, moving much slower than it normally did. On the twelfth floor, she inhaled deeply as she stepped onto the landing. Brushing the bottom of her shoes on the thick sisal mat, she noted that its green grosgrain border was in tatters, matching the Clarkson marriage inside.

With the little boxes of sugary cereal hidden in a plastic bag hanging from the crook of her arm, she grasped the knocker ready to ring, as if it were someone else's front door. She caught herself and plopped her head against the door instead. Everything was feeling foreign now.

As she opened it, the smell of burnt toast met her.

"Theo! Gigi!" Eddie's scream came from the kitchen. The beaters of the mixer were clanging against the sides of a glass bowl. "Just cheese or cheese and ham? Cheese and ham will have more protein. Daddy burned the bagels as usual, but I got more!"

Caroline slid the boxes of diabetes-inducing cereals under the living room sofa and walked by the kitchen and into Theo's room.

It was 7:35 a.m., twenty-five minutes before she'd have to walk her son and daughter out the door. Theo was brushing his teeth, perched on his tiptoes atop a small step stool with fire engines and his name painted on it. She massaged his shoulders and looked into the same mirror he was looking into. Theo asked, his hazel eyes wide, "Where's the Lucky Charms?"

"Honey, did you tell your sister or your father I was bringing home the cereal? You know we have a rule: only on vacation. I'm breaking the rule just this once."

He turned around, deeply offended at such an assumption of stupidity. "No way! Dad wouldn't let me have it! You promised the cereal now. Today," Theo said. He pursed his lips, the way he always did when he was thinking hard or lying.

Caroline kissed her cherub-look-alike's forehead again. Cupping his ears, she whispered, "I did say today, and you'll have it today. Just not this morning. Daddy will be mad about the cereal, and it'll get all of us in a bad mood before school. Maybe you'll even get *two* boxes after school if you stop whining." She sat on the edge of the tub and said, "I know you can wait."

"I can wait if I can really have two later." Theo bobbed his head, just like his father did when he was considering the value of a deal.

Caroline pressed her finger on the tip of her son's nose, "Two boxes. I promise. When I get you after school," she said. "When you were three, you never could wait for anything. Now that you're almost five, you can wait, even though I know, it's hard." She had no idea where her son would go to school in the fall, but recognizing the benefit of delayed gratification would be great preparation for kindergarten—and a lesson his father hadn't quite learned still.

After checking that Gigi was getting dressed, and kissing her cute little plump belly twenty times as she always did in the mornings, Caroline walked into the kitchen to face Eddie.

He didn't wait a moment: "How come you went out? You never

leave in the morning. Theo woke me up." As she approached him, he put his hands on her hips and pulled her into him, his back against the kitchen counter. His favorite part about sex with Caroline was her looking him in the eye and explaining what she wanted, in minute detail, like a dare. He loved her always being direct, and on point. And when he was a selfish shit, she'd nail his ass, even though it sucked that she'd told him in therapy that she knew he was fucking someone else. He brought his hands to her face and said, "What's going on in that beautiful head of yours?"

"Just that money and sex make the world go 'round, Eddie, that's all I'm thinking," she said. She took one yoga breath exactly as that teacher had instructed.

The spreadsheet scrolled by in her head: *so much more money than she knew.*

"And what the fuck is that supposed to mean?" Eddie asked.

If she left him, she wouldn't make a huge fuss about the cash. She'd get plenty. And if he'd hidden a bunch, he could damn well keep it. She had enough clients now to keep her afloat anyway—that is, if she lived in a town out on Long Island with good public schools. She'd sign them up for East Hampton Elementary today, she could always cancel their spots later.

"What are you not telling me? It's me. Just me, honey. Your best friend. What is it?"

Caroline pulled her shoulders back. "I'm just considering things, Eddie. I'm having a moment of reflection. Is that okay?"

"Well, tell me," Eddie said. He was very good at reading Caroline's mind—and she hoped he wasn't doing just that now.

She played out the conversation in her mind:

Enough of this bullshit where the men wander while the women nurture hearth and home.

Enough of this bullshit where a woman can't be a mother and screw someone hot once in a great while when she feels she needs it.

How many men have done that?
How many times have you, Eddie?
"What is it?" Eddie asked again.

He did know her better than anyone else did, she had to give him that. Marriage was comforting that way. The scene in couples' therapy when he admitted his first affair came back to her. It made her even angrier now to recall it.

"Now," Dr. Haass had said, "this is the safe place where you can reveal the pain of feeling betrayed, so we can parse it up and examine it, all together."

Caroline had remained silent on her end of that uncomfortable couch. She didn't like the doctor's tone; he treated her as if she were a child and he was her pediatrician. Neither Eddie nor the good doctor recognized her ambivalence about the marriage and that her qualms about being with Eddie in the first place were far more consequential than any hurt his cheating had caused her.

"Resistance to discuss your pain doesn't help you get through this," Dr. Haass had said, clearly after the victim character men love to paint on women in distress.

"Tell me now, Caroline," Eddie had said, emboldened by the doctor's comments. "Express it, I need to hear it."

Caroline was wiser than both men in the sessions and was only keenly interested in laying out a strategy that might save her marriage. The truth was that she adored Eddie's lustiness for life, but she was never truly in love with him. What's more, she would never be. She felt hurt for sure, but this dalliance was no dagger in her heart. Caroline knew herself; she might be anxious, she might second-guess herself, but she would never be the casualty in someone else's battle.

"Let's all pause for a moment," Dr. Haass had said. "Remember that two people see the same thing differently. Take this lazy Susan I made." He pulled a large wooden circle from behind his desk and placed it on the coffee table, then turned it round and round. A wooden fence divided the circle, with two plastic toy animals on either side.

"You actually got a medical degree, and you thought it was a good idea to spend your time making a lazy Susan? Are you for fuckin' real?" Eddie had asked, over the marital therapy concept before it had even started.

"Shhh!" had said Caroline. "Let the doctor explain his thing."

"There's a wall in the center," Dr. Haass had continued. "And as it turns, the husband sees this little elephant on this side while the wife sees this zebra, and—"

"What's next?" Eddie had barked. "Are you going to bring out a little dolly and ask me to show you where someone might have poked me with his dick?!"

"Eddie, stop!" Caroline had laughed a little; she couldn't help it. "I like the lazy Susan image. I think it's helpful. I mean that. It is supposed to represent one situation. Not only do we see it from opposite sides, but we also see it as opposite things. One sees it as an elephant, and the other—"

"I get it! Bang me over the head with it, I get it. Go on." Eddie had adjusted himself in the chair, thinking that was one super fuckin' annoying agreement he had made to see this guy.

Caroline had given him that look.

He softened a little, "I got you, baby," he had said. "Just don't make me twirl around a zebra to say I see how your view could be different." Eddie felt they were ganging up on him and that they had this all planned before he got there. "I hear you, okay? But I'm going to use the English language to express myself, and not little dolls and plastic fuckin' zebras, if that's okay."

Just then, Theo busted into the kitchen. "What shirt should I wear?" he asked. "I can't find my Eli Manning one."

"Wear the Odell Beckham one," Eddie said. "He's the Giants'

bigger star." Eddie crouched down to tussle Theo's hair. "What did I tell you?"

Theo smiled. "Lucky number thirteen."

"Yep, my uncle Charlie told me that. Thirteen is lucky, so is blue. Don't forget, thirteen was also Alex Rodriguez's number."

As Theo wandered out of the kitchen, Caroline plunked two pieces of bread into the toaster. She said, "If you want to know, for me to treat you like a best friend, I woke up thinking about infidelity, Eddie."

"You did?"

"Not exactly yours, just in general," Caroline said. "How come when men cheat they are seen as virile? How come when women in literature cheat they end up walking into an oncoming train or guzzling arsenic? How come men say they could never handle the image of another man inside their woman? Why do they think they own them?" Then she opened the refrigerator door with so much force that it banged the counter.

"Whoa, whoa," Eddie said, grabbing at the door.

"Don't whoa me," Caroline said.

"Remember Doctor Haass said it was important to express . . . even years later you can . . ."

"Please," she said. "Please don't bring up that guy; I never liked him. You know that."

"You made me go!" he said, stomping his feet.

Caroline closed her eyes and said, "And while we're on the topic, I've never cheated." Now she was pissed that she'd said no to the artist guy who suggested he take her home to paint her nude. Why hadn't she ripped her damn clothes off for him?

Eddie closed in on his wife and hugged her. He smelled of his Giorgio Armani cologne. She resisted the urge to nuzzle into his neck, as was their way, and instead crossed her arms across her breasts. He held her in a tight ball. She hated to admit to herself he felt good, in charge, protective, trying his best with those parents he had.

Caroline did a 180-degree twirl to escape him and poured herself a black coffee. Videos of those TED talks her shrink used to send about different forms of marriage flowed through her head: the one about forgiveness, the one about needing space, the one about unconventional unions and "the decision to ignore infidelities."

"What the hell is going on with you?" Eddie asked. "What did I do?" He worried for a moment that the doorman Constantine had told on him, the one who had seen him kiss Brittany before the car he had ordered drove her home. It was one night, okay, maybe two, and the family was in East Hampton anyway. And he was *horny as fuck,* what was he supposed to do to get off? Caroline was gone for three days!

Caroline blew the steam off the coffee. Eddie took the cup and set it on the counter. He put his arms behind her and tickled her bottom gently, the same way he touched her between her legs. She closed her eyes. It turned her on more than it should have. Maybe, she figured, relenting a little, because she was mad as fuck, everything was churning inside her.

"What are you doing, Eddie?" she asked, as his fingers reached down the front of her pajamas. She smiled—a little.

"See?" he said.

"I'm not smiling at you, it's just . . ."

"Just what?"

Marriage is weird, that's what. She wouldn't tell him now. The know-each-other's-mind, sense-each-other's-sparks, the ambivalent yin and yang of it all.

He pulled the string loose on her pajamas and kissed her breast—it silently reminded her that maybe he wasn't all that bad. "I'm just trying to get a read on where you're at," he said.

"C'mon. The kids will be here in a minute," she said. "You don't want to get me all turned on and then you turned on, which is worse than me getting turned on and way harder to stop."

"I'm working on getting you turned on, not me," Eddie said. "Just trying to get a little rise out of you." He licked her neck softly.

She thought about his texts: little come-ons, silly flirtations, and things she knew would have made him feel masculine. In the end, they were adolescent pleas for attention that would leave him wanting his wife, his soul mate, even more. No doubt in her mind that the man she married loved her fiercely. The texts, on some level, had nothing to do with their marriage. Still, what the hell kind of marriage was this?

"Caroline, you owe me," Eddie said. "Tell me. Something's up. Why did you go outside? You never go outside." He wondered what—or who—got his wife to go out of the house in her pajamas at seven in the morning. No one could get her body going at full Mach speed like he could, right?

She pecked his cheek, not looking him in the eye. "I just had a craving for that cappuccino on the corner," she said. "You know, they make the little heart design with the frothed milk? And I was just, I don't know, mine doesn't taste the same." She knew he wouldn't buy it. Then she offered, "Don't ask me questions you don't want asked of yourself, Eddie."

"I'm not asking any questions, Caroline." *What the fuck did she know?* "And don't treat me like I'm an idiot. I know you didn't go outside for a fuckin' cappuccino."

Chapter 19

Meditation Does Have a Downside

"D arling," Arthur said. "I need to keep my mind in the game today to handle the markets." He cocked his head to the side like a dog begging for a scrap off a dinner plate. "And you're so good at it. How could I not?"

Often, just to avoid a hassle, Annabelle would oblige. He did have a good point: with her knees perched on a folded towel on the marble floor, it was an expedient way to get it all done.

Today, the texts from Philippe had gotten into her head, as had the spectacular peaks and valleys of his chest in that tight polo outfit, so she had trouble getting herself into Arthur's game.

Halfway through her expert performance, he whispered from above, "Annabelle, my beauty, you seem distracted. It's no good for me if it isn't good for you." Arthur noticed everything. Always. His uncanny mind-reading ability came inside the same gene that allowed him to predict market flows. "Let me take you into the bedroom and get you a little revved up," he said. "That should make things a little better for both of us." And he reached under her arms to help her stand.

"It's fine, the girls, let me just . . ." and Annabelle slithered back down his legs. "I, just sometimes, every morning, it can't be like . . ."

"Oh, it can. I can show you," Arthur said. He placed a finger across her lips, shushing her resistance.

Now she'd have to do the full monty back in bed when she was hoping to get this over with. They put on their robes in case the girls woke up early, and he led her down his dressing room hallway to bed. She rolled her eyes toward God up above, thinking, *This is exactly what I didn't want to do right now.*

Arthur locked the heavy door to their suite. He lay his very substantial build on top of his beautiful wife and stroked her cheeks.

"I love you, darling," he said. "I won't let us get complacent." He squinted a little. He sensed she was not all there. "I'll never tire of having you in the mornings before the fire."

Twenty minutes later, she heard water flow from his shower. Annabelle sat up in bed naked. She inhaled deeply. Her husband was, in fact, a damn good lay, and for sure more dashing than any man on Fifth Avenue with his graying, Michael Caine appeal. He knew how to get the job done on this front and many others. Even at the age of fifty-seven, he was quick and to the point. He was right about this too: she did feel better having allowed herself to enjoy her side of things. She had to admit, as he untied her robe and slipped her panties off, he wasn't so bad. Powerful, if familiar, waves of pleasure weren't such a terrible addition to her morning routine.

Now that it was time to start the rest of her day, Annabelle slid into her satin monogrammed slippers that lay on top of a little cotton honeycomb towel on the floor. She draped her bathrobe over her shoulders and made her way to her own dressing suite.

As she began to submerge herself in her tub, Annabelle added spoonfuls of rosewater salts that fizzed in the warm bathwater and turned it a gentle pink. The color deepened to a purple hue when she added lavender buds. Closing her eyes, and leaning her head back against the terry-cloth cushion, she thought she might meditate for a few minutes before meeting the girls at the breakfast table. She and Caroline had taken a few classes together with that famous Bob Roth meditation guru who showed up in Aspen or anywhere his New York and Hollywood clients needed him. He was very good, no doubt, though they'd both gone into a laughing fit as he tried to coax them into another state of consciousness. And, though they'd each read his Harvard studies about meditation's benefits, neither could sit still for a second without her mind wandering. What mother could?

Now, instead of calmly repeating her mantra, *tah-leem, tah-leem, tah-leem,* all Annabelle could think about was that if she hadn't devoted herself to Arthur, she could have spent some time with Lily in her room, as she got ready for school. Lily loved to try out different bows with her. It was the only fashion self-expression left to the poor girl with the strict uniform rules of her private school.

She tried the mantra again, *tah-leem, tah-leem, tah-leem.*

Instead of focusing on nothing at all, Annabelle opened her eyes for just a teeny second as she stretched out her toes and inspected her new pedicure, noting that the pink she'd chosen was too orange. *This is not a time to think about nail color, Annabelle!* She would meditate for the remaining seven minutes. She repeated, *tah-leem, tah-leem,* over and over, vowing to push out competing thoughts.

Thirty seconds later, some black emptiness in her brain achieved, Annabelle looked at her phone on the little table beside her bath. The not-so-discreet texts from the morning entered her mind. She had deleted all the texts to and from Caroline and Philippe—one can't be too careful with technology. She sat up in the tub, water splashing around her. "Arthur? Arthur? You in there?"

Silence.

He might be in his dressing room, or maybe in his study, ogling the Money Honey's curves on Fox. Annabelle tried the *tah-leem, tah-leem* again, but again, after thirty seconds, she instead inspected her muscular legs, lifting one out of the water then the other. *Was it true that many men really preferred fatty flesh on women? Um, no.*

She repeated her mantra. This time, blackness, a void, took over her brain, and the physical world around her disappeared. It lasted about thirty seconds before a thought of Lily's favorite bows intruded. Then another thirty seconds of nothingness. Bob Roth said TM Meditation meant no punishment for those thoughts, just push them away, which she did. A bit. Though she'd let worries slip into her mind, this was progress for her. And it did calm and soothe her.

However, there was an unintended consequence to Annabelle's meditation session: she didn't hear Arthur when he tiptoed to her bedside. He suspected something had changed in her. Why was she so distracted? It required immediate investigation.

Like most spouses, he knew her iPhone code. He'd watch her put it in thirty times a day. The phone wasn't there, though, so he decided to lie in bed, and maybe she'd make a call from the bathroom. He would overhear her and maybe gain a little insight into his wife's absent mood.

Arthur didn't like the way snooping on her made him feel. Rather than think too much about his wife's behavior this morning, he turned on the television above the mantel and settled into his side of the bed.

Instead of watching the business news, he turned on Apple TV, maybe he'd finish the last ten minutes of that spy series. He closed his eyes to rest a little. A few minutes later, when he opened his eyes, the Apple TV was playing Annabelle's photo stream from her phone.

Arthur grinned as he watched shots of his girls on their horses from last weekend. First Cappa, then Parker, then Mouse, he thought, though he never could tell the horses apart. He once asked his assistant to construct a chart of horses' photos and names so the girls would think he knew what he was talking about. He loved the girls, and those horses did teach them discipline and how to care for another living creature. The people who thought it was just a rich girls' sport could bugger off. There were plenty of working students riding and competing horses in stables across America. Some people just didn't understand the value of animals and competition and camaraderie in life.

Then Arthur saw some tight shots of lobsters on the beach, steaming in the seaweed as Hans had ingeniously shown them. Yes, the clambake on the beach in front of their house last week had been a good idea. A little sandy for his tastes though. He'd have the staff get better chairs next time, so his hands didn't get quite so dirty. Next, some photos of furniture Annabelle must have bought yesterday. He'd have to go through her stream more often, have someone organize the family shots and make some albums too; plenty of assistants around his office with nothing to do.

And then . . . screenshots of texts floated across the TV: texts between his wife and a man.

His face felt hot; that was the adrenaline and the rage: that fuckhead Philippe de Montaigne, he'd paid that trainer a fortune to teach his girls.

Arthur charged toward the bathroom to confront Annabelle.

Then he paused.

He retreated and sat on the edge of his wife's side of their bed. He slouched, his broad Teutonic shoulders collapsing. His expression, only moments ago so jolly and satisfied, now sunk down to the rug.

PART II

Summer Heat

Chapter 20

Make It or Break It

I t can all be traced to an inanimate object: wooden beams Caroline sourced for a client. The people who took that big Methodist church down in Vermont would never know the ripples that would generate in its wake.

Caroline was picking up some throws for a client at a design store in East Hampton when her phone buzzed in her jacket pocket. It was a text from Ryan:

> How have you been?
> The birch lumber arrived from that church in Vermont.
> I'm putting it up today in a small cottage far off on the bay side, near Three Mile Harbor.

Caroline texted back:

> It'll be perfect, glad it worked out, those guys are so helpful.

Ryan:

Yes, they were. Thanks for connecting me.

She tried to remember something she'd learned in design school about cottage renovations:

Did you have to raise the structure to redo the foundation?

Ryan:

Yes. That's all done. Measuring out beam placement now. The wood is perfect: splintered but structurally sound, chamfer edges, dark but not too dark.

Caroline:

I know, I use those guys all the time.

Those three little dots were blinking for almost ninety seconds; he was either writing an opus or rewriting something over and over, making sure it sounded right.
And then finally:

Would you like to see it?

Caroline:

Of course.

She'd answered a bit too quickly, but she'd been waiting so

many days to hear from him again. She didn't want to stall with little telltale dots flickering like he had—that would give him the impression that she cared too much. She moved into a more professional zone, to keep her tone friendly, and, on some level, married:

I studied that process—houses on the ocean being pulled back on train tracks to avoid beach erosion—but I've never seen a house lifted off the ground myself.

And so, under the wholly manufactured and entirely false pretense of work, Ryan and Caroline organized a rendezvous to discuss wooden beam placement. At the cottage in question, there were a few workers around, so they kept their distance, their conversation overly work-related.

"Hey," he said, as they walked to their cars. During the tour of the job site, Caroline hadn't been able to concentrate on much of what he said. She kept avoiding his eyes and asking questions she already knew the answer to, probably, she figured, sounding like a nincompoop with little design acumen. As he talked, she had to reteach her lungs to expand and slowly empty.

Ryan stopped walking and touched her arm as if to get her to focus on what he was saying. It felt good to touch this woman; he was actually having trouble not touching her. "Are you working more?"

Caroline pushed the sand on the pavement around a bit with her foot, making little piles. "Not at all," she said. "I'm done for the day. I got most of my work done by lunchtime." Her pitch was higher than normal. She had to push breaths hard out of her nose to get her lungs back in rhythm.

"Morning work, all done midday, that's good," he said, fiddling with his car keys. "I'm, uh, just heading into Amagansett."

"I'm actually going in that direction to Montauk," Caroline said, smiling and trying hard not to sound the least bit suggestive.

Breathing was still not automatic; it felt like the air was not passing down her throat.

Just as Annabelle had predicted, Caroline had met this guy on the first weekend of summer, and even by meeting one, she was ready to go. Whatever this was, it already felt difficult to walk away from it. She smoothed out the waist of her jeans. Her stomach was churning so much, she didn't know how to calm it.

"I need a coffee, maybe something else," Ryan said. "It's almost two, and I haven't eaten much today, and—"

"Oh, well, me too, I guess," Caroline interrupted, almost immediately wishing she'd been a little cooler. "I'm hitting my early afternoon wall, and I need a little fruit or tea or something to keep me going."

Only it wasn't just coffee in town.

As they walked into Amagansett Square, by Wölffer Kitchen, Ryan held the door open to Jack's Stir Brew, where the heavy scent of coffee pervaded the air. He said, "What the hell, this place is crowded."

"It sure is," she replied, sounding like one of her Ohio cousins who declared the obvious all the time.

"You know what?" Ryan said. "Screw the coffee, let's get a dozen oysters down toward Montauk instead. Have some fun. You like oysters?"

"I do. A lot. But you mean right now?" Caroline said, looking at her watch. "I guess. I mean, I have a sitter taking the kids to playdates. I was going to check on a curtain installation on my way home, but it's a sleepy Tuesday, why not spend it . . . I mean, in town, of course."

"Why not spend a sleepy workday enjoying summer?" Ryan said and smiled. He placed his hand on her upper arm again, and this time, he left it there. "We can compare our favorite everything: beaches, fabrics, painters, and whatever . . . work or play. Let's do it."

He smiled again and said, "I had a rough morning with another client who can never be pleased no matter what gymnastics I do, so I need to blow off some steam."

They took their cars to the Clam Bar on the side of Montauk Highway. During the ride, Caroline made work calls, checked on the sitter, and noted that her mouth was so dry she had trouble swallowing.

When the hostess offered them a table by the road, Ryan said, "How about in the back?" This was her first clue that he had felt the same heat she had at the jobsite.

Ryan ordered a dozen oysters, a bowl of fried clams, and two iced teas. Rather than hogging the moment by talking about himself, he fired questions at her and listened to the answers. He asked how she got her jobs done in summer when all the providers were so jammed that they weren't promising to deliver orders until October. She already knew he wasn't a man who required being interviewed to keep interested in a conversation.

In fact, when she tried to ask him some questions, first about his surfing, he just joked, "Look, I've always been the worst surfer on the lineup. My timing has been off since high school, but I still get out there." He leaned over to her, getting more confident. "So I get credit for that, at least." His eyes were looking very green now against his tan skin and the hedge behind him. He put glasses on to check out the menu, then combed his hair back with one arm, leaving it scratching the back of his head. Caroline noted the well-formed triceps.

The waitress came with a pitcher of iced tea, and Caroline turned to Ryan, placing her head on her palm, staring at him in an I-dare-you way, "How about one oyster shot?"

"Oh, *really*, is that what's happening?" The way he looked at her over the brim of his glasses made her stomach churn more, this time in a good way.

And when she boldly answered, "Yeah, *really*," she knew she was in trouble.

After one vodka shot each (with an oyster and cocktail sauce in the heavy, little glasses) and three dozen oysters (the third dozen inhaled with his knee pressed against hers), Caroline and Ryan walked back to their cars. As she opened her door, he said, "Don't actually get in. Come over to my truck. Just for a second."

"Your truck?" Caroline asked. "You mean, you want me to go there?" She felt as if she were falling into a hole and sliding down a tunnel with nothing to grab on to. It was the middle of a Tuesday. Maybe, after all, that bravado she felt at the table wouldn't last; maybe she didn't have it in her. Didn't this kind of thing happen at night or sunset?

"Don't worry," Ryan said, reading her mind. "Harmless." He knew what she was thinking because he was thinking the same thing: *This is crazy, but I'm going to do it anyway.* "Just come over, under the tree." He motioned his head toward his truck, hidden behind some bushes in a far corner of the lot. "C'mon."

She followed and stood before him, no one in sight near them. Before asking her if he could or explaining earnestly that he'd never done this before, he placed his hands on her hips and pulled her into him so hard that the seams of her jeans cut into her body. He then kissed her, first softly to mitigate the way he'd just grabbed her, then with more abandon, holding her chin with his hand to steady the intensity.

She reached around to fix her jeans a little and yanked them down an inch or so. He reached inside the back and clutched her flesh hard. He took a brief break, and whispered into her ear, "I'm not going to ask you to do anything else, but Jesus, you feel good," he said.

After a few more moments of deep kissing, groping, and rearranging of denim, Ryan pulled back and made sure his secluded parking spot was indeed secluded enough. "Look, I'm sorry, I was going to ask if I could kiss you before, but I didn't want to give you the opportunity to say no. I've never once done that." And then he kissed her ear and whispered. "Maybe, let's just stop here before I can't stop."

She whispered back, feeling an ache between her legs so fiery that it almost hurt, "I'm not sure I want you to stop." Maybe that dangerous forties decade Annabelle kept referring to was barreling at her a few years early.

It was a surreal moment for Caroline: the first time she'd kissed a man other than Eddie Clarkson since they'd gotten married. Sure, the one vodka had warmed her up. And that natural effect of oysters maybe got her more primed than she'd expected, far more actually, but whatever caused it, she felt a sense of abandon with Ryan.

She felt kinship too. They shared the same interest in the way the height of cornstalks matched the amount of time one had left in summer; in the way the sun hit the water at certain times of the year; in the psychotherapy required to handle difficult clients. "Do we have to stop?" she asked him. "I mean, I'm just saying, do we actually *have to stop?*"

"I'm not sure, it's daylight, like I said, my timing is always off," Ryan said. "But where? You mean now?"

"Yeah. I mean now. I mean, why not now?" She was so hot inside her jeans, she couldn't wait to get this guy somewhere darker, somewhere safer. Fast.

If they did stop, she was going to have a moment alone in a dark powder room inside, or simply hump a tree nearby. Either way, her body was headed full speed in one direction only, no way to veer it to a rest stop.

"How about that cottage we just visited?" he said. "No one's there, it's past four."

Chapter 21

A Little Surprise "for You"

It's coming!" Theo yelled. The thud-thud-thud of the helicopter's propellers could be heard in the distance at the airstrip known grandiosely as the East Hampton *Airport*. Eddie wrapped Theo in his arms and said, "I love you, my only son, and I got a surprise for you!"

"What is it?" Theo asked.

"What did you get *me*?" Gigi asked. "I'm your only daughter!" He often called Theo his only son, but never referred to Gigi as his only daughter. Caroline always found that strange and had mentioned it to him a few times.

"The same thing!" Eddie answered as he winked at Caroline beside him in the passenger waiting area. She'd driven him to the Monday morning Blade helicopter flight into the city that he shared with five other passengers.

"I got a surprise for all of us!" Eddie said, rubbing his hands together.

"Honey, please," Caroline said. "You know the kids have camp in a half hour; it's their first day." She did not want to appear to be pushing him out the door. Every single thing she'd said to her husband all weekend made her prickle with paranoia.

No matter what she said to Eddie, she worried she was inadvertently revealing something about her Tuesday with Ryan. Even when she asked her husband if he wanted more sugar for his coffee, she thought, *I usually don't serve him like a handmaid; maybe he's going to know I'm up to something?*

Eddie usually took a fifty-dollar Hampton Jitney coach bus back and forth to Manhattan. A few times every summer, when he had a meeting to rush to, he'd splurge on a helicopter seat. At six hundred dollars a head, this was the cheapest commuter route to the city—through the clouds—a fraction of what chartering a whole helicopter would cost.

A billion dollars' worth of private jets and Sikorsky helicopters lined up beside the single, cracked runway in East Hampton. Eddie knew the most coveted jet, among the people with *serious money*, was the G650, with a sticker price of about $65 million. "Look, kids, at those jets pulling out of the hangar. See that passenger staircase opening like a clam? The pilot's gonna walk down those stairs to greet his passengers. Their car will pull up right to the plane. How cool is that?"

"Can we do that?" Theo asked. "Can we drive up to one and get in?"

Caroline rolled her eyes at her husband. She didn't need to say what she was thinking.

Eddie was so mesmerized by the Hamptons cash oozing around him that he couldn't respond to her. (He was, of course, breaking therapy rule number nine: listen to your spouse when he or she obviously cares about something.)

A Lexus sedan pulled up to a jet to Eddie's left. The ground crew laid a mat at the bottom of the plane's staircase to ensure the owner had minimal contact with actual concrete.

On Eddie's right, an extremely stylish young woman strutted up to a copter, leading her King Charles spaniel with a Goyard leash. Right before stepping into his Sikorsky, she held the hand of that loaded prick who never once remembered Eddie's name.

Eddie pointed the kids' attention now to a large jet landing, the thrust reversers slamming on hard. He said to them, "I've been inside one of those G5 babies once; like thirteen seats or something. Some have showers in them." *Maybe one day,* Eddie thought to himself. "It was with a developer to see some land for a mall in New Haven. Remember that guy, Caroline?"

"Eddie, I don't."

And then, he whispered to her, "He was an asshole anyway, treated everyone who worked for him on the plane like shit." Eddie recalled that the guy had screamed at the flight attendant because she'd added a kiwi to his fruit salad, and served 2 percent yogurt when the wife had *explicitly* ordered nonfat—*She said* no *fat, not* low *fat!*

Eddie knew he'd never abuse his staff, no matter how much money he made—granted, he had to admit to himself, his two assistants, Maryanne and Eleanor, would beat the crap out of him if he did.

All these private aircrafts got Eddie wondering about his French partners, drooling about all the cash he'd see in a few weeks. If it all went the way the French said, maybe he'd be G5 rich? Eight-seater rich would do his family of four—a used Citation CJ4 was perhaps a couple of mill, tops. So what if the French weren't the most ethical bunch? The plan was rock solid.

"I'm not clear about your schedule, honey," Caroline said. "We're going to be late for camp, and I don't want to rush you, but why are we waiting over here when your charter group is back there?"

"Well, then I know something else!" he said, as he kneeled down and hugged both kids at once. "Get this everyone: the Clarkson kids are all going to be late for camp today. Fun Daddy's going to be late for work too. We're all in trouble!" The kids clapped with glee, though they knew their mom didn't appreciate this one bit. They also knew she hated the nickname he'd given himself.

"Honey, please . . ." Caroline's protestations were useless.

Eddie was in one of his moods, possibly trying to surprise her or to earn her affections. Early this morning, after a somewhat strained weekend, she and Eddie had warmed up to each other. He'd pulled her to him in bed, wrapping his brawny legs around her. He wiped her thick hair off her face, locked eyes with the woman he adored and said, "I love you. We can do this. I'm sorry I had to work and be at the club with those clients and left you . . ."

"I don't mind you leaving me, it's just you don't warn me, so I can't plan. I have four client meetings today and couldn't prepare all day Sunday. And . . ." she'd kept listing reasons that would explain her aloofness. She worried that he'd pick up on something. She was avoiding sleeping with him because she didn't want to deal with sexual whiplash between him and Ryan.

"I couldn't be prouder of my wife, okay? I'm sorry I was a dick." In bed, the Monday morning light coming through their shades, he kissed her forehead hard, as if for emphasis.

"I'm sorry I was in a foul mood," she replied, yanking the covers under her arm. The playing field was a little more even now, and things were different. She felt more powerful, if, admittedly, a hundred times more anxious. "Last night, our usual deal, and I just wanted you to bring in dinner like we planned."

Eddie wasn't listening to her apologies or trying to figure out what was really on her mind. He had other plans for her, now burrowing his head under the comforter.

"Eddie, stop, c'mon, I have to . . ."

"You have nothing to do but lie back and let me make you happy," he said.

"Eddie, I'm just . . ." She tried to pull him up by the armpits. It had been five days, but she was still worried he'd detect Ryan somehow. As she later confided to Annabelle, she'd taken multiple baths, and used up six Summer's Eve douche bottles in the past week (even stopping at the drugstore and using one in the Starbuck's bathroom on the way to pick up Eddie on Friday because she couldn't calm her nerves). She whispered beneath the covers, "Just kiss me instead. Please, we have to rush, the kids and their first day at camp. Your helicopter. I know you're away for ten days, just . . ."

Eddie wasn't having it. All his golf buddies agreed: no better tactic for calming down a pissed off wife than going down on her slowly and not making her fuck you back. He could jerk off in the shower anyway. Eddie knew he was a strategic motherfucker if nothing else; he needed Caroline in a good mood for the family surprise he'd planned—one that had a teeny-weeny possibility of not getting the reaction he was after.

A helicopter hovered over the painted circle in the distance, swaying a bit, before landing and sending dust everywhere around it. Caroline, Gigi, and Theo turned their backs to the sandstorm, and Eddie shielded the kids' eyes. He then scooped them up and started walking toward the gate to the tarmac. He motioned for the porter to follow with his bags in the trolley.

"Eddie, your group helicopter is coming at eight-thirty, not earlier, that big one out there, it's not the Blade. The Blade woman isn't even out here yet," Caroline yelled to him. Caroline and everyone out here who didn't own their own helicopter knew all about Blade, the app that allowed any shmuck to push a button and order a six-hundred-dollar seat on a communal helicopter—as easy-peasy as booking an Uber car.

But Eddie kept walking, both kids firmly under his arms. She knew he had organized something he hadn't told her about. *Again.*

The Blade hostess came out in her sexy Star Trek uniform: a tight jumpsuit with navy stripes. On one arm, goody bags filled with Rag & Bone clothes she'd sized for their most attractive customers (the others got Masters and Dynamic studio headphones).

Caroline walked over to her. "Clarkson, he's already out on the tarmac for some reason heading toward that huge, silver one. But that isn't his ride, right?"

"We don't have a Clarkson on the eight-thirty," the Blade lady said.

"I made the reservation myself," Caroline told her. "Can you look again?"

"Eddie canceled that one," announced Blade's owner, Rob Wiesenthal, as he approached Caroline. He was wearing one of his Thom Browne striped retro sweaters, looking as if he'd just enjoyed a good cricket match in Sussex. Rob and Eddie had met at the club and joshed with each other for being the worst players there. Rob told Caroline, "Your husband ordered his own copter to the city, that big mack daddy, Sikorsky. He added an hour tour. Look."

"I'm a bad flyer, Rob. I'm not getting into that thing," Caroline said.

"Can we send you along with a mimosa? I think your husband's got a surprise for you." Rob rubbed her upper arm and winked. "Go on, don't let on I told you anything. But you can do it; it's got two pilots and can land anywhere. The wind might make it bounce a little on takeoff, but don't worry. And, by the way, congratulations. He must be doing very well."

Caroline had no idea what was going on. All she knew was that the kids would be late for camp on their first day. And that Eddie had spent a big bundle of the cash she wasn't supposed to know he'd earned.

"Mom!" Theo yelled. "We're going on a ride! C'mon! Daddy says you're a party pooper!"

Caroline walked onto the tarmac, wondering if she was confronting her fear of flying out of guilt or a need to keep up with Fun Daddy. She crouched as she approached the captain, who guided her under the propeller and into the cabin. She'd never been so close to a helicopter and wondered if people ever got decapitated on that huge propeller above her. Once inside, she buckled her belt so tightly, her flesh curled around it. "Eddie, what on earth?" she asked. "What is going on?" Then she whispered to him, so the kids couldn't hear, "This is like eight thousand for the morning trip alone, right? If you take it for yourself to fly around and go into the city?" She'd guessed right, she knew, she'd often asked Annabelle how many thousands it cost to fly private jets and helicopters.

"Nah, it's just, well, just trust me," Eddie said. "You're gonna love how it feels! I want you to see something better from up high."

Caroline now knew what was coming. Over and over, he had asked if they could buy the property on the ocean bluff that no one else dared purchase. Over and over, she had said no. Building on that land was too hard a project for her to manage with the kids and her clients. She didn't add that she might have one foot out the door anyway, and you didn't start building a new home from scratch with your marriage in trouble.

Caroline tightened her children's seat belts, and they started to squeal as the helicopter lifted off the pavement. The claustrophobic cabin rattled under the propeller, as the gears tilted the rotors from ascension to forward motion. Caroline gripped Eddie's thigh. She wasn't a good flyer in a 747 Jumbo Jet.

She looked at her kids, to see if they were as anxious as she was. They were oblivious to the grinding of the machinery and the distance between them and the receding ground. They pressed their noses against the window in anticipation of the rest of their father's extravaganza.

After a few minutes, Gigi turned to Caroline and said, "Mom, do you have water?" Her face was green. Caroline prayed Eddie had the bag in his pocket. She whispered to her husband, trying not to instigate their eighteenth fight of the weekend. "Eddie, this is so sweet, this little trip, but you know I get scared and Gigi, well, you know what happens when she flies." She paused and added, "*Every time.*"

Eddie patted his wife's hand. "Gigi won't puke, right, honey?" He rubbed Gigi's thigh hard, willing his daughter to get with his program. And then he whispered to Caroline, "Let's all stay positive, look at her, she's having a blast! It's only fifteen minutes, and we'll be back on the ground."

Suddenly the helicopter banked sharply left toward the ocean, as if under attack from the Luftwaffe. And, just as she figured, they were now gunning at full speed over the coast toward Wiborg Beach and along Further Lane.

"Look at the size of those homes, Jesus," Eddie said, salivating. "None as big as Ron Perelman's back on Georgica Pond we passed, but look, that huge one is the Millshore Club where your mom's friend Annabelle practically lives, then Jerry Seinfeld's . . ."

Caroline was calming down a little. It was pretty spectacular to look at these 15,000-square-foot, ocean-front estates from the air; they looked like dollhouses, with hedges outlining the property and vast lawns and tennis courts behind them. Most had swimming pools between the house and the cliff. She knew these houses all from the walks she'd been taking on the beach since she was small. "They look like castles, not homes," she said.

"Now, we're getting closer! Daddy has a surprise for everyone!" Eddie unbuckled the kids' belts and put Theo on his lap. Her son was excited to see what his father had planned, but Gigi was only feeling sicker.

Eddie knocked on the cockpit window behind him. "Guys, do me a favor, make some circles around it, like I said, just go slow and really low!"

The helicopter jerked again, the rotors pivoting into the wind. The cabin bounced as it flew over the ocean, the propellers battling the gusts. Caroline imagined the *East Hampton Star* headline, "Wealthy, Local-turned-Manhattan Developer Perishes in Crash—his Wife and Kids too." She whispered to Eddie, "Is that grinding sound . . . normal?"

"It's fine," he said. He needed her on his side.

The machine fought the elements as it circled around. Caroline badly wanted the flying machine to land; she started looking for a clearing below as if she could bring the thing down herself. Theo and Eddie, boys being boys, got even more pumped with the thrill of the maneuvers. They both stared out the window, their heads bounced in unison, giddy.

Gigi, the other female, implored her mom, "I want to go down!" She started crying and coughing, "Now! I don't feel well!" Eddie pulled out another Ziploc from his left pocket and handed it to his wife without even looking her way.

"Look!" Eddie yelled. "Look at our new home."

"Where is it? That big one?" Theo asked, wrapping his elbow around his father's neck.

"No, the land down there, that mountain of tan next to the big house."

It was an untamed acre on a cliff overlooking the Atlantic, four lots from Egypt Beach. After great logistical and legal difficulty, the new buyers (or suckers) could prop up the dune, pour a complex foundation, and build a house. She and Eddie would kill each other, fighting over everything. Eddie had certainly not heeded item number sixteen in marital therapy: no commando, unilateral home decisions. Caroline liked to walk to the beach, not live on it. Her kids could bike to the beach as she had.

She put her hand on her husband's thigh. This was a time to be nice to him; everything was different now that she'd done what she'd done with Ryan. "You're crazy, but that's something I knew early on," Caroline said. "I'm happy for you. It's what you wanted. You've worked hard, honey, to get here." She kissed his cheek. She decided she would let him develop the property as he wished. Who knew if she'd even be around for the housewarming?

"I did it for you," he said, and he kissed his wife. "You'll learn to love it."

Magnanimity was meant for the person who received it; not for the person who doled it out.

Just then, Gigi threw up all over both of them. She had missed the Ziploc by a good two feet.

Chapter 22

Drop-off and Go

Back at the East Hampton Airport lounge, Eddie dropped Caroline and the kids off before flying into the city alone on the huge Sikorsky, and despite the stain on his pants from Gigi's bout of motion sickness, he was feeling *like a boss*. Caroline hoped this wasn't a pattern, no matter how much money he had.

As she passed through the Blade lounge with her kids, Rob Wiesenthal patted her on the back. "What a piece of property! He's got elephant balls not to tell you," Rob said. Then he laughed and walked away, marveling at that Eddie character. Before going into his office, he turned back and said, "My wife would murder me if I did that!"

Though Caroline and Theo were an hour late to All Stars Soccer Academy, it took the usual two minutes to get Theo settled at his new camp. Caroline knew her timid little Gigi would cling a bit even at a pony camp in her own Daddy's barn.

This morning, Caroline wanted to check on the stables anyway. Maybe she'd find a little time with Thierry to see how the intra-barn relations were going, to make sure he was comfortable in the vast operation Eddie had created. Even if she never wanted to get involved in Eddie's projects, it wouldn't hurt to have the wife wander around a bit gathering intelligence. If there were real discord, Eddie might be too distracted by bigger things to even notice.

Caroline replayed the argument between Thierry and Philippe and Marcus in her mind from the barn party. They were hiding something, and Marcus McCree, that upstanding former cop and reputable businessman, was lying to her and to them about errands he was on. Eddie wouldn't let anyone skim anything, any amount; he and that ol' schoolmarm Maryanne raked through every expense. So, what were they hiding? And how was Marcus involved?

Thierry was placing heavy boxes of veterinary supplies in the tack room when Caroline walked in, Gigi still holding her mother's hand. His thin frame highlighted with the sun streaming through and the dust flying around him, he asked, "What happened to my helper this morning? I thought you were going to come a half hour before and help me get the ponies ready."

Gigi looked up at her mom, hoping she'd come up with a better excuse than that she'd taken her first ride in a helicopter and vomited all over her parents.

Thierry smiled at Gigi, his own niece's closest summer friend, very familiar with her shyness. "Rosie was here, missing you, but don't worry. There's always plenty of work," he said, winking at Caroline. He pulled his hat off, folded it, and shoved it into his back pocket. His dark ponytail, four inches long and filled with curls, hung low on the back of his neck, like a Colonial gentleman's.

Caroline asked Gigi, "Honey, do you want to go to camp with Thierry or . . ."

"I mean, do I just start riding or do I help the other kids first?" Gigi asked, rubbing her shoulder against her mother's hip.

"How about you go do what Rosie's doing on Sauerkraut, which is just a walk trot position class?" Thierry said. "They haven't really started; Scooby-Doo is out there, honey. Come with me." He took

Gigi's hand and half-dragged her out to ring two, where eight kids under twelve were just beginning their lesson.

This was not a time to grill Thierry on why he and his boss, Philippe, had been so rough with Marcus, so Caroline took a look around the stables. She reviewed the lesson plans on the white-boards: they'd use a dozen ponies this morning alone, and there'd be about two dozen horse and pony private lessons in the afternoon.

Checking that the grooms down the hall were occupied and that Thierry, the grooms, and Philippe were nowhere near, Caroline peeked into drawers and cabinets. She flipped through whatever ledgers she could find. There was nothing much out of the ordinary: only schedules, medications lists for the horses, time sheets for the grooms.

One thing caught her eye—the feed delivery schedules. All stables were closed on Mondays, the one day when grooms and trainers took a break. No one in a barn scheduled anything on Mondays. She saw the delivery calendar and noted the hand-writing: European numbers, the 9 that looked like a lower case g; the long tail on the 1; the crossed 7; and the commas instead of decimal points. How come the deliveries had been written by a French person when nothing else was—not the lessons, not the schedules?

A groom walked by, that sweet Juan Andrés from Colombia, who always showed Caroline photos of his daughter back home. He'd managed the logistics and schedule at the old barn with Thierry. "Hey, Juanito," she asked. "I have a question: What happens around here on Mondays?"

"We come in for an hour in the morning and another in the afternoon; the guards are here. Nothing else," he said, swallowing hard.

"And deliveries? When do they happen? Who covers all that?"

"Well, Philippe, uh, does. He does all that."

"Alone?" Caroline asked. "Do other barns get deliveries on Mondays?"

"Not one," he answered forcefully this time. "I don't know why, but he does it himself."

Juanito looked uncomfortable, and Caroline didn't want to put him on the spot. She'd ask Maryanne about the schedule in a few days, once she thought about it a little more, and come up with a good reason she might be asking. She'd call the trainer at the old barn, that sweet Jenna Westlake from Rose Patch. Caroline could say she wanted Gigi to do more work, and she could ask how they ran things there. Did head trainers usually get their hands into the feed and manure deliveries?

Chapter 23

The Pleasure Principle

As Caroline drove down Route 27, she inspected her face in the rearview mirror at a stoplight. She was glad she hadn't put on much makeup—she didn't want to look as if she were on a first date. She drove through Bridgehampton, past the Candy Kitchen, an old-style coffee shop run by a lovely guy everyone knew named Gus. It was the one Hamptons spot where locals and summer people gathered in equal numbers, grabbing their morning coffee or bringing their kids for Gus's famous homemade ice cream. Annabelle told her that grown women didn't eat grilled cheese and fries. Caroline countered that her roundness was genetic; there wasn't much she could do about it. She hated dieting more than she despised exercise.

Now, meeting Ryan for dinner, her look had to reflect a collected calm. She was going for a balance. She wore light jeans and a V-neck sweater that descended into her sizable cleavage when she leaned over.

"I'm getting things set here, got great burrata cheese from my favorite farm stand," Ryan said over the speakerphone in the car. "And I do want to meet you at the beach first . . ."

His voice trailed off, and Caroline asked, "You okay?"

"Totally good. I'm getting ready while I'm talking, so I'm a little preoccupied, and I've got some fire drills I'm running at the station tomorrow so I was just working on them before I go."

"You on the volunteer fireman force?" It made sense he would be connected to the community.

"Who isn't? Yes, I run the drills. And I don't want to be late for the beach. Six, right? You okay?"

"I'm fine, heading to a great sunset, couldn't be better," Caroline answered, anxious at the prospect of being seen with Ryan on a public beach. "You sure the beach is okay?"

"Hell yes, it's a Tuesday," he said. "No one's at Indian Wells Beach. Just go to that log, I'll meet you there as planned."

There was a silence for a moment until both of them spoke at once:

She asked, "You meet that horrible client?"

And he asked, "Did you get a lot done on the sunroom today?"

Caroline realized she didn't quite know what to say to him, so she said, "All good with you?"

"I'm feeling great," he answered. "Like a great white shark!"

"A shark feels great?" Caroline asked.

"That was a joke," Ryan said. "I'll lay it out for you in person."

"Okay," she said. "I'll see you at the beach."

Caroline didn't say what she was thinking: a great white shark? The joke didn't really make sense. At the oyster bar, she'd noticed that Ryan was like that sometimes, a little goofy. Maybe it had been the vodka. At the barn party he'd been sharper, and exceptionally perceptive about the entitled jerks around them.

She and Annabelle had agreed that the word *edgy* was used too much these days to describe people and that it annoyed them both.

But today, she was thinking, the term is apt. Ryan Miller was not edgy. Men could still be brave and bold without being edgy, but edgy was just a little more intriguing than normal.

And, of course, Eddie Clarkson had the edge of an atomic bomb, 24-7. He wanted to prove everybody wrong all the time, act crazy, clank up the stairs of a crappy beach hotel in a knight's costume, for God's sake. Joey had that same Energizer-bunny level of edginess—always wanting to have sex in store changing rooms, always wanting to make groups of people do things they were wary of, like jump in the ocean on a cold winter's night or water-ski down the sand behind a truck on boogie boards—so if she had a type, maybe that was it. "The Great Instigator" was what she used to call Joey.

Caroline didn't even like thinking something that entered her mind now, and would never tell anyone, even Annabelle. But it was true. No denying she was much prouder of Joey than Eddie, much more likely to show him off. She was happy to nestle up against Joey on the beach as he regaled the crowd with his stories, or she'd take a girlfriend to see the commissioned murals he had painted at the town basketball courts or at the childcare center, inspired by his favorite Latin American artists. She admired Eddie, for sure, but she also found herself apologizing for him, and she would never show off his stables or even talk much about his projects in the city.

As she sped toward East Hampton, passing the Seafood Shop in Sagaponack (a place that few knew also whipped up the best guacamole in Suffolk County), Caroline felt a kink in her neck. She took one hand off the wheel and tried to rub it out, but it didn't go away. She pushed her head back, against the headrest, pressing against the leather as hard as she could to bring blood flow to that region. Turning her head did nothing. Maybe it was her body reminding her of the messy side of straying.

The beach would help. She parked her Jeep in one of the slanted slots at the top of the hill near Indian Wells Beach. Ryan was right: the beach was empty. Only one car was there, and an older couple laden with beach chairs and tote bags approached the lot, clearly on their way home.

Caroline took off her sandals by the entrance to the beach and, with a blanket that she always kept in the car over her shoulder, she sank into the luscious Long Island sand. As she did so, it poured around her feet and between her toes. She took big strides that brought more weight to each step, her feet buried, unearthed, and reburied with each one.

At that log, she laid out her blanket, planted her cup of iced tea in the sand, and reclined, her face warming in the waning sun. She balled her sweater up against the log to rest her neck. Ryan wouldn't arrive for twenty minutes, and she fell in and out of a dream state.

His strong voice woke her. "You look beautiful when you sleep," he said, sitting down next to her, grabbing his shins with his arms. "I bet I'll never get to watch you do that."

She sat up and rubbed her cheeks, hoping to draw color into them. Turning to him, she said, "I mean, I don't think we'll be spending a night together, no. But . . . it's good to see you, and, I'm, uh, excited to try your cooking." That suggestion felt like a distant second for a couple who'd done what they'd done last week.

Brushing her hair from her face, Ryan didn't tell her what he wanted to do right now, or that her eyes were spellbinding, bright blue against the azure of the ocean. "You okay?" he asked.

"I mean, I'm okay, in terms of, like, what we are doing," Caroline said, sitting up now. She constructed small pyramids in the sand with her fingers that fell apart as fast as her conviction that all was okay. She felt her words were sounding forced, not cool. "I put your number in my phone contacts as 'Robert Smith Upholsterer,' so when I mean, if you call, or whatever, no one will suspect." She had trouble looking Ryan in the eyes. She ached for him, she wanted to sleep with him again, but she worried about it. All of it. "I just, you know, never did this, and . . ."

"Remember, Caroline. We set the rules yesterday," Ryan said, trying to comfort her. He placed his hand on hers. "Tuesday nights. We start early; we're home by midnight. You get the sitter every Tuesday. Never see each other in between; no calls in between, except Tuesday mornings to plan. We are one hundred percent over by Labor Day. We are both in the same boat. You have nothing to worry about except having a great dinner with an old school friend. All good, Caroline. Don't worry." He leaned down and looked at her face. Holding her chin lightly with his fingers, he added, "All fun, all light, or it's not worth it."

She wanted to ask where his wife, Suzy, was this evening, but she decided against it. Dissecting Ryan's marriage was not something that was advantageous to either of them. Still, she couldn't help trying to put some pieces together. Ryan had told her that Suzy had fallen for one of her colleagues at Stonybrook, where she sometimes taught in the studio art department. It was about ten years ago when their kids were just starting kindergarten. He'd more than hinted that this was his payback as well.

"All will go really fine tonight," Ryan said, craning his neck so she would have to face him.

"How do you know? I mean . . ." Caroline said before answering her own question. "I know everything's fine." She sounded idiotic. This was her choice, her life, her doing. She had to start channeling Annabelle.

"I can sense the worry in your voice, even Egyptian women having affairs don't make pyramids in the sand—unless they're trying to get their minds off their problems," Ryan said. "Remember: I won't let it *not* go okay. I promise you. That's why I offered you a water bottle when you already had fifty in front of you back at that juice tent from the barn party."

"Okay, thanks for saying that," she said. She sat up straight, nodding a little. She pulled the blanket around her shoulders as the sun cast a long shadow across the beach.

"Let's get to 364 Sandpiper Lane," he said. "The client is in Europe for the month, and I'm the only one with the key. Remember what we agreed: we're going to treat this like a present to each of us." They walked to the parking lot, and he added, "No stress, no guilt, no strings. Just one summer affair. Either wants out, the other kisses goodbye with a smile. No tears or sadness. I'm not leaving Suzy; I love Suzy," he said forcefully. "I hope I don't hurt you by saying or underlining this or even talking about her. I just feel I need to, once more."

After Ryan opened the door of the Jeep for her, she sat and turned to him through the open window. "It's all good. I'm not upset or nervous," she said. "It makes perfect sense to me too." She liked Ryan's values (though she conceded that cheating on one's wife didn't show sterling moral character, exactly) and how he said what he meant. Life was complicated, she decided, and good deeds weren't always good, and bad deeds weren't always so bad. "You're a kind man, Ryan. You care for people's homes, and you care for people too. I imagine your attention to detail in every renovation you do extends to all areas of your life."

He looked down, a little embarrassed with the compliments. "Not sure everyone would agree."

"I bet they do appreciate you, as I appreciate the burrata you got from the farm stand, too, and the way you gather provisions like a proper caveman, but I'm just saying some men are not caretakers. They don't know *how* to be caretakers. They are fun and exciting, but when it comes down to it, they're self-centered. That's all I'm saying."

"Ah, plenty of people around me think I'm a pain in the ass," he joked.

Caroline knew she was right. It wasn't her job to help Ryan understand that he was a good man. This was a contract, not a relationship.

A FEW HOURS later, a fire crackled before Caroline and Ryan in a home that was not theirs. Plates where tuna and tomatoes had once resided lay beside them. An empty wine bottle was upside down in a bucket half filled with water. He had said the tuna was Niçoise style, and he had smothered it in vegetables and a sweet olive sauce with ingredients she couldn't quite decipher. He'd used a ton of ginger as well, along with some honey and orange juice. She wanted to lap up the sauce from her plate but decided it wasn't so ladylike.

Ryan had brought a crunchy baguette from a bakery in Montauk, and a chunk remained in a basket. She wanted more of that too. He explained that he grilled the tuna with thyme butter and she had used the bread to, literally, clean her plate.

"I thought you said this was Niçoise tuna," she said. "I'm confused. It's filled with ginger. Don't get me wrong—this is literally the best tuna I've ever had, but isn't Niçoise meant to be with olives and tomatoes and olive oil?"

"Yeah. And also ginger, rice wine, honey, and mirin."

"That's not Niçoise," she said, smiling.

"That's what I call it." He laughed and rolled on top of her. "I don't really give a shit what it's called because it's good," he said. "Delicious as fuck, as my teenager says. Like you. Fucking delicious."

He placed her arms above her head and held them down. She kissed him hard. His breath tasted of roasted tomatoes, corn, ginger, olive oil, and white wine all swirled together. He pulled back, slowing the energy between them. There was time. Suzy thought he was in Bayshore with his friend Marty. Marty was primed not to answer his phone should Suzy call. Marty had been telling him for years to get Suzy back for that Stonybrook professor, so he could hardly contain himself with excitement that Ryan was partaking. No way would he pick up the phone.

Ryan then propped himself up by his elbow and traced her profile with his right index finger. She smiled, thinking of Joey, and how she used to do that to him. She was fine with thinking of Joey now; she didn't owe Ryan anything more than honesty and kindness.

"Are you still hungry?" he asked. He dunked the last small crust of bread into the remaining marinade on his plate and added a corner of tomato and creamy burrata. He then knelt and placed the savory concoction in her mouth.

She closed her eyes. "Sweet, creamy, and tart—all in one," she said. "Thanks, it tastes too good."

"Sweet, creamy, and tart?" he repeated, kissing her, licking her lips lightly while she chewed. He placed his palm between her thighs. "Sounds like you." He pressed his fingers on her. "Here. Fucking delicious."

Caroline smiled, but didn't respond. She worried when Ryan got a little romantic. She turned over onto her stomach, her chin resting in her hands. She considered what the rest of the night held and started thinking about what would go on later—much later—once fall came.

What would happen if she saw him in the Amagansett Farmers Market in November? They both went there for pies every weekend; they'd discussed it at dinner when she first bit into the baguette. He said he took his kids there every Saturday morning for berry muffins and coffee, but that he went to Bridgehampton for better bread from Pierre's. She didn't tell him that her kids inhaled those same muffins when she brought them home on Saturdays and that she grilled them with butter.

"Lie there," Ryan said, busing the plates to the small kitchenette.

"You look beautiful. Don't move." Eddie had never once cleared the table on cue, let alone instructed her to sit still while he did so.

He kissed her forehead gently and fluffed the pillow under her elbows, grabbing more plates from the floor. Ryan Miller was a caring man, a comforting one. She'd have to tell Annabelle that it was a little fucked up to have thought about what a good husband he must be, right before she had sex with him.

But, like Annabelle often said, like all fucked-up things, they were just plain true and very human.

Caroline asked, "You sure you don't need help?"

"I'll be working here tomorrow. I'm the only one, so I'll do the dishes then. I've got other plans for us." Ryan said, stacking the dishes around the sink.

He came back, and lay next to her, tracing her hips with the back of his hand as she curled up onto her side. He kissed her stomach. She played a little coy and curled up tighter. He rolled her onto her back and pulled her shirt up so he could kiss her abdomen. This time, he traced the lines of her muscles slowly with his mouth. She adjusted herself several times to lay more comfortably and savor sex with someone new for the second time.

When he slowed down a little, she sat up and took his cheeks in the palms of her hands. He kissed her hard, pulling the back of her head toward him, getting as deep inside her mouth as he could. Caroline wondered if Suzy gave him enough attention, if she kissed him like she needed to now, if she needed him to touch her as badly as Caroline did.

"Let's not do anything here," Ryan said. He helped Caroline stand and then led her by the hand to the pristine guest bedroom of a family she'd never meet.

"You sure it's okay? Will we be able to wash the sheets?" she asked, a pace behind him. She was sobering up, suddenly feeling less sexual and more anxious.

"I got it handled, Caroline," he said, pulling her along. He dimmed the bedside light. "I want to be able to see you, every part of you. At least I'll have that in my head."

"What do you mean, *at least*?"

He hesitated before saying, "I don't know, just, as a memory I guess."

"Memory?" That felt sad, even as they had barely begun. But she understood and of course agreed—*in the fall*.

"Never mind on the memory comment," he said. "Sorry I even said it. Let's just concentrate on the now."

"Well, I mean it's okay to kind of . . . never mind," Caroline said. She had wanted to say it was good to be clear about the rules, not to make it all a mystery. Her anxiety, always present, was spiking now.

What was she supposed to do in the fall? At that market? Say hi to him and his wife when they were buying out the rest of the blueberry muffins? People who had grown up out here had the same patterns. They checked the ocean at the same spots on the same dirt roads with the views of the same little cliffs (not from the big public designated overlooks the city people used). When Caroline would pull over at that spot near Wiborg Beach, she'd often see a Verizon truck or a landscaper. Locals knew how to move around here. Ryan was one of those people. They'd be on the same local paths, whether on foot or in a vehicle.

For the first time since meeting Ryan, her heart hurt a little. He was right: this was a finite event, like a departing summer; the sun would fade with the crackling leaves of fall. Right about the time the cornstalks sprouted flowering branches on the top, they'd be saying goodbye. A real goodbye.

She nudged him to sit down at the edge of the bed. She sat on his lap, straddling him. She touched his cheeks as she kissed him hard again, signaling her longing as best she could. Might as well make this good, she figured. As she felt the rough skin of his face, she thought about how rugged and handsome he was, but not someone all women would be drawn to. Still, his substantial build, his green eyes, and messy graying hair must attract a bunch. His maleness, his upright shoulders, his solid legs would draw a woman's attention across a crowded room. Maybe she wasn't the first. Maybe she was.

Her kissing made him moan a little, and he felt himself get hard. He stood, bringing her to her feet too, and he pressed his midsection against hers so she could feel what she was doing to him. She kissed him again, slowly, biting his lips a little. It seemed to make him even harder and more eager. He turned her around so now her back was to the bed, with him up against her, still pushing into her. She braced her legs against the side of the bed to keep her balance, hoping to prolong everything.

Then, as she wrapped one leg around his, she listed backward toward the mattress, a plump, ironed, downy comforter waiting to catch her. Ryan placed one hand on her neck and the other on her lower back and guided her to the bed while continuing to kiss her. Now, laying on top of her, he somehow, with one hand underneath her, adjusted her position forty-five degrees, so that her head was on a pillow and her legs could stretch out to the bottom of the bed.

She didn't intend to compare Eddie with Ryan—it was unfair—but it was unavoidable. Ryan's body was so much bigger and stronger and better proportioned. Eddie had muscular arms, but he was pretty short at five foot eight. Short men didn't have the space in their limbs to be so nimble. He also had a sizable gut that protruded and often got in the way in bed. Eddie would never have had the strength or agility to make that same smooth adjustment in her position as if she'd been buoyed by clouds.

Ryan unclasped her bra with a flick of his fingers and pulled her sweater off in a single motion. Then, reaching to the side table, he lit a small candle. He laughed and said, "I need more light, have to see what I'm working with here."

Caroline lay there, still amazed he'd been able to pull this all off so gracefully while still kissing her.

He pulled back and kneeled again, yanking his own shirt off. His chest was damn good, Caroline decided. A little paunch on the belly, but otherwise chiseled pecs, a nice covering of male hair on his chest, and very good arms. Epic arms, actually. He then lay on her again, both of them now shirtless, in jeans only. Caroline would try to remember every moment of this for Annabelle, who had a thing for men with clearly defined triceps and biceps. Arthur worked out with that young trainer woman to keep pumping his up. *Come to think of it, was he sleeping with her as well as the masseuse?*

As Ryan kissed her breasts, his mouth on one and his fingers playing lightly with the other nipple, she watched his arms flex in the gentle light. There were huge muscles that showed themselves in certain positions. She watched his triceps on the back of his right arm as he shifted his weight from elbow to elbow.

Caroline's breathing became short and labored as he lingered on her breasts. She kept reaching inside the back of his pants, pulling him closer, and guiding his hand down further.

"I'll get there. I've got some more work to do here first," he whispered. "We have a lot more time, so don't you even think of rushing me."

She arched her back, pushing up against him, wishing badly he'd just touch her below. She closed her eyes, as she tried to slow her breathing. She smiled a little and whispered back, "I'm trying to be patient." She knew that if he touched her softly beneath her jeans, she wouldn't be able to last.

She took in several long breaths to try to calm the throbbing between her thighs. This time, not able or willing to wait a second more, she pushed his arm down her torso. He rested it on her inner thigh, rubbing hard, but stopped when he got too close. With the back of his hand, he tickled her waist.

She whispered, "It hurts down there. It's literally aching, you've got to keep going, *please.*"

"I can tell" was his answer. "That's a good thing, Caroline. That's how we want it. It'll only get better, you'll see."

Chapter 24

Keep Your Mouth Shut and Smile

MIDDAY, WEDNESDAY, THE FOLLOWING
WEEK, BEGINNING OF JULY

Caroline took her least favorite client, Astrid Gleeson—Mrs. Tristan Gleeson III—into Southampton to purchase finishing touches for her powder room. Mrs. Gleeson was nearly done with her five-thousand-square-foot "cottage by the sea," but wanted to hire Caroline by the hour to "cozy it up" on her "tight budget."

Mrs. Gleeson, though fifty-three, had an ancient aura about her as she strolled down the sidewalk in her lime-green Belgian loafers with yellow bows and trim. Her legs were so long and thin that she had to lift her knees high to swing her feet forward like a pendulum. Crinkled skin, far too tan, sagged off her protruding bones. A bright Hermès scarf was draped over her shoulders and matched her pink blouse and yellow pants; the bands of colors aligned like a roll of Life Savers. She wore her blond-whitish hair in a 1950s-style anachronistic bouffant and carried a small Nantucket basket with a scrimshaw etching of a whaling vessel that she inherited from her aunt Dabby. With a bridge game starting at the Meadow Club in two hours, Mrs. Gleeson was in no mood to dawdle.

"I love this store, let's start here!" she exclaimed to Caroline.

"Mrs. Gleeson, I have several items on hold in other stores, this is just a knickknack kind of . . ."

Mrs. Gleeson was already inside the small boutique on a side street in Southampton, which sold shells, sea glass in jars of all sizes, doorstops made of needlepoint covered bricks—all the unoriginal items a small gift shop might carry for tourists in town who'd taken a day trip here. Not at all the type of store where Caroline curated a right look for her clients. Mrs. Gleeson cradled a blue glass globe the size of a basketball in her hands. "It's so perfectly nautical. I used to sail with my father off Salem Harbor in Marblehead. I'm going to need two of these, but then . . ."

She made her way to the back of the shop, reaching from shelf to shelf, her limbs moving like those of a praying mantis. "Caroline, I'm going to need dozens of shells for bowls. Please keep an eye out for that fabulous shagreen. Stingray skin is so divine as a holder of absolutely anything," Mrs. Gleeson said.

Caroline twirled around a stand at the counter that had shell key chains with names painted on them. "Mrs. Gleeson, this is not a shagreen type of store; it's lovely here, but I have your shagreen on hold down the block at . . ."

"I want to put shells everywhere, sofa tables, side tables, in the powder rooms, you know, it'll make it homey right away!"

Caroline walked slowly to her client. "The point of shells is to bring past experiences with the ocean into your home," she explained. "I'm happy to get a few things here with you, but also I can walk down to the beach near the inlet later. They have clamshells that are almost four inches wide, and much more natural to this region. I can take a bunch off the beach and put them in a basket and—"

"But why can't I just buy tons of shells? Why would I have to pay you to walk down a beach? And how much would that cost? Couldn't be the same hourly rate, you're hardly creating then!" Mrs. Gleeson snorted ever so slightly, channeling her sensible Pilgrim ancestors. "Or would that be more expensive, and far less efficient? I mean, we're here. I have my AmEx."

Caroline considered how to explain the concept of authenticity without patronizing her client. She remembered a lecture in customer satisfaction from design school. It was essential to make people who were paying you believe that you are simply executing *their* sense of taste and style for them—even if the professionals knew it was often far from the truth. And then, once they felt it was all their idea, you did a little bait and switch with your choices over their tragic ones.

"You can buy anything you want, and I'll help you place it, but . . . it's like this," Caroline said. "You can't *buy* memories. You have to live them and then bring physical bits of them home to relive them. You see what I mean?" Mrs. Gleeson looked at Caroline blankly, as if Caroline were explaining the origins of the Pythagorean theorem. She tried another way. "We talked about this when we met last summer: patience in design is very, very important. It's a layering thing, takes time, not just something an AmEx card can quickly resolve." Caroline placed her hand on Mrs. Gleeson's arm. "I promise we'll get it right, but we can't *buy* it right."

"Why not? I thought that's what we are doing today?" Mrs. Gleeson said, a tad miffed that an employee was trying to teach her a silly lesson in life.

"For example, take all those wonderful silver cups from your husband's regattas, the nautical maps on the walls—that's organic design birthed from your family. Those shells in the bag there are from East Asia anyway—they aren't even native to the Atlantic."

"The shells are lovely," Mrs. Gleeson said. "Besides, who will know if they're from somewhere else?" She put her hands on her angular hips, getting snippier by the second. The saleswoman at the front desk rolled her eyes at Caroline. "Now, you and I have had this itsy-bitsy problem that keeps rearing up ever since we started work on the powder rooms and sun porch last summer: no stalling on the little touches. If I'm willing to pay for your time, why delay the production for some harebrained idea of authenticity?"

Mrs. Gleeson did not dare say what she was really thinking. Her man from Manhattan, who'd done the big stuff in the house, wouldn't hem and haw like this: Jeffrey Bilhuber summered in Nantucket, for God's sake, *he got it*. The huge conch shells he had bought at an antique store for a few thousand each held the patio doors open and announced the East Coast summer. He hadn't found those on the beach, for goodness sakes. He couldn't even lift them . . . that thought made her chuckle, Jeffrey in his Tom Ford version of Nantucket red pants, with those vintage alligator Gucci loafers he lived in, actually doing manual labor for once in his life.

"What's so funny?" Caroline asked, calmly.

"Oh, nothing you would understand!" And then snatching jars off the shelf, Mrs. Gleeson said, "I want this divine green sea glass lining up my powder room counters. I'm sure you agree." She felt a little bad about how she'd treated Caroline in public, with this saleswoman hearing. She had good taste in soap and in towels; this project may have been over her head, just a sweet girl who grew up out here. She'd call Jeffrey to come out and save her from this amateur. Trying to skimp on Jeffrey's eight-hundred-dollar an hour fees, and hiring on local help was a bad idea, after all. You got what you paid for.

Mrs. Gleeson picked up four mesh bags filled with small white shells from Vietnam and turned to Caroline. "I don't want to hear a word of resistance," she said. "Please, indulge me! I'm getting late for my bridge game at the club, and I'm sure you're right, but the thing is, I *like* these. They match my mantel. See the caramel vein in this lovely shell, here? Brown on brown, see?" She plunked two huge metal baskets filled with goods on the counter and informed the clerk that her driver would be by to pick up her bounty later.

"I'm only here to advise. They are lovely," Caroline said, knowing it wasn't worth pushing this anthropoid creature any further.

"Thank you for your time, Caroline. I just love the soaps we got, and the hand towels, and just, well, *everything*," she said. "I don't much agree with your opinions on shells, but we can agree to have a difference of opinion on that. You're doing a nice job, so don't fret one bit." She patted Caroline's wrist.

Later on the sidewalk, Caroline bid her goodbye, counted up two hours at $150 an hour, and figured she had a pretty good gig going. Whether this fossilized WASP took all her advice or not didn't much matter. She liked her job, and most of her clients trusted her. She liked helping people figure out what they liked and wanted, just as, on a different scale, she was doing for herself this summer.

Chapter 25

If Only Dogs Could Talk

A nnabelle called Caroline with a proposal: "Let's celebrate summer. Let's go to Sag Harbor, have a nice lunch."

"You don't even need to say it, I know what's coming: you want
to go to one of your snobby Madison Avenue places that transplants
itself out here for three months," Caroline said.

"You can't prefer those disgusting fried clams to tuna carpaccio.
Le Manoir is so chic: the rosé is flowing, even the butter is to die
for. See you in half an hour."

Arriving early to the new restaurant—a place on the docks that
had been taken over by a team of Frenchmen from Saint Tropez—
Caroline walked out to the end of the pier. Cruisers whizzed by,
and huge yachts backed into slips with the aid of a dozen people
guiding them. In the distance, she heard the sound of sails flapping
in the wind as they tacked. The sun was bright, the day hot, but
good hot.

With ten minutes before Annabelle showed, Caroline sat on her
favorite bench and stared out to sea. Her thick hair blowing like

mad, she held it back off her face. She studied each boat, just in case she saw that profile again. Caroline felt silly. Joey was gone. So she stopped searching, laid back on the hard, wooden bench, and soaked up the warmth of July.

Placing her sweater over her face to shield it from the sun, she was transported back to Joey's family's beach shack. The image of the splintered wood of the window frames and their peeling white paint was so clear in her mind, as were the lace curtains billowing in the wind.

The Whitten family beach shack stood a few hundred yards up a sandy path from the beach. On one side, Joey had painted a large mural of churning waves, now art foretelling his life story. The shack had been passed down through three generations, and, since Joey's death, they dared not sell it. His father had fought with the town to keep the cottage where it was, mostly because it was his son's favorite place to bring his girl. It was now surrounded on three sides by a parking lot, holding up against the exhaust fumes and eroding beach. She'd of course seen it over the years, but never dared to go too near.

Whenever she ran into Joey's father around town, he'd mention Joey and reiterate that his death just didn't make sense. He'd tell her that the water wouldn't have overtaken his son the lifeguard. Joey was too smart and too strong to get lost in those angry currents.

Still, that ocean rescue chief came to her door and told her family, "I'm sorry, we can't look for him anymore." It was now a search and recover mission for a body, no longer a search and rescue for a living soul bobbing and breathing in the waves.

She had walked Atlantic Beach with Joey the day before he died, forty-eight hours before his twenty-fifth birthday. There were churning currents that day; a torrential storm had left a formidable wake.

On the walk, Joey pointed out the riptides to Caroline, who

would have never noticed them on her own. "Over there," he'd said. "At two o'clock, just to the right. It looks like a school of fish are in a feeding frenzy under the surface. And look at the white water above. If you study the bubbles, you can see the water is moving toward the horizon, not into shore."

Joey, other lifeguards, and certainly the surfers she knew growing up welcomed those riptides because they would carry the surfers out beyond the sandbar without them having to paddle too hard. Surfers who understood the ocean's whims called that current an escalator out to sea.

Nothing made sense that day.

Joey used to swim for an hour in the afternoons after work, always with his dog, Lucky. The dog was with him that day too. Ever since, all their friends, even Ryan, had been haunted by the sound of Lucky howling that night, waiting for Joey to return.

If only Labradors could talk.

Chapter 26

That Certain Je Ne Sais Quoi

Standing before the lectern at the entrance to Le Manoir, a smoldering French hostess studied her computer screen. She wore jeans and a plain white T-shirt, skipping the bra for effect. Her perky nipples bounced a little as she typed.

"Uh, von Tattenbach, please?" Annabelle said, in that mildly entitled manner she never particularly wanted to hide. She was wearing a flowing ARossGirl silk georgette Amanda dress in pale blue that matched her eyes, and carrying a little coordinating Gloria bag in leopard satin with a blue handle.

The woman continued to peck away, not deigning to look up. "Do you have a reservation?"

"I don't, no, and there are twenty empty tables. It's a weekday," replied Annabelle, rolling her eyes at Caroline. She whispered to her friend, "You're so right; they can be total assholes for no reason here. Just lemme . . ."

"In July, at Le Manoir, a reservation is required," the hostess said. She stared Annabelle down, knowing she had her trumped on sex appeal if not liquid assets.

This particular hostess wouldn't last the summer; she didn't know the faces of the powerful. The von Tattenbach name carried serious weight in Hamptons establishments, and Caroline knew this young woman was about to get her ass handed to her when the owner intervened. Despite the ingenue's hideous demeanor, Caroline felt sorry for her. She probably needed the job she was about to lose.

Just then, Jean-Claude Perrier, a rugged Frenchman raised near the beach in Antibes, dashed over. He was wearing a blue-and-white-striped T-shirt and looked as if he was about to drag a fishing net out of the Mediterranean. He air-kissed Annabelle four times with his eyebrows raised, and his eyes closed. He led Caroline and Annabelle to a center table under the awning with a spectacular view of the bay. The suction of a cork pulling out of a bottle sounded, and chilled rosé poured forth before they'd even settled into their seats.

"It's on me, Annabelle," Jean-Claude pleaded. "So sorry she didn't know you. She has identification photos of all . . ."

"J.C., it's fine," said Annabelle, swirling the wine around her glass, sniffing it, and then sloshing it a bit around with her tongue. "The wine is lovely, thanks."

Caroline said to her, "Oh, you like the tannins, do you?" They'd agreed they hated when people who had no idea what they were doing went through those wine-tasting machinations.

Annabelle shot her the middle finger playfully, and out of J.C.'s sight. She turned to him. "Don't fire the poor girl, but do tell her that her attitude makes the town unpleasant for all of us."

Caroline watched an older couple, in Mephisto sandals and fanny packs, ask the same hostess why they couldn't have a table if there were twenty free ones. She chimed in, "Hey, sorry, but look, she's doing it again to that poor couple."

"Please, J.C.," Annabelle said. "Obviously those poor day tourists don't know the rules of the lions' den. How can she say she needs a moment to find a table? Give back a teeny bit to the community, would you, please?"

"Of course," he said before bowing and backing away. Then he whisked the tragically Midwestern couple to undesirable seats near the kitchen.

"You know, on some level, it fascinates me," Caroline admitted, smiling. "I protest coming here, but to watch you defend stupid shit in life is so entertaining. So go ahead, swirl away, and pontificate on that wine you know so much about."

"It's tasty on a hot summer day, is what it is," Annabelle said. "The salmon tartar is perfect, the Cajun chicken stellar, plus it's so fun and festive on weekends. Your own husband loves it here. He flips hundred-dollar bills at every waiter."

"Eddie and I used to do tequila shots here in high school with our fake IDs when this was The Amazon," Caroline said. "We'd throw darts in the back, and dance to music they don't play anymore." Caroline took a gulp of the pink wine she found way too sweet. "We loved it here."

"Well, it has evolved," Annabelle said. "We all still feel pretty special here—it's like I'm transported to Le Club Cinquante-Cinq in Saint-Tropez. Your husband rolls over to his primo table all handsome and cool. There's no one more fun than Eddie Clarkson when he's in one of his big, happy moods, table hopping, buying people he barely knows a bottle of good champs just for kicks. It's simple why we come: to feel part of something special in the Hamptons, instead of going to a juice bar and another spin class."

"I get that wanting to be included in everything," Caroline said, nibbling on a radish from a glorious basket of vegetables that had blossomed on their table. She dipped it in butter and sprinkled it with sea salt from a tiny clay pot. "It's just not for me on a weekend with all the loud music and social mongering. I'm too shy to handle places like this. This has the same vibe as that chichi espresso place,

Sant Ambroeus in Southampton, where all the horse moms never invite me," Caroline said, as she studied the overpriced menu. "I mean, I wouldn't go, but an invite once a year from those snobby bitches would be nice."

An unusual and uncomfortable silence overtook the table. "So," Annabelle said finally. "Are we . . . you and that Ryan Mr. Architect what's-his-name . . . you want to . . ."

Caroline shook her head and said, "It's just . . . not yet, not ready to."

"Fine, avoid the elephant, and concentrate on the creamy French milkmaid butter," Annabelle said and smiled. She was happy to discontinue this line of questioning if only because Annabelle wasn't in the mood to admit that during the girls' lessons earlier, rather than focus on their equitation position, she'd been fantasizing about being plied into some twisted, constricted, ecstasy-enhancing French position against Philippe's headboard. It had to happen soon. But when? And how? "And, by the way, you'll only be able to avoid it for so long. When you hit forty, you hit your sexual freak show moment."

"Please explain. Immediately."

"You got a few years, but you'll see, you get beyond horny. You know what I did? If you don't want to talk about Mr. Architect, fine, but I'm going to tell you something I know I never told you that I did once."

"What did you do?" Caroline waited, knowing Annabelle's outrageous antics had a way of successively topping each other, one reason she was such good company.

"This May, I was so hot for Liza's cello teacher, he's a guitarist actually, but anyway, so beyond horny for him, I literally played with myself in the Diller-Quaile music school bathroom." Annabelle nodded, quite pleased with her efficiency. "Thank God it was a single powder room with a locked door! But I had to handle business *right then*."

Caroline laughed and said, "I don't care what Bunny Digby predicts, I won't ever do that."

"You'll see, give yourself a few years. You'll be doing it in strange places. I'm sure I wasn't the only Diller-Quaïle mom who's gotten busy in that room," Annabelle said, considering that concept. "Actually, those uptight Diller-Quaile moms are more in a strictly missionary no orgasm zone, but still." She paused again, thinking it was so sad to go through life that way.

"Still, I'm not like you, but I won't close the door to my inner freak coming out at some point," Caroline said, surveying the swanky new restaurant, while crunching on a yeasty baguette, raising her eyebrows to signal that indeed the butter was delicious. "I can so imagine Eddie in heaven here, ordering wine for strangers, over-tipping every busboy. In the old days, he was the guy on the dance floor here twirling the girls around, ordering a dozen tequila shots he couldn't afford even when they were cheap. I'm happy he still has his fun, of course."

Annabelle listened as Caroline buttered another morsel. "I came here with Joey too for drinks sometimes," Caroline said. "And with my grandmother for the special lunch we used to have there every month. Right over there, in that corner, a few weeks after Joey's funeral, she said a really sad thing to me: *Sometimes you can't be with the person you love the most.*"

Annabelle sipped her wine and said, "Well, fuck, that's depressing."

"She just knew, and I knew, that nothing would ever be the same. It was just, you know, a maternal warning on life—life after Joey."

Annabelle threw her napkin smack into Caroline's face. "Can we please not talk about that ghost again?" she said playfully, hoping to bring Caroline out of this strange Joey Whitten abyss. "It's not healthy. And even though Eddie is a colossally selfish person, he adores you, and is fabulously outrageous at just the right moments.

Your clients are piling up, your kids are doing well. You don't want to tell me, but your rosy glow tells me that the architect is getting you seriously laid. Let's just see how we end up on Labor Day without talking about Joey until then. Deal?"

"Deal," Caroline said, folding Annabelle's napkin and placing it back on her side.

Another unusual silence followed before Annabelle said, "Look, I said I didn't want to hear about Joey, but that doesn't mean we can't talk. I can tell something's wrong."

"I went to the barn, and hung out at Eddie's desk in his office for a bit," Caroline said.

"Snooping again."

Caroline nodded. "He's put us in a position where I have to snoop."

Annabelle swayed her head left and right. "You could ignore it. I basically do that with Arthur and his wanderings."

"And in a file," Caroline powered on, not interested in comparing marriage survival tactics right now, "I found these records of payments that Eddie made, extremely strange ones, suspicious ones."

"To women?"

"No. To Thierry that went back, like, ten years. All in one ledger, under stuff in a bottom drawer."

"Well, that's weird."

"Very."

Annabelle counted in her head and said, "Gigi has only been riding for four years, and if Thierry was the manager at Rose Patch before, then why would Eddie be paying him for six years before that? Did they even know each other?"

"Not only that, but Maryanne does all the accounting, so why was that ledger in his desk? Hidden? And then this Philippe guy, he's into something with Thierry and . . ."

"He's hot as fuck is what he is," Annabelle said, waving her impossibly toned arm in the air to get the waiter's attention. "You think Philippe and Thierry knew each other back then? Or that Eddie and Thierry and Philippe all did?"

"I don't know," said Caroline. "And I'm not going to tell you to stay away from Philippe because I know what you're going to do, if you haven't."

At that, Annabelle could not help but smile. "I haven't. I swear. But you have no fucking idea what the meaning of hot is once I do, is all I'm going to say. Go on."

"I will, actually," Caroline shook her head, not wanting to add that suave and sleazy wasn't her thing. "I'm just saying, I think Philippe has somehow scooped Thierry into something not entirely right. And I don't know if Eddie's clueless or what, or if he's been paying both of them for years and acting now like they are simple barn employees. It's just . . . it's not right."

"You're crazy, honey. Maryanne and Eddie are on top of everything. Nothing gets by those two," Annabelle announced, smacking her lips from the sweet and tart rosé. "Enough with your conspiracy theories. Clearly, you need a break from this July humidity. I'm taking the girls to Jackson Hole next weekend. We've got to get you away from sad memories of that water out there too. Do you want to come? You could bring the kids."

"They're fine, we're good," Caroline said, before informing the waiter that she'd have the fifty-eight-dollar black sea bass.

Annabelle pulled the top of Caroline's menu down, and loud enough for any nearby diners to hear, said, "We're NetJetting straight from Westhampton to Jackson. The plane holds twelve, no airport security lines, you could just stuff a bunch of tote bags and pop on and . . ."

"Annabelle," Caroline said sternly. "*NetJetting* is not a verb. *NetJet* is a noun: a company that you pay to fly you on an eighty-thousand-dollar private plane trip."

"More like a hundred, since you mentioned it," Annabelle said, which made Caroline laugh out loud.

Annabelle smiled, squeezing lemon onto salmon tartar on toast points with an edible purple flower on top of each that had appeared out of nowhere. "Eric, you're kind to remember my favorite." The handsome man nodded, then looked at Caroline as if he might sleep with her one day if she were lucky.

"I can't believe you get service like this. I'm sure they aren't charging us," Caroline said, biting into the delicate raw fish flecked with tiny cubes of purple onion.

"Nope," said Annabelle. "Maybe for the entrées, but the rest will be on J.C."

"Eddie calls it the rich person discount: the people who need it least get the most shit for free," Caroline said as she looked over at the hundreds of six-hundred-dollar bottles of pink Cristal champagne lining the shelves like books in a row, waiting to be lapped up by the celebrity-seeking wolves. "I can see Eddie buying those bottles for strangers at the next table, or for someone he met once. He can be too generous. That's one side of him I hate and love."

"You know better than anyone what Eddie says: 'Don't ask what the party can do for you, but what you can do for the party.' I could do without his lavender shoes that match his linen lavender shirt, but whatever. He's adorable. Here, try the Aperol spritz J.C. brought us," Annabelle said, pushing a fresh glass over.

Caroline made a face signaling it didn't look good.

Annabelle pushed more. "You're so stubborn, always need to be the contrarian. It's a nice day, you're on a gorgeous deck, and the best-grilled bass and crispy Brussels sprouts you ever had are about to be served to you. None of those horse mom bitches are here being mean to you. Now, go ahead, just sip the Aperol and cool off. And please, cast Joey Whitten and those ledgers out of your head."

Caroline took a sip of the bright-orange eighteen-dollar concoction and squeezed her eyes shut. "It tastes like cough syrup."

"I knew you were going to say something like that."

When she opened her eyes, Caroline looked out at the bay, just to see if, by chance, that Boston Whaler might motor by.

Maybe she was losing her mind.

Chapter 27

Fight or Flight?

Annabelle's Maserati purred like a sleeping leopard. She let the car run a little and dialed the climate bar down a notch to sixty-eight degrees. Oh, for the Italians' masterful control of climate: no noise, no blasts of supercool air, just a calm flow peacefully keeping the temperature moderate.

She'd parked to the right of the entry to her home and laid her head back on the neck rest. Her hands lay heavy on her thighs as if cinder blocks were weighing them down. She couldn't turn the engine off if she had wanted to.

Maybe she should try meditation again, it might help her cool off. Closing her eyes helped.

Tah-leem, tah-leem.

As usual, she could not repeat her mantra for more than thirty seconds at a time. A tornado twisted and contorted too violently in her brain.

Earlier that morning, she was sitting on a high director's chair by the side of a ring at Sea Crest. Philippe was barking commands at her two younger daughters, Lily and Liza, aged eight and ten, who were riding in the same ring, jumping rails on One Hot Pepper and Mouse. As the girls got off their ponies and started to walk them out to the paddocks, Lily turned back and asked Annabelle, "Can Liza and I go to Katia's house to go tubing? Her mom said it was okay."

Philippe yelled to Annabelle, "They are such elegant riders! Graceful, strong bodies from their mother . . ."

Annabelle interrupted him to answer her daughter, "Okay, there are swimsuits in your tote bags. Ghislaine will get you before lunch, though. Daddy's home."

Before she could turn back around to talk to Philippe, he struck like a cobra right beside her: "*We* have time now."

"For what, Philippe?" Annabelle said, placing her arm casually around the back of her chair, knowing three hours was more than enough time to get busy and still be home for lunch.

"Let me show you the polo field for the international tour this weekend, you haven't seen it," Philippe said. "I took you and the girls only to the training area last week. The main part is all dressed up and ready with sponsor booths, lemonade stands, all kinds of . . ."

"I don't like sugary drinks," Annabelle said.

"Well, then, I'll find something else you might like," he said, smirking. "It's only a little bit away, on the far side of Bridgehampton, near the train. And not too far from my house, come to think of it."

"Come to think of it? You're taking me to a polo field that I've already seen, that is also near your house," Annabelle pointed out.

"I meant, it's . . . Yes, it's near my house," Philippe said, raising his left eyebrow, going for the kill. "I was being coy. Of course, I have some wine and cheese. That's a little more direct, which I gather you prefer. We could have a little . . ."

"A little what, Philippe?" she pushed.

"A little of you showing me how it's done, and a little of me showing you I'm good at many things," Philippe said, shaking his hair out of his face the way young boys do after they surface in a pool. His fingers yanked his bangs to the side, and his arms bulged against the sleeves of his polo shirt. He shook the constant pain a little out of his right arm.

Annabelle considered his more adult proposal, rubbing both of her earlobes as if that would help her to decide. Like a potential buyer examining a prize stallion, she studied Philippe: there was a patch from the Argentine Open World Polo Tour on one sleeve, and a navy number 35 on his chest. White breeches with a nice, healthy package behind the zipper, secured by a woven belt with colorful squares from Central America. There were a lot of men wearing colorful polo shirts in the Hamptons, but very few had actually played polo.

"Follow me in your car," he whispered. "Let's discover together what the morning holds for us."

Annabelle put on her sunglasses and glared at him, "What the morning holds?"

"I'm not playing games," Philippe said. "I thought it more gentlemanly to offer you a tour of my work. My assistant can handle the next lessons. Follow me in your car. Trust me." He nodded to her and added, "Don't plan it out too much in your head. Just let me take charge of things for a little bit. I'll give you plenty of say later. *Plenty.*"

Annabelle swallowed hard. The girls were taken care of, and she could back out at any minute. This guy knew what he was doing with his body, he was a pro on the athletic field. She had been captain of the Dartmouth ski and tennis team. Athlete on athlete. She didn't know how that would play out exactly, but it did figure in. "I'll follow you in my car," she said, grabbing her Kenyan straw bag with Maasai beading from Barney's off the back of the chair. "I'll see what I want to do when I get there."

When Philippe pulled his vintage orange Porsche into an empty lot in a back wooded area, he motioned out of his window for her to park her Maserati *right there*. It was as if he had done this dozens of times before. He walked up to her window and knocked on it.

"I think it's best from here if you get in my car, so your car isn't parked in my driveway. And then I'll bring you back here," Philippe said. Annabelle nodded and got into his car.

Once there, he shut the garage door behind them, and he led her to the back of his three-room home behind the train tracks in Bridgehampton. He opened his fridge and poured her a glass of wine from a bottle that he had opened days before.

Even though the sand on the floors crunched under Annabelle's sandals, she was charmed by the place. (At her estate, staff members swept sand up from the floor the moment the kids trekked it in from the beach.) The rumpled little cottage reminded her of her mother's home—both tributes to curated discomfort and decay. Old-world Europeans with "de" preceding their last names, like Philippe, and hard-core American Protestants, like Annabelle's mother, shared the same ethos of taste: value the old and shun the shiny and new. Inherited furniture held the most prominence, especially if it were torn or faded.

She peeked into Philippe's bedroom and noticed his lumpy mattress, the bed haphazardly made with antique quilts. Since she'd married Arthur, even after she took a nap, her bed was rewrapped like a party gift within the hour.

She sat for a moment in Philippe's old armchair, which was covered in pale blue Oxford cloth. Faded striped wallpaper lined the walls, and a worn Aubusson needlepoint rug with fraying threads on the edges was centered on the walnut floor. A slight breeze was blowing in from the window, and Philippe turned on the ceiling fan, which sucked the pale-yellow linen curtains into the room. Europeans and American WASPs also shared a dislike of air-conditioning.

Annabelle sipped her wine, figuring she hadn't had any alcohol this early in the morning since college. Though it had turned in the fridge and tasted a bit vinegary, it would loosen her up.

When Philippe said, "Let's skip the cheese and crackers for now," she smiled. An image of herself from a family trip to Patagonia popped into her mind: she was standing at the top of a bridge in Torres del Paine National Park, strapped into a bungee jump harness, toes hanging off the edge, the churning waters five hundred yards below. Her husband, in yellow trousers, brown tasseled loafers, and a pressed shirt of the finest Italian linen, filmed the whole damn thing. Arthur didn't even like to dive into a pool, he preferred to wade in, down the steps.

Annabelle whispered, "This is between us, and just once. A soul will never . . ."

Philippe walked over to her, took her glass from her hand, and placed it on the table. He cradled her face in his hands and kissed her softly. "You taste like honey," he said, holding her hands to help her to her feet. He walked her gracefully up against the wallpaper, which, Annabelle noticed, was peeling *a tad* in the far corners of the ceiling. Before she could blink, he had unfastened her jeans, unzipped her, and slid his hand under the waistband to softly explore her. "A butterfly touch for now," he whispered. Then he outlined her mouth with those same fingers and kissed her again. "Taste yourself," he said, pressing her gently against the wall.

When he glided his fingers back into her panties, she grabbed his hand to slow the whole thing down; she'd need a moment to figure out if she were indeed ready to take the infidelity plunge for the first time as a married woman.

A daring descent down a double black diamond slope lay before her. Likewise, how different could it be from skiing off-piste in Austria over Christmas break: standing at the precipice, preparing mentally, concentrating, and having the confidence to launch herself off that steep edge?

The more she thought about the opportunity to tell Philippe exactly how she liked what, the more turned on she became. Her stomach was tightening. It was like super service sex, delivered on a familiar Porthault breakfast tray in a room that didn't feel one bit foreign.

He grabbed her hard by the wrist, and led her like a prized filly to the bedroom. His slight limp made her wonder if her toned body might be able to pin him a little, holding him where she needed him. She liked the idea of telling him what she wanted, controlling him a bit, winning in her way, on her terms. This would be her version of on-demand, spoiled rich princess sex.

On his bed now, Philippe guided her arms over her head and against his pillow, amused that this woman thought she'd be the boss. You could read women like this a mile away; all in charge, muscled like a racehorse, getting all hot by the idea of demanding this or that out loud. Ha! This would be fun. Philippe showed women like this what they wanted. They didn't show him.

He discarded her pale pink jeans on the floor and began to confidently prep her for what lay ahead. Stop, go, more, less, harder, softer . . . it was all about confusing a woman like Annabelle, the maestro playing her like an instrument. At one point, she begged him to let her finish, his fingers sliding like silk up and down and around as only a woman would do to herself. But then he'd stop and guide her to another crescendo, and another. His talent with both animals and women: reading them, knowing parts of them better than they knew themselves.

Next, he lay on top of her, entering her slowly just at that peak millisecond when she wanted all of him. Timing was Philippe's main asset; he knew to give himself to women just at that moment they went into another zone, and he could tell by the way they pulled him into them. Still, inside her, he lightly touched her again with the butterfly fluttering, so she had everything at once, forceful and gentle, hard and soft, too confusing between the pain of desire and pleasure of getting it attended to.

Annabelle was right where he wanted her; not able to verbalize this or that, even though the silly girl planned to tell him all. He watched her eyes roll into her head, her arched-back neck constricting with veins like a thoroughbred beneath him, accepting of his mastery below to bring her to a state he was sure she'd never been.

Using his strength, he held her elbows as she wriggled beneath him now. This allowed her, he knew well, to feel safe, but let her fantasize that she'd succumb and that he'd triumph in this clash.

And, earlier, back against that wallpaper, though she had expected and hoped for the opposite, for some unexplored part of her, this is exactly what she was after.

Chapter 28

Family-Style Lunch

In her driveway, Annabelle's Maserati now idled at a higher pitch. Heat waves emanating from the hood triggered a fan that cooled the engine. Nestled inside the womb of the car, surrounded by warm, plush, tan leather, the outside world was still too hot and too harsh for Annabelle to open the door.

She'd driven the twenty minutes home, her cheating virginity lost, and now relieved to be closer to her nice things. Yes, her couches were new, not family heirlooms, but they fluffed around her body, comforting every crevice. All she wanted to do now was sleep; it might help her to believe Philippe had been a dream. She wanted to inhale the lavender spray that Gisele spritzed on her pillows, and lie on the luxurious Hästens mattress that cost more than a very nice car.

The itching on her right ankle was making her crazy. The swarms of mosquitoes in the crappy, woodsy neighborhoods of the Hamptons were thick this time of year. They'd buzzed in her ear the moment she walked through Philippe's door. People who lived on the ocean knew the breeze blew all the insects and pests inland, toward the homes they'd never buy.

She studied her face in the rearview mirror to see if Arthur would be able to detect anything. Even with the AC blowing, her cheeks remained red and shiny. There was no getting around it: Annabelle looked like she'd just gotten supremely laid. And yes, he had won the physical battle; she'd succumbed more than she'd planned, which was weirdly a turn-on. *How did he know that?*

She stalled a little longer in the car, rubbing her hands together and cupping them to her nose; yes, the scent of sex was all over them. Philippe was a highly tuned lover, *more than she ever imagined,* but he was messy in bed. He wanted to taste everything, lick her entire body, mix their juices up and rub them all over her breasts and stomach and even her mouth. These fingers that would soon be wielding a soup spoon at lunch with her husband had just caressed another man's cock, for God's sakes. Why hadn't she showered at his house?

It wasn't like her to shower before lunch unless she was changing out of tennis whites or had taken a dip in the sea. She was wearing her pink jeans and a caftan with no bra. Her wet panties were in her bag. Philippe told her to rinse off in the outside shower—the only one that worked at his house. "Really, it would be best," he suggested more than once. This wasn't his first time. He knew the women he'd bedded would be seeing their families afterward. The least they could do was wash up. But when Annabelle looked in his outdoor shower, the cobwebs and soap with dirt stuck to it on the filthy little ledge made her retreat.

Annabelle watched the second hand on the clock embedded in the Maserati's burl wood dashboard. Each tick heightened her nerves a notch. Given his vast experiences, Philippe must be discreet, right? He couldn't keep traveling in his circle if he bragged about every conquest. Yet one slip in locker-room banter with some banker dad and she'd be discovered.

Arthur could always spot the slippery men, the ones who looked like they'd be fired any day for cutting corners at work, or for harassment issues. Philippe, always the gentleman, but was he really? He swore he wouldn't mention her. She prayed he meant it—he emphasized his sincerity by bringing her hands together and bowing to them.

In the front seat of the Maserati, Annabelle brought her hands together again, placing them between her thighs. She'd been more excited with Philippe than she thought she would be, possibly wetter than she'd ever been with anyone. *What exactly had gone on back there?!* Thankfully, Arthur didn't usually want sex in the middle of the day; he was more of a morning or evening man. After a shower, she'd be safe for at least eight hours. Maybe she'd take a bath. She needed something soothing; she was still pulsating a little, like a runner after a marathon.

Annabelle focused on the house's navy front door and its color. It was Caroline's idea, and she was right; they'd ordered the painter to do it on a whim one day in early May without telling Arthur. Caroline saying, "Why not paint the door a brilliant navy, so it brings out the blue of the hydrangeas?" She thought the blue would remind everyone that the ocean was just beyond the back deck. She was right. Now, Annabelle stared at the brass lion's head door knocker until it became blurry.

Concentrating on the mundane allowed Annabelle to overlook the monumental. She felt different. It reminded her of the summer she lost her virginity to Morgan McFadden on the back corner of the grass tennis courts at Millshore Club. They'd peed together in the kiddie pool at the club when they were babies. In her teens, after four summers of obsessing over his deep brown eyes, the manly body that belied his seventeen years, and his puffy lips, Annabelle was determined to give him signs that he was to be the one. And one night, after a half hour of groping and grasping and yanking of clothes, she finally allowed Morgan to push himself inside her. It had changed her then just as she felt changed again now.

When she told Caroline, she would explain to her how everything with Philippe had been so different from what she expected, as it had with Morgan. She recalled Philippe's body on top of her, and how later, having mastered her completely, when he was lying on his side, sated and resting, he looked like a Rodin statue. Screwing someone other than your husband was a little fuck-you to the whole world, especially when they'd just delivered a championship performance for you.

But then there was sweet, kind Arthur. He would be reading his market reports on the back deck about now, in his favorite Dedon swing lounger. He'd be stewing, wondering why she was late to lunch. The two younger girls had to be home from their playdate by now; maybe the two of them were in the pool. Maybe Rolf from the German Olympic diving team was there, the man Arthur felt was uniquely qualified to coach his daughters to swim better. Louisa, the reader, should be curled up on the deck by now with one of her father's silly German fairy-tale books he'd saved from his childhood.

Annabelle decided it best now to use her outdoor shower, by the pool, to wash off before heading inside. She loved the scratchy body wash from Bliss that she kept in the pool house shower; it removed every drop of sunscreen. A good scrubbing right now would reassure her that she could walk into the house with a straight face. Or maybe she'd walk to the side of the estate and jump in the pool—a baptism was certainly called for. Yes, the pool. The cool water would heal her body and mind. Maybe she could exhale fully, blow out all the oxygen, sink to the bottom, and meditate down there.

Her plan was suddenly aborted when someone banged on the car window.

"What on earth?"

Annabelle was so startled that she hit her wrist on the steering wheel. It hurt. She grabbed it with her other hand and wondered if her husband had seen her hands between her legs, compressing the pulsing that still hadn't stopped. Would he ask her why? Would he be turned on? He always asked her to touch herself, and she often obliged. Arthur never wanted sex in the middle of the day, but would he now? Jesus, would he taste Philippe on her if he went down on her? Why hadn't she bought a dozen bottles of Summer's Eve douche and handled it in the Starbucks bathroom on the way home like that wise Caroline had? What could be worse for a man than tasting another man on his wife? Her jeans were wet; was it from him or her? Or both? Annabelle's heart was racing.

Arthur opened the car door and held out his hand for his wife. She didn't take it. She chose to sit another moment to consider her next move. Minutes earlier she had felt a little thrill of recklessness, but that rush was now sour.

"Why are you sitting in a car when you know the girls and I are sitting at a table, napkins on our laps, not touching the crab soup that Hans made for us? The chilled soup is now room temperature. You know how I feel about that kind of disrespect of the chef's work. You know how much he cares, my dear."

Annabelle nodded. "I know, honey. I was at SoulCycle," she said. "I was just kind of hot and needed a moment to cool off and think."

"About what?"

He knew.

At least, she felt he knew.

Still, she kept trying. "Then I went to Caroline's, and she got me working on this wallpaper project with her," she said. "I'm just so filthy, I have to go wash off before lunch." Still, she didn't move, and she didn't respond when he asked her again to step out. She had to think. She swallowed hard and closed her eyes.

"Think in an automobile?" he asked again. "Why on earth are you sitting in the Maserati so long?"

He held out his hand, this time more gallantly, mimicking a footman helping a duchess out of her gilded coach.

She delicately placed her foot on the gravel, turned, and gave her hand to her husband for leverage. As she stood next to him, she was almost as tall as Arthur. He took both her hands and looked into her eyes. Neither husband nor wife spoke. As she tried to pull her hands away, he held her tighter. He pulled her hands to his face and inhaled deeply.

Arthur nodded and closed his eyes for a moment.

"Be careful, darling," he said softly. "Be very, very careful."

He walked away toward the back deck where his four, well-trained daughters were still waiting with their hands and napkins in their laps, the crab soup thickening before them.

Before his wife followed, she brought her hands to her own face and inhaled just to see how painfully obvious this was. They smelled like a mixture of the stale, flour-like residue of a man and the metallic, salty taste of a woman: perfectly blended in rapturous union all over her fingers.

Annabelle was indeed fucked: in more ways than one.

Chapter 29

Top 10 Reasons Apple Engineers
Want You to Get Caught

Annabelle drove her mint-green Mini Cooper convertible into Bridgehampton toward the exhale exercise studio. Arthur had surprised her with the car a few months earlier because, he said, it was cute and matched his favorite Valentino sundress of hers. After slamming the door, she realized she'd parked under a tree that might not have been a legal spot. But the shade would keep the car cool. She hated getting into a car that felt like a furnace during summer. A parking ticket, if she even got one, would be about eighty dollars. Her mother, the frugal WASP, was surely wagging her finger at her wherever she was.

Move the car, dear. Don't be a spoiled little snot face.

After some hesitation, she left the Mini Cooper in the shade. As Annabelle walked down the sidewalk to meet Caroline, she thought about all those trips to Costco she used to make with the housekeeper. Arthur would point out to his new bride that whatever she had saved, he'd made that much in interest in the time it had taken him to point out how silly her trips to Costco had been. She should feel free to charge anything she desired at that swanky Upper East Side market.

"Thrifty was how I was brought up," she used to tell him. "Excess is anathema to an old WASP household."

Fifteen years, four girls, four homes, a personal NetJet account for Mother's Day this spring (for trips with her girlfriends), and one big, fat summer affair later, Annabelle had readjusted her outlook. She didn't have *that* much showy designer clothing that screamed, *my husband has a fortune!* But she could see the value in spending for convenience and comfort. Today, for instance, what's eighty dollars when her ass would be cool on the drive home? It was a convertible, after all. Not her fault.

As she walked across the parking lot, Annabelle saw Caroline sitting on a small bench before the pond, two peach iced teas beside her, both dripping with condensation. They had fifteen minutes before the one exercise class of the summer they took together, and Caroline, by the look on her face, was already regretting it in the midday humidity.

"I just checked—the exhale class is with Fred DeVito. You knew that, didn't you?" Caroline announced, without saying hello.

"He's the best." She picked up Caroline's iced tea and moved it further away down the bench.

"What the hell?"

"Too much caffeine gives your wrinkles." She twisted open a second bottle of Ginger Kombucha and handed it to Caroline. "Drink."

"Nope, I've tried it once, tastes like rotten scraps that have been in a disposal for days."

"*Fermented*, not rotten. Fred knows, he drinks it. And you should make your life goal to have a body like his wife, Elisabeth," said Annabelle. "She's sixty, by the way. Besides, I have gory details that are more interesting than your whining."

"Fred is a tyrant. You could have picked some easier teacher. But yes, you have piqued my interest. Gory?" Caroline smelled the Kombucha, made a face like she'd been given smelling salts, and put the cap back on, nudging her friend's shoulder with hers. The women sat silently for a few moments.

"It's amazing we've both done what we've done," Annabelle said, without looking at her friend. "And I know you have and you know I have. What's even more incredible is we haven't sat and talked about it."

"I think that's because I still have to remind myself that our affair pact is not *illegal*. But it feels like it to me," Caroline remarked.

"The one thing I didn't predict is that once I indulged, I wouldn't want to admit it, even to you."

"Me too! Eddie did it, and he doesn't feel guilty. But, you know, narcissists are attention junkies, I know he feels that he somehow deserves his affairs. I'm telling you, all because he lacked parental love, mostly because of his drunk, mean dad," Caroline said, rubbing her head to help search for a reason she actually agreed to exercise. She grabbed her iced tea and took a sip.

"Don't defend Eddie," Annabelle said, yanking her leggings down her legs to reveal tight yoga shorts underneath that generally didn't look good on anyone older than fourteen.

"My point is that both our husbands have reasons they've done it multiple times: Eddie because he was unloved in childhood, and Arthur because, I don't know, he's European and entitled?" Caroline said. "Men just do it and move on. Still, I don't love villainizing men."

"*Villainizing* isn't the right word. It's *vilify*," Annabelle said, stretching both her arms in the air and tilting sideways.

"Sorry, Miss Ivy League," Caroline said, pinching her iced tea between her thighs and adding another packet of brown sugar.

"That sugar is literally oozing from packet to cup into your inner thigh flesh, you know that, right?" Annabelle stood, starting to stretch her right leg against the tree trunk next to them.

"Forget my thighs, let's discuss your expression when you walked over here screaming *panic;* it's what you might as well have tattooed on your forehead right now."

"Panic?"

"Here's the thing, Annabelle: you're cool almost all the time, but sometimes, you're just not. And that's why I love you. You're kind of a mess under all that beauty. I can tell you're super nervous about something now. Philippe didn't spill it, did he?"

"The problem is not Philippe. The problem is this: I'm sure Arthur already suspects."

"Oh, God," Caroline said softly. "Let's just sit out here and talk instead of going to some stupid class."

"Nope," Annabelle said. "We're going to class in three minutes." She fidgeted with the seam of her yoga shorts and rubbed her thighs hard. "That's an understatement, actually—Arthur's not just suspicious. I would relish suspicion at this point."

"You said you deleted all your texts with Philippe."

"Arthur's sixth sense for picking stocks apparently applies to his cheating spouse, as well. *He just knows.*"

Caroline grabbed the branch of a bush and picked the leaves off one by one, just to stem her own sudden anxiety. "You're doing the exact same thing that Arthur has done: you having a thing, you were naked with another person . . . only, for you, it's not just a little thing," Caroline said. "It's just not." She threw the branch as far as she could into the water. "I'm certainly less freaked by Ryan, and yes, we've done it a few times, and it's been so nice. But, just for starters, it's very interesting that I'm the cooler one here. You're the one who's not scared of anything."

"Never have been, until now," Annabelle said. "Look, Philippe was good, and worth it, you have no idea of that man's talent in bed, I can't even remember half the things he did, but still, I feel uneasy."

"Don't think I don't feel uneasy too. It's *adultery*. Let's just call it what it is."

"I prefer 'adventure.' Adultery sounds like we should be wearing a scarlet A," Annabelle said. "I just hope Arthur has the same *elegant* reaction to this that I've had to his affairs." She said this forcefully, revealing some resentment, and even hurt. "He won't ask me, I know that. He knows I suspected and didn't push him. I remained silent after overhearing his phone calls, and . . ." now Annabelle's facial muscles contracted in a way Caroline had rarely seen. "When he came home late with a lame excuse, I'd sarcastically say, '*Really?*' Once, I saw him look at this masseuse he's obsessed with, who I'm convinced jerks him off. This masseuse comes . . ."

"Marjina. I know," Caroline said and smiled. She knew *all* about Marjina's strong hands. Annabelle had told her how Arthur had said he "strangely" never needed sex a day or two after a session with her. However, Caroline settled in to hear it all again; a big part of friendship is powering through redundancy.

"Maybe end the Marjina thing?" Caroline suggested. "Tell him you don't like the way she looks at him. Leave it at that if you want to be all subtle. I, on the other hand, would say, 'Stop with the masseuse jerk-off sessions, Eddie.' But you guys, you and Arthur . . . you're all formal and European, you do it your way."

Chapter 30

Miserable Motions

A few moments later, as a disco version of Aretha Franklin's "R-E-S-P-E-C-T" blared out of the speakers, Fred DeVito bellowed, "Right foot on the bar in front of you. Reach for your toes, ladies." Annabelle swung her leg up and touched her nose to her knee, while Caroline had to stand on tiptoe just to get her foot to the bar. Her hamstrings ached already. She looked at the clock: only fifty-seven minutes to go.

As Annabelle gracefully cradled her foot with both hands, she turned her head to the right, and whispered to Caroline, "I couldn't even say it before, but Arthur knows."

"Oh, no!" Caroline said out loud.

Hearing the cry from the newcomer, Fred, an elegant man with a shaved head and a dancer's gait, came over to assist that unfortunate newcomer with her short legs. He tugged on Caroline's hips a little, adjusted the curve of her back, and rubbed her neck. "You can do it, honey, but you're going to need to come every day," he said. "Your flexibility is going to be a summer project of mine."

"No project!" Caroline groaned as he pushed her left ankle down to the ground with the tips of his toes. "Not coming back for a year!" Then she whispered to Annabelle, "I hate you for this. You're sure about Arthur?"

"Left leg up now!"

Annabelle nodded and switched legs like a Rockette. "Positive."

With her hands clasped behind her knee, Caroline worked on raising her other leg to the bar. It wasn't that she was out of shape, she told herself; it was genetic—her legs were shorter than Annabelle's. She said, "It wasn't a text he saw, was it?"

"Nope, deleted each conversation every time," Annabelle said.

"Okay, ladies, sideways plié. Left hand on the bar, heels together and up on your toes, knees apart like a butterfly, now bounce, bounce . . . lower, lower, touch your butt to your heels and rise. Right now is that moment we all seek. It is why we have gathered today. This is how your body changes."

"What if I don't want to change anything?" Caroline whispered. "Remember, you sent me a screenshot of texting between you and Philippe? Did you delete the photo of the conversation? Tell me you deleted that too."

"I don't think so!" Annabelle whispered. "Fuck! Let's take a break!"

The women walked into the hall where the clients' forty designer bags hung on hooks. Gucci, Prada, Stella McCartney, another Gucci, another Prada . . . Figuring about two thousand to four thousand dollars each, Caroline calculated the total value at over a hundred grand.

Annabelle pulled her phone out of her purse and searched for the photo of Philippe's suggestive texts. "Deleted now!"

Caroline shook her head disapprovingly. "Now empty the deleted photo folder."

"The what?"

"Oh my God. Hand me your phone." Before Annabelle could, Caroline grabbed it from her, emptied the deleted photos folder in the photo app, and tossed the phone back into her friend's bag. "You had like a hundred photos in there you thought you'd deleted over the past month. They're still on your phone until you actually empty the deleted folder, which is like emptying the trash on your computer. Basically, you have to delete photos twice to get rid of them." Caroline put her head in her hands. "Does he ever check your phone?"

Fred's wife, Elisabeth, peeked into the hallway area. "You ladies returning? Remember how fabulous you feel after class!"

"I feel my thighs are killing me, is how I feel," Caroline told Annabelle. "Is Arthur ever on your phone?"

"I don't think so."

"All right, let's assume he never checked your photos. You do know your photos migrate between iPads, computers, and even Apple TV, right?"

"Ladies? You having a martini in here?" Fred asked, poking his nose into the hallway while "All the Single Ladies" blasted in the room behind him. "C'mon, I'm not babysitting. This is hard work—it's bikini season! Get back in class."

"One minute, Fred. Promise," Annabelle said. Her face white, she turned back to Caroline. "My photos do tend to stream across my TVs when Apple TV is on. I have no idea when I said 'Okay' to that function, but my photos do that. I mean, those Apple engineers should really ask you, *really clearly*, if you want your entire photo library streaming on every TV in all four of your houses all the time, don't you think?"

"I do," answered Caroline softly. "Though, for most people it isn't four homes, just pointing that out. But I do take your point."

"Fuck!"

Caroline added, "Look, in this digital age, at least one of us is bound to get found out. I wish I could publish a list of the Top Ten Reasons Apple Engineers Want You to Get Caught Cheating. That's what I was saying when you proposed this pact."

"My mother always said, *I told you so* is bad manners," Annabelle said, dragging her friend back into class.

The group was in Annabelle's favorite position: water-skiing. Fred glided over to the pair, pointing his toes with each stride just to show off his glorious calf muscles to all these desperate housewives who had the hots for him. (He'd never partake, why would he, with Elisabeth's epic bottom in his bed each night?) "No leaving class again, ladies. Now Caroline, face the bar, hold on tight, pretend as if the bar is the rope behind a speedboat and you're water-skiing. Toes under the bar, heels touching in a *V*, and lean waaaay back. Now, bounce, one, two . . ."

"I don't care what your mother taught you. I *did* tell you so," Caroline whispered. "Technology will bite you in the ass these days—especially if your ass is naked in another man's bed."

Annabelle leaned back and assumed the water-ski position like Esther Williams. She whispered to Caroline, "Technology might have led Arthur to suspect, but the clincher was a pretty ancient technique."

"He didn't walk in on . . ."

"Ladies! Hit the mats, stomach down, two-minute plank," Fred shouted. "Does everyone know Ruth Bader Ginsberg can do two minutes? Let's see who in here can last . . ."

On the floor, Annabelle whispered to her friend as she lifted herself into a plank position. "Arthur literally smelled my hands after I'd just had massive sex with Philippe."

"You didn't shower?" Caroline said, also in a plank, her abdomen and back feeling like they were in a vice. "You went home all smelly from sex? How reckless and completely stupid are you? No Summer's Eve even?"

"Philippe's shower was gross. It had all these cobwebs . . . I was worried about athlete's foot and . . ."

"Jesus, Annabelle! Listen to yourself! You had sex with him, and you're worried about catching something from his feet?"

"I would love to hear the whole foot story, but I won't even ask," Fred said as he walked over to them. He yanked Caroline to the other side of the room, these girls needed to be separated. When Caroline complained that the plank position had hurt her lower back, he helped her to hang from a high bar to loosen it up, supporting her from the waist in case she slipped. After stretching out, Caroline lasted the remaining forty minutes of class, giving Annabelle dirty looks from across the room the entire time.

Afterward, on the sidewalk outside, Annabelle told Caroline, "I want to take a mulligan."

"That was our one exercise class together this summer," Caroline said. "You are not getting me into one of those torture chambers again until next year." She fished around in her bag for her keys and braced herself to hear the end of Annabelle's saga.

"I didn't mean another class, which, by the way, I will get you into. I meant another man."

"You say you're worried about Arthur knowing, and you're already thinking about round two?" Caroline shook her head in disbelief. "Annabelle the Enigma. You make *zero* sense. You say you're in crisis because Arthur smelled your hands. But now you want *more*? You're an adrenaline junkie, I'm telling you. That's why you ski race."

"Maybe. But it's no longer about trying to even the score with Arthur. I've done that." She bit her lower lip. "Philippe was one kind of lay, now I want someone more real, more American. I don't know, more *something*."

"Maybe he made you feel like just one of many," Caroline said. "You want special. Not just hot sex, but something to remember, right?"

"Uh, no," Annabelle said. "I'm not into slobbering gush like I bet you have with Mr. Architect. Just, this is my summer for variety, and I have a finite deadline, and well, keeping score, Arthur's done it a few times. Same deal for me. And on Mr. Architect, I mean I don't know the details yet, but I'm assuming he's just a more normal guy to interact with and you're . . ."

"Yeah," Caroline said, biting her lower lip. "He's a gem all around."

"You're falling for him, aren't you?"

Caroline shook her head. "I refuse. But it's something very solid and meaningful to both of us. It's in a very safe zone where transactional meets trust."

"Well, then cheers to us for getting what we want in life, and on our terms," Annabelle said, smiling. "Leave it to two determined women not to fuck around when we agree to fuck around!"

PART III

Summer Storm

Chapter 31

Doomed at Duryea's

"August is the best time to be celebrating the barn, everyone's well settled into summer and needs a little break," Eddie said boisterously, driving his family up the dusty road to Duryea's for lunch near the tip of Montauk. "Mom thinks I'm crazy to have a barn party here, today, but who wants lobster?" He winked at Caroline and blew her a kiss.

"Go, Fun Daddy!" Theo yelled, slamming the back of Caroline's seat over and over with his feet.

"Honey, please stop kicking me back there," Caroline said to Theo. "I love every day of August, Eddie. And I loved your idea of taking everyone out, but it's going to be a madhouse here on any Saturday of late summer. I don't see how they're going to fit one table for all the grooms, and all our kids, and Thierry and Annabelle and Arthur, you and I, that's what, sixteen?"

Eddie patted his wife's thigh, ignoring her silly concerns. "I got it, baby. Steven Jauffrineau is a cool guy, and he runs stuff perfectly at all of his spots. Here, Lulu's in Sag. I send him great Burgundy all the time. He knows who's who!" Eddie yelled looking back in the rearview mirror. "Right, kids?"

"Yes, Daddy!" Theo kicked more. "Lobster with lots of butter!"

"We'll cut in front of anyone waiting, Steven will let us," Eddie said.

"Honey, stop. That's not a lesson to pass on, cutting. C'mon. We'll wait in line."

Eddie shook his head and silently mouthed, *No way*, then added, "Besides, the great Philippe de Montaigne is there, handling it all. You know, frog on frog. He got there half an hour ago. A great-looking Frenchman who speaks their language helps. One reason I hired him."

"You said Philippe wasn't coming; that's the only reason I asked Annabelle and Arthur," Caroline said, trying to keep her skyrocketing nerves from being detectable. "Eddie, tell me that's not true. You specifically said Philippe was staying behind to mind the horses and this was all about the grooms, guys who never get to go out on a weekend. We agreed that was a lovely idea for them, but not for Philippe! He's in charge of the stable, hardly needs attention and rewards today!"

"Why the fuck do you care if he comes?"

"Dad sweared," Gigi said. "I get five dollars."

"Arthur suggested we add Philippe," Eddie explained. "Not to make him stay and work. He checked in yesterday specifically to make sure he was included. He said his girls adore Philippe and a barn lobster fest wouldn't be the same without him!"

Arthur knew.

Arthur wanted Philippe there to make his wife writhe and twist with guilt, nerves, the knowledge he never didn't know things.

That cold-ass, conniving European motherfucker.

Caroline took out her phone to text Annabelle, but as they pulled into the parking lot, she could see her friend waiting, with her cute, devilish husband. He was rubbing his short beard in anticipation with one hand, the other tightly grabbing the hip of his bride, his woman.

"Daddy, make the car park by itself," Theo said. "Put your hands in the air!"

Thinking about the awkward lunch ahead, Caroline started to sweat and took off her light cardigan. The fact that her four-year-old knew about the auto-park feature on his father's new $100,000 Tesla, or that her kids' favorite restaurant featured thirty-five-dollar lobster rolls and sixty-eight-dollar boiled lobsters were the least of her problems. But they were problems, nonetheless.

Chapter 32

I'll Have the Intravenous Sedative, Sir!

Caroline hadn't believed Annabelle was capable of experiencing fear or trepidation.

Until now.

Eddie put Theo on his shoulders and carried Gigi, the kids hanging off him like monkeys. He walked toward Annabelle and Arthur waiting outside Duryea's at the curb. Caroline, five paces behind Eddie, tried to signal her friend with an expression that said, *Holy shit! Philippe is here,* but Arthur would have intercepted it from across the lane. Caroline looked at him and waved, trying to act cool, *just a lovely little lunch ahead.* But Arthur was smiling at her, letting her know that nothing passes him by.

He knew she knew.

And she knew he knew.

A mob of Montauk hipsters in ripped thirty-dollar surf shorts and worn four-hundred-dollar sneakers, some glamorous would-be or should-be or actually-are models, and a few families crowded around the entrance to Duryea's. New Yorkers accustomed to having their way could be heard yelling at the hostesses, "We made a reservation a month ago. I've got my wife, my in-laws, it's been forty-five minutes, and you don't even . . ."

Caroline shot Eddie a look and said, "Honey, maybe we should all just grab something at the Clam Bar on the highway. That way we can just stand and go as we please."

"Who wants fried calamari, kids?" Eddie yelled out, hugging them tighter. "Who wants lobsters and hot butter?"

"We do!" Gigi said as she bolted from Eddie's arms and ran to Rosie and Thierry, who were also waiting on the sidewalk.

"Hey, Arthur, Annabelle, everyone," Eddie shouted. "I got this covered, wait a sec, just let me check and I'll be right out to get you all." He charged through the throngs like an offensive lineman, albeit one in five-hundred-dollar purple suede moccasins from Salvatore Ferragamo.

Caroline stood next to Annabelle and Arthur and said to them, "Eddie just loves a party, sometimes he doesn't understand how crowded things can get. So, you guys, if it's too much . . ."

"The girls are inside," Arthur said. "They wanted to see the lobster tank and that twenty-pounder they've got. Besides, Philippe is so crafty, he'll handle it, wouldn't you agree, Caroline?"

Annabelle's pallor matched her blond hair. She was busted and helpless.

"That lobster is huge," Caroline blurted out. "I mean, it's almost prehistoric . . ."

"I wasn't asking your opinion on the crustacean, Caroline," Arthur said with authoritarian conviction that he inherited from his ancestors. "I was referring to Philippe, the trainer. You must know him well. Don't you agree he's crafty? You must find him *almost irresistible,* no?"

"Well, I, yes, he's a good trainer, knows horses in and out."

"Looks like he knows the in and out of so much in life, wouldn't you agree, my darling?" He turned to Annabelle, and said, "I look forward to getting to know him at lunch. Hopefully the service will be horrendous, and we'll have lots of time to get to know each other."

Arthur walked to the far end of the crowd where his girls stood before the lobster tank. Upon hearing that their table was ready, he guided his four beauties past the families who had been waiting for an hour. Arthur ignored the dirty looks of those deemed less socially desirable in the eyes of the owners.

Annabelle gripped Caroline's wrist so hard, it hurt. "Arthur is so goddamned ruthless, it scares me what he does to make a point," she said.

"You know the barn lunch was specifically planned to exclude Philippe, timed when he has all his lessons. Eddie promised me, but then Arthur called and intervened," Caroline told her. "I mean, are we going to actually have lunch with your husband *and* your lover?"

"I think so." Annabelle managed to whisper, her face almost paralyzed. "And was that 'in and out' reference really necessary?"

"Oh my God, okay, okay," Caroline said. "I'll talk a lot, change the topic, move the service, do anything I can."

The dashing manager, Steven Jauffrineau, took both ladies by their elbows and guided them to the Sea Crest Stables table for seventeen: seven children, including the two Clarkson siblings, the von Tattenbachs' four girls, and Rosie; her uncle Thierry, four grooms, two wealthy couples, and one playboy.

Chapter 33

No Free Lunch in This World

P hilippe, you choose the wine," offered Arthur, handing him the list. "Just don't order a Lafite; you've robbed me enough this summer with stable fees, complete with those *private lessons*. Of course, perhaps you're worth the expense? Is he darling? As we said, he knows the in and out of so much in life!"

Philippe was sitting two spots from Arthur, with Annabelle between them.

From across the table, Eddie said, "Yo, Philippe, don't listen to him! Order the best. Get rosé and white! You French gotta know wine better than me."

Arthur leaned over his wife and looked Philippe in the eye. "Well, now, Philippe, don't go taking from another man too much this summer. I mean there are limits." Arthur perused the wine list, peeping over his reading glasses, and said, "For example, this Montrachet at four hundred and seventy-five dollars would be a little much. I'm sure you understand *too much*? Like taking a man's money and then taking even more from him."

Annabelle's gaze was fixed straight ahead as if she were posing for a mug shot. Philippe put on his Persol sunglasses and clinked his water glass. "I, uh, thank you!" was all he said to Arthur. He banged Annabelle's right knee with his left knee so hard that her upper body nudged her husband's. She never wavered, though, not even looking to Caroline for salvation.

Eddie, unfazed by the tripartite drama two feet in front of him, yelled down to the kids' end of the table, "Hey, Theo, Gigi! Should I get that huge lobster for lunch, or you wanna keep him as a pet?" Then Eddie waylaid the manager as he was trying to deliver a bucket of ice to the adjacent table. "Yo, Steven! How much for the big monster lobster in the tank? Name the price, you crazy frog!"

Eddie was on one of his rolls, whipping everyone up, feeding on the excitement of the white-hot restaurant. Caroline patted his arm and said, "Honey, let's just move this along. Annabelle is tired, and it's crowded so . . ."

"C'mon, baby! It's a gorgeous day, all our favorite people are here," Eddie said. "The kids are so happy to celebrate with the grooms. Look at 'em, everyone down there is talking and laughing. It's great for barn relations. What's the rush? Don't you agree, Annabelle?"

Annabelle nodded, agreeing to anything just to move time forward. Under the table, Philippe rubbed his leg against hers, and whispered in her ear, "Your husband has no idea, right?"

She kicked his leg for his audacity to touch her now, even discreetly. Then, she took a gulp of ice water and another and another. She nearly choked and had to wipe her chin with her napkin.

"By in and out," Philippe whispered in Annabelle's ear, "your husband wasn't referring to me and his wife, right? Please tell me that."

She whispered, "He meant what you think he meant."

"In and out of you? He meant that?"

"*Oui*, Philippe," she whispered, then grabbed a hunk of baguette, submerged it in olive oil, and raised her eyebrow at him.

"*Merde!*" Philippe mouthed silently.

Caroline stood up, fumbling for an excuse to get her friend out of the room. "Annabelle, let's go order for everyone. We don't need to spend a ton of time filling out the forms here. That's how they order here. We'll get a variety of stuff and share. Besides, moms know what everyone likes."

But Eddie stood instead of Annabelle. "Nah, baby, we got this," he said. "I'm hosting. They're all cramped and cozy on their side of the table." He shook his index finger at them. "You guys, stay, chat a little in the sunshine out here. I'll go with you, honey. Lunch is on me anyway!" Eddie brought Caroline over to the counter where patrons filled out checklists of what they wanted and paid. "What's with you, baby? You seem stressed. I did this lunch for you! You were so game when I suggested it a week ago. You loved Duryea's as a kid, and what fun to take the grooms out, and Thierry and Rosie and . . ."

"Honey, minor thing, but Duryea's back then was a true fish shack, not a Euro scene, but you're right, and thank you," she said. "You're always trying, it's just . . ."

"Just what? Tell me, baby, what's bothering you. You're my best friend, I'm yours, just tell me, would ya? I hate it when you keep secrets."

Caroline saw the line of patrons ahead of them and gauged the time it would take to even order. She considered the value of telling Eddie, so he could at least help ease the stress on Annabelle, who was now talking to the kids at their side of the table. Philippe, thankfully, had excused himself and was speaking French to the owners. Arthur was alone on his side of the table for a moment, and he placed his meaty arm on the back of the picnic bench and stared out to sea, the salty summer breeze blowing his strawberry-gray hair off his face. He rubbed his beard a bit, thinking, pleased with himself for engineering so much discomfort for his silly, wandering wife and that shithead trainer in the tight pants that hopefully strangled the life out of his dick.

Chapter 34

A Not-So-Perfect Perfect Day

Caroline looked over Eddie's shoulder as he was making marks on the ordering checklist: sixteen lobsters, eight lobster rolls, eight orders of clams, calamari, and oysters. "Honey, that's crazy, that's two dishes per person, kids don't each need, lemme just . . ."

Caroline stopped mid-sentence.

A couple at the front of the line turned around and started walking toward them. Ryan Miller waved sheepishly, and his wife, Suzy, paused, taking the lead from her husband, unsure if he wanted to stop and say hi.

"Oh, hi" was all Caroline could muster.

"Hello," Ryan answered awkwardly.

Ryan kept walking in a line, but Eddie tapped him on the arm before he could pass. "Hey man, don't I know you? Did we go to school together?"

"Eddie, it's fine," said Caroline. "Let them . . ."

"No! I know him! It's gonna stick with me all day if we don't . . ."

"We, uh, met at the barn party. We went to East Hampton High," Ryan answered, sounding like someone had just jammed a pointy heel into his foot.

Caroline pulled Eddie toward her and began checking every box on the form. "We sure did! Now, Eddie, everyone's hungry! Why not add mussels? Maybe some of the kids want fries . . ."

Eddie ignored her. "No, it wasn't school," he said, stomping his fragile moccasin (he got four pairs for summer because they scuffed up so easily) and slapping his forehead, trying to conjure a recollection of Ryan. "I'm sure of that. It was somewhere else. You surf? Maybe I used to see you out at Turtles? Or was it North Bar? Fortress?"

"Uh, not really those breaks, not much. This is, uh, my wife, Suzy," Ryan said, looking at Caroline and pulling Suzy's hand off his elbow as if he had been caught cheating *with his own wife.*

Caroline couldn't help but peek up at Suzy. Her wild mass of blond curly hair framed an angelic face with blue eyes and high cheekbones like a lioness. She had broad shoulders and large breasts that Caroline decided were all natural and far nicer than hers. Wearing cropped jeans and a white linen button-down, she had endless legs like Annabelle's and a tight waist highlighted by a braided, brown leather belt. No woman had great legs *and* great boobs; it was one or the other. Suzy looked like she jumped out of a Ralph Lauren magazine spread: the kind of freckled, clean, all-American beauty who never used a blow-dryer because that silly primping clashed with her free spirit. Caroline shook her head, vowing not to give in to any competitive nonsense. She studied the menu instead, praying Eddie would focus on moving lunch along and give up on Ryan and Suzy. "Honey, the food? Can we order?" Caroline asked.

Eddie ignored her. "So, maybe not surfing. You still live in East Hampton? I'm sure I know you from something else," Eddie said. "Remind me of your name? I'm Eddie Clarkson. You know Caroline apparently."

"Uh, just, yeah, met her, or, like re-met her from way back I guess," he said. "I'm Ryan."

Eddie pumped his hand. "And you?"

"She's, uh, here with me, uh, Suzy, my wife, we're celebrating our anniversary actually. We don't come here much," Ryan offered, for no particular reason except to fill the air.

Caroline reached the front of the line and started to order, hoping that Eddie would focus on the food and not the man she'd been shagging all summer. She said, "Actually, Eddie, your order ideas are all good, you want to double-check . . ."

"We played Ultimate Frisbee together, that was it! Yah, we did," Eddie said to Ryan, nodding. "You were one strong dude, I remember that! Let's get you both a glass of bubbly. Caroline, c'mon, just order whatever you think best for seventeen, honey. Ryan and Suzy's order will take twenty minutes, ours longer, I'm gonna get a jeroboam of champagne. Let's share that big, four-bottle bad boy with the barn guys, with the happy couple from high school. C'mon!" Eddie smacked Ryan on the back and guided him over to the big table. Eddie introduced him to the group: "It's an East Hampton High reunion *and* the best month of summer!"

"No, no, honey, no!" Caroline said, rushing over and glaring at Annabelle. "They want to be alone!"

Annabelle remained with her elbows tight against her sides, not wanting to have contact with either the man to her left or the one to her right.

"It's honestly fine," Suzy said, understanding a guy like Eddie wasn't going to give up. "I like champagne, and Ryan doesn't drink much, so I'm happy to have a glass." She smiled warmly at her fellow suffering spouse, Caroline, which only made Caroline more anxious. The last thing she wanted was girl bonding.

Eddie pulled two chairs up to the edge of their table, and asked the waiter, "Yo, bring a jeroboam of Moët, buddy. Put a sparkler on the top, 'cause, what the hell, it's a perfect day!"

Before Ryan and Suzy could even wedge into their chairs, the waiters had brought a chilled, enormous, almost joke-size bottle of Moët & Chandon. A huge sparkler was sticking out of the top, spraying glittering embers all around. "July Fourth is happening again in August!" Eddie yelled, slapping Ryan on the back. "I tell ya, what a day to celebrate. Hey kids, it's their anniversary! And he, I mean, Ryan, your mom, and I went to school together!"

Eddie then nabbed the bottle from the waiter with one hand. "Yo, this is heavy, gimme a hand, Ryan, hold the bottom for me." Then, Eddie grabbed champagne flutes from the table and proceeded to over-pour into each so that bubbles flowed down his hand. He hoisted the glasses in the air, "Happy summer, everyone. Love you, kids, and grateful to the grooms who work harder than anyone at the barn, and to Thierry and Philippe for making Sea Crest Stables a dream come true! And to our high school buddy, Ryan, and his bride. What a day! You guys just sit for a few minutes, hell, your food will take ten minutes, and I'll keep this fresh champs chilling for the second round. C'mon man, here you go."

Suzy took a glass and smiled at Caroline, and placing her hand gently on her shoulder, she whispered, "It's nice of him, thanks." Again, she signaled she understood that men like Eddie you just couldn't stop if you tried, and that she was perfectly okay with a quick glass on such a nice day.

"So, Ryan, you played Ultimate for how long?" Eddie asked.

"Oh, God, just a few years," Ryan said. He tilted his glass toward Caroline and then Suzy, and said, "We're just sitting for two minutes, but thank you, uh, Eddie."

Annabelle had by now pulled her pink linen scarf up under her eyes like a burka to hide her increasingly purple face. Caroline was more conspicuous; she looked like Munch's *The Scream*, mouth open in terror.

"And what do you do now, man?" Eddie asked Ryan. "You doing good for yourself out here?"

"I'm an architect. I do fine, thanks," Ryan said, smacking his lips. He started to get up, guiding his wife's elbow upward with his. "Honey, you wanna . . ."

But Suzy didn't "wanna." She pulled her arm back and told him, "I'm fine, honey. They gave us these glasses, let's finish them." She was surprised at her husband's ingratitude, he was usually so solicitous and polite. They barely knew these people, and they had generously presented them with expensive champagne. Two minutes wouldn't kill anyone.

Arthur turned to his right and, in an exaggerated fashion, leaned over Annabelle. "It's their anniversary, isn't that nice, Philippe? I love anniversary parties. Are you single, Philippe? Or no," Arthur asked rhetorically, stroking his beard in mock thought. "Lemme take a wild guess: you just play around because, well, you look like you like to play around, eh?"

Philippe took a big swig of champagne, the bubbles prickling in his nose. "I, uh, I'm not married yet," he said.

"Well, marriage is a great thing!" Arthur declared, putting his arm around his wife and then pulling her toward him. He planted a big kiss on her lips. "When you have a treasure like I do, there's nothing better in life than that partnership. It would take a lot to put a dent in it. Annabelle and I are like a Swiss safe-deposit vault, indestructible, right, darling?"

Chapter 35

Secrets Here, There, Everywhere

It's stuuunning. A winner!" Philippe yelled over to Sophia's parents, who were watching her ride from the side of the ring. "You know you're going to have a famous rider on your hands!"

Philippe, arms crossed, felt a pang of guilt. How to convince little Sophia that she would do well on this horse, given that she was talentless and that the mare was crap? Her banker father in those horrid American pleated pants would need a bit of mental massaging, but Philippe was up to it.

Ruing the day he let his baby princess get on that first pony, George Talbot asked his wife, "How many days a year will she ride this thing?"

"Puddles is not *a thing*," she answered, exasperated already—it's not like he'd get it eventually, either. "And I don't know, George, maybe fifty days? During the year we can try to come out to the Hamptons on Saturdays. But when it gets cold, I'm not going to be very willing. *Just saying*." She kissed her party-pooper husband and rubbed her new boob job up against him.

Philippe studied Puddles's gait: not too bad, though a little short-strided and inconsistent through the turns, nothing a layman would notice. At the more casual shows, the female judges he flirted with would add a few points, and the little brat would take home a colored ribbon—not first-place blue, but maybe an eighth-place brown, the color of manure.

Horseshit. Bullshit. Ah, a crappy horse that could bring Philippe about twenty grand. The joys of summer in full bloom.

CAROLINE ARRIVED RINGSIDE with an acai bowl and hibiscus iced tea from the barn's terrace café. She sat on a high-viewing chair ten feet from the Talbots. In her hand, a key to Eddie's file cabinet in his office that she'd grabbed from his hiding place in the hallway armoire. She fingered the key, planting it deep in the corner of her pocket. Perhaps she'd have a chance to go back into his office today to check on his files, papers, ledgers, anything that looked strange.

Gigi and her friend Rosie were inside the ring, helping the smarmy Philippe move rails around the ring for Puddles's jumps.

Caroline overheard Mr. Talbot say to his wife, "Just so you know the game here, this trainer guy in the fairy white pants is bullshitting me. If he wants to play ball with the head of the most profitable equity derivative department on the planet, I say game on."

"Not everything has a balance sheet, George!" his wife shot back. "Show jumping is an art; you can't put a price on Sophia's self-confidence." After a slight pause, during which she remembered the little thrill she'd felt when Philippe brushed her hair back and let his hand linger on her neck, she added, "*And* those are polo pants. *And* you're homophobic. *And* he's *very* heterosexual, *I assure you.*" She almost immediately rethought the wisdom of confirming the last bit.

"Honey, this is a beginner lesson for a nine-year-old. The guy is not about to play a polo match here, for Christ sakes, that's a ridiculous Halloween costume he's got on! And relax, it's not a judgment about you. I like the barn. I find Eddie a bit aggressive. You know, that tacky, new money glow in his eyes, but you have to admire what he's done here. I do wonder how rich he's gotten." George looked around at the vast fields, show rings, and luxurious stables. How exactly had that local turned city boy created all this? "Surely, this isn't Eddie Clarkson's taste. He must have hired a top designer."

Caroline thought about throwing her iced tea into this asshole's face. She pretended to be occupied with her phone.

"There's no backing out of the riding plan now," the wife fought on. "It's like you inked a deal. Think of it that way."

"Just don't be a dingbat on the expenses, and beware of that haughty Frenchman out there," Mr. Talbot said. "In addition to the cost of leasing this new Puddles for the year, say forty thousand dollars, it's a fixed three-thousand-dollars-a-month stall fee at this barn no matter what. Then about six hundred dollars to ship the dumb animal to a local show, eight hundred more in show fees on weekends, one-fifty on the braiding for every show. We just got a fifteen-hundred-dollar vet bill for shots and an oxygen tank for the other pony. That had to be a mistake, she hasn't ridden that one for a month. I sent it back to the vet."

"That 'other pony' is her baby. His name is Clay. And the poor pony had a bad sore on his back from a saddle that was too tight. The oxygen tank helps wounds heal faster."

"And whose fault is it that the saddle was too tight? I'm paying them three thousand dollars a month, presumably, to put on . . ."

"George," she said, defiantly, crossing her arms, "a custom Voltaire saddle is seven thousand dollars. Which, I wanted. *Badly.*"

"You wanted, or Sophia needed?" he wisely asked.

"Blame yourself for the shitty saddle Clay was wearing and the vet bills *you caused.* And, just so you know, we are still technically leasing Clay until September and obliged to cover the costs, so don't think you can—"

"Wait a second," George interrupted, placing his forefinger across his wife's poufy, collagen-enhanced lips. "We're paying Philippe for a pet that doesn't work? The feed, the stalls, the vets? All summer?"

"That's why we're here, considering Puddles as, uh, a replacement."

"Oh, nooow I get it," George said, raising his right eyebrow—something he always did when he felt an adversary was trying to fleece him. "You want a second pony? And me to cover the costs of both?" Everything was becoming clear now. George considered the motives behind the spectacular blow job he'd received earlier that morning.

"Clay can't even have a saddle on him for three months, *even a custom Voltaire;* it'll rub his sore. And then it'll get infected. Then it really gets expensive. I'm *saving* you money by keeping Clay out of the ring!" She pinched her elbows into her ribs, so her fabulous, new cleavage deepened. "Sophia *needs* Puddles. Otherwise, she'll miss every show of the summer, and fall behind, and, *worse,* feel left out of her new, horsey friend group. Besides, *I really like* the horse mom crowd. People have the wrong image of show jumping and the whole horse deal; but these moms *all* get that the sport is really about discipline and grit!"

George smacked himself on the forehead.

TEN MINUTES LATER, Thierry approached Caroline with a cold bottle of Sea Crest Stables signature water. "It's hot out here," he said.

"Thank you, but you don't need to bring this to me," she said, smiling. "I'm not the boss. I'm just here watching Gigi and Rosie. You know, we should be proud of them; unlike the other girls here, they work in the ring and the barn cleaning up ninety percent of their time and probably ride ten percent. They get there's some responsibility behind it." God help her for letting Gigi ride, she hoped she never turned into anything like that Sophia Talbot, who'd never been inside a stall. Caroline knew, with that rapacious mother guiding her through life, none of it was the child's fault.

"Gigi's working harder than Rosie," Thierry said, picking up Caroline's empty plastic bowl from the grass next to her. "My girl complains a little when she gets bored; she's always looking for the next activity."

"Staying with something even when you're bored is a maturity thing. She'll get there," Caroline said. "And thanks for taking the bowl. You know you don't have to do things like that. I keep telling you."

He smiled kindly as he turned away, bowl in hand.

"Thierry, one sec." Caroline beckoned him back. She hopped down from her chair and led him into the shade, away from everyone else. "You can talk to me about anything, you know that," she said. She let that sit a little, and he nodded. It was as if he were considering if he could trust her. "If you're having issues here, I can always try to smooth things out a little," she told him.

"It's fine," he lied.

"I don't think it is, Thierry," she said.

"The girls are doing great," he said. "The barn is—"

She interrupted him. "I don't know what was going on between Marcus McCree—that man who owns Executive Limo—Philippe, and you on Memorial Day, but it was something, and it wasn't what you were telling me. I hear Eddie yelling in the stalls all the time. I don't know what he's so nervous about, do you? You've known him for a while, right?"

She noticed that Thierry jerked his back more upright at that. "From the other barn, yes," he said.

"So, you've known Eddie since Gigi rode four years ago at Rose Patch with Jenna Westlake, right? You remember when you met him the first time?"

Thierry shrugged his shoulders as if he'd lost the power of speech. Finally, he muttered, "It's all business. Everything we do here is . . . just . . . ask your husband. He handles the business. I don't get involved."

Caroline nodded slowly. It had to be that snake Philippe who was corrupting this kind, docile man. She pried a little more, careful not to reveal what she'd seen in Eddie's desk. "Was it four years ago, or . . . I mean, you should know, *how many years has it been?*" He'd been receiving checks for ten years from Eddie. He knew and she knew.

"Mr. Clarkson and Philippe run everything. I'm just managing the animals and the grooms. My part is all fine," he answered. "I don't remember much."

She gave up. He just wanted to do his job and not be grilled.

"Okay, well, please remember that Eddie can be a bully. He doesn't realize how harsh he sounds when he's frustrated," Caroline told him. "He's very grateful to you."

Thierry nodded and walked away, his hands slung in his front pockets, his jeans hanging from his slender frame.

Clearly, he didn't want to talk about it anymore, but Caroline couldn't help but feel that Thierry wanted her on his side.

But on his side of what?

Chapter 36

High Tension Ringside

Caroline sat back down on her high-viewing chair ringside when she received a text:

> This is Robert Smith, the Upholsterer, are you free now?

She replied:

> Give me a little time. I'm in the middle of something.

Maybe there wasn't room for a summer affair. She was still traumatized by the lunch at Duryea's and hadn't seen Ryan since, though they'd discussed the debacle in texts later that day. They must stick to Tuesdays, she would tell Ryan, no contact at all on weekends.

"Look at your daughter, Caroline!" Philippe yelled from the center of the ring, drawing her attention away from her phone. He'd put Gigi on Puddles to show Sophia how the shitty pony could indeed prance over a four-inch rail. Caroline didn't much care for horses or ponies, but she knew enough to recognize that this animal moved more like a donkey than a show pony.

Caroline was so agitated that she couldn't stay seated. She stood and circled the chair twice with her arms firmly crossed over her chest, fuming at Philippe's unethical bullshit, unnerved by Thierry's obstinacy.

She considered the upholsterer contact in her phone. Was that obvious or genius? Could anyone guess it was the architect? Is there any chance that Eddie brought him over to their table to screw with her, as Arthur had done to Annabelle with Philippe?

She kneaded her temples. Maybe Eddie did suspect? Is that why he'd been in such a foul mood this morning? He would have had her tailed by a private eye the moment he considered she might be straying. The thought made her nauseated. She and Ryan had been so careful. But still, that lunch was so bizarre, and she hadn't stopped thinking about it since.

After watching her daughter round the ring three times, she gave Ryan the all clear.

He texted:

> *I'm recovering from that lunch, vowing to move on and forget it. You okay? One thing that helps: I remember how it felt when you wrapped your leg around mine on that first Tuesday. That's when I decided that you were a crazy level of sexy. Your leg around mine: that did it all.*

What did he mean by *it all*? Was Ryan falling for her?

It'll be a release, not a distraction, Annabelle had promised. She was wrong. Caroline was a pressure cooker, and this was no release.

Caroline promptly deleted Ryan's texts. She rested her chin on her hands on the back of the chair and tried to focus on sweet Gigi.

In the distance, she could see the main administrative building.

Eddie was inside, in his round cupola office. She was sure he was still steaming from the morning.

The key would have to stay in her pocket until much later; maybe she could tell Maryanne that she needed to make a call, that she wasn't getting good service on her phone, and close the door.

THIS MORNING, AFTER Eddie had stormed out of the kitchen and up to their room, she'd found him peeing in their bathroom. He rotated his head toward her midstream. "Don't call me an entitled urban prick," he said. "You know it sets me off. *Your marital therapist,* what is he, the fourth we've been to? You know I hate that shit. You don't even do what he says, so why do you make me go? He told you not to say things that set me off."

"You're right, and I'm sorry," Caroline said. "He also told us to apologize. You're right; I lit a match to a stick of dynamite on purpose. But you asked for it. If you forgot to charge up your Tesla this week, and you can't drive it today, the earth will keep spinning. You *do* know that."

"Don't moralize me," Eddie said, walking into his dressing room to put on a new shirt. On the way in, he looked back at her feet and said. "And by the way, nice four-hundred-and-fifty-dollar Givenchy sneakers."

"They're just . . ." she said as she followed him.

"Don't even try to justify them, Caroline. You're a player in the game, don't pull this country milkmaid shit with me." Then Eddie made air quotes and mocked her voice: "'They're the *mellow* ones, all white, no one can really tell.' But, thing is, Caroline, your fuckin' sneakers say Givenchy on the back. And you know what that says? *Entitled Urban Park Avenue Mom.*"

She looked down at her designer sneakers. She wished Annabelle hadn't convinced her to buy them at Barney's that day. Eddie had never been easy to spar with—that was one reason she'd been attracted to him. He went on, "So you drank the same Kool-Aid, baby. Tesla or Givenchy, it's all the same deal. Look in the fuckin' mirror before you yell about my car. You don't appreciate the shit I did to get all of this for all of us." He marched out of his dressing room and sat on the chair in their bedroom, thrusting his foot into his sock with so much force, he ripped a hole in the toe. "Fuck!"

She rounded the corner after him. "I do appreciate all you've achieved! And I'm proud of you," she said. "You're right about my sneakers, I'll accept that. But the babysitter overheard your tantrum over your new car, honey, and I just wish you could cool it. Francis is making fifteen dollars an hour. That Tesla costs over a hundred and thirty grand! God, I told you that you were nuts to buy it. Just like I told you ten years ago not to get that Hummer army Jeep, the car that almost got you killed the first week you drove it. You remember?"

"I remember," he said.

"You should remember, you almost got killed rounding the bend; you're lucky no one was in the passenger seat, you skidding full speed into a tree on that side. Can you imagine if you'd spun on your side?"

That missive stung more than Caroline knew. Eddie marveled that, to this day, she didn't even know anything about the real story. It wasn't fair, but what the hell was he supposed to do at this point? Caroline had no idea who was in the Hummer, no idea what happened to her. Still. Amazing he never got found out, only those cops and that hospital in upstate New York. On that Thursday before Memorial Day. *Jesus, it was ten years ago.* He'd wear that purple tie all year now just to remember her, say out loud to the skies above that it wasn't fair to Hélène. He didn't know how the Hummer handled on a wide-open country road.

She went on, "You looked like Schwarzenegger in the vehicle, or like you were in *Mad Max* in the middle of Manhattan. It wasn't safe: you were so lucky. You could have left your unborn child without a parent."

He stood up and buckled his belt. He had vowed to never speak about that Hummer crash and he wouldn't now. All he said was, "The fuckin' sitter doesn't know how much a 2018 Model X Tesla costs."

"She knows it's not cheap. Francis is part of our community, *where we went to school and grew up,* and I just don't want her talking about your values as if . . ."

"As if . . . what?" Eddie walked up to her and lifted his chin.

"As if they were *mine.*" She stared him down.

Silence.

And he walked out of the bathroom and charged out the front door. While Caroline helped Theo get dressed for his playdate and Gigi get ready to ride, Eddie was stewing in her Jeep Cherokee. He knew Caroline had picked the vinyl seats over leather just to piss him off. The fuckin' car didn't even have seat coolers. Women were impossible.

AND NOW, BESIDE the ring, Caroline crossed and uncrossed her legs. Her heart raced. She remembered Ryan's text:

> *Your leg around mine: that did it all.*

She tried again to define exactly what Ryan meant by "it all."

How hard was it to get transcripts of texts? Eddie might know that possibly Verizon could do that. Maybe she could call now and ask. Parents must be able to get deleted texts if they are really worried about their kids. Everyone always says all texts live out there in cyberspace forever. Was that only for the FBI? What about account holders, or Eddie Clarkson on a family plan? Did he have access to deleted texts? Caroline hankered for the horse-and-buggy days, when affairs unfolded in cornfields or a blacksmithery, undetected by pixels and screens. Of course, back then, she'd also be burned at the stake for what she was doing.

No doubt there was a little fuck-you to Eddie going on here. And that was part of the thrill, the butterflies. Her shrink could call it sadistic and try to get all into the base, sexual turn-on of hurting someone. But the motive was clear: to experience the easy liberation men do, the entitlement to wander.

Arthur had gotten a robust hand job from Marjina (or more) in the adjacent dressing room, and curled into bed with Annabelle fifteen minutes later. Eddie had fucked someone, *God knows who*, when Caroline was pregnant with Gigi. Why couldn't their women do the same?

But the guilt rolled in with the certainty of the Atlantic tide. It hit her now, frothing up and bubbling all around her. She was drowning, and she didn't entirely understand why she couldn't breathe. She walked in circles again.

What do I feel so bad about?

He's done it several times and did he feel this way!

Caroline was parched. She sipped her cool water, wondering why Thierry had really brought it to her. Was he trying to curry her favor? Why? Once Eddie calmed down, she'd talk to him about how he treated this sweet man. She'd explain that Thierry was not just another employee, but also the uncle of Gigi's best friend and, in effect, the girl's only parent. Eddie's tirades made Caroline uncomfortable, especially when she and Thierry would make plans for the girls, or talk about the girls' riding as friendly parents do on the sidelines. Yes, she'd talk to Eddie and maybe he'd give up some clue—how he met Thierry, say—that would lead to why on earth he'd been paying him for ten years.

She'd heard Eddie screaming at Thierry just that morning about the girls' tack trunks. It seemed those trunks were always a source of conflict. Maybe she should go into each one? But there were security cameras. Was that what Marcus McCree was doing that day, by coming out here with a pretense of delivering Gigi's jacket? Caroline didn't know exactly the significance of the trunks, but suddenly they seemed like a bigger deal than her sleeping with some nice architect she'd known since high school.

Chapter 37

Constant Cajoling

A WEEK LATER, MID-AUGUST

As Caroline slid her tray alongside the shrimp and lobster section of the Millshore Club's buffet, Annabelle bumped up behind her and whispered, "You can't say no."

"Jesus, what else are you making me do?" said Caroline, as Annabelle filled two glasses with Arnold Palmers. Two older women next to Caroline with bluish-gray hair and Lilly Pulitzer dresses shook their heads in disapproval: one did not talk so loudly at this club, and one did not hold other people up in line, especially while distracted by indiscreet conversation.

Caroline said to the server behind the counter, "A half lobster, and two crab claws, some of the cold asparagus in vinaigrette, and the . . ."

"I'm not *making* you do anything," Annabelle said, placing the two drinks on her tray.

"It is a miracle I survived that lunch. I'm not listening to you anymore," Caroline said.

"That crazy lunch at Duryea's built character. Besides, *noth-*

ing can ever be that bad again," Annabelle said. Then she ordered. "Hello Scottie. I'll have the usual chef salad, that small bowl is fine, don't forget I like it light on the cheese, red wine vinegar only, please."

As Annabelle gave the cashier her club number, Caroline studied both trays, hers overloaded with shellfish and fattening sauces, her friend's with starvation-level mini-portions.

While writing her membership account number on the check, Annabelle turned to Caroline and said, "What I'm asking you to do has nothing to do with getting laid."

One of the old ladies next to Caroline huffed out loud. This younger generation of club members was so sickeningly confessional. Why, in her day, you kept your business to yourself. She would complain to the executive committee and ask that bylaws be added prohibiting loud conversation at the food counters.

"You have to come to Linda Cockburn's for her belt and sandal trunk show I'm co-hosting on Thursday," Annabelle said, motioning for Caroline to follow her onto the club's ocean-side deck. "I know you hate her, but you can't just RSVP no like you did. You're my best friend."

"I don't hate her, just like I don't hate the WASPs at this club of yours. Linda's house for a lady's day sale is not my scene," Caroline said, dipping a piece of lobster tail into the bland, Protestant, mayonnaise sauce. "Has Arthur still not brought up Philippe?"

"Nope. And I've never come so close to puking my guts out on a dining table as I was at Duryea's. But no, we still haven't discussed it. That's just not our way," Annabelle said.

"And Philippe? Still nothing?"

"Not a word. Drama is not his style. I told you he's discreet."

"That's so goddamn weird," Caroline said, taking a gulp of her iced tea and lemonade, as she checked out some of the club go-ers: wet kids in their bright Vineyard Vines suits running from pool to ocean and back, parents who'd met at Andover mingling with other parents who'd met at Groton, older Protestants getting hammered on the club's signature Southsides (it was already one in the afternoon for heaven's sakes), and munching on peanuts or Ritz crackers and cheddar spread from a crock. "How could Philippe see what your husband was doing and not comment on that? What about seating you between them? Nothing?"

"Nope. And Eddie?"

"I'm convinced Eddie had no idea what he was doing by bringing Ryan to the table. He's such an extrovert, he wouldn't be able to keep it in."

Annabelle smiled at a family at the next table upon seeing their four-year-old girl dressed in the same lime-green Roberta Roller Rabbit cover-up with little seahorses on it, and the same lime-green and white Jack Rogers sandals as her mother. She said to them, "*Dying* on the outfits!" She then turned to Caroline and said, "Well, it's better if he's clueless. Let's work on developing *your* extrovert side, which barely exists: come to the sale. The Marvelous Mykonos sandals are really original. You'll love them. Just buy one pair."

Just then, towheaded twin boys in hot pink Vilebrequin bathing suits ran by, knocking Annabelle's tote off the back of her chair. Their father (in the grown-up version of the same Vilebrequin suit), horrified at his hooligans, lassoed them and forced them to "apologize to Mrs. von Tattenbach" as if they'd bruised the Queen of England.

Caroline leaned into her friend and said, "You do know every single child here has white hair and blue eyes." She looked around. "I haven't been here for two summers, I'd forgotten how preppy preppy can be." She crunched on a taro chip. "These chips are positively daring."

"What do you want me to do?" Annabelle asked. "I grew up

here, literally eating this bad chef salad in this blue wooden seat, lost my virginity on the grass courts here, Arthur likes the golf. People here like routine . . . like the underseasoned food."

"You mean *unseasoned* food," said Caroline.

Annabelle waved to a woman in a tragically out-of-date pink-and-orange Tory Burch caftan and a sun hat the size of a flying saucer. "See you at the beach later!" She then said to Caroline, "You have to understand, Linda and all those women don't mind you being there, they just look down on you."

"Lovely distinction, you're right," Caroline said, laughing.

"Has their mean-girl bullshit ever really gotten to you? C'mon!"

"I think it has," Caroline replied, remembering that, besides Annabelle, her life in Manhattan was pretty much friendless. If Caroline had a few more women around her, her city "experiment" might have been different. "Why don't you just write a check for twenty thousand dollars for the charity? You know that's a lot more than the sale will bring in."

"The stuff is kinda nice, kinda . . ."

"Please. Linda Cockburn pretends to source cashmere from some rare goat in Tashkent and that other woman, Tina what's-her-face, who lives at these trunk shows, says she sources her crocodile hides from an undiscovered swamp in the rain forest."

"It's not a swamp, it's the Amazon," Annabelle said, not knowing why she felt the need to defend any of these women. "You just don't like her because she's so into her Park Avenue life."

"No, Annabelle, I'm not judgmental that way," Caroline reminded her, polishing off her last crab claw. "You, with your warehouse of Tiffany china that you switch for the seasons: pinecones for Christmas, Easter eggs in the spring, pumpkins for fall, what's summer again?"

"There's like five summer patterns, mostly shells or fish. And summer is not for Tiffany, too delicate, Italian ceramics from Positano are what I have out now," Annabelle said, dousing her bland iceberg lettuce with pepper.

"And I still love you because you're a ballsy, hilarious bitch. But those other women are so 1950s, parking their brains once they marry Mr. Richie Rich, or," she looked around her, "one of these genetically interbred, blond Millshore men."

"You think?" Annabelle joked.

"I don't think, I know, and like them: you went to prep school at Exeter—or 'prepped' at Exeter, as your mother says—before Dartmouth. But you're an SAT tutor for the scholarship kids at four inner-city schools. Why? Because you yourself said they can't afford the tutors the rich kids can. You *use* your education. What are those other women doing besides hosting high-end Tupperware parties?"

"*I agree with you*," Annabelle said. "And it's not like I'm scared to tell them so. I warn Linda all the time: go do something serious so that when you're fifty-five years old, an empty nester, and your Henry falls for the yoga teacher, you can go get hired somewhere. But they don't listen to me. Come because you set an example: you kept your job, even when you didn't need to."

"Who says I don't need to? My anxieties come in handy sometimes, because I don't trust Eddie to support us forever. I love design, but I'm also being prudent. Everything could go down the tank," she pointed out. "If I leave, yeah, I'll have some of his money, but what if he's hiding it all in some tax haven in Bermuda? What if he loses it all in some scheme? At least my design jobs will support me and, presumably, Eddie would have saved enough to support the kids."

"Okay, so then Linda's house is like eighteen thousand square feet, go get some inspiration for your other clients, keep your skills honed," Annabelle said. "These women are into interior design porn, you are too, I know. Check out how much the owners spent on this room or that, have some rosé, shop a little, do some good.

All the money goes to the Bridgehampton Child Care Center, many of those moms are infirm somehow, part of the year-round population who need our support . . . it's a *thing*, a little *to-do* for Linda's company."

"I like that Bridgehampton Center, my mom used to work there," Caroline added. "And when is this to-do again?"

"This Thursday at four. You're a sport. And I admit it, when Linda calls Marvelous Mykonos her 'company,' it drives me crazy," Annabelle said. "It just isn't a company: Linda bought twenty thousand dollars' worth of merchandise on her last boozy trip to Mykonos with the girls, of course, NetJetting everyone there, and now she's just reselling it and acting as if she somehow curated a floor at the Athens pop-up of Bergdorf Goodman."

Just then, an officious-looking man in horn-rimmed glasses, a bow tie, and a blue blazer walked up to the table. "Mrs. von Tattenbach, sorry to interrupt, but the deadline is today at five in the afternoon," he said. "I have you and Mrs. Wentworth as the member-guest team for this weekend's championship. And your girls are partnered up, I assume?"

"Sorry, Mr. Bancroft, you'll have those names by then. You know how difficult four girls can be to nail down," Annabelle said. After Mr. Bancroft spirited away to check on more of these absent-minded members, Annabelle asked Caroline, "You've been so skittish about Eddie and his business recently. What are you so worried about?" As the same two older ladies in the Lilly Pulitzers walked by, Annabelle said, "Your husband is loaded, and as far as Arthur and I can tell, more loaded all the time. You're fine!" The two older women shook their heads, once again lamenting the manners of the new generation.

"I haven't wanted to tell the whole deal until I understood it more, but I ran across more papers at the barn," Caroline said.

"What were they?"

"Eddie's private files, much more than the ledgers I told you about."

"How did you see them?"

"I have several keys to his office and cabinets," Caroline said.

"You're going through Eddie's locked files? First, his iPad and ledgers and now his keys? Were you looking for sexy letters?"

"I wish," Caroline said. "Women are the least of my concerns at this point."

"What is it?" Annabelle asked, crunching on a stale breadstick from the plastic basket on the table.

"I don't know yet, but it's too many payments overseas, frankly too much money going in and out of weird code-worded entities that have nothing to do with horses and hay," Caroline said. She was worried that Eddie was in legal trouble, and it frightened her. She turned to Annabelle and added, "I'm sorry. I'll be at the sale. I know you're right . . . the rosé and the tea sandwiches get those rich women all sauced up and primed to shop. Then they remember the Bridgehampton Center at Christmas and send another five grand, and it's all smart marketing on your behalf . . . so yes, I will buy ugly sandals from Mykonos so that we can help other women who have bigger problems than which beads are on the tips of their shoes."

Chapter 38

Trapped at a Trunk Show

As Caroline got out of the car, the breezeless air stuck to her like cellophane.

"Ahem. Your keys, ma'am?" the valet asked.

"Oh, sorry," Caroline said, handing him the keys. Linda Cockburn's summer home was much bigger than Caroline realized. "How many women have arrived?" she asked.

"Has to be a couple dozen."

That sounded like more than enough women to make the show successful. Caroline considered getting back into the Jeep but knew that would infuriate Annabelle.

As an inside joke, Caroline had worn the Gucci hot pink satin slides that Annabelle had found for her. They were a special edition, with zebra skin as piping and on the inside sole. Gucci had made a teeny quantity, only a few pairs in each size for the Fifth Avenue store, sold out way before they even put a pair on a shelf. Annabelle had written on the gift card: *Armor for those ladies' events I make you go to. So you can outdo the women you so love to hate. They are going to PANIC when they see you in these.*

Caroline would walk in soon, but the many yapping women could wait a bit longer while she surveyed the five-acre property, ogling some of that real estate porn Annabelle had promised. The land sprawled to her left and right, with abundant hydrangeas in bloom everywhere. She figured the landscaping bill alone had to be two hundred thousand dollars a year. She counted the windows and guessed there must be twenty rooms upstairs.

The white stucco exterior, large porches, and enormous columns out front read more nouveau chateau than beach house, hardly inspiration for her own clients. The furniture on the deck, groupings of lounge chairs with golden legs and leopard-print cushions, made Caroline wonder what charlatan was responsible for the decor.

Awestruck at the mini-golf course to her right and the weeping hemlock orchard to her left, Caroline figured if design didn't work out, she could make a documentary film about Upper East Side ladies—the ones inside chomping on endive with tuna tartare. This bona fide tribe, their customs, and unique behavior was surely worthy of study. Her documentary, *America's Most Annoying Housewives,* wouldn't air on Bravo, but on the Discovery Channel, right after a show about killer bees or the headhunters of Papua New Guinea.

Armed with her hot pink satin slides, Caroline steeled herself to face the creatures inside. But before she could knock, the door swung open and a blast of artificially cooled air hit her in the face. (It was like a meat locker inside, and in a sense, it was, of course, best if the surgically remastered tissues of the women in there were preserved in the cold.)

One man was to open the door, another to stand sentry by the front entrance. He faced sideways, expressionless, like a Beefeater at Buckingham Palace. Each man had the house moniker, *Ocean*

Spray, stitched on his white polo shirt. Linda and her husband, Henry, had given their home a title as if it were a Scottish manor, obviously missing the cranberry juice reference.

In high school, Caroline used to drive by these estates with her girlfriends and wonder about the titles painted on wooden placards out front: *Willow Manor, Whispering Meadows* . . . The girls imagined fancy European counts lived inside. Now that she could actually enter these places (something she'd never imagined in her youth), she understood the naming trend was a pretentious play for social acceptance.

A housekeeper appeared in a tan staff uniform with a tan lace demi-apron. She offered to help Caroline in any way she could, putting her hands out to take something . . . anything. A short, awkward moment ensued when Caroline handed the woman her purse, then drew it back.

"Sorry . . . I don't mean I don't trust you with it. I just want to keep it actually."

With nothing else to do, the woman then opened her palm to guide Caroline from the marble foyer into the living area, as if Caroline were being escorted to an audience with Cleopatra.

The housekeeper's short white socks were stitched with tan lace that matched her apron. On her head, she had a little lace paper hat, like a nanny in a Disney cartoon. Many rich New York women like Linda insisted that their staff wear proper uniforms for day, night, and for different seasons—gray or tan in summer and darker colors during colder months. The staff was a projection of the employer's wealth and stature. Caroline smiled to herself upon seeing this woman in costume; when she first moved to the Upper East Side, she noted two types of couples made their staff dress in strict uniforms: American aristocrats whose ancestors actually hobnobbed with the Astors and Rockefellers, or those fakers desperate to project an old-world image.

Through the baronial front hallway, rich red fabrics and bright jewel-toned heavy rugs and curtains adorned the rooms. Linda's aesthetic reminded Caroline of the 1980s television series *Dallas*, the dark wood paneling completely out of place in East Hampton.

Caroline so wished Ryan were here. They had talked about how important it was to match homes with the Long Island environment of sand, water, salt, and brush. In her own design jobs, she steered clients toward floors the color of driftwood and white-washed furniture, or toward a more Bohemian look, with vintage blankets on the back of rattan loungers. Though it wasn't her style, she loved Annabelle's fancier home, done in light paisleys and summer stripes that made sense alongside the white wicker furniture she'd inherited from her preppy family.

"Tell me how crazy those big design jobs can be," Ryan had said, pouring her more wine.

"You're really interested in this stuff?"

"Very," he had answered. "I only see the quaint, restored homes; I rarely go into McMansions out here." Ryan sometimes reminded her of Joey. Both men got her going on silly topics, which made her excited just to be with them. Ryan added, "I think it's almost impossible, no matter how much style you have, to make an enormous house really chic. I'd die to go with you to a thirty-million-dollar design disaster."

Caroline agreed. The two were speaking an East Hampton local dialect; it was shared by those who didn't get snookered into projecting a bullshit impression of who they really were. This was the reason she'd fought Eddie so hard to keep their reasonably sized house near Bluff Road where she'd grown up. Ryan was entirely on her wavelength. "There are so many cool possibilities to make a beach house work. But, in the end, the product should fit the client and nature—*not* what the lady of the house hopes will make her appear richest as fuckest."

She wished there was a way to show Ryan this craven Cockburn palace. The rug had hexagon patterns of gold and maroon, while the couches were covered in a brocade in varying shades of royal blue, forest green, and deep red. The coffee tables were made of shiny metal and glass as if in some high-rise condo, and on top were expensive art books that were no doubt purchased by the designer's intern. The walls, covered in bookcases, held leather-bound volumes, their spines uncracked. All of it was dictated by someone other than the people who lived here.

As she entered the main room, women stood in clusters. Caroline hadn't gotten the memo that crisp pants and a silk blouse were a no-go at this lunch. All of the attendees, many of whom clocked in at about twenty pounds under anorexic, wore designer sundresses (most were Dolce & Gabbana) that showed off their rail-thin figures, maintained with a combination of rigorous exercise and CoolSculpting. In her decade in Manhattan, Caroline also became a plastic surgery expert, knowing there were two kinds of above-the-neck interventions. Some faces, the skin so stretched back, looked as if they were in front of a wind tunnel, and this meant full-on facelift. Others, the skin shiny with Botox, the cheeks plump (always unevenly so), more like a chipmunk who had run into a tree, had gone for injections and filler.

Caroline tried to appear occupied as she looked around, but she couldn't find Annabelle. Being surrounded by women who would rather choke on their fourth radish of the day than talk to her left Caroline with one destination: the gold powder room. She texted Annabelle from inside:

Where the hell are you?

Annabelle told her she was outside on the back deck. Caroline found her surrounded by a small cluster of mothers from the all-girls Spence School, munching on a piece of raw salmon rolled in a thin cucumber ribbon. One of them said, "Can you believe the new chef at school used to work in the *White House*?"

In a whisper, Caroline said in Annabelle's ear, "This was worse than I had imagined: trapped at a trunk show."

Annabelle put her arm warmly around Caroline and walked away from the cackling hens around her. "I do owe you, I recognize that."

"These women treat me like I'm the gardener or a tutor or something," Caroline said. "Besides, the lemon yellow and chartreuse dresses drifting around these rooms lined in jewel tones are giving me vertigo. You owe me."

"Well, then make yourself useful," Annabelle said. "Go shop and pretend to be excited to try on oodles of new shoes, none as nice as yours!" She ushered Caroline in the direction of the Marvelous Mykonos stand as if she were pushing a child to say thank you to her grandma.

In the sales corner of the room, several women were trying on belts, sandals, scarves, and blouses. Caroline didn't want new clothes. She never much liked beaded anything. The least expensive belt was $850, and the least expensive sandal was $450. Eddie wouldn't care what she paid, but she didn't like anything at all. The women around her didn't say hello; they smiled at her as if they'd just smelled cat poop.

Recognizing fresh prey, Linda homed in on Caroline. "This stuff is sooo good, isn't it?"

Caroline raised an eyebrow and said, "Fabulous."

Linda checked out Caroline's bland pant and blouse outfit and thought, *This woman can't help herself, poor thing.* But then, Linda saw her shoes: "Wait a minute . . . are those . . . not the actual zebra."

"Yes, Gucci." Caroline kept it cool and picked up a pair of sandals she'd never wear.

"And how did you . . ." Linda said, confused. "I mean, what list were you on?"

"I don't know," Caroline said. "Just, I guess Barney's and the Gucci flagship store kept me in mind for their 2019 resort collection."

Linda cleared her throat and put her hands on her hips. "Honey, resort comes after fall, end of the year, not in May when you had to have gotten those."

"I just meant . . ."

"And no one calls the Fifty-Sixth Street Gucci masterpiece 'the flagship store.' That's for H&M, or maybe Uniqlo." Linda Cockburn snorted. "Clearly, Annabelle got them for you." She grabbed navy beaded sandals and spoke to Caroline like she was explaining 2 + 2 = 4 to a nursery school student. "Honey, these sandals will look incredible with those, uh, white, uh, slacks."

"I'm good, Linda. I'm going to figure it all out on my own," Caroline said and smiled. "It's more fun for me that way."

"Apparently!" Linda huffed. Then she turned to educate another pupil. Of course, she returned three minutes later to see if she could nudge Caroline along, and perhaps loosen up her wallet a bit too. "So . . . your decisions are?"

Caroline stared back at Linda and cocked her head to the side. Linda continued, "No pressure at all, but, hey, you didn't grow up in Manhattan, we all know that! And, well, being raised in, well, *out here*, I imagine you grew up with a different aesthetic, right? How about one belt and one pair of sandals in every color?" Linda snorted loudly, pleased with her clever observations. "Then it'll be like those Garanimals outfits some kids used to wear: you won't even have to think about getting dressed and looking good!"

Chapter 39

Barn Blockbuster

Gigi called just as Caroline was driving her car through the front gate of Sea Crest Stables. "Don't come yet, Mom."

"Honey, I'm here already. We said four-thirty."

"I want ten more minutes to hose off the horses. Please?" Gigi pleaded. "Rosie is helping, and I want to too. Her uncle said I could."

"If you have more work to do, that's fine," Caroline said. "You don't have to make excuses to take care of the horses. You need like twenty minutes? Or more?"

"Can I have more?"

"Well, how about I come find you in thirty minutes, and we'll see where you are? I'll read in the sun a little."

As Caroline walked down a manicured grass lane between show rings, she saw Annabelle's Maserati parked in a corner far from the main entrance. Caroline walked in that direction and waved.

Annabelle turned around quickly, then gave up, knowing that Caroline had seen her. She took a breath before marching resolutely toward her friend.

"Hey," Annabelle said. "Thanks for coming to the trunk show. You know you'll wear that belt you got a few times." They walked over to a wooden rail fence that penned in a horse cantering around by itself, with no other horses nearby.

"No, I won't," Caroline said. "I won't ever wear it, and you know that. So, why are you . . . here?" Caroline asked. "It's not like you to leave an event you're hosting early."

"It's fun to see the animals happy," Annabelle said. "I worry about them in the stables all the time."

"You ever notice that you never see two horses in the same turn-out area?" Caroline said, resting her elbows on the top of the three-tier fence and tugging the brim of her hat down to shield her eyes.

"When the horses run around freely with no saddle or bridles they can hurt each other if they're in the same ring," Annabelle said. "They know this is their time for free play. It's like recess. So they get a little extra fresh and excited, and they have to be protected from each other."

"Well that makes sense," Caroline said. "Of course, what do I know? I'm half-scared of horses anyway."

"I'm going to go check on mine in a minute," Annabelle said, fluffing her hair and shaking it out as if she were readying herself for a photo shoot. "I haven't seen my baby, Seaside, in days."

"You're not prettying yourself up for a horse, Annabelle."

Annabelle reached into her bag, put on some gloss, and smacked her lips a little. Then, she checked that her shell earrings were on snugly.

"Yes, make sure those aren't going anywhere," Caroline said. "I mean, I know you said you were done with Philippe. But you never know when you might change your mind, do you? And you could lose an earring with all that wrestling in the sheets. And those look expensive."

"Philippe and I remain civil and friendly. He's training my

daughters, for God's sakes. But, if you must know, I'm meeting someone else: a father who has a daughter who rides here. Thaddeus Bradley: he's blond, a charmer, and I used to roll around with him on the grass courts of the Millshore Club growing up."

"You trust a guy names Thaddeus, who comes from parents who would choose that name?" Caroline asked, waving at Gigi and Rosie, who were leading Scooby-Doo and Sauerkraut into separate paddocks fifty yards away. Though Gigi was wearing rubber boots, she was caked in mud up to her thighs.

"Thaddeus gets around, but he's one of those gentlemanly preppies who knows to keep his mouth shut. I'm sure plenty of the women at my club have slept with him, and he's never told a soul." Annabelle put on her sun hat and fished around in her bag for her sunglasses. The horse in the ring sauntered over, expecting a treat from her bag. She patted his nose and said, "Sorry, baby. No carrots."

"And where will you go with this Thaddeus?" Caroline asked.

"A little inn."

"Walking through the lobby of a cute little inn in the Hamptons isn't smart. There will be people there—people who *know* you."

"He suggested the Southampton Bay View Motel," Annabelle said.

"The what?"

Annabelle nodded. "Way down on that highway back behind the Southampton movie theater, near the Hampton Maid breakfast spot. It's practically another country."

"You'll survive in a motel?"

Annabelle snorted. "His house has a lot of Brazilian help, and we both agree they probably know my help," she said. "Stop worrying, I got this."

"Okay," Caroline said. "But before you take the mulligan with a preppy guy . . ."

"Not some random preppy. He's a lawyer, a good one." Annabelle said with authority. "He's a spectacular piece of ass, always has been. I can just tell he's great in bed. His girlfriend caught us on the court in high school, so it didn't go further way back when, but it was hot back then, and will be more today because we've been flirting now for twenty years since. But if we're objectifying men, well, we might as well use them fully, until their benefits have ceased to be benefits."

"I get that. They might as well be good in bed," Caroline said. Why not let her friend off the hook? They were in this together.

Caroline wrapped a sweatshirt over her shoulders and asked Annabelle, "Should we get going? I have to get my kid, and you've got your new clubby guy. He's probably all excited he's landed a fellow WASP aristocrat. Maybe you're not the only one doing the objectifying."

"Thaddeus's not one to kiss and tell," said Annabelle. "And it wasn't only on the grass courts. I blew him once at the Andover–Exeter game. We laugh about it now."

"And you don't think half his Andover class knows that?" Caroline said. "You think he doesn't talk about you now? You think men ever stop being boys?"

"I'm doing it once more now, because I'm just in the mood," Annabelle said, flinging her bag over her shoulder. "And it could well be the last time I stray."

"Don't talk like your life is over because today might be the last time you sleep with some preppy guy," Caroline said, jabbing her with her elbow softly as they walked toward the barn. "You could do that every week for the rest of your life given your power and popularity at that club. We vowed to protect each other."

"Whoa," Annabelle stopped and faced Caroline. "Don't pretend that what you're doing isn't a whole other level of unsafe."

"Agreed," Caroline whispered, making sure no one was within

earshot. "My choosing a married man was reckless in its way too, I know."

"So what are you going to do, Little Miss Schoolmarm who's trying to protect me? What if Ryan's wife finds out or, worse, if Ryan falls in love with you?" Annabelle was trying to reason with Caroline, but it sounded like she was reprimanding her. "Then *you've* got big, serious stuff to deal with. I've just fooled around with an experienced playboy." She put two fingers in the air and leaned in. "*Deux,* if I'm lucky! You're the one playing with fire."

Caroline shook her head. "You're wrong. Ryan's got an amazing character."

"Oh, really?" Annabelle said.

"Really. Ryan and I have a lovely deal going. It's hot, for sure, but it's also very neat. *And* there's a clear ending."

Sex with Ryan was becoming more than a transaction, but Caroline wasn't going to admit that to Annabelle. The prospect of ending her arrangement with Ryan by the end of summer was tugging at Caroline's heart. It was August. The corn across the island was taller now, husks popping out in all directions—autumn was coming.

"You got a Labor Day deadline with him?" Annabelle asked. "Did you agree on an expiration date?"

Caroline nodded and scrunched up her lips, smiling.

"You're full of it, I can tell," Annabelle said. "It's not all neat."

"I mean, it's not an actual expiration date. Maybe we let it slide into September? Early September is still summer."

Annabelle put her arm around her friend and said, "Ryan would look good in a turtleneck, but you just can't."

The women walked in silence around the back of the barns. As they did, a delivery truck, leaving the compound, stopped at the back gate and idled. The driver turned and saw Caroline. Then he put a Yankees cap on, slouched a bit, and put the truck in reverse.

His eyes hadn't betrayed him out on the bay on the Boston Whaler that day. She was even more beautiful now. She was paying no attention to him. How could he not take another look at her now?

"Annabelle, have fun," Caroline said. "I've got to find the girls, and you've got to, you know, have that last naughty lay of your adult life."

Caroline went stall to stall looking for her daughter. Instead, she found Thierry, polishing up Gigi's trunk. "Thank you so much, Thierry," she said. "But honestly I'd prefer if you let her do that."

Thierry stood suddenly. "I'm so sorry," he said.

"I'm not the boss, Thierry. You don't need to be so worried." Caroline placed her hand on his shoulder. She wondered what Eddie had done to him to make him so skittish. "I don't care at all how you run the barn. It's just, as Gigi's mom, I want her taking care of her own stuff. I'm sure you want the same for Rosie."

"I do, of course. I'm so sorry." Thierry kicked the side of the trunk a few times with his foot.

"Is there a problem with the trunk?" Caroline asked.

"Nope, just an edge here."

"Should I . . ."

"Nope. I got it," Thierry replied, blocking Caroline's path to the trunk.

He was acting strangely, but she let it go.

She finally found Gigi and Rosie out in the back, soaked and filthy from working the hoses. The girls scuttled out to the field where they often constructed jumps out of logs and, pretending to be horses, cantered around and leaped over them. She was worried she'd never get them out of here, and it was time to pick up Theo.

She yelled to the girls, "Two-minute warning! In the car before then, girls. I mean it!" The rascals didn't even look back at her, and they rounded a corner, out of sight.

Caroline began mentally cataloging what fresh food she had in the house. There'd be three hungry kids now; Gigi would demand a sleepover with Rosie. There was some salmon. She could coat the fish in something sweet, so it candied under the broiler. For once, the kids might agree to something that wasn't white and starchy. Frozen veggies were a travesty during the summer on Long Island, but she did have some peas in the freezer, and with butter and some dill from her garden they'd do the trick. Lost in contemplating her maternal duties, she walked around the back of the stables in her ongoing search for the girls.

There, she saw something she thought she'd never see again.

The truck was there. Beneath the brim of the driver's cap was Joey Whitten's profile, the unmistakable square jaw. He was driving slowly across the back lot where hay, feed, and shavings were stored. She blinked a few times, wondering how her vision could betray her again, for the second time since the day she saw the Boston Whaler. She walked briskly after the truck, but it disappeared around a corner. *It was almost as if the driver knew she was following him.*

The hair on the back of Caroline's neck was standing up. She was disoriented and blinked water out of her eyes. Her brain wasn't working; she was seeing things that weren't there.

She surveyed the complex before her. She saw Thierry helping grooms with a wheelbarrow and feed. A young worker hosing off an enormous black stallion. Rays of the late summer sun streaming through the droplets of spray created a rainbow around the silhouette of the wet beast.

Over to the far right, the truck reappeared. Maybe it was a cousin of Joey's, someone she had never met who had grown up to resemble Joey so strongly that it shook her to her core? Maybe she should introduce herself, and ask what his family name was. After all, lots of men had strong jaws. She marched toward the truck, willing herself to think more clearly.

But then, instead of continuing on its way, the truck stopped. Caroline froze. Again, it was as if the driver knew she was trailing him. The truck backed up and turned enough so that the driver was in her line of sight.

Joey Whitten stuck his head out of the driver's side window.

"No, you're not crazy," he said. "And it's good to see you too. More soon."

Then, the truck accelerated down the road and out the back gate, racing so fast a cloud of dust hid it from view.

CAROLINE LEANED AGAINST a tree to support herself. She inhaled deeply, through her nose, trying to soothe her throbbing heart. Her pulse was pounding loudly inside her ears. She held her breath for several seconds, then blew it out from her sternum. And again.

Stretching her arms wide, she splayed out her fingers. Her hands were vibrating. To steady them, she pressed her palms to her cheeks. Sliding down the tree's trunk, she slumped into the mulch at its base. She sat cross-legged, the hard edges of the wood chips scraping the thin skin of her ankles. The pain was helping to ground her; it made her feel alive and present and not out of her mind crazy. Her bag fell from her shoulder. Her keys, makeup, and coins poured out mingled with the mulch as the bag tipped over. She was sobbing, her shoulders convulsing.

She said out loud, to no one but herself: "I still love him."

Chapter 40

Focus on the Big and the Little

Several minutes later, Caroline felt a child's hand tapping her gently on the head. "Mom! Are you okay? You're being really weird."

She looked up at her daughter, wiping tears from her eyes and smiling so much her cheeks ached. "I'm okay. I'm okay," she said. "I mean, I just felt dizzy for a second." She sniffled and started laughing again.

Joey had not drowned in the Atlantic. Why didn't the rest of her listen to the part of her that knew he was alive? She was sure his father knew, all the times he'd said it couldn't happen . . .

"Mom!" Gigi said. "You're embarrassing me. Please stand up or sit in the grass, just not in the mud. And are you crying or laughing?"

TEN MINUTES LATER, Caroline, Gigi, and Rosie were in the parking lot. When Gigi informed her mother that she absolutely had to have a sleepover with Rosie "or she might die," Caroline agreed. At that point, she would have let the girls take a rocket to the moon. When the girls piled into the back seat muddy and wet, Caroline didn't even notice.

Once they were buckled in their seats, Gigi asked, "Mom? We're in the car. Turn it on and drive. Why are you so spaced out?"

"I'm fine," Caroline said, looking down Spring Farm Lane to see if the truck had returned. It hadn't, though. It was gone.

Caroline turned the engine on. Then she turned it off and got out of the car. She decided she would talk to Thierry about what she had seen. He always seemed like he wanted to tell her something, and now she was pretty sure it involved Joey Whitten. After a minute, she reconsidered and got back into the car. Asking Thierry about the truck might not be smart. She wouldn't call Joey's family either. She needed to sleuth much more first.

She started driving and decided that cooking salmon for three hungry kids was out of the question. With a Theo energized from his playdate now picked up, she announced that she'd take them all to the Navy Beach restaurant that looked out over a calm Fort Pond Bay. It was August, and the water would still be warm enough for the kids to wash off the dirt of the day. Meanwhile, she could have a drink to quiet herself down.

As she parked, she told the kids, "Each of you grab a bathing suit from the trunk, and a towel. I'll let you go in the water a bit before dinner."

The kids ran toward the water, sand flicking up behind their heels. The early evening sun was still bright enough that she needed her sunglasses. Watching them, Caroline slipped off her sandals and felt the sand between her toes. She looked down at the slanted boulder she and Joey used to sit on by the shore. A flood of memories washed over her with the force of a tsunami.

He'd taken her here, to Navy Beach, before they went to his parents' house for photos with four other couples. The night of the prom she'd worn a yellow gown that cinched in the middle. She hadn't minded that it got wrinkled and sandy at this beach at sunset. She spent the night yanking at the thick, elastic ribbon surrounding her rib cage, trying to free herself. Joey kept his arm around her waist most of the evening, and he would squeeze her breasts when they popped out of the top, apologizing for not being able to keep his hands off her.

And at Navy Beach, Joey, in his tuxedo, so unnatural for the rough guy he was, balled up the jacket beside him. His mother had put gel in his unruly, dirty-blond hair and he'd wanted to skinny dip in the bay to wash it out.

He'd told her things that night, at this very spot, that she'd never forget.

I'm never leaving your side.

"TABLE FOR FOUR? Just you and the three kids?" the hostess asked. "Hey, are you okay?"

"I'm totally fine," Caroline said. "I'm sorry, I'm just distracted with the kids. I'd love to sit by that rock down there and order a glass of something and then come back up for dinner. Can you save us a table?"

"Of course," the hostess said. She then disappeared behind swinging doors and when she returned she had a thick cotton blanket in her hands. "Take this, it's really nice to lean on," she said. "That rock is a little sharp, but it's my favorite spot too."

The sun now cast a purple haze that spread across the bay. Children were running in and out of the small lapping waves, while dogs fetched sticks and leaped in pirouettes for Frisbees and bald tennis balls. On the deck of the restaurant, sailcloth hung from wooden beams to protect the tables from the wind and sand. Mothers nibbling on baskets of crudités chattered away about how to perfect their backhands or spend their husbands' money more creatively.

As Caroline walked to her table, she heard one mother joke, "Eric told me I could spend whatever I wanted on the beach house.

When I was done, he said I was the only woman in America who had exceeded an unlimited budget!" Loud cackles followed.

"You guys, leave your sweatshirts here on the benches, so no one takes our seats," Caroline told the kids. She felt so tired. "I need to go for a little walk down to that boulder, not far. Can you girls watch Theo?"

Theo put his thumb in his mouth, and he slowly blinked. New plan: she pulled over an armchair she knew he would fall asleep in. She positioned another chair in front for him to stretch his legs out. From twenty yards down at the bay, she could watch him dozing. Caroline ripped open a packet of breadsticks with her teeth and handed them to Theo, kissing his forehead. Then she placed her iPad on his lap. "Any game, as long as you want."

A waitress put a special menu checklist on the table next to a jar of pencils. "You all mark off what you want."

"How about you girls do the ordering?" Caroline said, knowing they would order too much, but enjoy the responsibility.

"And for you, ma'am?" Gigi asked, giggling.

"I'll have the fried shrimp plate. My son would love some too," Caroline said. Normally she couldn't be bothered with healthy-mom quinoa combos, and today she didn't even want her favorite oysters. Fattening foods, when eaten at the right time, solved a lot of life's problems. "Order whatever you girls want," she told Gigi and Rosie.

"Really?"

"Really," Caroline said. "It's a special night. A very special night."

The left side of the boulder was round, while the middle and right side had slanted, smooth spots that sloped all the way to the sand. When she and Joey first came here, they'd sit on the top, his arm wrapped around her. Then, they'd slide down to the sand and lay back against the slanted face.

Sitting down now, leaning against the rock, she draped her elbow across her face to exist in darkness and deep thought. Joey Whitten's appearance had made the world spin round her so fast she buried her fingers in the sand to slow it down.

"I'm never leaving your side," Joey had said as they'd laid out a blanket. "Even if you marry someone else, I'm not leaving. I'll be the painter, the contractor, the paperboy. I don't care."

Caroline had smiled. "We'll see," she said. "We don't even know how we're going to make college work."

"Everything will work," he'd said. "I promise. I'm not going anywhere." They had made six good years work before that day in the currents.

Caroline glanced over at Theo in the chair, occupied and happy with breadsticks and his screen. Down near the water, the girls were playing with other kids, making a pile of small rocks. As usual, Rosie was bossing around the whole project, making new friends, and Gigi was quietly playing along, but to the side. She was relieved that they didn't seem interested in going deeper into the bay. If they got in over their knees, she'd have to go over. Even though a lifeguard was watching from a plastic chair, and the water was still as a skating rink, there was no way she could relax with the kids in the bay.

The waitress came out to the beach and walked over to her with a small tray. From her supine position, she couldn't quite tell what was on it.

"Okay, so you got a glass of wine, fries, and garlic aioli," she said. The girl, clearly clairvoyant, placed a white ceramic bucket of steaming French fries on the sand beside her. A sheet of pastry paper soaked up some of the cooking grease. The crystals of sea salt poured on top sparkled in the sun. "You know, I've had this job for three summers now," she said to Caroline, "and sometimes, there's a mom here who clearly needs a break." The waitress smiled and pressed the base of a plastic goblet of white wine into the sand.

It had a stick in the bottom and was designed to be planted in a beach. She looked down at Caroline and said, "French fries and white wine on a summer evening cure anything, at least in my book."

Caroline sipped the cool wine and felt it enter her veins like a sedative.

"Also, just so you know, we have a service to drive people home in their own cars," the waitress said. "The guys put their motorized bikes in the trunk and ride back. So, have a few drinks, and one of the valets will drive you and the kids home. It's thirty dollars."

Caroline shielded her eyes from the sunlight and smiled at the young woman. "I'm not sure what I need and when, but all you're doing and suggesting is helping. A lot. You're kind to bring this down here, and even kinder to worry about me."

"You know what's sort of funny?"

"Tell me," Caroline said.

"I couldn't tell if you were from out here, or from the city. At first, I thought out here, but then, well, you look so tired, so I thought maybe just city."

"City women are more tired?"

"Yes. And more frazzled. They're always stressed about when the food's coming, when it really shouldn't matter with this view, right?"

Caroline started to protest that she wasn't a rich mom from the city with no job, and that she worked hard on her designing, but she let it go. "You're right," she said. "There are no struggles that French fries and wine won't fix, or at least put a Band-Aid on."

"That's what my mom says too. And don't forget the drive-home service, I remind anyone I give wine to. The cops have checkpoints everywhere around here, and they're waiting for you."

"Roger that," Caroline said, and smiled, lying back, remembering more . . . Joey's hands always grabbing her thighs hard, the way he wouldn't let go like he couldn't ever get enough of her.

A child's foot tickled her leg. Gigi took a French fry. "Mom, you know the glass has a stick on the bottom, so it stands up in the sand?"

Like puppies, the girls had circled back to their protector. They hovered around Caroline while looking out at the other children still playing in the sand. Soon, she knew, they would scamper away again. Theo was now asleep on the two chairs, coming down from too much candy and activity on his playdate.

Gigi and Rosie stood beside her in bare feet and locked their arms. "Is the water cold?" Caroline asked them.

"Not really. Can we go in?" asked Rosie.

"Only to the top of your legs unless I'm standing with you."

Caroline started rubbing the crusted wet sand off their cute little feet. Then, she touched each of Rosie's ten toes. "You girls chose a lovely purple for those toenails last week." She pushed their feet together side by side and studied them. "Look at how similar your feet are, girls! I never noticed that, did you?"

"Yes, Mom," said Gigi, rolling her eyes. "Like every time we wear flip-flops. Our fourth toes both roll out, then the pinkies are back straight, but super chubby. We hate our pinkies."

"Yeah, we hate our pinkies," said Rosie.

"Well, I think you both have adorable little toes," Caroline said, leaning on her elbow to look more closely. The girls' big toes were identical. The index and middle toes curled over. And the fourth, in the opposite direction.

Caroline kneeled now. She pushed the girls' hips together, so their feet were in line.

It was bizarre.

Thierry was Rosie's uncle, not her father, but she found herself wondering about his feet. Did his fourth toe curl in too?

Her mind doubled over: Eddie had these chubby toes too. That same fourth toe. The two that curled in a little. The feet before her were miniature versions of Eddie's.

"Rosie, you literally have the same feet as Gigi! The second toe is so cute, the third even cuter, the fourth a little curly, and the pinkie all . . ."

"We both love horses, we have the same feet, and we have the same nail polish," Rosie said. "We're like sisters!"

"Can we go now, Mom? Can we go to the water, please?" Gigi asked.

Caroline nodded and watched as the girls bounded toward the sea. Enough about the feet for now. How could she focus on anything but Joey and his casual nod, as if coming back from the dead was a daily occurrence?

If she hadn't encountered Joey earlier that day, she might have thought a little more about Rosie's feet, or about her stocky—somehow familiar—waddle as she ran toward the ocean.

Chapter 41

That Dashing Little Binaca Trick

Thaddeus Bradley called Annabelle from his convertible Jeep, a vintage Land Rover Defender, yelling over the wind as it whipped by the roll bar. "My dear, I'm so sorry that my cousin is at my home, and I fear . . . just with the staff and the people, it's not wise."

"It's fine," Annabelle said from four cars behind him. "Besides, I can't leave my car at your house; someone might check the license plate, or drive by and talk. The Bay View sounds perfect."

"I've had this thing for you burning inside me since when, senior year, that football game?" Thaddeus said. In the rearview mirror, he checked out his dashing smile, his Kennedyesque, Chiclet-shaped teeth. Then he smoothed his short, very manicured brown hair down on the sides, that gel keeping it nicely in place, even in the car. He grabbed the Binaca out of the center console and slid it into his jeans' pocket. Sometimes, he'd spray a little bit on his tongue during sex so she'd feel an extra tingle down there. In about twenty minutes, he'd have that hottie club tennis champ back there in the Maserati right where he wanted her: horizontal and all his.

At the next stoplight, Thaddeus reached into the glove compartment for some Pinaud Clubman cologne his grandfather Bradford used to wear, all Bradley men in his lineage wore it (and so convenient the Millshore stocked it in the men's lounges). Always smart to keep a bottle in the Defender for moments like this. "This is my plan, darling," he explained to Annabelle. "First, I am going to massage you with a warming ginger, lavender oil blend."

"Just . . . keep it a surprise," Annabelle answered, six cars behind him now, inching toward Southampton on Route 27. Her breasts were uncomfortable in her French balcony bra. She'd bought the La Perla set for her second time with Philippe, and it was a fortune. It wouldn't be right to wear it with Arthur, would it? But she could wear it with Thaddeus, right? This infidelity pact had so many little details to consider.

She took a moment to adjust her breasts for the fifth time since she'd left the house. She would burn the bra after she'd slept with Thaddeus. You could wear the same lingerie with two different lovers, but not if one of them was your husband. She nodded slightly at that solid rationale. The cost ($678) of the two-piece number could be amortized across two men this summer.

When the light turned green, Thaddeus's Jeep took off, his brown hair flying back, his neat left side part unfortunately now all messed up. Annabelle could hear the deep-throttled roar of its motor. Arthur's German family had made engines for a century now, and he'd explained the exact whir and pitch of each to her endlessly.

Thaddeus cradled the microphone of his headphones in one hand to block it from the wind. "I'm going to put gentle and firm pressure on all your special areas. You'll become so wet . . ."

Annabelle felt a definite ick-factor. Nonetheless, her foot remained on the accelerator. She'd heard for years that Thaddeus was deft in the sheets, and he had a masculine strut she'd found appealing since their Andover/Exeter days, not to mention just the right amount of graying chest hair peeking out from his blue Oxford button-downs. And he would keep quiet. She knew that.

"And the soft, supple lips will part for my tongue . . ."

"Please, just, can you not tell me?" she asked. She and Caroline would no doubt laugh about Thaddeus's dirty talk; it was so *off.* She'd memorize his lame comments to share later.

Thaddeus, oblivious, went on. "The touch and taste of your body, the hum of your breath as you exhale, my tongue teasing you, with wide, circular motions, reducing, then increasing pressure, pinpointing it to drive you mad. And then, at the same time, moving my fingers gently, in slow and deliberate motions. Your almond will be so . . ."

Annabelle veered over to the right so hard, she almost caused an accident. Three cars behind her each honked as they had to brake not to swerve into oncoming traffic.

My fucking almond? I can't do this, Annabelle thought. *This guy is a TOOL. My fucking almond? I'll jerk my own almond off.*

Chapter 42

Flip-Flopping at the Beach

Caroline's phone rang in the sand at the Navy Beach shore-line restaurant. She put her earbuds on and said, "Hold on, Annabelle."

She hoisted herself up on an elbow, feeling more than a tad buzzed after a glass of wine, and looked over at the kids. Theo was now awake, but still stretched out in his chairs, playing on the iPad, having demolished a basket of fried shrimp. The girls were playing tag with other kids by the shore, and, thankfully, showed no more signs of wanting to wade into the water. Caroline's dinner was surely cold by now, but how could she eat when her nerves were careening toward Pluto?

"I'm so glad you called. I need to talk," Caroline said. "I have to tell you something really . . ."

"Me first," Annabelle barked.

"No, Annabelle, my story. Two of them, actually, and they're *big*."

"Okay," said Annabelle, who was driving back in the direction of East Hampton, away from the Bay View Motel and from that preppy almond-fondler. "Go ahead," she snapped.

"Well, it's kind of like this," Caroline said and then she paused. "I need to prepare myself to tell you this."

Annabelle, now at a stoplight, put her car in park and revved the engine just to have something to do with her right foot. She picked up her phone and blocked Thaddeus's number. Things would be awkward during club events for a while, but he'd move along and fuck someone else's wife soon enough. "Tell me, Caroline," Annabelle said. "Mr. Architect told his wife, and now you're leaving Eddie and putting the kids into East Hampton Elementary?"

"Hold on," Caroline said, readying herself. She took another big gulp of wine and dunked the last two fries into the aioli. Then, she laid down again. "So, it's like this . . ." And she paused again.

"It's like what?" Annabelle asked. "It sounds like you're eating those disgusting fried clams again. We might have to get you to exercise for the second time this decade."

"Never again am I doing a Fred class at exhale," Caroline said. "And about the news . . . actually, you know what, never mind. It's not important."

"Never mind? Why are you being so crazy?"

"Just . . . it's really an in-person type of story," Caroline said, knowing Annabelle would howl and cry once she heard the news. "So you go instead. Did you do the French playboy one more time? Or did you decide to delve into Preppyland?"

"I actually just blocked Thaddeus Bradley's number," Annabelle said, relieved. "He's going to be driving to the Bay View Motel, checking in, and then expecting me to meet him around the back."

"So where are you?"

"Driving back to you," said Annabelle. "Did you take the kids out? Where are you? Are you outside? I hear the wind through your phone."

"Navy Beach. So you didn't fuck either one of them?"

"I kind of did. I mean, Thaddeus is going to pay for the room and get blown off."

"Well, you're right." Caroline laughed. "That's a *form* of fucking him. Fucking him over."

Chapter 43

Oyster Fest

FIVE DAYS LATER

The teakettle whistled, breaking the silence of the early dawn. The sunlight peeked through the flowering bushes outside Caroline's window, and shadows danced across the breakfast table. Her brain raced in circles.

Why hasn't Joey come by the barn again?
Or left a note?
It has been too many days.

Teeny fruit flies hovered around the fruit bowl. Caroline swatted them away and started to cut a peach, slamming the knife into the cutting board. Taking a bite—the August nectar was so sweet—she closed her eyes to savor it.

The white hydrangea bush outside the window had grown fatter with each day of summer. The branches, heavy with succulent leaves and blossoms the size of a honeydew, flopped down. She'd cut a few later. Or maybe she should just let everything grow wild.

Why would Joey want us to believe he had drowned?
Where had he been? What had he done?

Who else knew?

Caroline poured hot water into a ceramic pot Gigi had painted for Mother's Day, allowing the tart green tea to brew as she sat at the table. She had already organized all her design proposals by room, stalling a bit, hoping the routine might push the storms from her head.

How could he do this to me?

He knew it would kill a part of me too.

She tapped the table so hard a piece of nail polish chipped off.

To touch his face again . . . would it feel the same?

Six design boards, three-by-three-feet wooden frames holding tan corkboard, beckoned Caroline. Using one for each project, she'd pinned photos from magazines, swatches, and paint chips for inspiration. With her ideas confined to neat squares, clients could better visualize the rooms. Eddie was in the city, and the kids would wake up in an hour. She had just enough time to tackle overdue work.

She reached to exchange a magenta linen swatch that was too hot—cheerleader tacky, even—for an orange one. The ripe melon color would work well with the client's dark wood floor. She'd tell them to imagine ripe cantaloupe and chocolate.

Her next decision—to pick green instead of light blue for the library couch—felt like a small triumph. Sticking with the green, *knowing* it would pop, reminded her that she was capable of making choices, small and large, safe and risky, and building on them.

Could she announce to Eddie one day over a quiet breakfast, *"We aren't packing to return to urban stress. Gigi and Theo aren't going back to prissy private school. We're just staying right here."*

She might do that, in the same way she might put this red-striped poplin in the corner of the McDermotts' sunroom. That room had stumped her, the glossy white floor almost radioactively bright; now, at least she had an inspiration. There was so much more to do for these clients before the meeting this weekend, and it worried her. She had to decide on paint colors, blinds, and type of curtains, and that was on top of having to convince Mrs. McDermott that the white beadboard on the playroom ceiling would soften the room.

Caroline pierced the red poplin swatch with a metal pushpin and added it to the board, next to a photo of a white wicker chair. She massaged the rough-hewn fabric with her fingertips, feeling the tiny clumps of cotton caught in the weave. The sunlight in the room would highlight its earthy texture. Maybe she should use natural wood beams in the ceiling instead of whitewashed ones; it would look more like a high-end surf shack than a Pottery Barn showroom.

Caroline felt satisfied with her choices. She thanked God she had signed the kids up for East Hampton Lower School, online, way back when she'd first discovered Eddie's iPad in his study. Gigi and Theo could mold clay in the same art studio where she had made mugs in fourth grade. On the forms, she'd left out the name of parent number two, so Eddie wasn't getting emails about the start of school. She'd used East Hampton as their home address, and Eddie never checked the mail there. The week before, she'd gone to the school district administration building to tell the registrar, Mrs. Coley, an old friend of her mother's, to keep their return quiet around town, and not to announce it to the teachers just yet.

If the kids didn't end up going, it would be simple enough to click a box online that meant "Never mind." Yet she felt the kids knew something was up with their fall plans. Like horses, they could smell it in the air. Earlier in the summer, Gigi had asked if she could ever be in Rosie's East Hampton class. Just the day before, Theo had told Caroline, "I like my room here better because I can see my jungle gym outside." Caroline took both statements as confirmation that even the kids knew which life was better for them.

A text came through.

It's Robert Smith the Upholsterer. I know it's early, but is now a good time to talk about the curtains? It's a Tuesday deadline, and I need to make a plan.

She called Ryan. Before even saying hello, he said, "I want to take you for a paddle. And then to one of my favorite—"

"We can't go out in public together again," Caroline said, interrupting him. "We've done it like three times. People talk. C'mon, don't get careless on me." A prickly and sudden headache spread its tentacles behind her ears. Theo had caught a terrible case of summer croup, and Caroline had snuggled him through his nighttime hacking. She'd lost hours of sleep thanks to three excursions to a steamy shower with him in hopes of loosening his congestion a little.

"I'm not being careless or reckless," Ryan said. "I just want to take you somewhere."

"You can't take me anywhere," she answered matter-of-factly. Ryan was someone else's husband. Caroline exhaled loudly as if that might extinguish some of the self-reproach roiling inside her.

"I know," Ryan said. "I just had an idea of something fun. I like seeing you smile. Is that allowed?"

"Yes, of course," Caroline replied.

"You smile in bed," Ryan said. "And that makes me happy. I'm just trying to make you smile, baby."

"I don't really," she said, starting to feel a little uncomfortable. The guilt was hitting her hard now; she felt like a rag doll slamming against a brick wall. She felt bad for Ryan's wife first, and Eddie second.

Was that good or horrible?

To release the tension now constricting her chest like a vice, she tried rationalizing: Ryan's wife had cheated on him once. *This is his payback, just as it is mine.*

"You do smile," Ryan went on. "Like when I'm touching you, when you're close and, you know, I stop everything, because I want you to go first. It's better for me that way."

"Okaaay."

Should I end it now, before he gets attached, or was he already too attached?

"You know, there are ways I could prolong that, that period where you're about to. You can trust me. If you'd stop fighting me, you can just lay there and let me make it last so long that you won't even know what's happening to you."

"Maybe I will," she said.

"Maybe? I don't know why you resist sometimes. It's like you want to rush it."

"I don't know, it takes me a while sometimes," she said. "And when it's finally about to happen, I do want it to." What she didn't say was that sometimes she felt bad it took her a long time to come, and she wondered if he was bored. She shook her head. What a stupid, womanly reaction, always worrying about other people rather than taking care of herself. At the ultimate moment of pleasure, she should be thinking only about her own enjoyment. "Maybe I just get impatient?"

"No, no, no, that's what you don't understand; that's when you let me prolong it," Ryan said. "It's not like we have that much time left." His voice softened, sounding melancholy about autumn, and more about what it meant for them. "Caroline, you are so beautiful in bed, it just, it almost freaks me out." She didn't react. He asked, "You there?"

"Yeah, sorry."

"What's with you?"

"You can't get gushy talking about what my face looks like when I'm close and . . ." She stood up and paced. If she did live out here in the fall, she'd have to pretend she didn't know Ryan if she bumped into him in town. Time to pour a little ice on this whole thing.

"You have to promise me that you're metal inside when it comes to me. Cold, hard, unfeeling," Caroline said, tossing a bunch of swatches across the table. "I mean, I need our deal to be clean. Emotionally this just, you know, can't be a problem."

"Call me Mr. Robot," Ryan said.

Caroline walked over to the window and stared at the jungle gym on the patio, splintered and weathered now. It had been bright red just a few years before. If they moved here for good, she'd splurge on a fabulous new one with a fort.

"C'mon, it's me you're talking to," Ryan said. "I'm going to miss you, but I respect what we have to do, the timeline. We're in this together. I need the same, uncomplicated fun. I'm just trying to discover all the little gems inside you before, you know, fall."

This man she'd say goodbye to in a few weeks wasn't an architect who built splashy houses in his own image, as monuments to himself. He was a caretaker of other people's older homes, restoring them to what they were meant to be. That was his way in life. She let her guard down a little. "Okay, tell me your stupid story about my face." Maybe he got it. Maybe he did only want to see the best in her.

"You're smiling. Finally," he said. "I can hear it in the way you just said that."

"Possibly," Caroline admitted, plopping back down in her chair.

"Okay, it's my favorite part about you," he continued. "When you kind of surrender, you have this beautiful look on your face. That's all I'm saying. Period. I could help you surrender more, you know."

"Sounds intriguing." She grabbed a pile of red swatches and flipped through them.

"You want me to show you or tell you now? A robot can't do either," Ryan said playfully. This guy had a Joey side, always game, teasing her like a girlfriend would.

"Shut up," Caroline said.

"You wanna know how I can help you surrender?"

"Yeah, just tell me." She laughed a little. This guy was cute. She'd made a good choice.

Ryan paused for a moment, then said softly, "A little silk around your wrists, not tied to anything, just together. It'd help you not resist so much."

Caroline had never allowed a man to do that. And, for that matter, had never been asked. She nodded and swallowed hard. With her voice almost an octave higher, she asked, "And if I didn't like it?"

"If you pulled hard enough, you could get out. And it's me, Ryan. You say you don't like it, and I'll try something else. No silk, just my body." After a long pause, he added: "Hey, no pressure. Just a suggestion to help you let me put you into a whole other zone I know you can go to. And it's for you, baby. Watching you in that state. Just know that while it's happening, you're exquisite, with your red lips and your dark hair surrounding your face like a halo. Really, exquisite."

"Hmm, hmm, thanks."

"You were smiling when you said that 'hmm, hmm,'" Ryan said. "I can tell, even on the phone. You know, you're allowed to actually like hearing what I say. And now that you seem to be in a better mood, I had a plan for today to make you happy at sunset. You up for that?"

"Yes, I am actually," Caroline answered, rummaging through a pile of swatches and finding a cherry paisley that would match the red-striped poplin for a throw pillow. She pinned it to the board with fortitude. Silk on her wrists? She wasn't sure. This poplin, though, was perfect. "You're right, enough of this going over robot rules. Fuck it; let's do something fun. I need it."

"You in the mood for oysters?"

"Of course, but where? We can't go to the same fish shack again."

"Let's do takeout oysters," Ryan added. "The new house has an outdoor fireplace. We can eat them there."

"I'm sorry," Caroline said. "Is there another out-of-the-way oyster place where we don't know anyone? I . . . I don't like takeout raw food. The ice melts so fast, and it gets all watery and gross."

"No, you silly woman," Ryan laughed. "It's me. When I say 'takeout oysters,' I mean we are going to *take out oysters,* from the bay. Ourselves."

Chapter 44

Paddle Party

Ryan's pickup truck bounced and swerved in the sand as he drove along Napeague Bay. Out in the dunes, small cottages on stilts lorded over green and tan stalks of sea grass. Caroline turned and watched Ryan drive. She smiled to herself, thinking that he looked every bit the local man, wearing wraparound sunglasses, flip-flops, and surf shorts. The guy didn't have a designer bone in his body.

He turned to Caroline as the pickup bounded between the divots in the bay sand, his face bursting with excitement. "You know, I had the most amazing morning with my son. It's whiplash with teenagers—you'll see when your kids are a little older. At night, he sat at dinner, giving me the nastiest of glares, as if words were incapable of expressing the level of hatred he felt. Why? Because I asked him to share a Spotify playlist with me." Ryan looked over at her again quickly to make sure she was paying attention. He smiled, realizing he now had the power to deliver her from her most distracted and grouchy moods, as he'd done on the phone earlier. "Then, today, Jason literally rubbed his head up against my shoulder like a dog. He asked if I'd please take him to the ocean, like when he was six or so and still loved me all the time."

"I don't know how I'm going to handle my kids as teenagers," Caroline said. "It'll kill me if they don't want a hug." An end-of-summer tan, rougher beard, and longer hair in back gave Ryan extra appeal today. But Caroline decided against telling him that. She looked out the window at the houses lining the shore, many partly hidden behind grassy dunes. "The land people own in this area is in such small parcels, but I can tell they all have gardens behind the houses."

"How do you know if you can't see them?"

"The smell," Caroline explained. "It's my favorite scent of summer: ripe tomatoes on the vine. You know what I mean? It kind of pierces your nose for a minute, like pepper."

"I'm not sure I've thought about it like that, but you're right."

"So much of summer comes in through my nose. There's the salt from the bay, which is different from the salt from the ocean. Out here, it's a muddy, almost stale scent from the marshy sand that doesn't get moved around much, or as much as ocean sand does," she said, grateful for this talk of the little things that made her love East Hampton, anything to keep her mind off bigger things—namely, that her first love was not dead after all, and that she was screwing another woman's husband, and that if her own husband found out about it, he might grab a tiki torch out of their garage and bludgeon him.

Ryan pulled the truck up to a small inlet in the bay. "You know that Paddle Diva company?" he asked.

"Yeah, but I told you," Caroline objected, or tried. "I've never paddleboarded, so I'm not . . ."

"Oh, yes you are. That's why I told you to bring a suit."

"I thought we were swimming before dinner or something? Or going to another house with a hot tub?" Caroline said.

"Nope. The paddleboard company owner is a woman who helps with the volunteer force, Gina Bradley. I told her that my cousin was in town, and she left me a few of her favorite boards. They're over there by the tree. Now, c'mon, let's get on them and let me take you around to my favorite spot."

"I've never been on a paddleboard. I'm not the most coordinated—"

"Stop. What's the worst thing that could happen? You'll fall in? Then what? It's water, for Christ sakes, and it's the most beautiful evening. You wanted to go in the water anyway, so just tumble off to the side when you feel you're losing your balance."

After a ten-minute lesson from Ryan (which included two spills after which she clumsily climbed back up on all fours while Ryan steadied the board for her), Caroline managed to push up to her feet, planting them properly. Once stable, she tightened her core muscles, dug the paddle into the water as Ryan had shown her. Suddenly, it started to feel like a moving sidewalk. Though she'd never admit it to Annabelle, she liked this. She might even do it a few mornings a week to get that little layer of softness off her tummy.

As they circled around a corner surrounded by long weeds, Ryan reached into his backpack and started tossing little pebbles from a plastic bag into the bay.

"Is that fish food?"

Ryan laughed. "You sure you grew up here? You went clamming your whole childhood, and you don't know what I'm doing?"

"Nope."

"I'm dropping oyster spat."

"Oyster what?" she asked.

"Oyster spat is the fertilized baby oyster that attaches itself often to the shell. I'm throwing pieces of oyster shells that have oyster seeds in them. They can be farmed in trays or grow naturally in water. When I do the 'takeout' oysters, I just go to certain secluded parts of the bay where I seed all the time, then I can find them no problem. It's my own, private oyster bed to harvest myself, here among the reeds. Also, the oysters act as filters, they actually clean the water, purify like fifty gallons a day, did you know that?"

"None of it. And are we taking some oysters now?"

"Of course. I'm taking some, then I'll open them for you in a new client's guest house because, what the hell, they're in Europe. I'll feed them to you, then ravage you. And I'll wait for that smile. All good?"

"Really nice," Caroline conceded. Ryan's wife was lucky; she had married a good, strong, giving man. She felt exhilarated about the evening ahead, but also jumpy with guilt; she had a vague sense of foreboding. Part of her felt like she was cheating on Joey, which made no sense *and* absolute sense. If he were here, alive, she should be having an affair with him, not Ryan Miller.

Ryan paddled over to Caroline, kissed her hand, and watched her board sway with the gentle wake his speed had created. He pumped his feet a little on either side of his board to create more rocking. And then, just as he'd hoped, she lost her balance and fell in for the third time.

Caroline came up for air, laughing and choking. "You did that on purpose! I'm not an idiot, I saw that!"

They stood in three feet of water now.

She screamed a little and jumped. "The bay floor is really slimy! What is down there?"

"And you say you're not a city slicker now."

"Stop!" With both hands, she splashed water at him.

Ryan couldn't help but grab her and kiss her beautiful red mouth. He knew he shouldn't even get near her—there had been a few guys fishing a hundred yards back or so. But Caroline was too cute—all soaking wet and free, a little clumsy in her way, and worrying about some algae between her toes. It made him happy to see her laugh like this; she seemed so stressed all the time because of that asshole husband of hers. She deserved some lightness, and he was so glad to be delivering it to her on this perfect summer day. He put his mouth on her salty lips.

Let me just have one little taste out here . . . no one will see.

And, as he did, Caroline kissed him back, furiously. It helped to expunge the massive confusion and shock over Joey's return. All those anxious feelings started to drift away with the ripples of the warm, brackish water: her guilt about being with Ryan, her doubts she could walk out on Eddie, her anxieties over a possible switch of schools so late in the season, even her nerves over the blank canvas of the McDermotts' sunroom.

As Ryan kissed her deeper, he tasted like a hypnotizing mixture of Valium and adrenaline, and she wanted more. Caroline pulled the back of his neck toward her and devoured him, breathless in her quest to take him in. Every touch, every tingle, was amplified with the apprehension that autumn was almost there. This was a prelude to what she would do to Ryan in the bed he'd arranged for them. And yes, this time, she wouldn't resist her pleasure, but succumb to it in any way he wanted to give it to her.

They kept kissing, both soaking in the late-day sun and slight breeze. September was near, signaling its arrival with a chill in the wind that gave her goose bumps on her bare arms. It was different in July, when the steamy wind enveloped her, suffocating her, and when the summer felt pregnant with time. The cornstalks weren't so high then, she could see over them and view the whole field, their cobs just sprouting, the size of a pickle.

When she wrapped her leg around him under the water, she felt him harden against her. *Tragic*, she thought, *to see our lives together end just when I understood how to manipulate this glorious, muscled body.* She'd be damned if she didn't leave him with sloppy, sexy summer memories, the cornstalks now high and mighty, the cobs crunchy through the slathering of butter and salt.

And Ryan was not only persistent, but perceptive—she did always rush her part along if she could. What if she did just let him do whatever he wanted, for as long as he wanted? What if she did not resist at all, and instead just laid back, and let him make that delicious tug inside more potent? She'd often wondered about having her wrists tied gently above her head. Just the thought created a sudden ache between her legs.

What if he bound her with a soft piece of silk that felt safe, as he promised, and she could untie if she wanted? Maybe that was the ultimate surrender, to him, and then, in turn, to her own body.

And while this couple, drenched in the marshy water of August, seized with impatience, kissed more intensely, a man stood in the reeds a hundred yards away.

He was watching them.

Eddie Clarkson had a clear line of sight to his wife and this shithead, two-bit architect. He had trouble focusing on them, though, the binoculars shook in his trembling hands.

Chapter 45

The Secrets of Silk

Caroline drove her Jeep up her driveway and sat in the car silently for a moment. It was midnight now. Her hair, twisted up in a slapdash bun, was still damp. She'd worn her flowing Calypso blue caftan that made her eyes sparkle—a favorite blouse women grab like an old friend, the one Linda Cockburn had once said was "so out of fashion, you should burn it." Reaching inside, she adjusted the shoulder. She'd put it on in a dark room, and now she realized the thing was on backward. The adolescent groping in an unfamiliar place, the dizzy after-effects of sex with Ryan made simple tasks, like dressing, challenging—and all of that made her smile.

Thank God Eddie is in the city.

Turning on a light in the car, she looked at her face in the rearview mirror. Her forehead was shiny, her hair was in a rat's nest atop her head, and her mascara was smudged. It would be tough to hide her flushed-cheek, just-got-laid look. Ryan's beard had rubbed her chin so hard that it was red. Touching it now, it was raw and a little sore. But Caroline didn't mind: a little makeup would cover it in the morning, and after all, this was how one was supposed to look after sex, at the height of an affair. And she'd spent this summer cannon-balling into a very good one indeed.

No guilt or shame allowed.

She would focus only on the kiss in the water, and how satisfying it had been. Ryan had taught her to slow down that ache in bed. The silk tie on her wrists had allowed her pleasure to last and linger, to play like music that waned and rose.

The night made her think about all those "fallen" women in literature who had to jump on train tracks or drink arsenic after freeing their passion. And, in real life, women in foreign places who were put in hot boxes in the desert for the feeling she had now, or as punishment for a night like the one she'd just had. Some of them were even stoned to death before a crowd of cheering male relatives.

It was so unfair to punish human desire; it made her seethe. She was no outlaw, no victim; no woman should be punished for this.

Men around the world who had affairs were virile; they hadn't "tarnished" their family name, they were not doomed to hell. Fathers who strayed were just being boys and enjoying themselves. The labels put on mothers who cheated infuriated Caroline: dirty sluts, unfit mothers, hysterical wives. She knew many of those women were merely looking to even the score. Most of them were likely in love.

Caroline shook her head, pissed that she could do what she wanted and so many women around the planet couldn't. Who did people think these men cheated with? Prostitutes, assistants, yoga teachers, and, more often, other wives and mothers—co-participants in mutual sexual desire, an urge that didn't end when they gave birth. Caroline could flip from sexual being to hearth tender any time she wanted, and so could any mom out there. It was just the demented world that saw a woman as madonna or whore.

Peering inside her house, she could see the library lights dimmed, the blue haze of the television flickering inside. The babysitter, Francis, might think Caroline's hours odd, but Caroline could do what she wanted with her evening.

And she had.

As had her husband several times over the years.

Francis thought every Tuesday night this summer was "girls' night." She didn't expect Caroline home until late, and she often slept over, curling up in the library in front of the TV. Caroline knew that if she started worrying about the sitter's time, it would quash her enjoyment with Ryan and, in turn, ignite the guilt she had worked hard to suppress. If Francis were up now, Caroline could tell her that her hair was damp because she took a silly dip in the ocean with her pals from high school.

But then, why did she care what a babysitter thought anyway? That was the whole point: doing what she wanted every hour this summer. Figuring things out. Maneuvering through life on her terms. As Eddie always did.

Caroline touched her favorite blouse again. Ryan had told her she looked like a beautiful creature spawned from stars, her eyes so clear, reflecting the glare of the sun on the waves. She knew her eyes were brightest in that light, in this blouse. Screw Linda.

Before they'd dunked themselves in the bay, Ryan had asked her why she was distracted this evening. Was she sad? Did something happen he could help with? She wasn't sure she could trust Ryan with news of Joey. Caroline knew he would help her with anything, even if it involved an old lover. She was desperate to tell someone about Joey, someone who had known him. Keeping the secret was killing her. Was Ryan, someone she already shared a secret with, the best person to confide in, better even than Annabelle?

Caroline put her hand on the car door handle to open it but

instead turned on the engine again to roll down the windows and allow a cross breeze in to cool her down.

If Eddie found out about Ryan—*if*—she wondered, would she confess right away? She could volley back citing his infidelities first: "*Was Brittany fun and smart or just fun?*" She could also just smirk, ignoring his rage, and tell him he had a lot of nerve to even open his mouth.

On second thought, this was different. There was no need to incite Eddie, and help kindle World War–level dynamite. Caroline knew that men had their virgin obsessions; they could sleep around, but they wanted their own property untouched, untainted, safe, and preserved.

As she walked up the front steps, Caroline noticed the hazy glow around the half moon. The night was too special to end. She sat on the soft armchair on her porch. Something told her not to go inside. The night was still clear, but she could feel the ocean fog approaching. Caroline let down her messy bun, and her damp hair cooled the back of her neck enough to make her shiver.

WHEN SHE AND Ryan had arrived at the cottage, drenched from the bay, she saw he had already loaded the fridge with sea bass, tomatoes, cheese, corn, and a bottle of white wine from a local vineyard. A generous bundle of basil stood in a mason jar by the sink, its perfume infusing the kitchen air. Crumbs lay around a crusty baguette in brown paper, and when Caroline had walked in, she instinctively started brushing them into her hand at the edge of the counter.

"What are you doing?" he asked. "That kiss in the bay made it hard to concentrate on the drive home. There's no cooking or cleaning now." And he led her against a wall, and one of his strong hands clasped both of hers. She tried to free herself, but he wasn't letting go. He held her chin with his other hand and kissed her softly. "Don't even kiss me back," he said. "Just let me taste you, let me do everything I want right now. Please."

When she'd try to kiss back, he'd say, "Just . . . let me do this like this. It's a way of having you all to myself."

Trying to fight against surrendering made Caroline want it more. He'd started undressing her against the wall.

She relived the scene as she sat on the soft chair in the moonlight. They had lain on a carpet between the kitchen and the guest room, both glistening from chest to toe. They had a joke about this, calling it hallway sex. It had happened a few times before, neither able to wait to get comfortable on a mattress. A month ago, she had a rug burn on her back that she'd had to hide for a week.

At the cottage, after dinner, they'd made it past the hallway into the guest room. Now, in the cool night air, she touched her wrists where the silk had been.

"It won't be tight," he had said. "Remember, you can just say untie it, and I will. Also, you can slip out if you pull hard enough. But try to forget that. Pretend that you can't."

And she did, so lost in the charged fantasy that she had no choice but to let his tongue and fingers act on their own. He had kissed her and raised her arms over her head. Positioning a pillow under her and straightening her on the mattress, he was able to keep kissing her and to tie her wrists together. Just as he had said, the knot was firm, but not too tight. He smoothed her hair off her face with one hand. "Just let me, please," he said.

She was already wet from his slow kissing, the way his nails danced lightly on her breasts, and mostly, from the foreign feeling of trying to yank her wrists apart but reaching a full stop. She gripped her legs closed, and Ryan, on his knees, said, "No, no, no."

He touched her softly on the fabric of her underwear, knowing she was the one who usually pulled them down. It turned her on more that she couldn't; and, immediately, she pleaded with him to take them off her. He was going so slowly it hurt. With her arms over her head, she lurched into a half sit-up, and said forcefully, "Now, fuck, do it, take them off." He finally did, and spread her legs with his elbows, almost forcing them apart. The struggle, part real, part pretend, put her in a state she'd never felt, the waves inside so ferocious she ached hard. She'd begged him. "Don't stop, please God, don't you stop."

But he did.

And then, he didn't.

And when it was over, she realized her body was entirely constricted and unleashed at the same time.

Several minutes later, he laughed and said, "Maybe you need a shower?"

In the dark, her skin smelled clean now, like soap, though she'd only half rinsed her hair. Her black tresses were still sticky from the sweat and the sex, not to mention knotty in the back from being mashed up against pillows and walls and carpets.

Caroline yanked an ottoman closer to her with the heels of her feet and stretched out. Maybe she'd just sleep out here. It was a night of new adventures after all. She'd learned things this summer, from trying new things, thinking in different ways, and from Ryan. Maybe she'd make a decision by the mid-month deadline she'd set for herself.

Move out here and do a trial separation?

She grabbed a wilting geranium out of a window box next to her and plucked at the leaves. Parts of her life were better than ever, if she chose to see it that way. Each day, Gigi and Theo gained the confidence and know-how to do more on their own. Just this morning, through her own design work, she had tapped into reserves of creativity that she hadn't explored for a long time. She, herself, needed to be pushed. She threw the denuded stem into the unruly bushes and vowed to trim the shrubs in the morning.

It was time to go check on the kids, to wrap the blanket tighter around that darling Francis. It was nearing one in the morning, and the lavender bath salts were calling out to her before bed. Soon, inside her own safe walls, she'd reclaim her role as mother and wife.

Chapter 46

A Whispering Warning

As Caroline approached her front porch, she noticed something on the far right of the door that hadn't been there when she left that afternoon. At first, she thought it was a deflated soccer ball, but as she knelt beside it, she understood: it was an old conch shell.

It wasn't the same shell that Joey had in his father's cottage, but it was similar enough for Caroline to get the message. The summer he disappeared, walking down the beach with Caroline, Joey had casually offered, "If I die, spread my ashes in the ocean, right here at Two Mile Hollow Beach."

"But this isn't even our regular beach. We walked farther west today," Caroline had said.

"Well, I wouldn't want you to feel sad every time you went to our beach, so just do it here," he'd said.

"Fine, then, but that'll be when you're ninety-eight."

"Well, let's say this: I hope so, but if you outlast me, I'll talk to you through a conch shell," he'd told her. "I'll send a special one to you with the waves. You'll put it up to your ear and hear me kissing you."

Caroline remembered telling him that his idea was silly and corny. Besides, there were large clam shells in Long Island, nothing as big as a Caribbean conch shell.

But here was a large conch shell, whispering to her, startlingly out of place in East Hampton. She picked it up and looked inside, wondering for the briefest second if Francis had bought it to paint as a crafts project.

No way.

Joey had put it there.

And now, in her hands, it didn't feel silly; it felt serious and substantial. She cradled it in the crook of her arm and stepped into her house.

Caroline set her purse and keys on the kitchen counter. The lights were dim throughout the halls. For a moment, her heart tightened because Eddie always dimmed them at this level. But it was Tuesday, and he wouldn't ever come without telling her.

Caroline walked into the library to check on the blinking blue television light; some cable news was on. She expected to find Francis there asleep, curled up in her soft, pale-green blanket, but instead, she heard her husband's bellowing voice: "And where the fuck were you all night?"

Chapter 47

Inside the Marriage Tomb

A nd," he yelled even louder, "what the fuck kind of bad joke is this?"

Caroline stood before her husband in the entrance to the library. She recognized that telling Eddie about Ryan here and now might be the healthiest approach, and part of her was willing. What was he going to say: that he had never strayed?

She walked into the library, the sound of her footsteps echoing in the quiet night, and she placed the conch shell on the coffee table. Eddie looked at it for a moment, failing to understand its significance. He swirled his Pinhook bourbon around the ice cubes.

"Where is Francis, anyway?" Caroline asked.

"I sent her home in a taxi an hour ago," Eddie said, his voice battle-ready, playing with the lines that went up his favorite crystal Baccarat glass. He wasn't ready to look at his wife.

"Why are you out here on a Tuesday?" she asked. "You haven't done that once in twelve years." She walked over to him and tried to kiss him hello, but he pulled back like a prizefighter eluding a right hook.

"Okay," she said, stepping back, understanding this was going to be painful. She plunked her weary body into a side chair. "And why on earth would you not tell me you were coming?" She shook her head, justifying the prior events of the evening to herself, or trying to.

"I didn't warn you, you mean? Just fuckin' because . . ." Eddie started to drum on his knees with his fingers.

"It's after midnight. Why are you so hyperactive?"

"I'm very upset, let's put it that way." Eddie cocked his head sideways and squinted. "And confused."

She clasped and unclasped her hands, studying them. She couldn't help but think where her hands had been an hour before. She stood and grabbed the conch shell, just to have something to fiddle with on her lap. She massaged it like a crystal ball.

Silence lingered in the air like the fog that had rolled in outside. She looked at the built-in bookcases, painted maroon, each lit with a small, clamshell sconce. She'd found the lights at a garage sale in a set of six. The right side of the room was stuffed with art books, the middle with the fiction she'd read since college, and the left mostly with art supplies and children's books. A table where the kids drew and had afternoon snacks was in front of the bay window.

It was a true family room, and yet her family was disintegrating.

Where she'd been tonight, what she'd done, wasn't designed to wound Eddie—she never wanted him to know. Honesty had limited benefits. Girls' night was plausible; she complained about missing old friends out here all the time. Only, she'd have to tell those women that she lied to her husband and then they would wonder. Her lies would multiply, and she'd tumble into a hole she couldn't climb out of.

This is why she told Annabelle you got caught no matter what.

Eddie stared at her.

"What is it, Eddie? What is going on with you?"

From behind a cushion, he pulled out a new Frisbee and placed it on the glass coffee table. He pointed to words that had been scrawled on top of it in black marker, in handwriting she instantly recognized as Joey's: *She's still mine.*

Caroline blanched.

Eddie nodded and said, "Yep."

"You mean . . ."

"Yeah, I mean Joey fuckin' Whitten's Frisbee story coming back to haunt the fuck out of me. Last time, twenty or so years ago, after I beat him up at an Ultimate Frisbee game, Joey left the Frisbee from the game in my car the next day. Remember what he wrote on it? *She's mine.* Don't you remember?"

"I do, of course, I do. But what are you talking about now?" The conch shell, now this . . . Caroline knew. "I don't get it."

Eddie grabbed the Frisbee, stood up, and dropped it on her lap. "It's brand new. It arrived at my office *this morning.*" He flipped it over so she could see the underside. On it, in Joey's handwriting: *She's still mine.* "This is a new Frisbee, not the one from the game. But very fuckin' weird it's the same handwriting, I remember, because I wanted to pummel him again after I read his stupid message back then."

"Stop with the macho violence, I don't like it," Caroline said. "Maybe it's the same Frisbee, just somehow . . ."

"It's a fuckin' Jonathan Nethercutt Ultimate Frisbee MVP Frisbee. I Googled it. Says 2018! Nethercutt is the MVP of the best team out there, the Raleigh Flyers. Nethercutt was probably two years old last time I got a Frisbee like this. What the *fuck*? 'She's still mine'?!"

"I . . . I don't know what to tell you. I had nothing to do with this."

"Here's the thing," Eddie said. "Only three people get that comment, *She's mine.* Me, you, and, you know, dead lover boy."

"Eddie. Stop. He's a lovely man. *Was.*"

"I couldn't be with a girl I loved. And he was rubbing it in. That's just not fair game, every guy knows that's not shit you tease about," Eddie said.

"You didn't need to try to strangle Joey in front of everyone on the field," Caroline said. "It made people hate you, and then when he died, they all remembered that game." She was thinking of how Ryan had mentioned it at the barn party.

Caroline stood and started to clean up the markers and papers on the kids' table. "You can go play housewife over there to avoid me, but, thing is, I threw the old Frisbee in the trash compactor back then, and no one saw it. And what the fuck does the writing mean? Unless one of his friends maybe knew about that back then and this is some weird anniversary or . . . is it his fuckin' drowning anniversary?"

"No, it isn't, by, uh, like two weeks or something." Caroline started jamming the tops onto the markers. Turning back to Eddie, she added, "And, well, I wasn't your girl then. I was your math and homework buddy. I mean, c'mon, you *won*. You married me, Eddie, and he *died*."

She worried Eddie might know more than he was letting on. Had he seen Joey too?

"Yeah, I know he died doing what he did best, which was fuckin' swimming," Eddie said. Caroline knelt down beside a cupboard and took out Tupperware bins filled with colored paper for the kids' art projects. Then she went back to the table to shuffle the unused paper into a pile, stalling. He slammed the table. "Come back and sit down, for God's sake. Focus."

Caroline walked back to her chair and sat down, cradling a pillow and leaning forward to give the moment the attention it demanded. The conch shell now stood heavy on the table, almost radiating: Joey was sending signs, inciting the beast. "I've been listening to you while I was neatening up," Caroline said.

Eddie continued, "I'm just saying, like everyone has always said, that that day didn't make sense. Either he's come back, or Joey's got a ghost, or you are one sick wife trying to play with me, because, yes, I know I haven't . . . I'm sorry if I . . . you know . . . but fuck Caroline." He looked at her plaintively. "I mean, c'mon! That's just sick, creepy shit. It's not funny."

She threw the pillow on the floor, frustrated he didn't believe her, and replied softly, "I did not send it to you. I wouldn't pretend I was Joey trying to get back at you. It's just . . . that's awful."

Eddie stood, walked over to the bookshelf, and slapped a bunch of heavy art books so hard that they fell along the shelf like dominoes. "I don't believe you," he said. "How's that?"

"Why don't you believe me?"

"Because you're lying."

"I'm not lying. What do you mean by that?" Caroline said. He didn't answer; he wanted her to suffer while she guessed what he was leading up to. Now it was her turn to stand and pace while Eddie went back and sat on the couch. She leaned her arms straight against the windowsill and stared out at the night. A few lantern candles she'd made out of thick black wire and mason jars hung from the elm tree and swayed in the wind. As they tapped against branches, they pinged a resonant tone into the blackness.

Eddie hit his hand on the table. "Turn around, Caroline. At least have the balls to face me."

Looking at him, she said, "I have all the balls I need to face you. I'm not lying."

Eddie placed his elbows on his knees and looked up at her. Then, he said, "I mean, for starters, you're lying because you're fucking somebody. Probably fucked him an hour ago."

Chapter 48

Confessional

Caroline rubbed the itchy sting out of her eye and considered the merits of denial versus admission. She couldn't decide what mattered more at this moment: why Joey had sent this Frisbee or how Eddie knew about Ryan. "For your information, Eddie, I'm not into lying," Caroline said.

"Really? That's interesting."

"Please. Don't mock the respect I believe we do have for each other. For starters, how do you even know what I might or might not be doing?"

Had he called Verizon and got access to her deleted text messages? Or hired a private eye to follow her? The other possibility was that he only suspected something and was playing tough guy. "Honestly, Eddie, are you testing me? Threatening me with innuendo?"

"Look at your fuckin' hair and face! What the fuck else could you have been doing besides getting plowed!"

"Shhh!" She walked to the entry and looked up the stairs to make sure Gigi and Theo were asleep. "Be careful. Don't yell crazy things at me now, for the kids' sake. Just . . . please be thoughtful here. I'm trying to do the same. It's not easy. On either of us."

She sat back in her chair, studying his face, his massive shoulders made even bulkier as his arms crossed behind his head on the sofa. He was wearing thin sweatpants, and he'd set his thick, brawny legs on the couch, one resting on a pillow, the other flung over the back. It was strange how, even with all that was going on, Caroline felt close to him, familiar with his moods and how he looked when he was resting, legs splayed out. The kids loved that position, like a big old lion laying in the sun on his back. They often ran and jumped on him, his powerful, welcoming arms embracing them when they did.

Fiery sparks of tension rose inside her, mixed with grief over their decaying marriage. Caroline respected Eddie for detecting something, and it made her feel sad for him, and for them.

She recalled Eddie tumbling down the stairs in that armor. Normal men wouldn't go that far, or put themselves out as he had. Eddie's need to grab life by the neck and shake it for all it was worth wasn't easy to live with, but she did love him for it, or that part of him. The laughter and tears of that marriage proposal flooded back to her; she heard the clanking metal, saw the image of the gallant knight facedown, crawling for the lost ring among the spilled ice. She knew now—as she did then—that this man's love for her had been entirely monogamous since he was fourteen. She blinked tears away.

Neither she nor Annabelle would have predicted that a summer affair would make them feel such intimacy with their husbands.

"No, it isn't easy," he said softly, and in a tone she wasn't sure she'd ever heard.

"So, we're on the same page then," she said, hoping that he would agree it was all too painful to face this minute, so late at night.

No luck. Eddie raged on. "There's this Joey Whitten Frisbee

mindfuck, but I gotta also deal with the fact that you're screwing some local guy we grew up with? Really? Is that really necessary? Right where we *lived*? I'm just . . . I looked him up, and I know his business now. And his wife, Suzy Miller—who, by the way, is known in these parts as an extremely hot piece of ass. I mean, you do know," he said. "Of course you know! Because, well, we had champagne with her. *At my favorite restaurant.* All of us, on the same Duryea's dock! What the hell, you let me buy that fucking architect champs?"

Caroline laid her head back, thinking about how easy it was to be found out, even without technology. She waited a few minutes before saying anything, looking at the wooden beams in the ceiling, soothing her mind with the observation that brown against the white made the house feel more authentic, more beach-y, and that Eddie had wanted everything all white and stark like his office. Her mundane thoughts, a brief respite, were now ruptured by the memory of Suzy's hand on her shoulder, her sweet voice saying, "It's fine, we'll sit for a moment and have a glass." That girlfriend-to-girlfriend tone, wife-to-wife, sensitive to Eddie's bulldog generosity—there was no stopping him, so why try?

"What, you hired an investigator? You paid someone to watch me on Tuesdays? Because, though I'm sure you only know this given how much you've been watching me, it was only on Tuesdays."

From his supine position, Eddie thrust his arms up in the air and said, "You want a fuckin' medal because it was *only* on Tuesdays, when I'm never ever out here, so you can get laid by some local dude we knew?"

"We didn't know him, Eddie, not that that matters. He just grew up out here same time as we did," Caroline stated softly. "And no, I'm not looking for an award. I was just saying it happened on

Tuesdays. The 'only' wasn't some kind of excuse. I just meant, I don't know . . . what'd you do? Hire someone on that day to check up on us?"

"I didn't hire anyone. I didn't have to, Caroline," Eddie answered, in a defeated tone. He sat up and grabbed his knees. "I just heard about it from another contractor I know who works with him sometimes. I won't name him, but he saw you and Ryan together at some project another vendor had worked on. He went late to pick something up, and looked in the window."

"And he saw what?" she had to ask.

"I don't know what he fuckin' saw, Caroline. He had the class not to tell me whether you were taking it missionary or doggie style."

"Jesus, Eddie, you can be so crude. I wasn't, I mean, I'm sure he didn't . . ."

Eddie interrupted her. "And then, if you really want to know, I just rented a car so you wouldn't know it was me, and watched for myself. You guys in the bay, paddling on those boards." He put his head in his hands. Two full minutes passed. His body slumped back down, and he lay there for a moment, staring at the ceiling, thinking he never got what he wanted, even a fuckin' white ceiling. "And, you know, it sucked. It really fucking sucked." Now he was yelling louder and faster. "And you know, Caroline, you would *never* paddleboard with me in a million years. And fucking forget about surfing. *But now you do with the fuckin' shitty architect?* Oh, and I checked him out good. He's never touched a home larger than a garage. You do know that, right? No one could trust him with the real thing. What the fuck does he have on me?"

She had the wisdom not to answer. She knew it was better to let the lava flow.

"Remember when I asked you to call that Paddle Diva lady

and rent some paddleboards because I thought it would be easy for you, and we could do it together? You looked at me like I asked you to run a marathon." Eddie wiped his eyes with the bottom of his T-shirt. He kept talking to the ceiling, not even able to look at her. "And, out in the bay, with him, on that board, you were laughing. I've surfed my whole life. That pussy probably wouldn't know a wave if he saw one, that's why he has to paddle on a fuckin' flat pond. But forget him. It's you! You looked happy. It was just like a goddamned arrow through my heart."

"I didn't *want* that Eddie," Caroline said. "I never wanted that. And I won't lie about what I did. That would only hurt you—and us—more. And, for what it's worth, my, uh, extramarital whatever was something I needed for me. It was never about you. I know that's hard to hear, but it's the truth."

Eddie closed his eyes and nodded.

"And, you know Eddie, you're not exactly innocent when it comes to fidelity. I know you're up to something now, in 2019, not way back, even if it's flirting and not fucking. I don't honestly know what it is frankly, but just do whatever you're doing with Brittany. I'm not an idiot either."

At hearing Brittany's name, Eddie's ears pricked up like a dog's. *How the fuck did she know about Brittany? It was only two times!*

He looked up at her and said, "You're not an idiot. You're a smart and beautiful woman, Caroline. I just can't lose you. Ever. If I ever strayed, which I'm not saying I did . . ."

"You did, Eddie," Caroline said. "You admitted it in therapy, remember?"

"Okay. Well, but if I ever did *after* that, *it was for me*, not you." He said in an exaggerated tone, parroting his wife's reasoning so she would hear how hollow it sounded.

"It was for you?" Caroline said softly, considering that they had very real and very similar rationales for their actions. Her mind raced around the painful possibility that they were more in sync than not.

His affairs were for him. Caroline actually believed her husband, and, when she defended him to Annabelle, saying just that, she knew she was right. The attention Eddie got from these women, whoever they were, filled a bottomless hole dug way back by his drunk dad.

A few minutes later, she asked for clarification. "I mean, when I was pregnant, were you just . . . being needy? Which, by the way, I know you are. I know you love attention, but like, was any part of you back then figuring out if you, if you really wanted a kid with me . . ."

"Are you for friggin' real? I loved you, Caroline! How could you ask that? Always! Since ninth grade in Ms. Maher's class," he yelled. "I. LOVE. YOU. I just, you know, need distractions. I crave attention like a man in a desert craves water.

"And," he said, pausing. "I know this sounds really sexist and shitty and just awful, but I never thought you'd do it too. You're doing it feels so much bigger than me because I know mine doesn't mean shit. I know that. I'm the one who, well, did it, so I know about myself and how I was feeling during it: *nothing*. FUCKING NADA.

"It's a horrible thing to say that it's bigger with you, but that's how I feel. In fact, it's nuclear with you." Eddie stood up, circled the room, and stretched out again on the sofa, one leg resting on the back again. He covered his head with a soft pillow and moaned into it. He sounded like an animal who had been run over.

Caroline chose not to go over and comfort him; she knew it would restore a connection she was trying to break. Her face felt hot, and the tears came. She rubbed her temples and closed her eyes to swim inside her thoughts.

And then she considered Eddie Clarkson's belief that his wife, his woman, would never stray. Her anger at this presumption rumbled and boiled up in her.

Perhaps it was rage.

Chapter 49

Horse Show Crescendo

T his Joey thing is the ultimate mindfuck," Annabelle said as she and Caroline settled into high-viewing chairs beside the horse ring at the Sea Crest Rolex Classic. "At the beginning of the summer, I thought you'd imagined a ghost on a Boston Whaler. Then, when you told me yesterday, finally . . . Jesus, how could you keep that secret from me?"

"It took a week to settle."

"I get that, I forgive you. I mean, *not really.*" Annabelle jabbed her. "But let's just acknowledge there's something crazy happening around you."

"Why would he show up after all this time and then not reappear for a week?" said Caroline, jamming on a sun hat. It was eleven in the morning and the Classic was already under way. Gigi, Rosie, and Annabelle's youngest, Lily, were competing.

"Well, he *is* sending cryptic messages. The Frisbee and the shell and all that. So we know that Joey is kicking around somewhere near you," Annabelle said. "Do you get the impression Eddie is still watching you?"

Caroline rearranged the items in her bag instead of responding to the question. Annabelle always said Caroline's lips curled strangely when she lied, so she didn't look up. Maybe she'd switch topics, or perhaps the girls would ride soon.

"Hello? Do you?" Annabelle pushed.

"Who knows?" Caroline finally responded, vowing to steer the conversation away from the talk she'd had with Eddie. "I know I saw Joey, and I don't believe Eddie knows he's even alive. But Joey is screwing with Eddie for sure. He got a trucking job just to gain entry here."

"I can't get my head around any of it. Okay, so he's hovering around the stables, but why is he taunting Eddie?" Annabelle asked.

"I don't know, I'm so nervous I feel like I'm going to puke all the time."

"Just do your mom thing. Handle your clients better than ever," Annabelle advised, placing her arm around her and pulling Caroline to her. She tipped the brim of her hat up and looked into her friend's eyes. "Choices will become clear if you focus on the things that matter most to you: your kids, your kids, your kids, and, oh, your kids. Then work. Everything else will fall into place. Hey, Gigi's pony is second in line over there."

Caroline smiled and waved at Gigi who, with a young woman trainer that Philippe had hired, was readying herself for her trip in the ring. Adult and child riders from all over the East Coast had trucked in horses and ponies to compete in the four rings for the first year of the Rolex Classic at Sea Crest Stables. In the cross rails, the easiest over fences division, the girls were to make their ponies walk, then trot, then canter and jump over six small jumps individually. Judges scored them based on the girls' posture, their command of the animals, and the steadiness of gait the animals displayed as they rounded the ring. Local kids who were paying thirty-five dollars for hourly lessons and didn't own a pony were competing on Eddie's ponies alongside wealthy girls who owned or leased their own. Caroline held her breath every time her pony, Scooby-Doo, was approaching the jump until he cleared it with Gigi safe and secure on his back.

Eddie stood at the entrance with Gigi, brushing dust off her back and tightening the pink striped bows on the ends of her braids. Meanwhile, Thierry tended to his niece's jacket, yanking it down in the back, brushing it off; Rosie was slated to go next. The riders' presentation counted for points as well. Not a collar or a bootstrap could be out of place. Eddie then polished both girls' boots. Ribbons, from blue for first place to brown for eighth, hung at the gate waiting to be awarded.

"You letting Eddie handle all the parenting needs over there?" Annabelle asked. "On the ice meter this weekend, where are you guys?"

"I told you, I don't really have much to discuss. He's been working and sleeping in the guest room," Caroline said, reaching into her bag to put on her sunglasses and ready her phone to film her daughter's trip in the ring. She was not ready to tell her friend that Eddie knew about Ryan. "You're right, all the design work I'm so behind on will save me from obsessing over decisions I'm not ready to make. Part of me never wants to see Ryan again. And another part of me, well, just wants to wait at home, like some prairie wife, hoping Joey rides in at sunset and explains what the hell is going on." Caroline turned to her friend. "And you? You talking to Mr. Polo Eurotrash Extraordinaire?"

"Nope. I'm really done. You should have stopped me at the start!" Annabelle elbowed her friend, teasing. "Hey, your daughter is going in."

Caroline stood, took off her sun hat, and videoed Gigi as she did her two-minute tour around the ring with Scooby-Doo. She turned to Annabelle. "It's so funny," she said. "She sticks her tongue out every time she jumps. I tell her, and she's so embarrassed . . . oh shit, I'm taping, and she'll hear this conversation." Then she said into the phone's microphone, "Sorry that I said that, honey. You're doing great."

Scooby-Doo trotted neatly into the ring, then cantered at the right spot and jumped over six sets of rails. Having completed the trip, just before the gate, the pony halted and turned toward the small crowd in the rafters beside the ring. Gigi lost her balance at the abrupt move by her animal and grabbed Scooby-Doo's neck to steady herself. The judge called out on the microphone, "Rider scores a seventy-one."

"I can't stand this. I know they aren't doing anything that dangerous yet, but it still scares me," Caroline said. "Her legs aren't strong at all, and she always loses balance at some point. She was tired at the end there. Oh, God, she's going to hear me worrying on this video too. She *hates* me worrying. *Sorry honey!*" She turned off her phone and slid it into her jacket pocket.

Caroline waved like a crazed person back at her daughter, yelling, "Good job, Scooby-Doo! Woo-hoo!" Gigi flapped her hand back in disgust, horrified someone might figure out she was related to Caroline.

"Stop, please. You're even embarrassing me," Annabelle said. "The moms don't yell like that. I know this is her first big competition, but that wasn't a soccer goal, for Christ's sake; it's an elegant hunter trip in a ring. Gigi's going to kill you. And she won't claim a ribbon, but she rode well, and got her lead changes when she needed to. At her age, maybe a year or two older, I was fox hunting in Virginia and flying over logs in the fields. She's got a way to go, but she's a nice little rider." Annabelle put her arm around her clueless friend's shoulder again. "Wait till she's Laeticia's age and jumping over fourteen three-foot-six-inch jumps as fast as she can in the Jumper division. You'll have a heart attack if you can't even handle the easiest class in the sport."

"Okay, okay. Look, Rosie's up next."

Eddie was now paying equal attention to Rosie, polishing her boots and wiping dust off her breeches.

"Wow, what the hell? You see that pony she's on?" Annabelle pointed. "That's Cashmere, one of the best ones on the East Coast. It's awfully nice of the barn to allow Rosie to ride him, considering that if anything happens, that's a half-million-dollar animal. It's strange putting someone as green as Rosie on him. And I was hoping, with all the working students and local kids here on hourly lessons, the playing field would be even, but that horse is going to beat everyone, if Rosie can get around the ring on him!"

"Eddie doesn't take chances like that with cash, ever," Caroline said. "Is he really a half-million-dollar pony? What's that to lease for a year?"

"Usually you figure like a third of the purchase price to lease it, so like one hundred and seventy-five thousand to lease for a year. It's, you know, a little risky to a put a kid on Cashmere in this silly little starter division. He usually does the large pony hunter class. I didn't even know that pony was here at Sea Crest. Philippe probably brought it in to try to lease it to someone, nice of Eddie to let Rosie show him off. It has very distinct markings on its nose, and just one sock on his hind leg."

"One sock?"

"I mean the color of the right hind hoof and shin; see how it's white, and the other one is brown?

"Yeah. You know, if Rosie gets to be a good little rider, I know Eddie would be happy to chip in and get her something her uncle couldn't afford. Sauerkraut is fine for now. I just don't get why Eddie is putting her on that priceless one?"

"Cashmere's a ballerina," Annabelle explained. "Baryshnikov with four legs. But that horse is powerful. Laeticia was a great rider at this age, but when she rode Cashmere for one summer, she had some issues with him. He's a peppy little rocket, and he takes off when he's spooked. The rider has to have some skill to handle him, and I think that Rosie is just . . . look at her, she looks terrified."

Caroline watched how solicitous Eddie was with Rosie, making sure she was well mounted before she stepped in the ring. "Something isn't right," Caroline said to Annabelle. "Maybe it's my nerves, I just . . . everything now is so off in my life. And, I'd venture to say, Eddie is spending more time with Rosie than he did with his own daughter."

Rosie and Cashmere trotted carefully around the ring. She posted correctly during the trot and looked beautiful doing so. Word spread fast among the horse moms that the half-million-dollar pony was in the ring. It seemed Cashmere was taking care of Rosie. "He's doing fine, so there's no need to worry," Annabelle said. Still, she was nervous for the child. Rosie was only a mediocre rider, and not at all experienced with the tension of real competition. Then, the animal did a lead change on cue, right as he rounded, and she felt the kid might even win.

As Rosie neared the second set of cross rails, she jumped all three flawlessly, and Caroline let out a deep breath. "She'll be fine. It'd be great if she beat all these little girls, even Gigi," she said. She sat back down on her chair and started to relax.

Annabelle didn't sit. "Still, she has a little way to go before she wins. She's doing fine, and I agree it would be nice. Just . . . one more tour around the ring, and one little step over the rails again and she'll be clear." She studied Rosie's position, knowing the child could never be a graceful rider like her own daughters—she was too stocky, and her movements too jerky to compete in the equitation divisions that judged the position and grace of the rider. Still, she wouldn't say that out loud, not even to Caroline.

"Is she going to win?" asked Caroline. "God, can you imagine the faces on all those bitchy mothers who came in from Greenwich if some unknown newcomer wins? It'd be great."

"Everyone always thinks an expensive horse always wins, but it's not really true. You can't win the Indy 500 just because you have a great car; if you can't drive it, you're going to crash. Same deal with this sport: in the end, it's still the skill of the rider that counts," Annabelle explained. "The best riders take the championship on mediocre horses all the time."

Caroline grabbed Annabelle's arm and Annabelle went on. "Fuck. Look at that, did you see that little trip as he was cantering there? It's sad that Rosie's parents are not here for her, her first big show. Remind me what exactly happened to them. She's lucky to have that uncle Thierry raising her."

"Thierry only told me the mother died when she was pregnant with Rosie, that the father wasn't present ever. They were able to save the baby. How sad for a child to be without a father or mother. It gives me chills every time I remember Eddie had an accident in this huge Hummer Jeep he insisted on buying back then, but it was only a hurt arm for him." Out in the ring, Rosie seemed to have some trouble with the reins. "Wait, did you see Cashmere trip again? He's not acting smooth, is he?"

"I told you, that pony is like a rocket, he can just take off, but that was just a stumble. Rosie is pulling too hard, and even a championship pony gets confused." Annabelle started biting her bottom lip as she watched Rosie. "Look again, just there, that was Rosie's fault. Her distance at the sixth jump was way too far away, so he had to take another stride then go over the cross rail awkwardly. It's called chipping when they're right near the jump. Distance is something everyone works on. Sometimes you guide the horse too close, sometimes you do it too far. Sometimes the horse is pissed and refuses to jump, and you fly off, and sometimes, the animal will just take over, cover your mistakes and get over it somehow. In the end, it comes down to whether the rider and animal are in sync, and Rosie and Cashmere just aren't. But she'll get through it, she's almost done."

On the last rail, at the stroke of noon, the Long Island Railroad train barreled by in the distance and honked, like a foghorn. Hearing it, Cashmere spooked. He refused to do the last jump. And poor Rosie, who had no experience in a real show ring or even handling a pony like this, had no time to prepare for the stop. She went flying over the top of the pony's neck and landed in the mud on the other side of the rails.

Eddie and Thierry rushed into the ring as Rosie lay on her back. Gigi ran yelling and crying to her best friend, as people crowded around her.

A medic yelled from the sidelines, "Don't move her! Let her lie still until we get help."

Caroline and Annabelle also ran into the ring, partially to help, but also to keep Gigi from touching her friend. Caroline picked up her daughter as she cried and hid her eyes, fearing the worst. "Don't talk to her, honey. She'll be okay." Gigi struggled to get down, but Caroline held her firmly. Rosie started to move her head left and right and bent her knees up, wincing from pain.

Caroline watched her husband tend to Rosie. He immediately lay in the dirt on his stomach, the obsessive-compulsive neat freak getting his clothes filthy. He set his arm on her tummy and began speaking softly into her ear. "It's okay, baby. Don't move. You may be hurt, so lie still. I'm here, honey. I'm always here for you, baby."

"I'm okay," Rosie whispered back. "I'm okay. I promise." She pushed on the mud with her elbows and sat up.

The medic said, "Just lie here, Rosie. Catch your breath. You got the wind knocked out of you. Did you hit your head?"

She shook her head no. Caroline thought it was strange that Thierry stood back a few feet, letting Eddie handle Rosie. Caroline knew this wasn't an issue of rank; the kid was Thierry's niece after all.

It was something else.

She listened to Eddie's distinctly parental tone.

He sounded just as he did when he comforted Gigi or Theo.

Rosie wiped away tears and smiled, embarrassed by all the attention. Eddie helped her sit up, and the crowd clapped for her.

"You're fine, baby, you're okay," Eddie said softly, rubbing her cheek.

Was he crying?

Eddie got to his knees, filthy with dirt, and then picked Rosie up, hugging her tightly. "C'mon, baby, lemme hold you now."

And with the way he held her, the way he talked to her, Caroline knew: Eddie had uttered these words as if Rosie were his own.

PART IV

Summer Thunder

Chapter 50

And So the World Crumbles

T<small>HE NEXT MORNING</small>

C aroline peeked in on her husband snoring in the guest room, and then quietly left the house. Waking up alone in bed made her jumpy in the mornings, and she got up earlier than she normally did. In shorts and a sweatshirt, she headed down the street for a dawn walk on Wiborg Beach from her home on Pondview Lane.

Once at the beach parking lot, Caroline could see the mist lingering from the cool night. The sun, rising in the distance, cast a pale pink glow over the dunes. Caroline left her sneakers at the edge of the lot and walked down a path between stalks of sea grass. Closer to the water, a lifeguard stand lay tipped forward, waiting for the guards to come to work and put it back upright. The sea was calm, more like a lake, with small waves lapping gently on the shore.

She placed her towel on a sandy ledge that a storm had created the week before. She sat on it, and when she poked at the edge with her fingers, several large chunks of solid sand crumbled like glaciers in a warming climate.

Her suspicions about Rosie had now marinated for the entire weekend. The young girl walked like Eddie Clarkson. Their feet were the same. Her chin, her eyes, the same. They were two paper dolls cut from the same Clarkson fold. How blind she had been; Rosie looked more like Eddie than even Gigi and Theo, who were much smaller in build, more like their mom.

Rosie, always the leader of the gang, rarely walked; she ran excitedly from one activity to the next, a wide smile plastered on her broad little face. She scrambled into a back seat or dining chair as if she were climbing Everest. Eddie was that way too, roaring headfirst into every situation.

The LIRR honking in the distance, and spooking that expensive horse, resonated in Caroline's head.

"You're okay, baby. I'm here, and you're okay," Eddie had said, over and over.

Not just "baby."

His baby.

The Atlantic blew its familiar salty mist at her, a hint of bluefish in the air today. In the distance seagulls swarmed a trawler, its nets pulled up. The foam from the waves sparkled like a line of white diamonds in the morning light. Piping plovers played chicken with the water line. Although her beach, her sea, her sand looked, felt, and smelled as it always did, Caroline knew everything in her life was different. She was now at a breaking point.

Eddie had admitted to an affair when she was pregnant with Gigi. He had neglected to inform her (minor detail) that he'd gotten his girlfriend pregnant as well, and that they had created Rosie. Thierry, that kind man in that ever-present colonial ponytail, was her uncle. He was the brother of the woman Eddie had been sleeping with.

Over the last four years, Eddie had often taken Rosie for her lessons at the barn Thierry used to manage, and for treats afterward. He and Thierry did talk back then when Thierry was handling all the ponies. But they had been in touch for the six years before that, when Rosie was born and then a younger child.

Eddie had never shown particular attachment to Rosie, except to be nice to a friend of his daughter's. Or had he? Not that she thought about it, he did take them into town a bunch of times over the years, and he always jumped at the chance to watch a Disney movie with them. But Eddie spent all weekend with the kids and their playdates, taking them to play mini golf, and making forts out of old sheets. Eddie was just being himself, excited and game. Caroline could not hate herself now for not seeing it earlier. Earlier had meant just watching *The Incredibles* for the hundredth time, Eddie and kids with their friends all snuggled up on that TV room's enormous sofa. Earlier was undetectable, all before that moment he cried in that wet, filthy mud, cradling his hurt baby in his arms.

There were other discreet parental things she had overlooked. Now that the girls were competing, earlier in the summer, Eddie had bought Rosie a show jacket too when he ordered one for Gigi. "Just to even things out," he told Caroline. She'd chalked it up to Eddie's boundless generosity.

Now she knew the attention was his fatherly duty.

When Rosie tumbled off Cashmere, Eddie was the real first responder, the one lying with the child, whispering comfort in her ear. In the twenty years since Caroline had met Eddie, she'd never seen him get so dirty. Thierry, who'd raised the child, had given Eddie some space with her.

Thierry knew.

How could Thierry not have known all along?

Rosie was prideful, obstinate, and impatient, like her father.

The facts were clear, her husband had another daughter, and her children had a half-sister.

Would Gigi squeal in delight at the news? Or would she be furious that she was only finding out now? It was a double betrayal on Eddie's part: of his wife and of the kids who'd played together for so many summers. Gigi would have to ask, "Why didn't you tell me before? Does Daddy have another wife too?"

Looking out at the horizon, the pink fading to bright blue, Caroline considered Rosie's complexion; it was a little more olive than Gigi's, and she had darker eyes. Who was the mother? How did Eddie meet her, and where? How long did it go on? And how did the mother die exactly?

Caroline's cell phone buzzed in her pocket. She looked at it and rolled her eyes.

> It's the Upholsterer. I have a question about an armchair.
> Sorry to ask on a Monday morning. Is now a good time?

Caroline typed forcefully: *No. Definitely not a good time.*

Thirty seconds later, Caroline grabbed her phone out of her pocket and added: *Sorry. Not you. Just me and things.*

She placed her fingers, a bit sandy, behind the lower part of her skull and massaged it. She and Ryan had another full night and day until they'd meet for drinks. She couldn't bother to do the math: Was it thirty or thirty-five hours? It didn't matter. She could wait. She now felt like she could wait forever.

Caroline piled sand next to her and smoothed out the sides into a teepee shape. When Eddie had asked about Ryan, she'd balked, like Cashmere the pony, if only to protect Eddie's feelings. But another child? In the bad behavior book of marriage, that was not something one protected a spouse from.

And when she would confront him with the fact that Rosie had his waddle, his toes, his eyes, his bullish instincts, *his bossy personality for God's sakes*, Eddie would go on the offensive. He would argue he hadn't outright lied to her. He'd say he technically committed a crime of omission. She could see his arms flying up in the air out of exasperation. As if she, Caroline, were a little off.

She would calmly explain that he hadn't merely neglected to tell her about a woman he was texting. (*Who was Brittany, by the way!*) He had outright lied about a child he'd fathered—who also happened to be the living, breathing best friend of their daughter!

Caroline grabbed a large clamshell with jagged edges and threw it at the shoreline. It cartwheeled a few times along the sand. When the next wave came in, the sea inched it back home, and her mood sunk even deeper.

The tears were flowing now. She choked a bit as her chest convulsed, and used the sleeve of her sweatshirt to wipe her nose. Rosie was five months older than Gigi. Eddie had gotten two women pregnant in the same season, during the winter of 2008—they shared trimesters, Gigi born in October, and Rosie in late May. A sad, angry, humiliated spin cycle of emotions sped up inside her. It whirled out of control, banging in Caroline's head and heart.

Caroline threw another large clamshell, this time harder. It plunked into the flat sea. Something about the ripples it created, something about the heavy *thunk* it made, caused her to stop feeling sorry for herself, and to forgive herself for her choices. She could, if she tried hard enough, turn off that horrible, revolving, self-pity machine.

If she lived out here this fall, she could more quietly leave Eddie. Thank God she'd signed the kids up for the East Hampton schools. Her children would finally be free, released from those constricting urban uniforms and rules. And if she did move, would she take Rosie part of the year? She was family, after all. Now it made perfect sense that Rosie's father was not around—he had been here the whole time. Caroline couldn't *not* mother Rosie now; she *wanted* to mother her. Rosie didn't have a mother of her own.

Caroline's phone pinged again: *Tuesday fine, the project is very hard in the meantime. I know you can solve that.*

Ryan was a good man, even if their affair hadn't clarified as much as Annabelle had promised. The Rosie bombshell provided all the self-enlightenment she needed.

She answered Ryan's text: *I'm looking forward to a Tuesday meeting, but a lot is going on.*

She wondered if the next time they'd be together she'd end it, and explain her heart and mind had too much occupying them now to allow room for an affair.

As she wrote, the three little dots pulsated on his side of the text conversation, indicating he was writing too.

Then the dots stopped. Ryan started again, typing: *I'm not sure the project can wait until Tuesday.*

She remembered Annabelle saying something about knowing the affair would be over when it was destined to be over. "It will be black and white, on or off, living or dead." They'd discussed that little voice inside that had told them in high school or college that the relationship they'd been in had reached its expiration date. With this Rosie news and Joey in the truck, though she felt undecided in the middle gray, she wasn't sure she had the mental energy for Ryan.

She threw a handful of pebbles into the sea. They landed on the shore, and the piping plovers pecked at them to see if they were food. Her family would take it slow, and focus only on the school move now. Eddie would come out on weekends, and stay in the guest room. She had to find a way to forgive him for the sake of her children, and for Rosie, who was motherless and so young.

She couldn't co-parent the kids and despise Eddie forever; at some point, the fury of betrayal would have to subside. Remembering his childhood deprivations might help explain his behavior, but it didn't change how she felt. She did not want to be married to a man who had to gorge on attention to fill a void, and who would lie, like an alcoholic, to cover up his binging.

Over and out.

Forgiveness is easier when you don't love someone anymore.

CAROLINE'S PHONE PINGED and vibrated in her pocket again. She was in no mood to handle Ryan's growing attachment, nor his "hard" project she had to solve. It was almost the end of summer: time to wind it down, not rev it up.

Her phone pinged and vibrated more.

So stop fucking texting me, she thought.

Caroline had her kids, she had her work, and now she had her hometown, fulltime. Joey Whitten was alive, perhaps to stay, perhaps to leave again, but still, he was breathing. She had to concentrate on the good, rather than the messy. A flock of seagulls squawked and picked at a fish carcass ten yards down the shore. One flew away with a chunk of skin and flesh, and then five others chased after him until he dropped it, which sent them all diving to the sand like kamikaze pilots. It made her smile. She could now visit these birds every morning, with her children, if she wished, all year round.

It was 7:30 a.m., the sun now half an hour higher and burning her forehead. She pulled up the hood of her sweatshirt to cover her fair skin to her eyebrows. Her body felt warm.

Caroline's phone pinged and vibrated yet another time. This was too much. She thought to herself, *Shut up, Ryan, please!*

She pulled her phone out of her bag and shielded her eyes to see the screen.

From Thierry: seven missed calls that had never rung with the bad cell service on the beach, along with four texts.

> *CAROLINE, COME TO THE BARN RIGHT NOW.*
> *GO TO LAETITIA von TATTENBACH'S TRUNK*
> *SOMETHING BIG IS HAPPENING.*
> *NOW.*

Chapter 51

Get Your Titties There Fast

Caroline climbed back up the five feet of sandy ledge, which tumbled away in chunks beneath her. She ran back to the parking lot.

On the cement now, her mouth and throat raw, she regretted that today, of all days, she had decided to power walk to the beach to burn calories instead of riding her pale-green cruiser—the same bike she used in high school—as she usually did. Here was more proof that exercise messed up your life. Running now on the streets toward her home on Pondview Lane, she tried to speed-dial Thierry, but the call went straight to voicemail. She tried to text and run but only succeeded in dropping her phone when her bag slid down her arm. She screamed, "Fuck!"

In her driveway, parched and with her heart pounding, Caroline crept up her porch. Thankfully, she hadn't closed the large wooden door on her way to the beach, because it always creaked. She pushed the screen door silently. No one was in the kitchen yet, though she knew her kids and Eddie might be brushing their teeth upstairs. Francis would arrive soon and help Eddie with breakfast. Caroline tiptoed into the back pantry, grabbed her car keys from a metal bin nailed to the wall, went into the armoire where Eddie thought he'd very successfully hidden his second office key, and sped back out to her car.

Her hands shaking, Caroline dialed Thierry again. Again, the call went straight to voicemail. She left a voice message: "Would you call me and explain? Are you okay?"

She flew down the back roads to Main Street in East Hampton, leading to Route 27 and Sea Crest Stables. In town, with the streets almost empty at this hour, she charged through a light that had changed to red two seconds before. She figured people in Manhattan did that all the time, the Hamptons' cops had to be used to it.

Immediately, a police cruiser followed her with his siren on. From his car microphone, he asked, "Pull over, please." Caroline hesitated for fifty yards, hoping he didn't mean it. Again, the microphone bellowed, "Pull over immediately!"

She used the sleeves of her thick sweatshirt to wipe her face, now moist from worry and sweat. She yanked the sweatshirt half over her head, her T-shirt now coming off with it, exposing her bra on her bare skin.

A man's voice said, "You do know it's illegal to offer sexual favors to a police officer, ma'am?"

"No, I'm so embarrassed officer, I . . ."

"Haven't seen those huge boobs since spin the bottle got out of hand in seventh grade!"

"Oh my God, James. It's you."

Officer James Vincent and his wife, Tracy, had had a beach barbeque with their kids two weeks before. Eddie had come, even though James never much liked him, and Caroline had always sensed that.

"Don't you dare give me a ticket."

"I'm not. I wouldn't. Ever." James knocked on her roof and

winked at her. "Caroline, you look kind of crazy right now. Your hair, the shirt half off your shoulder, what's . . ."

"Can you give me a police escort to Eddie's barn, to Sea Crest Stables, and let me speed?"

He shook his head, "Negative on that."

"Can I go a little fast out of here and can you ignore it?"

Officer Vincent flicked the top of his police cap up to expose those warm brown eyes she'd known since middle school. "I can ignore you, but you also want to make sure the rest of the cops don't see you. Take Route 114 in the back, then left all the way down on Stephen Hands to Route 27. Cops don't monitor that whole section of town at this hour."

"Got it, and thanks."

Caroline careened like a race car driver down the back roads, the centrifugal force pulling her toward the door as she sped around curves. Arriving at the entrance to the stables at 32 Spring Farm Lane, Caroline punched in the Monday code at the gate. It was the off day. There was no riding, no lessons, no visiting. A few grooms would come in to feed and turn out the animals, but there would not be any Eddie, clients, or Philippe. Thierry knew this. She was pretty sure this was part of his plan.

Chapter 52

Horses Don't Bite, or Do They?

A groom, far in the distance, walked a horse out to pasture as Caroline entered the stables through a trellised walkway. There were four corridors in the main stable, each connected to a rotunda in the middle with the blue mosaicked fountain where she now stood. To her left and right, front and back, there were long halls with stalls housing one horse each, twenty on each side.

A navy and brass trunk with the client's name engraved on a brass plaque on the front stood beside the entrance to each stall. Caroline walked down one hall and saw the infamous Talbot family green and silver trunk, which, despite her apprehension at this moment, still amused her. Every other client in the barn had agreed to Eddie's rule that they purchase navy trunks with brass borders from a specific supplier. This did not sit well with Mr. Talbot, one of those stubborn New York rich guys who had to score a point in every situation. Even when Eddie offered to pay for the blue trunk himself—just to meet his compulsive need for neat lines and order—Mr. Talbot refused.

There had been no further texts from Thierry and no calls. Caroline knew more clues lay before her—about everyone's strange behavior this summer and about Joey and his delivery truck—but there were none yet.

If Thierry didn't show up soon, she would go up to Eddie's office again to look for papers that might shed some light on that emergency text. Those horse trunks the men were always arguing over—now she'd take time to look at one carefully. She noticed that the bottom siding on Laetitia's trunk seemed to stick out. As she started to jam it into the base with her toes, Caroline heard a familiar voice inside the stall behind her. "Don't do that. Please, don't touch it. Be very discreet right now, Mrs. Clarkson. Not sure why you're here today." He didn't want to tell her they'd set a trap.

She whispered to Marcus McCree without turning her head: "I'm just checking on things." Caroline sat on the trunk instead, cross-legged, and pretended to busy herself with emails. "I just, uh, need something here, I'll leave soon."

Caroline nodded and asked, "Are you okay in there? You want to tell me why you're hiding in a horse stall?"

"This horse is looking at me like a bull," he said.

"He's not going to do anything," Caroline said. "Just stay in front of him, so he doesn't kick. That's the only way you can get hurt. If you surprise him from the back, he might kick his hind legs."

"He keeps rolling his lips up like he's showing his teeth to a dentist. Hell, now this guy is pushing his nose at the back of my head here. Do they bite, ever?"

"Marcus, no. Now, please: I know something is going on. You have to tell me."

"Tell you what, Mrs. Clarkson?"

"C'mon, at this point you have to call me Caroline. Every single thing you know. I got half the story, and if you would just please help me fill in what I need, okay?"

"Okay . . . so, for starters, Joey is here."

As Caroline inhaled, her whole body jerked. She laid her head back on the wooden stall behind her and said, "I guess you mean Joey Whitten."

"Yes, ma'am. *That* Joey."

Chapter 53

So the Ghost Can Walk and Talk After All

That Joey Whitten appeared at the far south opening of the stables. As the early morning sun lit up the tips of his blond hair, particles of dust danced around his shoulders. He pushed a wheelbarrow with feed down the center corridor.

The tears streamed down Caroline's face. Her chest ached; she clasped her hands over her sternum as if she could force the throbbing to stop.

Marcus stood behind her. Sweetly, he reached his hand out and patted her shoulder. "It's going to be okay," he said. "Starting today, everything will be different. Best you stay on the trunk, and just let it play out for a minute, but then you should go."

She hadn't cried this hard since the Ocean Rescue chief came to her door: *"I'm sorry, we can't look for him anymore. It's now a search and recover mission, not a search and rescue."*

Through the rivulets of tears, Caroline could see enough to judge from a distance that Joey was thicker all around, but still lean. His long legs propelled the heavy cart along, and his arms looked bigger, perhaps he'd been doing manual labor for years.

Now, thirty-eight, he'd grown his hair out. The color was always a mix of brown and honey, but it had turned more uniform over the years as if the alchemy of sun, sand, and saltwater had dyed it lighter.

She stood now as he approached, and reached out to touch him, to weave her fingers into his hair. The stubble on his face was rougher, and he had creases beside his mouth. He was heavier in the middle, and his shoulders looked wider; there was just *more* of him everywhere.

As Joey passed by her, he shook his head, and lifted his chin, signaling her to go back and sit. His own eyes welled with tears. "You're more beautiful," he whispered quietly, as he rolled a wheelbarrow into the stall next to Caroline, dumped a bit of feed into the horse's box, and then exited. As he passed by her, Joey leaned in, and his shoulder brushed hers. "I owe you a big explanation."

"Can't we do it now?"

"It's not safe yet, not until everything goes down here," Joey said, rubbing her arm with his. He then rolled the wheelbarrow toward the other end of the corridor.

Sitting on the trunk again, her legs crossed, Caroline pulled her ankles in and banged her head several times against the wooden beams behind her. Her stomach was tightening like the middle of a rope with people tugging on either end.

Marcus whispered again, "He's right: something is going down here today. Right here. With the trunks. It's going to look like business as usual, so just stay cool."

"Marcus, it's never business as usual when we are talking Eddie Clarkson," Caroline said. In her mind, she was going over Maryanne's ledgers, books, and files. "I'm working on my own clues."

"Okay, but I'm not sure it's fully safe," Marcus said. He didn't want to force her to leave, but he worried she'd mess up something they'd worked on for two years.

"And screw that idea of *safe* Marcus. I'm the wife, what the hell are they going to do to me?"

"All right, I get that. If you want to know what's really going on, stroll around a little. Then, notice the sides of half the trunks are loose. Just please don't kick them, in case someone is around. Then come back, we got time. Be back here in five minutes. Don't go long."

Caroline closed her eyes and did three Darth Vader yoga breaths to pull oxygen deep into her chest. Then she pushed it out through her nostrils from the depths of her diaphragm. Whether the technique helped or not, she wasn't sure, but it was less dramatic than hyperventilating into a brown paper bag.

She stood and walked down one of the corridors, her heart pounding. She sensed she was being watched. "Hello?" she yelled out. Her voice echoed into the high cathedral ceilings. Aware security cameras were taping her, she pretended to playfully sweep the dust with her feet, but actually kicked the side wall of each trunk. The bottom gold brass molding was indeed loose on some of them.

She sat again on the von Tattenbach trunk and waited. "Ten minutes. You'll get a full picture then," Marcus whispered. "You deserve to know it all. And I get that you on your own know things, just please, in a little while, you must leave."

Right on time, to Caroline's left, on the opposite end of the corridor from where Joey had entered, Philippe appeared, along with four men. They walked straight to the first trunk, not noticing Caroline fifty yards away, slightly hidden beside a column. Caroline knew it wasn't a coincidence that they were here on a Monday.

The four men leaned down and circled a trunk at the end of the corridor. One used a screwdriver to jimmy open the bottom sash of the trunk. He started to slide something out, but Caroline's view was obstructed by the other men. One of the men handed Philippe a backpack. He opened it, and placed several brown tightly wrapped packages on the ground, all the size of stacks of bills. Then Philippe shook the men's hands. He heaved the backpack onto his shoulders, jumping slightly from the immense weight of it. Did Eddie know about this? He was most likely on the jungle gym about now, under a fort made of blankets, with a bagel picnic he'd made for the kids.

Caroline coughed loudly—on purpose.

"Is that you? Caroline?! No lessons on Mondays!" Philippe yelled.

She stood up nonchalantly, noting Philippe's body language. He stood too erect, like a six-year-old boy who'd been caught eating cookies before dinner. The other men straightened their spines as well. One of them threw up his hands in shock at Philippe. Another angrily shook his head.

Marcus whispered back, "They turned the cameras off, as they always do, but we've got armed security in every second or third stall, hiding with one of these huge horses."

"I'm going to ask them what the hell they are doing," she whispered back at Marcus.

"No, no, just act all cool. And then, go. Promise me, you gotta leave."

"I trust you, but cool is not my style, Marcus, even on a slow day in my life. Everything makes me anxious. And today, it's about as bad as it's ever been. But I'll try."

"Just don't ask too many questions. Then leave," he said. "My phone fell in a damn water bucket in here, I left it on the ledge and the horse moved his head, dropping it in. I'll get another phone from the guys and text you when I can."

Caroline rotated her head in circles to ready herself for this strange confrontation. She ambled, just to make the men at the end of the corridor uneasy. When she reached them, she calmly said, "Hello, gentlemen. I'm just here to give the horses some treats. What are you doing here? My husband likes no work at all on Mondays."

"It's just business, Caroline. Normal business for the barn," Philippe said.

"Can I see what kind of business . . ." She motioned to his backpack, and then the horse trunk in front of them, aware she wasn't exactly following Marcus's overly cautious instructions.

Philippe glared at her.

"I mean, it's a simple question, Philippe. Eddie is at home with the kids. Should I call him over?"

"No, it's fine. We are talking about horses. I may be leasing some new ones."

"I see." She squinted at him. "Goodbye, gentlemen."

Caroline made her way down a corridor and outside. As she reached her car door, she received a text:

IT'S MARCUS, I GOT THE GUY'S PHONE TWO STALLS DOWN.

JOEY SAYS MEET HIM AT THE ROCK.

Chapter 54

That Rock

On Mondays, which were off days for many Hamptons restaurants, it was always calm on the beach lining Fort Pond Bay, shaped like a crab with its claws facing inward. The soft bayside waves slapped against the shore, splashing rhythmically. Caroline remembered how, on so many nights, Joey would take her here and lay beside her on a blanket, the moon painting a thick white stripe on the flat bay before them. She walked slowly over the pebbly concrete toward the public access to the bay, beside the closed-up Navy Beach.

A loud pop sounded down the lane. Her nerves on fire now, Caroline dropped her phone. A white box truck rolled away in the opposite direction a hundred yards down. She waited, in case Joey was driving, but the truck turned right toward the main Montauk drag.

Caroline walked through the gate and toward their slanted boulder. She lay against it, soaking up the sun, willing herself to breathe normally. She took off her sweatshirt and used it as a cushion for her head. She craned her neck every minute in each direction to see if Joey was approaching.

CAROLINE KNOTTED HER sweatshirt sleeves around her head like a turban to prevent her fair skin from getting burned in the morning sun. An hour had passed, and still there was no sign of Joey. What's more, she had no way of contacting him; she had no idea where he'd been for the past thirteen years, much less his phone number. She'd texted Marcus from that new number twice. He told her to keep waiting.

She texted Annabelle.

> *Can you meet me at Navy Beach now?*
> *JOEY IS 100% ALIVE . . .*

Twenty minutes later, Annabelle approached her friend. Caroline stated clearly, "I don't think Joey is coming."

"And we're waiting right here because . . ."

"Something's going on at the barn," Caroline said. "Something illegal. Thierry knows about it and is involved. But I feel he's not a willing participant, just from the looks he gave me when I asked him if there was anything he wanted to talk about. This morning— early, at around seven-thirty—Thierry made me rush over to the barn. I did what I was told, but when I showed up, there was no Thierry at all. I texted him, but he didn't answer. I think he wanted me to see Philippe in some business deal with men I'd never seen, passing cash around. Joey was there for a minute, and I was told to meet Joey here. This is our rock—the place we used to meet when we were together, he used to . . ."

"I know about the fucking rock! You made out here, you shagged him here a billion times in the moonlight. Jesus! It's me, okay?" Annabelle said, smiling. "But why isn't Joey here if he said he'd be?"

"I don't know. I'm worried," Caroline said, banging her palms together several times.

"By the sound of your voice, I can tell it would be a bad time to make a joke about Joey reappearing during our summer pact."

"It would."

"Just give this a second of consideration, in all seriousness," Annabelle continued. "His arrival this summer is a twist of timing here that could be really . . ."

"Annabelle. This has become so much bigger. There's a crime here. I promise you."

Annabelle nodded slowly, not at all sure she shared Caroline's paranoia. "Eddie's finances are the one thing he's got under control. Even Arthur agrees he's fantastic at real estate development," she reminded Caroline, attempting to lessen her relentless, often silly, anxiety. "Honey, look, relax. There's so much you don't get about the horse world. It is very complex. Tons of people are skimming fees and making shady deals. The barn gets a good pony for ten grand from Holland, trains it, puts a great working student on it at good shows so it has a public record of wins, then leases it to women like me for fifty to a hundred grand a year. Of course, Eddie and Philippe are skimming off like that to their clients, but they . . ."

"It has nothing to do with horse buying and leasing, I promise," Caroline said. "You get patronizing sometimes. In this case, you're wrong and I'm right; this time, *trust my nerves*. The barn is covering up something."

Caroline's phone rang. She screamed into it, breathing quickly, praying Thierry was calling to explain. Without looking at the number calling, she yelled, "Hello! Is it you?"

"It's the Upholsterer," the caller said. "Is that the 'you' you meant . . ."

"Fuck, Ryan! You have to wait a day! Jesus Christ. It's Monday, not Tuesday! I can't deal with any of your stuff right now!" She hung up.

Annabelle shook her head. "Honey, call him back."

"I don't want to call him back," Caroline said. "He'll never understand, or be able to know what's going on at the barn. He'll never . . ." She looked down at the phone and realized Ryan was still on it and she hadn't disconnected him. "Fuck!"

She put the phone to her ear with one hand and banged her thigh with the other. Annabelle rubbed her arm to try to get her to calm down.

Ryan said into her ear, "Uh, Caroline, can you tell me what the matter is? I'm sorry I called, but I know it says Roger the Upholsterer. You're not guilty of anything if you're talking to a tradesman when you're a designer."

"Okay, Ryan."

"You sound upset. How can I help?"

"It's not totally clear what's going on. I'm sure we're safe, just the situation isn't."

"What situation?"

"Oh my God, like six situations. Can you keep a secret, Ryan? Can you do that for me? Please?"

"Are you kidding? There's no one better on the planet to trust than me right now with *anything*. You think I'm ever telling Suzy or anyone what we're up to? You got more secrets? Pile 'em into the vault of Ryan Miller."

Caroline nodded her head while blinking tears from her eyes. She slumped down from the weight of the morning and sat in the sand. This did make sense; she could trust Ryan Miller. "Can you meet Annabelle and me at Navy Beach? You know that big boulder in the sand, the one that juts out a little to the right before the bay starts?"

"Of course. And of course, I know that boulder. Who didn't get laid in high school at that boulder?"

"Hurry. And can you bring that volunteer fireman siren thing you have in your car? Just in case."

"I can't use it for fun. It's not a toy."

"This whole situation is not a game. I promise, Ryan."

"Give me about ten minutes and I'm there."

"You're perfect," Caroline said.

Annabelle grabbed Caroline's sandals and helped her up, saying, "I like this Mr. Architect guy. Portable siren? That's sexy. Sometimes you just need a real man in life!"

Annabelle looked once more at her best friend. "And before Ryan gets here, take that stupid sweatshirt off your head. You look like a freak."

Chapter 55

The Trio Twists and Turns

Ryan Miller drove up in a beat-up white Volvo wagon, laying his strong arm on the edge of the open car window.

"Did you get a new car?" Caroline asked.

"It's a client's car. I have no idea what's going on, but I figured I don't want to be driving a vehicle with my own plates right now in case you were worried about Eddie." He shielded his face and looked up. "Nice to see you again, Annabelle. It's been a while since that stress-free sip of champagne at Duryea's."

"Nice to see you too, Ryan," Annabelle said. "Awkward doesn't define that day."

"So, tell me, what is this serious, non-game, Caroline?" He got out of the car and placed his arms softly on each woman's back and guided them twenty feet further toward the dunes.

Annabelle noticed his manners and the agile way his body moved, not to mention the way his arm had bulged nicely in his crisp polo shirt on the edge of the car window. A hint of envy flooded her bloodstream at the realization that Caroline had chosen better than she had, which wasn't entirely fair since the whole thing was Annabelle's idea.

This guy was hot, in a good, responsible way. Annabelle checked out his outfit further, how his jeans slung on his ass, how the polo shirt blowing in the breeze now outlined his large build: rugged *and* preppy? What woman got that in life? *Jesus!* Philippe de Montaigne and Mr. Almond-Fondler Thaddeus were both handsome, but neither was as cool in their veins as this Mr. Architect.

Only one good solution: another pact next summer to even the score.

Annabelle noticed Ryan's worn flip-flops as he walked a bit ahead, his arm tighter now around Caroline. Men shouldn't ever wear flip-flops with jeans unless they were at a clambake, somewhere maybe getting their toes wet or sandy. Or, she decided, a man might wear flips-flops like those around town because, possibly, *he didn't own great moccasins?*

Well, one thing: Mr. Architect wasn't rich. You couldn't have it all in a man. Not that she cared about a man's money, well, *maybe a little.*

"OKAY, CAROLINE," RYAN said, stopping in the middle of the beach now. "Tell us what's going on."

"Something illegal is happening at the barn," Caroline explained slowly. "And I don't want to call the police because security is already there, this guy Marcus McCree who sometimes drives Eddie. He's got a large company too, men who drive and I guess provide security when needed."

Ryan asked, "Are sure you can trust this Marcus?"

"He's the kind of man, like you, frankly, you tell just from the way he holds himself. That's a yes that he's on my side," Caroline said. "Besides, Joey and he are in touch."

"Okay, who is Joey?" Ryan asked.

Caroline looked at Annabelle and then back at Ryan. With her fingers, she pushed her lips together and bobbed her head slowly, staring at him with wide eyes.

"Not *that* Joey?" he said.

She nodded.

Ryan rubbed his scruffy stubble hard, taking this in, then he roughly raked his hair with both hands. Annabelle took another good peek at his triceps rounding out from the bottom sleeve of his polo shirt. One word: unfair.

Though Caroline's statement defied any realm of common sense, Ryan got it. "Joey Whitten, from the lifeguard squad, is not, shall I assume, in the depths of the sea?"

Caroline shook her head. "Alive. Joey Whitten is alive. I saw him, a few times this summer, from a distance, though."

Ryan chuckled a little to hide the fact that this stung. "How long exactly have we known that Joey is on solid ground and back among the living?"

"You know, always, and never, and just, like, kind of for the last two months," Caroline said rapidly. "And he's been hiding since he came back. I don't know where, but I bet it has something to do the barn and with Eddie."

Ryan nodded. "And you think Eddie is involved in illegal activity?"

"How could he not be?" Caroline said.

"What's your proof?" Ryan asked. He stopped talking, as a supped-up Range Rover drove toward them on the sand.

The clueless, city driver leaned out his window and asked, "You need permits to drive on this beach?"

"Yes! Of course you need a sticker!" Caroline snapped. The couple shook their heads and drove away.

"Caroline, chill out. That man was asking a very normal question," Annabelle added.

Watching Caroline tap her foot furiously now, plotting her next move, Ryan knew he'd miss this beautiful woman. Sure, she was a little too wound up a little too often, but she also emitted sexual energy that no man could resist.

"What, Ryan?" Caroline asked, impatient, pulling her thick hair up into a ponytail.

Ryan now understood that the Caroline Clarkson he'd had this summer was, at this very minute, slipping out of his hands like the soft sand beneath him. He'd most likely not see that stunning face in bed again, nor hear that laugh he worked so hard to earn. Ryan inhaled deeply. He loved Suzy, but he'd miss another woman now. Deeply.

"Hello? Ryan? You with us?" Annabelle said.

"Yeah, it's just a lot to digest.

Tears started to drip down Caroline's cheeks; anger over Eddie's betrayal overpowering her. "Plus, well . . . there's something really big besides the fact that Joey is alive." Caroline rubbed her head and placed it between her knees to get more oxygen. And then she sat down in the sand again.

Annabelle, now next to her, put her hand on her best friend's knee. "Tell us, what else? Is it Eddie? Is there something huge we still don't know?"

Caroline looked up. Tears flooded her eyes, and she coughed, choking on the words. "Eddie. Has. Another. Child. A daughter."

"No!" Annabelle yelled.

"Yes. He had a thing with some woman related to Thierry about ten years ago. I have no idea who she was, I just know she's not alive, died around the time of the birth. Thierry and Eddie are keeping Eddie's paternity a secret. They have payments between them."

Annabelle rubbed her forehead. "So who is Eddie's other child? Is she much older or . . ."

"It's Rosie Moinot. Rosie is Eddie's daughter," Caroline answered, smacking the sand.

"Wow." Annabelle put both hands on her mouth.

To Ryan, Caroline said, "You see, Rosie is not only my daughter's best friend. She's Eddie's daughter."

Ryan nodded, so gobsmacked by all this information that he had to take a few steps away from the two women sitting together by his legs. Staring out to the bay, he pondered all these developments in Caroline's life. As a married man with his own family, it was not right to be so close to this mess. He swallowed the melancholy of his goodbye down hard. It had to wait, but not for very long.

"I see it now," said Annabelle, nodding slowly and concentrating. "Rosie has that same wide, warm smile. That round face, the . . ."

"Right," said Caroline. "Same build, same bossiness, same way of confronting situations hard. They have the same feet. Don't you notice how kids' feet are often the same as their parents'?"

Ryan and Annabelle looked at each other and shook their heads no.

"Well, I do," said Caroline. "Fingers and toes run in families. And Rosie has his feet. Also, when she fell yesterday, Eddie sobbed, calling her 'my baby.' When I watched him comfort her, and touch her the way he touches our kids, it just hit me. That child is his. Rosie is his. I just know it."

"I *did* think he was being kind of dramatic out there in the ring when she fell off Cashmere, like he was taking over Thierry's role somehow. But I guess I just thought it was sweet, or controlling, or both—the way he always is both. Still, I just can't believe Eddie would do this," Annabelle said. "But they are for fuck sure related."

"And," Caroline added, "somehow whatever is going on at the barn might be linked back to Rosie."

Chapter 56

That Briny Juice Forever

Ryan's borrowed white Volvo rolled down Spring Farm Lane. A hundred yards before the entrance to Sea Crest Stables, Caroline said, "Ryan, pull over here."

Ryan stopped as instructed, and all three got out of the car. They took a moment and considered the enormous barn complex. Caroline, planning carefully, said, "I think Annabelle and I should maybe walk in through the trees, and climb over that low horse fence."

"You're the wife of the owner," Annabelle said. "You're allowed to walk around, Caroline. I'll go check on my horses. That wouldn't be out of the ordinary."

"Nope. I do not want to signal our arrival," said Caroline. "This way, we can go in discreetly and find out what we need."

"What I need is a good, dirty, martini. Up. Stirred, not shaken," added Annabelle.

"That'll be for later today at some good, out-of-the-way bar I know," said Ryan. "For now, when I drive in, I can easily play lost tourist."

"If anyone is here, they're going to know you're not a tourist," Caroline explained.

"Why?"

"Because there's a gate code only for Mondays, and very few people know that. If you, a tourist, drive into the stables, it won't make sense. That's the first reason."

"So, what's your plan, Sherlock?" asked Annabelle.

"Ryan shouldn't get near the barn if Eddie is here."

"It won't be any tougher than my acting job in front of Eddie that day at Duryea's restaurant. But if Eddie is here, I could say I was interested in the barn from a professional angle, or hired by Annabelle and wanted to see the wood board and batten barn siding or some bullshit."

"Eddie knows exactly who you are," Caroline said.

"And, by that, you are hopefully saying he knows my name?"

She gave him a look, shaking her head slowly, no.

"You don't mean that Eddie Clarkson knows exactly what I've been doing with his wife?" Ryan asked. "Do you mean that?"

"That too."

"What the hell? When did that happen?" Annabelle asked sternly, a bit miffed she found out when Ryan did. "Eddie has another child who happens to live part-time in your home because, inconveniently or conveniently, she's your daughter's best summer friend. Your husband knows about your summer lover, and your dead boyfriend is alive and waiting for us?"

"Check on all," Caroline answered.

Annabelle leaned into her best friend, adding, "I'll say one thing, I never thought our summer pact would lead to all this!"

"Summer pact?" asked Ryan.

"It's just a girlfriend thing," Caroline answered.

"Clearly." Ryan smiled, knowing that drink at his favorite dive bar would never happen. Before he left, he wanted to tell Caroline how grateful he was, how she'd erased the humiliation he'd felt for a decade. She was distracted, but still, he felt he needed to try. "Caroline, come here for a sec."

"Okay, but make it quick."

"Excuse us, Annabelle," Ryan said as he led Caroline away. He decided there'd be no more succumbing to his lust, no more of that thrill in discovering that hidden code to another woman's sexuality. The score with Suzy was on an even keel now, and he was relieved. He was too lucky a man, for his family, and for his time with Caroline.

She turned to him, crossing her arms. "I'm going to find out everything now, I know I am."

"You might, Caroline, you know, mess up the plan somehow," Ryan said. He knew that if this Marcus guy were with security already, there were most likely law enforcement setting a trap. This being East Hampton, where there was very little crime except the random drunk banker driving around, he knew they would be happy to arrest a dickhead like Eddie Clarkson who'd hogged all their waves when they were young.

"I don't give a shit whose plan I mess up. Eddie is still my children's father, and if I can protect him or warn him, I'm going to. Don't stop me."

"It's not my place to stop you. I never would," Ryan said. Grabbing both her shoulders, willing her to focus, Ryan looked into those crystal eyes once more. The cornstalks weren't quite flowering at the tips, it wasn't the very end of summer when he thought this moment would happen, but it was time now.

Did she understand he couldn't be a part of this? Would she, like he, be grateful for the subtle balance of distance and affection they'd accomplished together? It wasn't so easy to do, after all, given their mutual circumstances. Would she, like he, marvel at the delicate line they tiptoed on? Would she always remember their oyster gorging, their hallway sex, or the liberating, fantastical ravaging in bed that night?

Caroline understood all of it: especially that nuanced, respectful equilibrium they shared. And she knew that Ryan Miller, pleading sadly with his eyes only, always the gentleman, always considering her needs first, wanted her permission to bow out now.

She tilted her head to the side, softening her gaze, expressing that she knew when he gave her the water bottle at the barn party and kept his finger on hers a millisecond longer than he needed to, they were in trouble. That she'd never forget how she succumbed to him that night, that silk tugging at her wrists. And that she'd forever think of him when she slid an oyster on her tongue, the briny juice bringing her back to their first date on a random Tuesday afternoon. How could she not?

Even without words from her, Ryan knew he had, as with her initial resistance in bed, broken through that steely resolve of hers. "Go," he said. "I won't and can't stop you."

"Thank you," she said. Caroline kissed Ryan one more time softly on his lips, and he held her tight until she broke free. "I have to go now, Ryan. It's the only way. I've got to confront this head-on."

Chapter 57

Fathers May Not Know Best, but They Know

Caroline and Annabelle took slow steps on the pebbled sidewalks that led to the main stables. "Let's go up over to the right side, to the second level," Caroline said. "There's a landing up there with a window and a deck. A viewing area for the main ring, mostly for the dads. If I remember right, in that storage area behind the Branch Water Lounge, you can see down into the stables."

The women crept up a side staircase onto the balcony and interior lounge with several screens on one wall. Behind six leather lounge chairs, and a bookcase filled with antique horse ribbons and silver championship chalices, Caroline and Annabelle opened the door to the storage area. They climbed over cases of beer and Kentucky's finest bourbon to get a good view of the forty horses below and the trunks in front of each stall.

Immediately, both women sensed something strange was happening. Philippe was down at the far end with those same men, near the side of a trunk. More canvas duffel bags were opened on the ground and emptied.

"You know, Annabelle, it's all coming together," Caroline

whispered. "I swear these men paid Philippe earlier. I think it was a shit ton of money."

"You saw actual bills?" Annabelle asked.

"I saw neat, tight packages all lined up on the floor in the shape of stacks of bills. Yes."

"Not exactly the official way of paying someone," Annabelle said.

"I mean, it was like hundreds of thousands of dollars, I bet," Caroline said. "And, earlier, they'd slid a drawer out of the bottom of one trunk."

"The bottom of a trunk is solid. It's just a wooden box, how can you slide something out?"

"I'm telling you, Annabelle, they've rebuilt some of these. They have a secret side drawer on the bottom casing. The whole bottom of the trunk slid out."

"Why?"

"Whatever those men are doing down there right now has to do with that bottom, sliding area. I don't know what it is, and I don't see Marcus or Joey yet, but I *know* it's not legal."

"Shhh . . ." Annabelle hushed Caroline. "Look down there, it's your husband. Eddie is walking down the center hall. If Eddie is here, I can ask him outright something stupid, like I need carrots for my houseguests on the way to feed Seaside. Let's go."

By the time the women were on the last step, ready to stroll into the stables and confront the men, Joey had intercepted them.

"Oh," Caroline said, breathlessly.

"You *are* here," Annabelle said, her face red with emotion for her best friend. She placed her palms on her cheeks as a few tears started to trickle down her fingers. "I didn't fully believe her."

Caroline reached for Joey, almost falling into him, as he led her back up the stairs to the Branch Water Lounge. At the top landing, Joey and Caroline embraced for several long minutes, clenching their fingers around each other's back. Caroline then held his face in her hands, curling his hair around his ears. "I had a feeling, and so did your father."

"My father knew," Joey said softly. "I'm so sorry, I couldn't tell you." He kissed her forehead and grabbed her hands tight.

"I saw you in May on a boat, I swear . . ." Caroline wept, interlacing her fingers with his. "How could you? How could you not tell me you were okay?" She started sobbing, and then, suddenly, she pushed him away. She clenched her jaw; she was too happy that he was alive, but she was also furious he had abandoned her. She whispered, "You knew what it would do to me. What could possibly be worth that?"

"I'm sorry I couldn't tell you," he said, looking for a way to explain, his own eyes watering. He looked up at Annabelle first. "Is, she, can I . . ."

"You can, and please do. I'm her bona fide best friend," Annabelle said.

Caroline nodded and moved her hands in circles to get Joey to go on.

"It was something I could not explain," Joey stated. "Just, it was better for you to believe I was gone."

"Why couldn't you have just called?" she asked. "Just to tell me you were alive? Or . . ."

"I will just say this for now: I got involved in something I shouldn't have, and then it got very bad very fast, and I had to leave. That's all I can say. It was safer that way, for you." Joey climbed up a few steps so he could look down on the men through slats in the staircase. "And I'm sorry I couldn't meet you at the bay, at our rock. It was just too crazy here for me to leave as planned. Things went on for longer than we figured. I was going to tell you everything there."

Annabelle moved in, hugging Caroline protectively, holding her as she continued weeping. "Come on, honey, whatever you have to face is here," she said. "And I'm with you, okay? Apparently, so is that ghost you won't shut up about."

Joey looked at Caroline, unable to stifle his boyish smile. She stared back at him, wiping away the wetness from her skin. The connection to a man she hadn't seen in thirteen years felt as potent as it always had.

To cheer her up, while Joey stepped up a few stairs to check out below, Annabelle whispered in Caroline's ear, "Okay, so you for sure have slept with hotter men than I have, *your whole life*." Annabelle examined the athletic, strong leg muscles that were highlighted in the way Joey's jeans were tightening on his body, as he contorted himself to see better. "And how could that happen or be remotely fair, when I'm technically the one with the much better body between us? You don't even work out! What the fuck?"

Joey walked back down and said, "I think it's safer if you two get out of this barn."

"I'm not. I'm going down there and confronting Eddie," Caroline said. "That's why we came back."

Joey's lips curled in. He wasn't able to hide a smile, knowing Caroline's stubbornness was still alive. "Just meet me halfway then. Do not leave the property, just go to the landscaping shed in the back."

Annabelle touched Joey's shoulder to get his attention. "We've got a lot of questions that we would like answers to. My friend here is in shock just to be on the same planet as you. But you gotta tell us, why can't she just go down there?"

"I found out Thierry wanted you to watch it play out; that's why he told you to come over. Marcus and I were both surprised to see you today. But you have to stand back and let it happen, or the plan won't work. Thierry is fine. But that trainer guy from France, Philippe de Montagyew or something, is going to have some explaining to do. As will your husband."

"It's de *Montaigne*," said Annabelle, a bit self-conscious now about her summer mate.

"I still don't understand, Joey," Caroline said.

Joey kissed her forehead again, this time holding his lips there for several seconds, pulling Caroline tightly into his chest. With his thumbs tight, Joey clenched both of her hands. "Listen to me: I have been planning this moment for two years. Marcus McCree is in on it; his sister, Justine, and her lip-reading helped us more than she knows."

Chapter 58

Crouching Tigers

Caroline and Annabelle sat in the landscaping shed in the corner of the main ring. From here, they could see the side entrance to the main stables where Philippe and the men had walked in earlier. They'd closed the wooden door, but enough sun was shining through a crack, so there was plenty of light inside. They heard men's voices, first screaming, then quieting down. Caroline tried to make out the words, but she couldn't decipher them.

"I hear Eddie," she whispered. "I wish Joey could come in here. Jesus, Annabelle!"

"He'll come back. And that will be one conversation I'd like to be in on," Annabelle said, standing now on a lawn mower to get higher. She could see through a small slat in the side of the shed.

Caroline tried to push another crate over to the side, but it was too heavy. "I'm six inches shorter than you, and there's nothing in here for me to stand on, not even a bucket!"

"There's a large truck coming," Annabelle said, narrating the scene.

"Is it white and old? Like a box truck? If yes, that's like the truck

I first saw Joey driving," Caroline said. She tried to climb up on a mulch pile, but she kept slipping.

"Yeah. Oh God, now there's Philippe's orange Porsche. He's opening the trunk. These guys are having a real fucking party."

"Any sign of Marcus or Joey or Thierry?" Caroline asked.

"Nope. It just looks like a normal delivery or something," Annabelle said.

"It's not a normal delivery," Caroline said. "And, though I do trust Joey, I just don't understand why we have to wait in here."

"We don't."

"I mean, I've got my old boyfriend, my husband, and my family's livelihood out there, all smashing up against each other."

"Don't forget to throw my summer French fling into the shit show that your life has become. You're right, let's go," Annabelle said as she opened the creaky door of the landscaping shed. "I'm not doing as told and waiting in here one more second."

Once outside, the women walked briskly toward Eddie's office, and up a circular staircase to the cupola. They heard the beeping of the truck backing up in the distance. Annabelle went back down the stairs and reported, "Looks like another truck is arriving. This one's more like a dump truck."

"I'm telling you there have to be more clues in Eddie's office, we just have to piece them together," Caroline said, quietly unlocking his office door. She then thought of Maryanne, relieved that she was not around on Mondays, and Caroline wondered how much that sourpuss knew. Probably all of it.

Annabelle watched Caroline unlocking and locking various file drawers. "What can I do? You want me to look for something in particular? And did you take all those keys from Eddie and copy them?"

Caroline spun the keys around in the air on her index finger without looking back at her friend. "The main one to the office door, he hid in our armoire. I grabbed it this morning. The others? For the cabinets? It's just something I learned in the art gallery where I worked. Basically, every credenza in America has a cheap lock, and the same keys work on all of them or most. I've always had this set of various kinds from the gallery, and it's come in handy various times in my life. Like now." Caroline was on her knees, butt in the air, pushing a key into the bottom drawer of a wall of files.

"You used to break into files at work?"

"Just to see the prices people were paying," Caroline said, looking back at Annabelle, a bit sheepishly. "Kinda like how I used to try on people's clothes when I was a chambermaid at the Maidstone Arms in high school. It wasn't illegal; I was just curious." Caroline rifled through the files in Eddie's bottom desk drawer. She found the ledger with payments to Thierry in the small book and flung it in Annabelle's direction. "See? Eddie's been paying Thierry since 2009, right when Gigi and Rosie were born. These are some sort of child support payments, right?"

"Have to be," Annabelle said. "He only started working for Eddie formally this year, right? When the stables were created."

"I guess so," Caroline said, looking at more files, fanning the pages of more small books for clues inside. "I don't know what happened to Rosie's mom. Thierry told me a few times that she died of some illness during Rosie's birth, but he didn't elaborate. Thing is, the payments to Thierry go up in amounts, ten times higher this summer, since spring really, from five thousand a month to fifty thousand. And then, look," her finger trailed lines on the pages, "To Maryanne and to Philippe: these are kooky numbers. Seventy-five thousand dollars for a trainer per month all summer? And fifty thousand for like two years now as a monthly bonus to an assistant?"

"I hear footsteps!" Annabelle said. "Let's get out of here."

"We can't, there's only one staircase," Caroline stood, jamming the files back into the drawer and locking it as fast as she could.

The door opened slowly. Marcus McCree appeared and said, "Come on, ladies. You gotta see what's going down. Mrs. Clarkson, your formerly dead boyfriend and your husband are about to lock heads, and it's not going to be pretty. But if you made the effort to get as far as you did, then you might as well see it all."

"This is going to be good!" Annabelle said, grabbing Caroline's arm and dragging her full speed down the shiny mahogany staircase.

Chapter 59

Bungling the Bricks

"L et's go up to that storage area," Caroline said, heading for the Branch Water Lounge. Annabelle and Marcus ascended the stairs, but Caroline waited at the bottom step. "I'll be right there."

"You're not coming?" Annabelle asked. "You're going to bust in on whatever they are doing? I'm not sure that's wise."

"I've got an idea," Caroline told them. "Besides, this is my life colliding, not yours."

Entering the stables from the far end, Caroline sidestepped in along the wall to make sure the men down the halls could not see her. She walked three stalls down to Liza von Tattenbach's trunk, which she'd seen Philippe standing over this morning with the duffel bag. Lifting the top, she slid the tray with horse treats, ribbons, and sunscreen to one side. Then, taking it out entirely to be able to see the entire interior, she removed a helmet, two rumpled show jackets, a huge Ziploc of rotten carrots, and tall leather boots.

Now that it was mostly empty, she could knock on the bottom floor of the trunk. It sounded hollow: Annabelle was right, no one would ever expect there to be a false bottom on one of these. She stood to the side and grabbed the bottom brass border, about four inches thick, and, yanking it hard, pulled it out from the bottom. There was a neat, metal drawer. She nodded to herself, remembering that Eddie insisted that every client had no choice but to purchase "special" navy and brass trunks from his supplier. No standard horse trunk had a secret compartment in the bottom.

The security men and Marcus had left the adjacent stalls, most likely, she assumed, to survey the grounds. Next, she slipped into the tack room where bridles hung on hooks and saddles straddled polished wooden bars. A window opened up to another corridor, and Philippe and the men were ten stalls down. Caroline crouched at the bottom sill to watch them.

The men murmured, surrounded by open duffel bags again. They pulled out the bottom drawer of the trunk beside them. Out came neatly packed, cellophane-wrapped bricks. One of the men placed them in a wheelbarrow of horse stall shavings, mixed with manure. Another man shoveled the shavings a bit to cover the bricks. Caroline trailed the wheelbarrow outside and watched the man dump it into the manure and shavings refuse bin.

Caroline returned to the landing where Annabelle waited and said, "This is beyond unbelievable. Everything is clear now, or almost. I just need to tie up a few more strings. The question is, who is doing what?" She started to explain, "Riders' horse trunks get carted all over the East Coast for shows on the circuit, right?"

"Yes, Wellington near Palm Beach in winter," Annabelle said. "Lexington in the spring, Harrisburg in the fall, Lake Placid in the summer . . . yeah, yeah, hurry up."

"Philippe is hiding cellophane bricks inside that bottom compartment of the trunks, then mixing the packages into dirty shavings filled with manure, and carting them out to the horse manure pen," Caroline said. "And that manure pile gets picked up with special handling. Not normal horse shit and shavings they're handling. That's like a really expensive kitty litter box."

"So, what's in the packages?" asked Annabelle. "Has to be drugs, right?"

"I think so, or cash," Caroline answered. "The bricks aren't in the shape of a bag of stolen jewelry or something like that."

"Drugs," said Annabelle. "Sorry, it has to be. I once saw a mirror laying on a side table at Philippe's cottage and chose to ignore it."

"Okay, so all drugs. The cash was just in his backpack," Caroline announced. "I'm just scared for Eddie, for us. I'm sure Sea Crest manure and shavings don't go to a dump. They go to some warehouse or whatever, and some guy has to dig the plastic-wrapped drugs out of the horseshit and shavings and voilà, presto, ingenious drug transport. An excellent way to deliver drugs up and down the East Coast."

"Absolutely," Annabelle said. "Who would ever suspect drugs in manure piles, or beneath rich little girls' hair bows and peppermint horse snacks?"

"Philippe and the polo circuit French guys had to bring this to Eddie, and I guess he couldn't say no," Caroline said.

"Eddie may be an idiot for getting involved, but that's a pretty damn smart plan," Annabelle said. "That's like putting drugs into some Park Avenue woman's Balenciaga suitcases in the luggage section of her private plane."

"Which I bet happens, by the way," said Caroline. "I mean, what DEA agent goes into some little brat's ribbon trunk?"

Annabelle added, "Or, if they did, the feds would do some racial profiling bullshit and look into the grooms' quarters, just because most of those guys are from Latin America."

"So true," Caroline said. "They'd blame the grooms, the hardest working people on the circuit. All family men, photos of their kids all over their tack room. You take care of animals that well, you also take equal care of people around you. They'd try to bust the good guys. They'd never look to bust the fancy polo players."

"Honey, I love you, but I gotta get out of here," Annabelle said, feeling quite nervous now. "I think you should sneak out with me." She grabbed her Céline tote off the floor and dusted off the bottom. "I don't want to be involved in this, or implicated with Philippe in some way. Whether you come or not, I need to walk down Spring Farm Lane to that little coffee spot, get myself an Uber from there, and go back to my family. I've never been so grateful for Arthur!" She puffed up her gorgeous mane and wiped the dirt off her long, lean legs.

Caroline agreed, "Go, Annabelle, slip out the front, and go home to that darling husband of yours."

As she took the first step down, sirens roared from every direction.

Chapter 60

I Pronounce You Husband and Wife

By the time Caroline reached the bottom step and looked out into the courtyard behind the stables, it was too late. Fifty yards away, Eddie was being led up against a police car, the guy she'd played spin the bottle with in seventh grade was placing handcuffs on his wrists. Upon seeing her, Eddie yanked his hand away, saying, "James, c'mon, my wife. Shit, can you forget the cuffs for a moment?"

Officer Vincent hesitated and looked around. His colleagues were watching him now, rounding up Philippe, Thierry, and the four men who'd arrived earlier with the duffel bags. "Eddie, I, this is official business. I can't give you special treatment with everyone watching."

Eddie put his hands in his pockets and said, "I was at your house for a barbecue two weeks ago, man. Could you just stall a few minutes?"

Caroline walked up to her old school friend, her eyes moist. "You can't put him in jail, James. You just can't."

"Well, of course I can. But I'm not, we're not," he answered softly. "If he plays ball. Still, we have to bring him in. And he's going to have to . . ."

"You're not?" said Eddie. He turned around, placed his face in his hands and leaned his whole body over the car's hood, praying to God. He convulsed as he started sobbing, relieved that he might have a chance to be spared for his greed.

James turned to Caroline and said, "Now I understand why you were speeding through town this morning."

"How do you know he's not going away?" Caroline asked. "Can you honestly confirm that?"

The officer's answer was interrupted by Philippe de Montaigne, who was yelling obscenities in French, offended that anyone would accuse him of a crime worthy of lower-class riffraff. Two cops tried to reason with him and to cuff him.

"Well, Eddie here knew what was going on, it's just he wasn't a big player in it," James explained. "He knew those French guys were into bad deals, and he let them use the girls' horse trunks. There was this drawer system . . ."

"Yo! Caroline doesn't know anything, James," Eddie said. "You gotta go easy on the details with her or she's gonna . . ."

"Eddie, stop," Caroline said, glowering at her husband and willing him to be respectful to the officer. "I figured out everything. I pulled out a damn drawer this morning on my own. So, please, for once in your life, just shut up."

Eddie turned around and faced the ground. *How the fuck did his wife know about the drug drawers?* He turned to James. "So I'm not confirming anything, but why do you think I'll be okay, James?"

"Because Marcus McCree wanted it that way."

"Marcus is the fuckin' Executive Coach company owner!" Eddie said. "He has no idea . . ."

"Cool it, Eddie, or I'll put the cuffs on in front of your wife. Yes, that Marcus McCree came to us to protect you. And so did someone else," James said, protecting his old friend Caroline. He was not sure if Eddie even knew that the man he'd tried to strangle on the Ultimate Frisbee field more than a decade ago was alive.

Caroline looked over at Marcus, who was talking to some policemen and guiding them around the stalls. He caught her eye and signaled—it was all under control now. She put her hands together in prayer and bowed her head to him in thanks. He nodded once elegantly.

She asked James, "When you say someone else was helping, do you mean Thierry Moinot?" *What would happen to Rosie?*

James shook his head no.

"So Thierry's taking the fall for . . ."

"Last week, they got the bad guys already, up in Lake Placid, of all places. Apparently, two men put the pieces together for the agents. Marcus McCree was one of them, and the other I'm not going to name. Just know that they made sure everyone took care of Eddie and Thierry. Philippe should be fine if he can cool down his little hissy fit over there and talk some truth to us."

Caroline saw that the four men with the duffel bags were in front of a larger police vehicle with DEA agents and dogs around them. Thierry sat in a police car, quietly taking orders.

"Give me a minute," Caroline said.

She walked over to Thierry and asked the officers, "Can I talk to Mr. Moinot?"

"Not wise, ma'am," a policeman said. "But . . . I guess a few words."

"Thierry, I got Rosie's back. You know that? She can move in for a while until all of this settles," Caroline said. "I'll take care of things, okay? And thanks for the text, I did need to see this through myself."

Thierry, eyes closed, nodded, "You deserved to know." And the cop shut the door.

When she got back to Eddie, James was explaining, ". . . and if you fill in those blanks, Eddie, you'll all be relatively free to go."

"Relatively?" Eddie asked.

"Eddie, stop. You're a lucky man." Caroline advised. "James, tell me what you can."

"Philippe de Montaigne was apparently a pawn for some drug dealers from France. Philippe knew Thierry, and roped him in, pretty much without him knowing is the thing. But as far as we can tell, Eddie was aware. The fancy polo guys are behind the big machinery, though. Now, for sure, Eddie could have said 'No thanks,' but instead, Eddie got involved, making millions for himself, some for his assistant . . ."

"Maryanne?" Caroline asked. Then she remembered the fifty-thousand-dollar payments. "Eddie, I thought you had partners, *real* partners," Caroline said, not able to stop herself.

"Well, he had partners of sorts. Your husband's cash is in a warehouse. Or *was* in a warehouse," James said. "The cash has been seized, and the real bad guys are going to be put away. If Eddie and Thierry cooperate, they'll be fine and free to go. They may have to move somewhere else for a while, a few months at most, just to let the dust settle here."

"The kids? What do I tell them?" Caroline asked.

"Look, I'm going to let you two talk for five minutes, one of my guys over there needs some assistance with that French drama queen in the white pants," James said, as he walked away.

Eddie took a few steps. He guided Caroline to a nearby horse fence, leaned his back against a thick post, and slinked his sturdy build down to the ground. He looked up at the woman he loved, knowing she wouldn't be his wife much longer. "I'm so sorry," he said. "I got excited. I had so much cash. And they practically forced me to."

"Who forced you to help transport drugs?"

"I mean, anyone would have . . ."

"Eddie, not *anyone*. I will ask you one thing: take accountability for once. There's no one to blame but yourself. Not your drunk dad, not anyone else." She pointed to the vast equine complex around them. "Look at all this. It's a massive web you got yourself into. How did this even start? Was it all Philippe?"

"There's so much you don't know."

"I know everything, I know about the trunks, the packages in the manure shavings, even *Rosie*." She paused. "And I'll help take care of her as one of my own. The child didn't ask for any of this. But I only ask you to come forward with one bit of information, if you want me not to hate you forever."

Eddie was dumbstruck she knew it all. After several moments, he said, "Anything, baby."

"Please don't call me baby, just tell me, Eddie, my one missing link: tell me about Rosie's mother, *your girlfriend when I was pregnant,* and how she died?"

Eddie placed his head between his legs, shaking it back and forth.

"You owe me this, Eddie Clarkson. Now." Caroline didn't feel bad or guilty about anything that had happened these past few months.

It had been a summer of salvation. Period.

"Tell me, now."

"I just can't."

"Then I officially hate you forever."

He coughed and wiped his nose with the back of his hand. "Rosie's mom is, was, named Hélène Moinot."

"Makes sense, that's her brother's last name and her daughter's. Go on, Eddie."

"How did she die?"

"In my Hummer jeep."

"NO!"

"It was so slippery, so dark under the trees, and a deer, it just came out of nowhere and I spun. Well, *we spun*. Into a tree, on the passenger's side. But Rosie lived."

Epilogue

BACK AT THE ROCK
THE FOLLOWING DAY

A gentle breeze caused ripples across the surface of Fort Pond Bay, consistent as corduroy. Strands of clouds reached across the orange sky, glowing with the setting sun. At the edge of the beach, Caroline took her shoes off and walked in the cool sand by the bay, which always struck her as harder than the sifted flour of Atlantic sand. Kids were down by the water, but, thankfully, the tables weren't crowded yet. Still, seeing people mingle, drink, kids frolic and splash, started to restore Caroline's spirit. East Hampton was better when people enjoyed it, together. It had been eerie on this very sand yesterday, but it was low tide now, and Joey had already laid out a blanket. His legs were stretched on it. It was a warm, humid evening, the scorching heat of the day started to fade.

She was ten minutes earlier than they'd planned and she startled him. He shielded his eyes from the sun's rays behind her and patted the blanket, hidden from view behind the rock for their privacy. "Sit, I owe you too much now."

Caroline kneeled next to him. She looked into his eyes, tears flowing yet again. It was different being with Joey now, with so many years of her own history he had missed. He looked exactly thirteen years more advanced in his life, his cheeks a little less plump and baby-faced, the crevices in his face a little deeper. His older face made his square jaw more prominent, more distinguished. She swallowed hard, and realized that Joey didn't even know Theo's and Gigi's names.

He put his hand on her knee, "You tell the kids?"

His ability to perceive her thoughts before she'd said them was uncanny, as it always was. It made her smile. "I didn't even know if you knew I had kids."

He sat up and faced her, sitting on his own knees, touching hers with his. Feeling even a small part of her body against his sent so many sparks up his spine he had to rub the back of his neck. "C'mon. My dad knew everything. He kept me up to date, even sent me pictures of Theo and Gigi. What did you tell them?"

It made her so terribly sad to think of her children without Eddie for months, and the impossibility of hiding his actions from them. Caroline felt her face looked distorted and ugly when she tried not to cry too much. She pushed her lips together hard to try to keep it in, but she could feel her cheeks and chin moving into strange positions.

"You know your eyes are even clearer blue with the tears in them," Joey said. "And the reflections of the water behind you. I don't know . . . you're more beautiful than ever."

She shook her head and looked down to compose herself. "Telling them last night that Daddy was going away for a few months for work was the most difficult conversation I've ever had," she said. "I explained that staying in East Hampton would make it easier, that they could play outside more, and that Rosie would move in during the time because her uncle Thierry had to go too. I just said they had business problems." She paused for a moment. "You know Rosie is . . ."

"I know. Marcus McCree told me everything a few years back, when I first reached out to him."

"Why him?"

"Because friends out here, some cops, were starting to quietly watch Eddie, sniffing him out. They told my dad, and he called me. They figured out the guy who owned the company where Eddie orders drivers and cars had been in the force. They reached out to him, cop-to-cop thing. And then I called Marcus myself and told him I was worried about the family. He jumped into the whole story after that."

Caroline slid her back against the boulder, holding her knees with her arms. She turned to him. "Tell me, why did you pretend to die?"

"To protect you, and your family, and, yeah . . . even Eddie, your kids' dad." Joey gritted his teeth a little. "But then I kept hearing Eddie was getting deeper in. We all had to work together to protect him from his own greed because it could have put you in danger. And from some dangerous people he got involved with . . . or, well, who we *all* got involved with."

"Who is we? How did you know them?" Caroline asked.

"Come here," Joey said, putting his arms around her. She hugged him as tightly as she could, and nestled her face in his neck. He brushed her hair, whispering in her ear, "There's so much to tell you."

She pushed Joey away: "Don't touch me now. It's too much at once. Just talk, slowly, please. Not about us, or me, just *it*, whatever *it* is, and whatever happened."

"I'm going to try hard not to hold you," he said. He paused to gather his thoughts. His straggly hair was lighter now, and Caroline noticed some spindly gray strands. There were a few wrinkles above and below his mouth, gravity pulling his skin toward the sand as he looked down. He dusted off his jeans as if to prepare for his lecture. He looked up at her with his deep brown eyes: "You have to understand that guys like this were always lingering around here, even in high school."

"Jesus, Joey. Who in high school?"

"Remember Eddie's Rice Krispies treats?"

"Jesus Christ," Caroline said. Could she know so little about the man she'd married—and so little about Joey too, the only man she'd ever loved? She tried to remain cool. It took everything in her not to kiss him so hard she'd knock him over. "Of course I remember those, even the little red ribbons he put on. I helped him a few times in his kitchen because his parents were too wasted to cope. Tell me everything."

Joey nodded and said, staring hard at every nook and curve of her impossibly beautiful face. "Of course. Sorry, your eyes, it's just, okay. Back to the story." Joey sat cross-legged and placed both hands on her knees. She looked down at them and considered telling him not to touch her, that the feel of his hands was too distracting. Instead, she lifted them playfully off her again, and shook her head no.

"Okay, sorry." He sat on his palms facedown. "It'll help me not to touch you. It's not easy," he looked inside her eyes and knew she was trying her hardest not to give up the fight. "So Eddie Clarkson was selling weed with those guys who delivered those Rice Krispies treats to kids all over the island. Nothing big, like now, but he did slip joints inside, wrapped in plastic, where they were smell proof. Maybe that's how he came up with the idea to put the packages in the manure and shavings. Again, I don't know every step, but I do know he was dealing some drugs way back."

"You're sure?" she asked. Caroline rolled up her sleeves as if that would help her concentrate on the story and not the fact that Joey Whitten was breathing the same air that she was, the breeze blowing off the bay, their bay.

"So, I used to deliver the Rice Krispies weed treats for Eddie. I got a little involved back in high school, and the job went on when you and I were together and during college. One reason he hated me so much was that I worked for him in a small-time weed business, and then, well, his girl fell for me, his underling."

Caroline leaned against the rock and crossed her arms over her face. Closing her eyes, her forearms shielding the sun, created nothing but blackness in her mind. It allowed her to try to imagine Eddie and Joey working together, and then hating each other because of her. "Go on, so it started in high school."

"And then," Joey said, "in our early twenties, his guys wanted more. Eddie was making bigger and bigger deals. And I started to balk and wanted out. I knew I could go to jail with the amounts we started to work with. They told me they'd hurt my family if I didn't continue."

She lifted her arms and faced him, "Hurt your family? Like beat up your dad?"

"Yeah, beat up, hurt, or worse," Joey responded. "And they said they might hurt my girlfriend, you, but I never really believed that."

Caroline swallowed and nodded, relieved the men had been caught.

"You know, I was the one who was familiar with their faces because Eddie wanted me handling deliveries. He was smart. He didn't meet anyone or touch anything. I was the mule, and I knew all the guys in charge because I made the pickups, Eddie was too smart to do that." Joey shook his head. Like all mules, he was used and in danger while the other guys were safe and hoarded the cash. "So, these were my options: keep handling bigger packages or skip town. I didn't know what to do."

"So, what did you do?"

"My dad knew. No one else, no need with Mom in heaven. I packed some clothes in a bag, some cash, and my credit cards and passport, and literally swam five miles down with the currents. I mean, I didn't even swim, it was one of those days where the ocean is literally moving sideways. It just pulled me down the beach, and my dad got me at this spot where no one ever sat on the beach, and gave me a car to drive south. That's it. I thought I'd leave and come back in a few years, but they would have followed me. So I literally had to drown, disappear. Leaving you, and Lucky." He coughed and wiped his eyes.

"Lucky must have been the hardest," she said. "You both were inseparable."

He half smiled. "Not exactly the hardest, but yeah, kind of."

"Your dad took good care of him, you know." She would never tell him about Lucky howling at the moon all night by the shoreline where Joey went in forever. Or kind of forever.

Okay," she said, stretching out on her side, her elbow propping her up. "Go on."

He lay beside her, about a foot away, with his head resting the same way, on his palm. The outline of her profile formed a silhouette with the western sun setting against it. He remembered her finger on his profile at the beach shack, the way she always used to touch him, and wondered if his own face was dark like this with the candle behind it. He would take her to the beach shack later. His dad promised he'd always save it for them. She would go, he felt it.

"You look even more like Snow White. Especially now."

She didn't say anything; she just nodded coldly. She was right: he shouldn't be romantic now, and he figured it could take months to win her back. Maybe he'd have to wait for a divorce, which could take a year, but there was no way he could wait that long.

Then Caroline asked, "Can I just ask where the hell you were? I'm going to lie here and just try my hardest to comprehend the fact that you're here, lying in our spot. Where did you go?"

"I was a boat captain off South America, near Colombia, on this island called San Andrés. It's the most magical place in the world," Joey said. "I helped build a sustainable hotel down there, and a restaurant. And remember my murals?"

"Of course, your one on the shack is still there."

"Well, I painted them all over the place down there, schools, my restaurants, commissions all over the place. My Spanish is good, and I have a lot of friends. But, you know, I never had a family."

Caroline breathed out hard. No family. No wife. She could only say, "Your Spanish was always good, even back in sixth grade."

"Yeah, well, seems like more than half the world speaks it. Anyway, I figured out, in the past thirteen years, that the earth is a big place. I built up a good little business. I just had to stay dead. My house is gorgeous, actually. Not big, but just perfect for me. They call me Enrique Marquez. That's the stupid name I came up with day one, and it stuck."

"People call you Enrique?" Caroline laughed.

"Yep. I answer to it. And most of the people I hang out with have no idea I lived in the United States for so long. I have a totally new identity now. It wasn't hard because I wasn't hiding from any legal authorities. I was just hiding from . . ."

"From Eddie's guys?"

"Yeah."

Caroline now covered her face in her hands, gave into her emotions, and started weeping again. "So, it's because of Eddie that we were kept apart, and then he married me? And I fell for him? And the whole time I'm thinking you're gone, and I'm figuring Eddie, as a husband, he'll be . . . I don't even know, *exciting*?" She coughed a few times through her tears, and lay back. Joey wiped the tears away from under her eyes with his fingers. She shook her head a little, and he pulled his hand back quickly. She had a family now—or what was a family—and he shouldn't touch her like they were still together.

Finally, Caroline looked up at Joey. "It's just a big game for him, isn't it?"

"Well, he loved you. And he didn't know I didn't drown. No one did, except Dad. I mean, I'm sure Eddie still loves you," Joey said. "I mean, who wouldn't with that smile."

"I'm not smiling!"

"You are," Joey said. "And it's even more beautiful than the twenty photos that I've handled like twenty million times. I saw you from my boat that day before Memorial Day, you know. Eating those fried clams you love. I could tell you saw me."

"That freaked me out," Caroline said, allowing herself the faintest smile. She lay on her side again, with her head resting on her palm.

The two of them played with the wrinkles of the blanket with their fingers. He lay looking at her a safe foot away, his head also resting on his palm. It was quiet for a moment. The seagulls squawked at each other in the distance. The air was heavy, hovering around them now, though a degree or so cooler than even twenty minutes ago. Finally, Joey added, "Eddie always loved you. He always told me he loved you more than I did, more than any man could. I sent him a Frisbee with a note just to fuck with him. Maybe he told you?"

"That definitely got his attention. But why that message, 'She's still mine'?"

"That message?" He knew she was asking as a ploy to make him fight for it. "Why did I write that message? Because, Caroline, one can only hope."

She nodded, trying to pretend that he didn't have her that way anymore, that it wouldn't be that easy for him. The air was still, and she had trouble breathing. She loved him just the same, maybe more, and she smiled a little. She couldn't help herself.

"And I left the conch shell, just to say I'm always here, and that nothing's changed."

She nodded. "The story. Go on."

Joey took note and got back on track. "Sorry, I know he's the man you married and the father of your kids, but Eddie Clarkson didn't deserve you," Joey continued. "Everyone, all the local cops at the barn yesterday, was psyched to help with the sting and show him who's really boss in this town. But, yes, back then, I had to leave. I didn't want to. I had to. Leaving you was the hardest thing. But the one person I wanted to know the truth was the one person I could never tell. It would have put your life in danger. Drug dealers are no joke. You take their threats seriously. I thought it would be easier for you to start a new life if you really believed I was gone. I'm so sorry, baby." He put his hand on her stomach, and she picked it up and removed it.

"And how did Marcus . . . how did he . . . help you all?"

"He's got a little sister who can't hear. Justine McCree is like ninety-five percent deaf, but she can read lips. He knew bad shit was going down with Eddie Clarkson because the East Hampton cops had called him, as I mentioned. He worried about the family, you, the kids. Marcus used to place his sister nearby to spy on Eddie during meetings. Marcus told me she'd even eat in the same coffee shop downtown in Alphabet City with the French guys. He would go to this restaurant, and his sister would sit across from Eddie so she could watch and take notes. Then, Marcus tipped off law enforcement. He thought Eddie was getting in too deep, and it wasn't safe for you and your kids."

"Marcus would help the police, to do what's right."

"Yeah, he's an amazing guy," Joey said. "I never believed selling a few dozen joints to a few high schools every week would sink us in so fast, but Eddie . . . he just, he never got enough. Then a few years ago, I changed my plan. I started hearing how deep in he was. I realized that someone had to stop Eddie before he really did put you in danger."

"I can see Eddie thinking it's all cool, but he's been super jumpy recently," Caroline said. "He must have known he was in way over his head with the horse complex." Caroline's mind raced through the years, focusing on small things that started to make more sense. She thought of Maryanne and her cold stares. All those fifty-thousand-dollar payments. She kept the books—she had to know most or all of it.

And then, Rosie's olive skin. Now she wondered what Rosie's mother was like, or who she was. Regardless, she'd pay it forward to her, give that child more fierce mothering than she could hope for, wherever she was up there. She did need her father too.

"I think Eddie's going to be okay," Caroline said. "James Vincent told us that if he filled in some blanks. I mean, he's my kids' father, I . . ."

Joey threw a rock at the water harder than he meant to. "Well, he's your husband too," Joey said, sitting up cross-legged, feeling impatient. He sat on his hands again to keep from mauling this woman next to him. He knew that he'd have to give Caroline time.

He stood up and walked a few steps to the water's edge. "Officer Vincent was in heaven. I love James. He was so fully in control. He's hated Eddie since seventh grade. Eddie was actually arguing that he was innocent. I was there watching the whole thing from a horse stall with Marcus, who was terrified of the animal, he's got some city in him, that guy."

"Marcus has only good in him. But you really think Eddie will be okay?" Caroline whispered. "Tell me, reassure me."

"Yeah, he's fine. James is going to make him suffer though. We made a deal with the feds: let him go in exchange for the big fish we handed them on a platter, the real dealers. And, well, they got them, so they don't honestly care much about people like Eddie. The stuff at the stables was child's play. They get it. They are going to seize Eddie's cash though."

Caroline sat up, starting to realize that the simpler life she'd been imagining was in place before her. "Worse things could happen," she said. "As long as my kids' father is alive, and he's able to see them and . . ." she couldn't find the words to complete that sentence.

Joey paced along the blanket's edge, kicking up sand, and said, "And, well, I'm moving home. Now I can. People are going to wonder what the hell game I was playing, and I won't ever be able to explain the drug dealing, or what I knew, or the threats against me, but it'll be nice to be home. Maybe I can keep the restaurant down in San Andrés and build another one here too. The world is moving too fast for me now, but with the big fish caught, it's safe for me, finally. I can come home."

"So, you're coming back?" Caroline looked up at him, coughed, and rubbed her mouth a little.

"Don't try to hide that gorgeous smile."

"I'm not."

He fell to his knees and guided her shoulders back down. "Just rest, because there's a lot of thinking you have to do. And I don't want you leaving this safe little space of ours," he said. He lay down next to her, propping up his head on his palm again. But this time, he was closer to her. "So, one thing. That Ryan guy. He's really great. I saw him outside the complex when I was hiding near a tree, talking to the cops. Some of them were arriving when he was leaving. I remember him. He remembered me and shook my hand before he left. Volunteer firemen force, he said. He was talking to the cops about you, making sure the guys kept you safe. And I hate to pry, but I just had this weird feeling you and he were . . ."

"Only on Tuesdays!" Caroline blurted out. She leaned up, very much wanting him to know it was over with Ryan. "I swear only Tuesdays and only until the end of . . ."

Joey reached over and brushed her cheek with the back of his hand. "You're as ridiculous and anxious as always. Only on Tuesdays? You've got some things going on, I see."

"It was Annabelle's idea." She looked at him and laughed.

"You don't need to defend anything. It's not like you cheated on me," he reminded her. "Or maybe that's not true. You did go and get married on me."

That cracked her up. She wouldn't admit that it felt like she had.

"I like it better when you laugh," Joey whispered. "You should be crying about fifty crazy things going on in your life, but I do like the laugh. You look just as pretty laughing, despite the mascara raccoon eye thing you got going."

He edged closer to her. Neither talked for a few moments; both resisting the pull toward the other as if against the force of a giant magnet. The silence was almost awkward now. Could he hold her? He placed his hand on her hip. This time she allowed it to stay there.

She said, "Could you just . . ."

"Just what?" His dark eyes sparkled with the knowledge that he knew what she meant and exactly what she wanted, as he always did. It was more fun to make her say it, though.

There was silence again, and she looked down.

"Could you just please, in here, with the globe spinning a million miles an hour . . ."

"It's actually a thousand miles an hour . . ."

"Stop," Caroline said, and she smiled.

"Stop? Oh, that's what you want?" He yanked his hand back in a big, exaggerated arch. Torturing her was better, and more like old days. She did marry Eddie, so she owed him, he figured. Then, what the hell, he put his hand right where it had been. He pressed his fingers harder into her flesh. It took everything for him not to slide his hand down the back of her pants and grab that body he knew too well, had waited to touch for too long.

"No, I don't want you to stop," she admitted.

"So, what do you want, Caroline?"

"Like I said, I want you to help me, help stop me feeling like everything's spinning so fast. And," she paused again, "I really want you to . . ."

"To what?" He edged an inch closer, their bodies hovering side by side, only millimeters separating them.

"To kiss me."

"You think that'll stop that crazy world outside?" He inched closer, his chest touching hers.

"I have no idea, but maybe it'll help. Just kiss me. Please."

And so he did.

For a very long time.

Acknowledgments

During the writing of a novel, the characters become great company for the author. They talk to each other in my head all day long and often in dreams at night. They argue, laugh, cry, reenact, and challenge how I depict them on the page. Thank you to my family for allowing me time to sit in the library to write and to stroll in the city parks and on the beach shorelines to think and converse with my characters.

Thank you to my friend Lynne Greenberg, who is always the first to dive in as only an English professor can. Juju Chang and David Saltzman gave me thorough and early reads. Electra Touh provided a late and much-needed read. Leslie Bennetts mentored me in the art of writing fast and furiously. Bill Uhrig handled technology and airplanes, Jenny Landey helped with Hamptons geography, Susan Fales-Hill with characters, Amanda Ross with style and tone, Ashley McDermott and Ann Coley with funny and clever ideas (as is their way). Grant Ginder talked me off the cliff and waved his wonderful editing wand. Richard Demak provided a generous and robust copyedit. My William Morrow editor, Tessa Woodward, always has the most astute observations; Elle Keck brings it together; and Molly Waxman and Erin Reback help blaze the word out.

For all I am grateful.

BOOKS BY HOLLY PETERSON

THE IDEA OF HIM
A Novel

"*The Idea of Him* is a coming-of-age book for grown ups. It's fast-paced and intriguing, glamorous and real—not only a great, great read but a tutorial in how to be your own best friend."
—Elin Hilderbrand, author of *Beautiful Day*

From the *New York Times* bestselling author of *The Manny*—a vibrant novel of love, life lessons, and learning to trust yourself. Captivating and seductive, told in the whip-smart voice of a woman who is working hard to keep her parenting and career on track, *The Idea of Him* is a novel of conspiracy, intrigue, and intense passion—and discovering your greatest strength through your deepest fears.

IT HAPPENS IN THE HAMPTONS
A Novel

"In this irresistible beach read, a single mom lured to the Hamptons for the summer learns the ways of the 1 percent of the 1 percent. Peterson chronicles this crowd with firsthand knowledge and a sense of the ridiculous." —*People*

From the *New York Times* bestselling author of *The Manny* comes this deliciously entertaining upstairs/downstairs story about the millionaires who summer in the Hamptons—and the everyday people hired to fulfill their every desire.

IT'S HOT IN THE HAMPTONS
A Novel

In the Hamptons, no rules apply, especially in matters of money—and the heart...

From the author of the summer hit *It Happens in The Hamptons* comes an unforgettable new novel about the women who live and love in the Hamptons.